EVENFALL

EVENFALL

GAJA J. KOS & BORIS KOS

EVENFALL

Cover illustration © 2018 by Merwild (Coralie Jubénot)

Cover design by Morana Designs

ISBN 978-961-94374-5-2 (hardcover)

ISBN 978-961-94374-6-9 (paperback)

ISBN 978-961-94368-5-1 (eBook)

Published by Boris Kos

October, 2018

For all the fellow INTJ people out there

CHAPTER ONE

THE THING I NOTICED ABOVE ALL ELSE WHEN unconsciousness released me from its talons of darkness, was that for the first time in my life, I found myself gazing at the night sky.

The second, just as enchanting, yet infinitely more unbelievable, was that the world around me was no longer mine.

A raspy laugh escaped my lips.

I should have been scared, terrified of this impossibility. But I didn't have the strength to do anything more than roll over onto my back and drink it all in.

Above me, a spill of flickering, pale golden light scattered across the canvas, painting a breathtaking blend of black, violet, and deep blue. My breath hitched as a thought wormed its way in. I blinked, refusing to acknowledge that hopeful voice in case this smattering of illuminated specs was a consequence of my...fall?

Given my undignified position and the sting that crawled

across my palms, I had to have fallen. Yet those lights remained unmoving. A product not of my impaired vision, but my surroundings, however odd they were.

I dared to utter it out loud.

"Stars."

They were stars. The mysterious luminescence I had only ever read about in fairy tales my parents kept hidden under lock and key in the dusty crates, believing that indulging in that kind of nonsense didn't become a High Master's daughter.

Gingerly, I pushed myself up from the hard ground and tucked my legs beneath me. My face, however, remained tilted towards the sky.

In my sunlit world, there was no room for dreaming of the surreal. Yet here, wherever *here* was, it took shape, answering the question I was never supposed to ask, yet thought of time and time again as I observed the High Masters or their heirs command the fabric of reality.

If they could open portals between chambers, lands, even regions, why couldn't they reach farther?

It was absurd, but the conviction that my *childish, inappropriate* thoughts had touched the truth was anchored in the very core of my being. I was as certain of kneeling in an unfamiliar, faraway world as I was of the necessity to draw breath.

Still, a small part of me—that rational, cultivated voice that sounded unnervingly similar to my father's—argued that it must have been the wine I'd drunk to mark my eighteenth birthday toying with my vision. That I must have fallen asleep, plummeted into another one of my dreams, and gave life to the fragments of stories I had stolen as a child. And yet the landscape refused to bend to my will.

A light breeze chilled my cheeks, bringing with it not the scents of greenery or blooming flowers, but a quality that was foreign to my lungs.

Latching on to the sensation, I allowed it to ground me before I lowered my gaze and shoved away the whispers of doubt.

"It's real," I muttered.

My fingers brushed the stones and rocks, exploring their rough texture. A corner of my mouth curled up in a smile.

"It's real."

From what I could discern under the starlight that broke up the violet and blue hues, this world was strangely barren, nothing but lifeless gray rock stretching endlessly into the distance. Only far to my right did the landscape change.

A copse of trees stood sentry before a ridge of hulking mountains, the jagged caps dipped in shadows so dark, it made them nearly indistinguishable from the night rising above.

There wasn't a single stretch of land in Soltzen this harsh. This cold.

I brought my hands to my arms to ward off the chill but stopped as I felt an odd sense of kinship burn within me. Reaching up, I entwined a strand of hair that had come undone from my braid around my finger.

Silver. The mark of a girl devoid of color, living in a world of flare.

It appeared I'd finally found a place where I fitted in.

Only I didn't know where it was. Or how I even got here.

Portals were wielded by High Masters, not their wives or daughters. Could it be that someone at the party had gotten carried away? That I had somehow tumbled through the rip in the fabric of reality, the portal knitting shut behind me before anyone could follow?

I bit my lip and looked down. I was still in the same burgundy dress I'd worn at the feast, although the velvet fabric now bore some tears in the bodice, as well as a few along the long, skintight sleeves, and appeared to be a touch ragged at the hem. I certainly wouldn't have dreamed *that* detail up. Or the scrapes across my palms, the edges still bearing flakes of dried blood.

No, it had to have been a portal, cutting across more space than any had ever succeeded before.

Just as I let out a laugh, unease reared its head and subdued the rush of exhilaration until it was nothing more than a trickle still warming my veins.

Because if it *were* true, then that left me stranded in a foreign world with no means of getting back home.

The taste of copper spread across my tongue as I worried on my lower lip a little too hard. I stopped, but the metallic tang was as resilient as the grating discomfort.

I'd never even seen much of *my* world beyond the Norcross estate walls, so how was I supposed to find my way around *this* one?

Maybe if I waited here, someone would—

A rapid *thud* of paws exploded from behind. I jumped to my feet and twisted around, scanning the darkness for any sign of the animal. But my eyes, unaccustomed to this somber hue, blurred together the details. There was only the persistent sound that was growing louder. Nearer.

And still, I had no idea what it belonged to.

Quickly, I snatched one of the sharper pieces of rock, although with it fitting comfortably in the palm of my hand, only a harsh tip protruding, the crude weapon was pitiful at best. The odds of me inflicting any serious damage before I lost my arm weren't in my favor.

Sweat broke down the length of my back.

I considered chancing a mad dash across the flat expanse of rock, but before I could take a single step towards the mountain range and the trees I could use for cover, an excited yelp froze me in place. A yelp, followed by the faint press of paws against my left leg.

Remembering that animals reacted to fear, I breathed deeply and focused on calming my frantic heartbeat, but my efforts shattered the instant my gaze fell on the slender muzzle jutting up into the air.

A dog.

Or, at least I *hoped* it was a dog.

Its body was smooth obsidian and completely devoid of fur. Only peculiar, white hair-like strands adorned the top of its head and coated the lower part of its legs, the tip of its tail, and the edge of its wide, triangular ears. The pure, blinding color contrasted wildly with its sleek, dark skin, giving the animal an even more unusual look. Stinging pain lanced through me where the dog's tiny claws dug into the fabric of my dress, but from the way it continued to wag its tail and look at me with those black eyes that seemed to reflect the starlight, it wasn't trying to harm me.

If anything, it—no, *she*—seemed happy to have found me here.

I looked around, but with the touch of clouds that crept across the horizon and fed the already prevalent shadows, I could see even less.

Seconds stretched.

Nothing stirred.

Exhaling, I loosened my grip on the rock.

I was still staring into the distance when the dog smacked me with her paw. Then once more, when I failed to react.

"Hi," I whispered, suppressing a chuckle.

Her tail wagged furiously, urging me on. I leaned over a little, then lowered my free hand down by my side where she could sniff at it.

"What are you doing out here alone?"

The strange dog didn't answer—at least *something* appeared to be the same in both worlds—but she did give another yelp before nudging at my palm with her wet nose as if...

"Oh, you want me to pet you?"

The dog simply repeated the motion, staring up with excitement and expectancy brimming in her eyes.

"All right, then."

I touched the mane of her white hair first. I kept the touch light since I didn't want to risk any sudden moves in case I misread her intentions. Or she mine. But when the animal leaned into my caress and let out a small rumble of pleasure, I relaxed. My fingers trailed the long strands down the nape of her neck, all the way to the middle of her back, and I was surprised by how warm her skin was. How smooth it felt, gliding beneath my fingers like silk.

"Lyra!" a melodic female voice called out.

The dog tore away from me and broke into a sprint. I swore as my heel caught on the tattered hem of my dress, but I quickly regained my balance, my gaze already seeking out the animal...

I found her.

As well as the girl she was now circling around.

Lyra's tail lashed from side to side even as she launched herself up to nip at her owner's elbow.

"Lyra, that's enou—"

Our eyes met.

A staccato of *thuds* announced Lyra's return. She ran between the girl and me, then settled by my side when the stranger walked over.

She looked about my age, maybe a little older, dressed in a gray tunic and black pants, with riding boots reaching up to her knees. There were no gemstones or gold ornaments adorning the garments, as was the fashion at home. Instead, the clothes, while tailored, were functional. If it weren't for the spill of hair reaching past her chest, the strands gradually lightening from dark into a vivid, fiery red, it would have been impossible to distinguish her from the backdrop of the night.

It struck me that that was precisely her intention.

"It's you," she whispered, then as if snapping out of a dream, she rushed forward and placed a tentative hand on my shoulder.

I flinched, but the girl didn't seem to notice.

"I *told* Mother the spell wouldn't last..."

Only distantly, I sensed the dog nuzzle at my palm. My attention was on the girl, on the bewilderment and recognition alight in the striking jade of her irises as her words echoed in my head, causing numerous questions to clash.

Yet one was louder than the rest.

"Spell? What spell?"

The girl looked at me, eyes wide as if I'd asked something fundamental knowledge should cover. Her full lips parted, then closed, and she shook her head before gesturing towards me.

"The one that was supposed to keep you from coming here, of course."

"WHERE IS *HERE*?" I pressed, but the girl was focused on scanning the barren surroundings, her feet carrying her forward.

As I followed her gaze, I saw a faint outline of a town I'd missed earlier, tucked closely to the foot of the mountain. It was nothing more than a blob, but by the way the girl was studying it, she clearly saw something more.

The light breeze with just a hint of petrichor entwined in the currents brought over her audible sigh. It was laced with relief—and no small amount of tension. With one last glance, she backtracked to my side.

"The celebrations haven't started yet, so there's still time to get you to safety." She grabbed my hand, the dog—Lyra—already running in the direction of the town. "We'll have to move fast, though. You can't be out here when he comes."

"Wait, wait," I cried out as she dragged me behind her.

I twisted my arm until my wrist came free from her grip, nearly stumbling over some protruding rocks—and losing the one I'd been holding on to.

"What are you talking about?" I snapped, then moved farther back so she couldn't grab me again. "I'm not even *from* here, and I'm certainly not going *anywhere* with someone I know nothing about, not even their name."

"*Stars*," she whispered, and there was something so honest in that one word that I stopped retreating. "Of course you wouldn't. I'm sorry. I got carried away. It's just that we've been waiting for you for so long, and—"

She sucked in a breath, an apology in the green of her eyes. I focused on that instead of the implications written in her ramblings.

"I'm Ada Aldane, and we're just outside Nysa, the capital of Somraque."

"Ember Norcross," I offered. "From Soltzen."

"Ember." She flashed me a smile that lit up her entire face. But the expression was brief, fleeting, and all too soon gave way to something graver. "I'll explain everything as soon as we get to my house. The Winter Solstice celebrations are about to start, and the Crescent Prince *will* come. He always does. He searches for you, Ember, every year. My mother sacrificed so much to keep you safe, and if he got to you now..."

It was in that moment that I first questioned my sanity.

Accepting that I somehow landed in another world was easy. After all, it was an idea I'd entertained since I first saw a portal and what it created. But what Ada was implying...

Impossible. Aside from my father's high rank in society, I was *no one*. Not in any way that truly mattered, at least.

And yet the way she looked at me, as if I were someone important, someone cherished, instead of just a prize to be married off to the highest bidder... It made no sense. And I told her as much.

"You, ah..." A light furrow appeared on her brow as she grappled for words.

"Ada, I'm sorry, but my people *will* come looking for me once they realize I'm gone. Someone will open a portal to the last location, and if I'm not here..."

My words died in my throat as a flash of light erupted in the distance behind Ada.

The shadowed settlement. Only it wasn't shadowed any longer.

Clear, pale light engulfed the buildings, the town gleaming like a jewel beneath the mountains.

"No," Ada rasped. She turned to me and sliced a dagger I hadn't even seen her draw across her palm. The wound instantly welled with crimson. "It won't be long now. I'll—"

My fingers wrapped around the silver pendant hanging from my neck before she could finish. The magic within it responded to my touch—only a trickle, a faint echo of the power I felt back at home, but it was enough.

The world around me slowed, the ever-shifting slices of time coming to a crawl, and I ran through the stillness, leaving the dark, as well as the girl with her delusions, behind.

CHAPTER TWO

My lungs burned, and a stabbing pain pierced one side of my abdomen, but I kept running, grateful I hadn't allowed myself to go *entirely* out of shape.

Though evading my parents by darting down the many corridors of our manor didn't come even near the distance I had to cover now.

Relief slammed into me when the press of buildings tightened and the wasteland lying beyond the town became nothing more than a memory. I braced myself against the wall, doubling over and sucking in deep breaths.

I made it. But I wasn't in the clear just yet.

An unpleasant weakness persisted in my legs when I pushed on, although at least my head felt clearer—and I wasn't gasping loud enough to be heard from several streets away.

Not that there was anyone in the vicinity to take notice.

The outskirts of Nysa—or at least that's what I *thought* the girl had named the settlement—were a flickering dance of shadows and faint blue light. Utterly abandoned.

The town, however, was not.

Voices ricocheted off the plain stone facades, reminding me of the time I was standing just beyond the coliseum at the race tracks, listening to the crowd cheer their favorite riders on. There had been an edge of hysteria etched into the sound then. Now, I made out nothing but pleasure.

Curious, I ventured down the streets but didn't take a direct path even when I noticed all the larger ones seemed to run diagonally, like rays of the sun, leading towards what could only be the center. Instead, I took the smaller alleys that branched off at irregular angles.

While I didn't hear anyone following me, the deeper shadows pooling between the two- and three-story buildings offered more comfort than the open setting of the avenues. It could be nothing more than a false sense of security, but I'd take it.

As I zigzagged ever closer to the heart of the town, the cobblestones filled up with people. Not stragglers, but entire groups of them, as if I had crossed some invisible demarcation line. What surprised me the most, though, was that unlike the girl in the rocky desert, none of them wore subdued colors. And yet there was a visible theme to their various attires nonetheless.

The Winter Solstice.

A warming blue of a new year, a sprinkle of green that hinted the world was gradually readying itself for the upcoming turn of the seasons, even brilliant dashes of gold reminiscent of sunlight, cut up the dominating sapphire hue of the town. My burgundy dress didn't quite fit in with their fashion, not in color nor in cut, but at least it didn't make me stand out like a sore thumb.

Besides, the passersby seemed far more interested in what lay deeper in Nysa than a solitary girl, lurking close to the building walls.

My fingers itched to grab hold of the pendant, slow the passing of time so I could move around freely and explore the unknown town without constantly looking over my shoulder or jumping at every hastily spoken word. But the power had barely worked out there in the fields. I couldn't trust it to last me the needed amount—or at least give ample warning before it faded.

A person moving from one end of the road to the other in the blink of an eye would attract far more attention than infiltrating the crowds.

I exhaled, the resolve pooling deep and steady in my stomach, then closed the distance to the largest group walking up ahead.

As we milled out onto one of the diagonal avenues, merging with the throng of people already flowing down the cobblestones, the blue gleam became brighter. Its sapphire shade softened into an even turquoise, and I was ashamed it took me so long to realize what the light was.

Not only the glint of winter but an imitation of the sky.

My sky.

The dome stretched above the buildings, a translucent sheen of brilliant blue that somehow didn't smother the glistening stars, only painted the dark canvas on which they lay a different color. Lips parted, I gazed up. How was this even possible?

It didn't feel like a portal, and the shape certainly wasn't one I'd ever seen. Not to mention the sheer size of it. Yet at the same time, I could taste the hint of power in the air, a soft thrumming that revealed this wasn't some natural occurrence.

"The Illusionists really gave it their best this year," a young dark-haired woman whispered to her companion, her head tilted up much the same way as mine.

He mumbled something I couldn't quite catch, though it definitely sounded like agreement, then added, "They accepted more practitioners into the main fray this year. The Magicians, too."

"Ohh!" The woman linked elbows with the man, who flashed her a wide smile. "Do you think they've set up the Summer tent again? My skin stayed tanned for a whole *month* the last time!"

I squinted up at the sky, trying to make sense of their conversation.

Illusionists. Magicians. They were the ones...*conjuring* this?

And what was a Summer tent?

The name was telling enough, true, but with the false sky looming over me, a reminder that there were things here I hadn't even considered, it would be more effort than it was worth to lose myself in speculations. Still, I strained my ears, hoping to catch more.

Right as the man commented on grabbing a drink first, another group walked by, whisking away the pair and drowning their conversation in a roll of boisterous chatter.

Knowing there was only one way to get my answers, I followed.

My mother always chided me that I was too curious for my own good. She claimed that the only reason I got away with such tendencies was because my father was a High Master, and that meant others were obligated to overlook my excessive thirst for knowledge instead of reprimanding me for it. It wasn't a trait valued in girls, usually snuffed out before it could develop, but my desire to learn about anything and everything that caught my interest wasn't something I could just stuff into a portal and send away.

Not that I could even *make* a portal.

A ridiculous rule—and one in the long line of many—that forbade women from using objects of power.

I stroked my necklace absentmindedly. It was a wonder no one had ever become aware of the strength hidden in its silver-and-gemstone-encrusted form.

Then again, I was cautious to never use it in front of an audience, regardless of how tempted I often was.

I let my hand fall down to my side, and continued down the street, ensconced from all sides by Nysa denizens. I didn't have to fake excitement to match their mood.

Everything inside me buzzed with anticipation.

None of us knew what, exactly, waited in the heart of the town, even if our ignorance was of various degrees. But their good spirits were more than enough to convince me it wasn't anything sinister. A Solstice celebration, if one cloaked in different entertainment than what I was used to.

With no High Masters around to look down their noses at me or parents to shoot me warning glances, I let the atmosphere claim me.

When the crowd tightened at the end of the street, shoulders bumping as laughter rose up front and fueled our curiosity, as well as urge to *see*, I felt no need to separate myself from the fray. On the contrary, I allowed the current to take me where it wished. It was oddly...liberating to forgo control.

Moments later, I finally saw what the bottleneck was—an elegant arch we had to stream through. Its stone surface was chiseled, boasting numerous ornaments that blended into a seamless whole from afar but stood out each on their own when

I passed by them. Swirls and stars, with the phases of the moon fanning out over the passage.

I would have stopped to examine the details if not for the press of bodies from behind.

A large square opened up ahead once I emerged on the other side of the arch, and when the crowd parted, scattering in every possible direction save from the one we came from, the air collectively left my lungs.

What...

This...

Everywhere I looked, people converged around gazebos and stalls, laughing, chatting, and releasing little sounds of wonder as every bit of the square offered its very own sight. On the left, butterflies fluttered their colorful wings and danced over upturned faces in a graceful, flirty rhythm. Beside them, a tent served steaming pitchers, the patrons cradling them in their hands as dainty, glimmering snowflakes descended from above. Just a few steps away, a display of effervescent mirrors sat, distorting the image of whoever peered into the glass.

I took another step, twirling around in an attempt to take it all in.

Trees made of crystal ice, the only dash of color the blossoms adorning the tips of their frosty branches; a green, fiery ring through which children jumped, giggling as the embers reached for them, only to settle down once more as they landed on their feet on the other side. But what truly drew my gaze was a fountain of starlight, pure and mesmerizing, a work of art that commanded the space with singular grace.

I was stunned by its simplicity, by the beauty of thousands of minuscule stars, cascading down the three levels before they were drawn up to the top again to repeat the cycle. I wanted to sit down before it, stare at this wonder until the flickering specks were imprinted on the backs of my lids...

And yet there was more. So much more to see.

Nysa reminded me of something from a dream. Only I knew even the deepest, wildest pockets of my imagination couldn't create something as breathtaking as this.

My world might have the gold of sunlight, but it was Nysa that shone.

These weren't some jester's tricks or stacked portals to create mosaics of living pictures—windows into different parts of our lands.

It wasn't reality reused. But facets of it *created*.

And it was beautiful.

I scanned the illuminated storefronts, the dresses, treats, and numerous peculiarities they displayed. There wasn't a single shop devoid of customers, and I yearned to join them. To buy myself one of the gilded masks, or the small, shimmering cupcakes designed to be eaten in a single bite. My stomach whined at the thought.

How long ago was it that I'd had my last meal?

I started moving towards the patisserie, the sweet touch of strawberries, vanilla, and sugar a tempting presence in the air when I remembered I had no coin. Nothing to offer in exchange for the wonderful items.

Even my jewelry was limited to my necklace, and that was one thing I would never part with, regardless of what I would gain in exchange.

I hurried away from the scent of baked goods but continued to walk alongside the storefronts. Admiring the wares kept my hunger at bay, although an undercurrent of longing remained.

Three girls in masks that radiated rainbow-tinted light burst through one of the doors, nearly sweeping me away. I tensed, but their matching apologetic expressions soothed the onset of nerves. With a smile, I stepped aside to let them pass, then pushed on, their voices disappearing as cheerful music from one of the stalls ensnared my senses. I slowed to catch more of the tune but didn't stop.

Once I reached the end of the square, I noticed an archway similar to the one I had come through, the phases of the moon stretching over the gate. Only where the previous arch marked the passage into the quiet and dark of the outskirts, this one was bathed in blue.

Intrigued, I padded forward.

Several people came from the other direction, so I kept to the edge, running my fingers over the chiseled grooves in the stone as I made my way to the other side. The widest avenue I had ever seen spilled out ahead, a smooth road separating the two stretches of cobblestones, lined with more icy trees. With the open space and fewer people crammed together, I instinctively rubbed my hands down my arms—but there was no chill to swat away.

If anything, I felt pleasantly warm, as if a phantom sun was laying its caresses upon my skin.

I glanced up, wondering if there was more to the dome-like imitation of my sky than color. It certainly *seemed* like the warmth was coming from there, although that left me with more questions than answers. I eyed the frosty trees and shook my head.

Trying to grasp everything at once rarely worked.

I stuck to the left side of the avenue, moving between the inner line of the open stalls and the bustling shops. Faintly, I could see the spiked tips of tents rising in the distance, their white-capped tops darkening into a silver-lined black.

These had to be the same tents the girl had been talking about.

"An illusion for an illusion?" an elderly man called out to me from up ahead, a smile fixed on his gradually shifting face. "A blooming dress, perhaps? Or hair of sun-kissed yellow?"

I returned his smile as I approached his iron-and-glass stall, noting how his features settled—save for the eyes.

They vacillated between various shades of green, as if they— he?—couldn't decide which hue would complement his gold-embroidered jade tunic best. Oddly, it wasn't unsettling.

How would it feel if he modified a part of me? Would I sense the change? Or only *appear* changed from the outside?

If only I had an illusion to offer.

I wanted to utter the words, maybe work out some other payment, but somehow knew it would be the wrong thing to say.

Every person I met, even that pair, watching the blue dome in awe, not unlike mine, *felt* different. They seemed to thrum with life, with some essence I couldn't quite place but was fairly certain shared the same core as the illusions on display around me.

The Illusionists and Magicians might have been responsible for the beauty filling Nysa's center, but I had a suspicion they weren't the only ones who possessed power. In fact, I was willing to bet I was the sole person here with nothing but a plain heartbeat in her chest and an almost useless pendant resting above it.

So I shook my head, even as a part of me ached to do so. "Nothing right now, thank you."

The man shrugged with a lightness to the gesture that

showed even refusals were part of the business, then went on to dabble with the length of his hair.

When a thick group of gray-haired women shuffled from a stall seemingly made of candy into a small bakery on the other side, and a narrow pathway opened up ahead, I used the opportunity to push forward. Without any idea how late it was or how much time I had already spent here, I hurried towards those illustrious tents, hoping to sneak a peek inside before they would close.

There was a persistent, weak voice at the back of my mind, warning that the longer I remained in Nysa, the harder it would be to find my way back home. But I didn't have it in me to return to that barren stretch of land just yet.

I told myself that it was purely pragmatic. Ada could still be waiting there, and I refused to come anywhere near that girl and her knife. Yet my heart spoke of the true reason.

I wasn't willing to give all of this up.

Streets veered off the avenue, all bathed in the same blue light, some of them ending in smaller versions of the two arches I'd walked through, while others twisted away and out of sight. I liked their somewhat quieter atmosphere, the intimacy of the small taverns with tables set up out front. Under different circumstances, that's where I would be, curled up with some book I wasn't supposed to read, alternating between losing myself in its lines and sneaking glimpses into other people's lives. But today, it was the pulse of the crowd that lured me in.

Three small girls rushed past me in a blur of wind that ruffled my dress. They giggled wildly as delicate, periwinkle birds followed in their wake, finding them regardless of how quickly they darted around vendors and icy trees. A short distance behind, their parents followed, elbows locked and bodies leaning towards one another as if to part were a burden neither of them wanted to bear. I stared after the amorous couple, longing dragging its vicious claws down my insides.

I would never have that.

I would never get to share that kind of affection with someone—at least not someone of my choosing. My father only needed to make the final decision between the two High Master's sons he deemed most appropriate, and that would be it.

A groan rose in my chest. I forced myself to look at the frosty, translucent trees, to follow the weaving path of snowflakes circling around a vendor's stall. But the bitterness in my chest remained.

I'd done my best to lessen my *value,* even took up a lover on my seventeenth year instead of waiting for marriage as I was supposed to—although Magnus had been far more than just a means to an end, even if it had been my resentment that had given me the initial courage to approach him.

The rest, however, was free of that particular taint.

Magnus was sweet, caring, supportive of my *whims* the others frowned upon. But he was also a commoner.

We knew our tryst and friendship couldn't last indefinitely. So we made the most of what we had.

Often, I wondered where his life had taken him. If he was happy.

I also knew better than to try and find out.

It was a miracle enough that Father had never learned his name after a nosy servant had told him of my *indiscretion.* He simply banished all seasonal workers from the estate and cut off my privileges for wandering around the grounds unchaperoned.

I still remembered the glimpse of Magnus's face I'd caught when our guards had escorted the lot of them away—the expression that hinted at absolutely no regrets for the time we had spent together. He'd marched off with his shoulders squared and head held high to some new part of Soltzen where he would start over.

No ties. No weight to slow him down.

A smile tugged on the corners of my lips, filling me with fleeting warmth. Magnus would have liked it here.

And, I realized with stark clarity, I did, too.

It was more than the illusions or the starlit sky—I could forge my own life here.

Maybe staying in this world wouldn't be so bad. I could keep my head down, find work somewhere, somehow, and—

A deafening silence pressed against my ears.

The crowd went still, as if the entire avenue was holding its collective breath. Even the illusions seemed to dull their brimming nature, becoming subdued, mute—a carefully shielded joy that continued to burn while doing its best to go unnoticed.

Keeping my back to the buildings, I craned my neck, hoping to see what had stopped the town's pulse. Hooves clicked against the cobblestones, merging with the too-loud pounding of my heart.

The previously immobile crowd pushed back as one, the avenue perfectly empty within the span of a few seconds.

No, not empty.

Cleared.

Riders in black leathers guided their steeds down the smooth stone of the corridor, their advance slow and every move—regardless how small—demanding attention. Some of the townsfolk averted their eyes, some lowered their heads, but no one dared to turn away despite their rigid postures bluntly projecting their need in a voiceless scream.

I saw him then.

A young man sitting atop a dark stallion, his pale features sharp, framed by a spill of silken, obsidian hair, just short enough to reveal the tattooed moon phases creeping up his neck from beneath the collar of his black jacket.

Regal and stern, with a presence that saturated the very air, he was without a doubt the most handsome man I had ever seen. And yet it wasn't his face or elegant demeanor that stole away my breath.

It was the shadows—tendrils of pure silver that seemed to unfurl from his body and dance in his wake.

Horrifying. And beautiful.

Fear stirred inside me, entwining with deep, silent admiration. I wanted to look away, but couldn't.

Wanted to distance myself from the coiling tongues of silver and brush my fingers against their curving form at the same time.

His blue gaze scanned the crowd as he rode farther, seeming to take in each and every face as if he were looking for someone.

The blood in my veins froze.

He searches for you, Ember, every year.

Ada's warning crashed against the walls of my mind until I felt as if the weight of her voice would bury me.

It was *him*. The Crescent Prince.

And his gaze was inches from locking onto mine.

CHAPTER THREE

MY LEGS REFUSED TO OBEY. I WAS TUCKED BEHIND A WALL OF people just thick enough that maybe—maybe I could have moved without him noticing.

Had I been capable of moving at all.

The Crescent Prince's sapphire gaze skimmed those standing to my left.

Three bodies away.

Two.

Something caught his attention, and he hesitated—a small halting in his progression I somehow felt more than saw. It was my last chance.

I didn't take it.

Pinned to the cobblestones, I failed to do anything but stare at that devastatingly handsome face, at the silver shadows unspooling behind him and creating a stark contrast to his obsidian hair.

Only one person left, then it would be *my* gaze he met.

Ada's warning replayed louder and louder in my head, the words unaffected by this slowing of time I seemed to be caught in. One not caused by magic, but my own indecision to flee—or surrender.

The brilliant sapphire turned towards me—

I stumbled back with a jerk. The fingers that had snapped around my upper arm yanked me sideways with such force a small gasp escaped my lips. A hand pressed against my lips to muffle the sound, followed by sharp, searing pain as my shoulder brutally collided with the sleek stones of the building set at the mouth of the alley.

My vision blurred, and the next thing I knew, my back was flat against what felt like a door, one hand still on my mouth while the other lay across my chest, blocking the pendant.

Every muscle in my body tensed and thrashed in a futile attempt to get away.

"Stop it," my assailant hissed.

Just as the pressure across my chest increased as if they leaned on me with the brunt of their weight, my mind caught up to the familiarity of the voice.

Trapped as I was, it took a nearly overwhelming amount of effort to soothe the choking waves of panic. My body kept fighting, but my senses cleared as I listened to the faint thrumming that came from the person struggling to hold me still. A different quality from what I had sensed when observing the illusions—a sound that was more akin to breathing than a melody. But I recognized its tune.

Ada.

Only now realizing I had been squeezing my eyes shut, I opened them and took in the girl's face. She was furious, perspiration beading on her forehead and dampening her hair as if she'd been running this entire time.

Despite our initial encounter and the growing discomfort of being trapped as I was, I willed myself to relax as the beating of hooves grew fainter, distant. Still, her hold didn't change. I dipped my chin in a gesture I hoped would convey my silent promise to not slip away the instant she let me go. A promise I meant to keep as long as she didn't pull her knife out.

Not that I was in any state to do much damage even if I wanted to.

My shoulder was throbbing hard enough to make me grit my teeth, and I was fairly certain that spill of warmth soaking the fabric of my dress was blood.

Eventually, Ada accepted I wasn't bluffing. She unclasped her hand from my mouth but shifted the other on my forearm as she pulled me away from the door. The tender flesh screamed in protest.

"Watch it," I snapped even as a rancid taste exploded at the back of my throat.

By the Sun, it *hurt*.

Ada must have realized her mistake because she quickly let go and grabbed my wrist instead. She was, however, still seething.

"What do you think you were *doing?*" Her gaze flickered from me to the now somewhat livelier avenue behind us, then back again. "I warned you of the Crescent Prince, and you came here to *flaunt* yourself before him?"

My cheeks heated. In part from the low-burning anger that this stranger who couldn't have been more than a year older than me was chiding me as if I were some rule-breaking brat. In part from the memory of how drawn I'd been to the prince, regardless of the primal fear those silver shadows and his own effect on people had instilled in me.

There was no real answer to her question. At least not a satisfactory one. So I held my silence.

I hadn't walked into Nysa with the intention to *flaunt* myself, but wasn't that precisely what I'd done?

Something warm brushed against my leg. I glanced down to see Lyra wiggling beneath my dress as if she could sense my discomfort and tried to ease the effect of Ada's words. I was touched by the dog's compassion, but it did little to lessen the blow of blazing fury rolling off Ada's skin.

Though the sight of the white-coated black tail jutting from underneath the burgundy fabric as Lyra rubbed her muzzle against my calves *did* soften the tense line of my lips.

And, perhaps, made me more inclined to partake in whatever unpleasant conversation I was certain would follow.

"Look, Ember." Ada let out a long breath, her jade eyes calming. "I'm sorry I snapped, startled you...and rammed you against the wall."

I lifted an eyebrow just as Lyra padded out from beneath my dress.

"But what happened..." She looked towards the avenue again where people continued with the celebrations—louder, more boisterous, as if they wanted to bury the memory of the prince's arrival in thick layers of merriment. "It was a hair's width away from disaster. We need to move before you announce yourself to the whole town."

The sympathy I'd just started to harbor due to her sincere concern evaporated in an instant. I wasn't blameless, but I didn't deserve *that* attitude, either.

Ada didn't seem to notice the change.

She tugged me deeper down the alley, but, holding on to that flicker of anger still coiling in my core, I snatched my wrist from her grip.

Some part of me wanted to roar in her face, but my voice came out surprisingly calm as I said, "You appear out of nowhere, talk like you know who I am, then pull a dagger on me. And now you expect that I'll just follow you down an empty street? Because what you've done so far *really* inspired me to trust that you have my best interests at heart?" I threw my hands in the air. "What's *wrong* with you?"

A furrow descended on Ada's brow, her features still aligned in a furious, sharp mask. Then something shifted.

Her eyes widened, lips forming a gentle *O*.

"You thought—you thought I was going to *hurt* you?"

I shot her a pointed look. To her credit, Ada actually seemed ashamed.

She glanced at her palm, only a faint line now marring her dark skin where she had slashed it open, and shook her head.

"You don't know... Shit." She looked at me. "Our power is fueled by blood. Everything you saw out there comes from it. When I drew the dagger, I only meant to place an illusion on your dress, so that you would blend in better. You were really lucky you didn't run into any guards."

"Oh."

We stared at each other for a moment, swallowed by the faint shadows the balcony jutting out overhead cast on us.

"But the people at the stalls... I hadn't noticed any of them brandish blades or sport wounds."

Granted, I paid more attention to the magic, but I *had* spoken to that vendor, seen him up close...

Ada's lips pulled into a straight line. "Concealed pins in

clothing. A single drop is usually enough for Illusionists and Magicians. For what they do out there."

"But you're not one of them." I ventured a guess.

Ada shook her head again.

"I'm a Mage." Her gaze dipped down, and I noticed her foot had started drawing small circles across the blue-tinted cobblestones. "I messed up, and I'm sorry. I'm really, really sorry. For everything. I thought your people knew about us, at least a little. I shouldn't have assumed, and I'll try to explain, I swear, but would you *please* follow me someplace safe before this whole situation gets even worse?"

I stared into her pleading eyes, my thoughts filled with those silver shadows, the sudden iciness that had descended upon the avenue.

I inclined my head. "Fine." I glanced at Lyra who was watching us from a little farther away, ears perked up and dark eyes focused. "But I want those explanations as soon as we get there or I'm leaving."

Eagerly, Ada nodded and snatched my hand, pulling me after Lyra who was already padding down the alley before us.

THE PATH ADA guided me down—or was it Lyra, since she was always ahead of us, not once taking a wrong turn?—took us away from the bustling life of Nysa's main avenue, but not as far into the outskirts where the people were so few as to make us stand out. We hadn't crossed under any arches, so I assumed we were still within the perimeter of the town's center. Though with more changes in direction than I could count, including some backtracking, it was hard to pinpoint just where we truly were.

Always half a step ahead of me, Ada moved with that utter silence of someone who wasn't a stranger to sneaking about. I recognized the trait, given I'd nurtured it myself ever since the time I realized I couldn't rely on my family to provide me the education or liberties I craved.

Unfortunately, party-wear, as much as I loved it, wasn't exactly a friend to stealth. If what Ada claimed were true, and she *was* expecting my arrival, it would have been nice if she'd brought a change of clothes with her. After all, what if I had emerged in Somraque in nothing but a nightgown? Or less?

I scrunched up my nose, then focused on doing my best to match her as we drifted down the cobblestones, constantly reading her body language so I wouldn't falter when she suddenly came to a halt or cut to the side. Crashing into her one time already was more than enough.

While I couldn't figure out how, Ada knew without fault when to slink into another alley or hide in a doorway, sensing the black-uniform-clad men long before they marched by.

"The Crescent Prince's guard," she'd whispered to me the first time we watched them from the shadows, although I'd recognized their attire from earlier.

Aside from that one instance, neither Ada nor I spoke. Luckily, the rest of the passersby made up for our silence.

Every so often, during the lulls in the crowds, she would glance at the flowing red of my garment, then trained her gaze on the street once more. When I caught her for the fifth time, I sighed and rolled my eyes.

"All right, spill it. What's bothering you? You want to magic the dress?"

The slight wince she gave me was answer enough. I waved my hand through the air in the universal sign to get on with it.

Gratitude swept across her features, and the very next instant she dragged me into an empty side alley. She pulled the familiar dagger from under the hem of her tunic, looked at me one more time as if to confirm I wasn't about to run away, then carefully drew the blade across her palm.

Like before, blood welled. But as I prepared myself for Sun knows what, she merely closed her fingers into a fist, gaze fixed on the bodice of my gown. A faint thrumming spread around me, the sensation foreign, though not irksome.

The dress shimmered before my eyes. Sleeves fanned out just beneath my elbows and draped over my wrists, embroidered with golden thread, the opulent, layered skirts becoming demure, darker, and far less flamboyant if still pleasing to the eye. Oddly, I could still feel the material weigh down on my hips, the touch of fabric against my legs precisely as it had been moments before.

Of course it was the same, I chided myself. These people dealt in illusions. While the sensations I'd felt back when I passed the different stalls were real—a touch of frost, a spring breeze—they had all appealed to other senses. Not sight.

I hadn't truly *touched* any of the visible displays.

Unease slithered through me.

A trick. All of it was one grand trick.

But carried on the wings of that thought came another, far more terrifying one.

What *was* real in this world?

CHAPTER FOUR

GOOSEBUMPS SWEPT ACROSS MY SKIN.

Was Ada truly the girl standing before me? Was I even in a town, or had it *all* been an illusion, thrust around me the instant I had slipped into this world?

I remembered then. The ache in my shoulder. The very *solid* feel of the wall I'd crashed into, which could quite possibly have been nothing more than the stones that made up some Sun forsaken—I don't know—dungeon or maze or something just as equally lovely I was currently locked in.

No, I told myself firmly.

Not all of my senses were tricked. And the dress, this *other* dress, gave off some sort of offshoot of the thrumming I'd felt within the people. Stronger, in a way, though just an echo of what had coursed through the air when Ada had released her blood—a simple, faint mark of magic at work that separated it from reality.

For her part, Ada didn't say anything as I sorted through the jumbled mess that was my thoughts. The struggle must have shown on my face, given how carefully she considered me, but she made no move to intrude on this silent battle.

I liked her a little better for that.

"I'm all right," I said once I was sure the words coming out of my mouth wouldn't be a blatant lie.

When Ada continued to look at me, I added, "And the dress is beautiful. I mean, your illusion is."

Another truth.

Maybe I was crossing personal boundaries, complimenting someone's magic, but now that the worst of my panic had subsided, I couldn't *not* admire Ada's work.

A few tentative steps revealed it even moved like a true garment, rippling and swaying with every kick of my feet.

Ada nodded almost imperceptibly when I was done exploring the lengths to which the illusion went, though a brief smile did touch her lips before she peered around the edge of the building we were hidden behind. Closer to the floor, Lyra did the same.

The dog went out first, her tail curled over her back, and we followed. The majority of the people seemed to loiter around chatting or were unhurriedly making their way towards Nysa's grand avenue, but there was a trickle of them already leaving the celebrations as well.

Perhaps not everybody was eager to partake in revelry after the Crescent Prince's appearance.

We used them as cover, and for the first few minutes, I was preoccupied with not accidentally bumping into anyone with the fanned sleeves that weren't there or skirts that were, but shouldn't be. It wasn't until I realized that probably half of the people wore illusions of some kind that I relaxed, feeling more than a little foolish.

Once we had a fair amount of distance between the closest groups and us—just enough to make us seem as if we were part of the crowd without giving any of them the ability to overhear us—questions once more rattled the surface of my mind.

Safe or not, I really couldn't wait any longer.

"The Crescent Prince," I started, stepping over a dented cobblestone. "You said he searches for me. But what does he want? *How* can he want anything from me when I had no idea your world even *existed* until today..."

Voices rose in the distance, and Ada cut a quick look their way. Just a couple of boys, careening out the tavern door with a familiar tipsy sway to their step. I looked back at Ada, eyebrows raised.

"Eighteen years ago, the most powerful Mages felt a stirring. A—a light, flickering into existence." She bit the inside of her cheek. "They all felt *you*, Ember."

My fingers tightened around the pendant I hadn't even been aware I was clutching. Forcefully, I uncurled them, then let my arm fall by my side. The scent of freshly baked bread suffused the air, but even my previously growling stomach hardly reacted.

"You're saying they felt my birth in a different world?" I tried to mask the skepticism in my tone and failed spectacularly. "You do realize how odd all of this sounds?"

"I'm well aware," Ada grumbled, though there was a fierceness in her expression that sealed my lips shut. "But odd or not, it doesn't change that that's what my mother sensed, what several other Mages from powerful families experienced—even if they didn't know *what* it was. And the Crescent Prince, Mordecai... He felt it, too."

Mulling over her words, it took me a moment to realize Ada had said his name. Mordecai. The word had been filled with venom, uttered with almost a kind of hesitation that led me to think she wouldn't have spoken it at all if it weren't for my benefit.

Fear had immobilized the crowd during the Crescent Prince's procession. Ada's hatred overpowered hers.

But it was there nonetheless, like mist that refused to dissipate entirely.

We turned down another street, this one cocooned in a darkness deeper than all those before it. Only a few stragglers with their shifting feet broke the predominant quiet. Maybe we had already crossed beyond Nysa's inner ring despite the obvious lack of arches.

Ada struck me as the kind of girl who would find every possible entry and exit point.

With Lyra trotting several steps ahead, I studied my companion. Her profile was stark in the once more subdued sapphire light, the growing pool of shadows underlining her determination to get me away. Her belief that all she had told me was the truth.

In a world of illusions, this was her reality.

But I had seen too many people convinced in facts tailored to their liking to fall into those clutches quite so easily.

"Look, Ember,"—she glanced over her shoulder, then slowed so we were walking side by side—"my mother will be able to tell you more. She was there when it all happened. She was the one to push the spell through the veil separating our worlds to keep you from accidentally coming here as a child..."

"How *did* I come here?"

Instead of replying, Ada nudged me with her elbow. I flattened myself against the wall when I spotted the dagger in her hand, blood already tainting her palm.

I willed myself to go perfectly still, then suppressed a gasp when I noted that we were suddenly ensconced *within* the wall, as if the building had lurched forward, altering its shape. But what surprised me the most was that I could actually *see* through the illusion.

The weather-worn stones now extended before me were oddly translucent, letting me catch a glimpse of two men clad in black tunics and combat-appropriate pants walk by. Silver embroidery lined their upturned collars, corded forearms on display where the sleeves ended just beneath the elbow. The younger of the guards, the one with russet hair and piercing amber eyes, glanced sideways, as if sensing something was amiss.

How well did they know the town? If this was a part they usually patrolled, they would surely see the protruding facade—

I sucked in a silent breath, Ada going tense beside me. For the longest of moments, I could almost see him walk over and touch the wall that wasn't there.

And perhaps he would have, too, if a massive, scaled beast hadn't swept down from above, spitting trails of crackling fire.

The russet-haired guard yelped, then quickly caught himself. His gaze darted to the pair of laughing boys I'd spotted coming from the tavern earlier.

"No pre-approved larger illusions allowed during the celebrations," he shouted across the darkness while his partner brandished a blade from its sheath. "Snuff out your magic *now* unless you want me to fine you."

The two boys chuckled wildly, but the beast dissolved, leaving nothing but the night sky once more above us.

"Drunken little shits," the second guard spat as he sheathed his dagger, then gestured to the younger one to come over.

But the man, while acknowledging the call, turned towards our altered building instead.

Neither Ada nor I even dared to breathe as those amber eyes scanned the windows devoid of life, the shut doors tucked amidst the massive gray stones. All false.

"Come on, Tristan. Unless you want me to report a dragon made you scream, we have to get going to make it to the checkpoint in time."

Grunting, the russet-haired man spun on his heels. It seemed to take him forever to actually *reach* the other guard. He swept his gaze in our direction once more, then faced his partner and nodded. Together, they marched down the street, muttering something about how the celebrations should be banned altogether.

A part of me sympathized.

Even if they were Mordecai's men, I'd been around enough guards to know their positions weren't the kind to inspire envy. Long hours and dealing with people who broke the rules—more often than not just to provoke them, all of it made even worse during feasts and parties... It was ungrateful work, regardless of the pay.

Still, that twinge of sympathy didn't make me any more inclined to come face-to-face with them.

If they were anything like the men at home, their master's word was law. Death would be preferable to disobedience.

When the darkness wrapped around the guards' forms at last, footsteps fading as they turned into another alley, Ada's shoulders dropped. She dissolved the immaterial wall before us with what couldn't have been more than a thought.

"I honestly don't know," she said.

Seconds passed before I realized what she was referring to. My question. She had no idea how I'd traversed worlds, either.

I nibbled on my lip, then followed her down a different, larger street than the one the guards had taken. Lyra came to pad by our side from wherever it was that she had taken shelter.

With Ada in the lead, I moved automatically—pausing when she did, hastening my step whenever she sped up. Lyra occasionally zigzagged between us but seemed to take notice of my predominantly detached state and made sure to give my skirt a wide berth.

There was just...too much chatter clogging up my mind. I had no means to process the fragments of information I'd gleaned.

The sheer volume of the unknown produced a turbulent pressure that threatened to shatter me, so I focused on the one thought that stood above them all. One answer Ada could give. Hopefully.

"Ada, why does Mordecai want me?"

His name tasted like poison on my lips, lethal yet alluring. I couldn't block the image of the regal Crescent Prince from manifesting in front of my eyes—the coiling silver shadows, the sensual curve of his cruel lips.

Ada's voice dispelled the apparition. "For your magic."

The bitter laugh that bubbled from my chest earned me a curious look from Lyra. Ada's wasn't far off, either.

"I'm a *woman* from Soltzen. We have no magic. Can't have it by law. This"—I tugged on the pendant—"is just a stolen trickle."

Bewilderment danced across Ada's features, followed by a delicate frown. "Why shouldn't women have magic?"

"Because it belongs to High Masters," I said dryly. The old, familiar bitterness began to rise once more. "Because it is their right, and their right alone to wield the objects of power while our place is to swoon over them, croon how magnificent and resplendent they are."

"But that's absurd!" Ada exploded. Even Lyra cocked her large ears, sending a low growl to curl through the night. "No, it's more than absurd. It's disgusting!" Her brilliant jade gaze dug into mine. "And you, Ember, you have the power to change *everything!*"

She sounded so certain that my initial denial was briskly whisked away by curiosity. I opened my mouth, eager to learn the chunks of vital information I seemed to be missing when heavy footsteps sounded up ahead.

Ada cursed and stilled by my side, Lyra scurrying away behind an empty pot. I caught a flash of silver and black.

Guards. Three guards blocked the mouth of the street.

And they were staring right at us.

CHAPTER FIVE

IT WAS ONE OF THOSE INSTANCES WHEN EVERYTHING SEEMED to slow down. Not from the kind of magic stored in my pendant. No, it was sheer, utter terror that brought things down to a crawl.

Even the thrashing, hard beat of my heart was spaced out, punctuating every dreadful slice of the seconds I stood there, helpless and exposed.

The guards' eyes skimmed me with nothing more than curiosity, perhaps a smidgeon of appreciation, but narrowed their gazes once they saw Ada. I reached for her hand, hoping she would pick up on my intentions. If we could play the whole thing off as if we were just two friends out for the celebrations, they might return to the lingering glances directed at our appearance, not our identities.

But it quickly became clear Ada had other ideas.

It was my turn to curse.

That damned dagger was out in her hand and with it any

chance we might have had of *not* drawing attention folded in on itself as abruptly and irrevocably as a weak portal. By the Sun, didn't she ever *think* before acting?

In mute horror, I watched as something shifted within the guards. Recognition.

They leaped forward before the full impact of what had just happened could hit me.

The one on the left produced a blade of his own. Only Ada was faster.

She slashed the steel across her skin, only this time, she didn't go for the palm. No, the bloody well of crimson gaped down the length of her entire forearm. My hand flew to the pendant, fingers hesitating just above the three dark, circular stones protruding from the silver surface.

Every instinct in my body screamed to call to its magic, to slow down time in earnest and give us a chance to escape, however short. But the way Ada's eyebrows furrowed in concentration, the way her green eyes seemed to shine in tune with the thrumming radiating from her body... I waited.

And the guards stilled.

I didn't know how long the five of us stood there, the sounds of the celebrations a muffled buzzing in the distance. While the streets we'd taken had been deserted, we must have veered closer to the center at some point. I strained my hearing, listening for any rogue steps, any signs that someone else was coming. But aside from a touch of wind that licked at my collarbones and caught in my hair, nothing stirred.

Not even the shouts I had expected to rip themselves from the guards' mouths.

A steady *drip-drip-drip* fluttered to my ears. Ada.

I couldn't tell what she was doing to the men, what kind of

power she was coaxing from her veins, yet there was no mistaking the subtle changes that fell across their features.

Wrinkles loosening. Jaws unclenching. Even the matching hard sets of their eyes became softer around the edges, although the tension didn't slip away entirely.

As if the threat that had had them wound up was now nothing more than a casual inconvenience.

While they were still staring our way, they didn't seem to be looking at *us* any longer.

The hairs at the nape of my neck stood on end, and it took every ounce of my will to not give in to my curiosity and turn around to see what it was that had grabbed their attention. I didn't know how illusions worked. Were they all the same, pliant to motion? Or would movement break this particular brand and cause me to fall beyond the reach of whatever spell Ada was weaving?

So I remained locked in place, observing not the guards, but Ada's face out of the corner of my eye.

Her skin seemed to have lost some of its warm glow, her lips pressed tightly together as blood ran down her arm and onto the cobblestones, tainting them crimson. She wavered on her feet, like a blade of grass in a soft breeze, and the thrumming seemed to become louder. More forceful. It reverberated through my body, a peculiar sensation, though not entirely invasive.

"Stay *perfectly* still," Ada hissed.

The guards broke into a run.

The edges of my pendant dug into my palm as I tensed, the urge to step closer to Ada, make us into as small a target as possible, thrashing within me.

All three men aimed for my side of the street. The

hammering of their boots ricocheted off the building that was too close for comfort.

Together, they would never make it through the narrow space between the stone facade and my body.

Stay perfectly *still,* Ada's words replayed in my mind. I had to trust her.

At least in this.

The tallest of the three pushed ahead of his companions. He breezed past me with room to spare, but the remaining two didn't tighten their formation as much as I'd hoped. Especially when the gruff, dark-haired one still hadn't put away his blade.

Silver flashed under the demure sapphire light, the guard's hand pumping—

The contact sent me careening sideways.

Biting down a scream as his blade snagged the full skirts of my dress, I steadied myself, grateful the sharp steel had taken off a strip of fabric, not skin. As the footfalls grew fainter, then disappeared in earnest, some of the stiffness left my spine.

But only for a pitiful instant.

Ada swayed, and with the liquid looseness of her limbs, she didn't look like she would be able to recover. I lurched to the side and snaked my arm around her, catching her the split second before she would have toppled down. My shoe skidded on the blood smeared across the cobblestones, back screeching in protest as I fought for balance with Ada now a deadweight in my arms.

Muscles trembling, I readjusted my hold. "Shit, shit, shit..."

I dragged us towards the buildings where Lyra was waiting, crouched in the deepest shadow. Not knowing what else to do, I lowered both of us down and set my back against the cool stone

GAJA J. KOS & BORIS KOS

as I cradled Ada's limp body, dreading every drop of blood that trailed down her skin.

Lyra let out a soft whine, sniffing around our feet and steering clear of the smears of crimson. The bleeding.

I needed to staunch the bleeding.

I reached over to tear away a strip of my already tattered dress when Ada's head lolled to the side, her limbs eerily boneless.

"No, no, no, tell me what to do," I whispered as I ripped the fabric.

Even if I bound her wound, I had no herbs or alcohol to snap her out of this state.

I exhaled. One thing at a time.

Carefully, I braced Ada better against me, then grabbed hold of her injured arm to inspect the wound. The slice was viciously long and...*closing?*

I blinked, lips parting in what might have been a curse if I hadn't been so stunned. Lyra watched me patiently—now seated by my side—as if confirming what my mind refused to accept. I looked from her back to Ada, at that wretched gash that was, indeed, knitting itself together.

The strips of fabric fluttered from my hand.

The longer I stared, the lesser the wound, until there was nothing but the slowly caking blood left marring her dark skin.

Impossible, I thought for a moment.

Before I remembered that I was in another world, holding a girl who could weave illusions in my arms.

A weak laugh bubbled from my lips.

Of course people who used their blood to perform magic would have a way to circumvent the whole slow healing thing.

"Good to know you're having fun," Ada's hoarse voice wove through the darkness.

I brushed a damp strand of dark red hair from her forehead, but despite my efforts, only laughed harder. "You have to admit you *are* quite fun to be around."

She chuckled. "I suppose I am."

A blur of white and black, and Lyra was standing with her front paws on Ada's shoulder, licking furiously at her cheek. Then leaped up to smack a wet kiss on my nose.

The leaden weight that had lurked in the air disappeared thanks to her antics. I stroked her head, running my fingers behind her ears before gently shooing her away. Lyra didn't go far, but she did give me enough space to help Ada back onto her feet. The street was still abandoned, so I took my time hoisting her up. Despite my care—and the steel grip on her arm—Ada swayed.

Stubborn, for not letting me keep her in a half embrace, but I made do with the situation, maintaining my free hand by her side just in case her tipsiness grew worse. Her falling all over the place wouldn't help our cause, especially when Ada was obviously resolute not to waste a single second more.

At least Lyra appeared to agree with me. She kept wagging her odd, elegant tail and kept sending me what seemed like grateful glances as I took the brunt of Ada's weight whenever her foot snagged against a cobblestone.

"I'm all right now," she said once we turned left at the intersection where the guards had stumbled upon us. "Really, Ember, you can let go."

I shot her a skeptical look but unlocked my fingers once I saw the determination lending her features a sharp edge.

I knew that look. And I respected it.

If she felt like proving to herself that she didn't need my help, it was her right to do so. Though that didn't mean I was about to stop looking out for her.

So while Ada focused on walking in a straight line, I kept an eye on our surroundings, offering my support in the one way I could.

The sounds of revelry turned into nothing more than a memory the longer we walked, and the utter lack of people marked these streets as part of the outskirts. Different from the ones I'd first explored, but blanketed by the same tranquility.

Shadows deepened, the blue glow remaining only in wisps that caressed the roofs. Maybe it was my imagination, but I could have sworn I felt the vastness of the rocky desert expand my lungs and fill me with something that eerily reminded me of blunt relief.

For all I knew, Ada might still harbor some nefarious purpose for getting me alone, although after everything we'd been through, the thought sat wrongly in my mind for the brief span I entertained it. Even if I didn't trust *her*, I trusted her intention to get me out of Nysa unseen.

My fingers traced the three stones on the pendant. If push came to shove, I could just slip away again.

Mordecai, on the other hand... I didn't think I could escape him on my own.

Even now, some dark and clearly irrational part of me kept wondering what would have happened had I stayed...

I frowned at myself, grateful Ada's gaze was still focused on the darkness ahead. I was pretty certain she wouldn't appreciate the uncanny way my thoughts seemed to swirl around one another when it came to the Crescent Prince, tugging me between this inexplicable allure that had ignited inside me and the harsh reality of danger I'd seen with my own eyes.

By the Sun, it wasn't like I was gullible for handsome faces. If *that* were true, my father would have undoubtedly uncorked his finest bottle of liquor and married me off in a flash.

"Ember?"

Crap. Ada was staring at me, probably had been for a while.

I bit my lip and scattered the last remnants of the black-and-silver image filling up my treacherous mind.

"Those men," I ventured slowly, tasting the question before letting it slip into the air. "What did you do to them?"

"Something I shouldn't."

I cocked an eyebrow. "Now you *know* I won't give up until you tell me more..."

Ada sighed, but beneath the discontent so evident in the flat line of her lips, there was also something else.

Pride, I thought with no small amount of amusement.

Given the state she had been in afterward, it wasn't difficult to assume whatever magic she spun from her blood was no minor thing. Now I had my confirmation—as well as a nagging curiosity to extract every last detail from her.

But before I had the chance, Ada motioned me to stay back. She crept forward to peer around the edge of a two-story building with an assortment of small balconies jutting out over the street, then waved me to move on. Lyra, too.

When we caught up with her, Lyra took the front once more while I kept by Ada's side. Only a single row of houses separated us from the rocky land stretching beyond the town.

My senses hadn't been fooling me.

That touch of vastness in the air grew stronger, as if amidst

Nysa's walls, it couldn't hope to rival the thrumming presence of magic. Here, it reigned.

The essence of this world, uninterrupted.

Although what surprised me even more than the staggering difference, were the trees standing sentry on the perimeter, their branches dark and sporadic leaves strangely colorless. Desaturated.

Not illusions. But life as it existed under the night sky.

The fragile, somber beauty of it nearly caused me to fall behind. Thankfully, Ada hadn't gone far, and once I shook off the wonder that had filled me moments earlier, I noticed she had visibly relaxed, too. She thrust her hand in her hair in a casual gesture, revealing the not-so-long-ago-sliced-up forearm.

My eyes narrowed on the nearly unmarred skin. We still had unfinished business between us.

"So," I tried again. "What did you say you did to those guards?"

Ada snorted but followed it up with a conspirator's look.

If she continued in this direction, I just might grow fond of her in earnest.

She brushed a hand down the sleeve of her tunic and flicked off the few bits of dried blood that had still clung to her skin. "What you've seen in town, the decorations, displays, the wares they were selling... Those were just products of Illusionists and Magicians. The former affect the mind, the latter the body."

I nodded. I figured as much, though it was nice to hear I'd hit the mark.

"But I'm a *Mage*. We..." She paused, training her gaze on the sky before meeting mine—searching for words. Or maybe just deciding how much she was willing to share. "We hold the range of both powers in our blood, as well as the combined strength, and it gives even the weakest of us the ability to do more than any of them ever could."

"But you're not weak, are you?"

She couldn't be. Not with what I'd felt when she had unleashed her blood.

Ada shook her head, the fiery spill of her hair glistening under the starlight. "I come from the most powerful line of Mages in Somraque."

"I didn't say you could boast," I teased.

She flashed me a small smile, but it faded quickly, the *crunch* of her steps suffusing the temporary hesitation. "I made those guards believe *and* feel we weren't in that alley. That they had gone after some fleeing drunk who had flaunted illusions despite the Celebrations' Decree."

It sounded pretty reasonable. And...tame. Even if she *had* hijacked the men's minds and warped their reality.

"So why shouldn't you do what you did? Is it because of this... Celebrations' Decree? That's what the guard was referring to, wasn't he? With the dragon?"

"Yes. But that's not it. Not all of it, at least." She rubbed her forehead, then let out a harsh breath. "I shouldn't have done it because magic like that leaves an imprint. If the Crescent Prince looks into their minds during their reports, he'll find my touch there. And he'll know I'm hiding something important enough to risk influencing his guards, which is quite an offense all on its own."

"Oh."

"Yeah."

There was more to the story, some past Ada shared with the Crescent Prince—or at least his men, if not him directly. Questions continued to flood my mind, but one glance at her solemn face told me she was struggling enough without me pressing why she was a person of interest. Or why it was so important that Mordecai didn't find out I was here, aside from my supposed magic.

So I simply followed her, both of us wrapped in our own thoughts.

Once we reached the desaturated trees that were even lovelier in their gloom up close than from afar, Lyra broke into a gleeful sprint. I peered after the dog, watching her smooth skin glisten under the moonlight that pierced the veil of gossamer clouds.

At first, I couldn't puzzle out what had set her off. Then I saw it.

A house.

She was running towards a house.

I half turned towards Ada, but she wasn't paying me any attention. A conflicting blend of tension and relief played across her face, although nothing that would hint at imminent danger.

I filed the impression away, then looked back at what must have been our destination. With its stone walls and small windows, the building wasn't unlike those I'd seen so far, if a bit larger. And yet there was one staggering difference—a deviation that had made me write the structure off as a piece of landscape earlier. Where the buildings in Nysa stood tucked together, wall to wall, in long, uninterrupted lines, this one had no neighbors.

It stood alone, with space stretching out of all sides, as if rejected from the others' company.

Or like a miniature manor, set apart from the rest not by some imposed law, but choice. As if it were law unto itself.

A faint thrumming crept up my legs as we crossed the flat

stretch of land beyond the trees, but if there was some illusion lurking nearby, I couldn't see it. Much like Lyra.

Looking around for any telltale sign of the dog, I padded up to the front door after Ada and nearly collided with her back as she came to a stop. I extracted my foot from where it tangled in the frayed, uneven hem of my dress, then stepped back when Ada turned around to face me.

Her green eyes met mine. "Are you ready for your answers?"

"I am," I said, and meant it, even if echoes of concerns continued to linger. But after everything I'd seen in the whirlwind of the past hours, I was craving to learn all that I could more than I feared it.

Without preamble, Ada dispelled the illusion blanketing my body and gave me a stern once-over. Seemingly satisfied with what she saw—my conviction more than my dress, I imagined— she opened the door. I steeled myself for whatever waited beyond the threshold, but the breath still escaped my lungs when my gaze fell on an older woman perched on a loved, velvet armchair in the room that opened up on the left.

"Mother," Ada said, bowing her head lightly. "The savior... She's here."

The word *savior* echoed in my mind, a warning that this was one of those key pieces I was missing. And yet it failed to snap my attention.

From the frail woman.

Or from the veins that branched all across her dark skin— every single one of them pure silver.

CHAPTER SIX

THE SIGHT CAUGHT ME SO OFF GUARD THAT IT WASN'T UNTIL Ada placed a tentative hand on my elbow that I realized I was staring. Rudely.

Lyra curled up by the old woman's feet, a long sigh uncurling from the dog's chest as if she'd just gotten rid of a terrible burden. I blinked. I hadn't even noticed her enter the room.

Then again, I hadn't seen *anything* beyond those silver veins. Not the gentle roar of the fire or the ornate grandfather clock. Just the veins. How they appeared to be almost invisible where they ran deep under her skin, then painfully bright as they neared the surface.

They threatened to pull me under again, but Ada saved me from plunging into the bone-chilling abyss.

"Ember." Her voice was soft, as if she were afraid I would run away at any given moment. "It's all right. My mother won't hurt you. The veins... They're—"

"A *gift* from the one who hunts you," the woman finished, every word as sharp as a dagger as it left her lips. "Ember, is it?"

I nodded, actually a bit surprised I managed even that much.

She gestured to the empty armchair, just as lovingly worn as the one she was in, although set a little farther away from the crackling fire. "Come, sit with me. You must be overwhelmed."

More stunned and in serious need of answers than overwhelmed, really, but I had no desire to argue over semantics.

If she believed I was a frightened doe, stranded in a foreign world... She was right about the latter, but not the former. Still, her assumption might play out in my favor. I'd seen it back at home, the loose lips and lack of caution people adopted when they thought they were dealing with someone who could barely process the basics. I held on to the hope that Ada's mother was no different—and would fill in the blanks that had only been multiplying every step of the way.

Sucking in a breath, I glanced at Ada, then walked across the carpeted floor and sat on the very edge of the armchair. Keeping a respectable distance from the woman without making it seem as if I was reluctant to be close to her.

Not because of the veins, regardless of their eerie appearance.

I simply didn't know her, and this way, I was in the direct line of the door in case something went wrong.

"I'll make us all some tea," Ada offered, already making her way towards the rudimental archway before disappearing out of sight.

She didn't look back.

Briefly, I contemplated following her, but if this peculiar woman could explain to me what Ada couldn't—or perhaps didn't want to—then I had no choice but to stay. At least Lyra seemed content, her muzzle resting on her paw and eyes drifting between awareness and sleep.

Her, I trusted.

The woman observed me with eyes a shade darker than Ada's, waiting for my next move. Her body might have appeared frail, but now that the initial surprise had worn off, I could see her appearance was as well-crafted as any illusion I'd seen so far. But like them, she, too, had signs that pointed to another reality lurking beneath.

The immaculate, braided ebony updo. The straight line of her spine as she reclined lightly to the side, as if watching the world from a throne.

Frail, but a force nonetheless.

I inched back, sinking into the plush armchair, and folded my hands in my lap. The crackling of the fire gave texture to the silence, and faintly, I could hear the sound of boiling water coming from the other room. Using this slice of normalcy as an anchor, I schooled my face into a neutral expression, although every now and then, my gaze still drifted to the silver branching up the woman's neck, her temples, her cheeks, so very much like the one I had seen coiling in Mordecai's wake.

"My daughter's a good girl, but she sometimes forgets her manners." The corners of her eyes crinkled, rearranging the smaller argent capillaries. "I'm Telaria Aldane."

"Pleasure to meet you," I responded automatically. The years of living at my father's estate made the lie slip easily from my lips.

A single edge of the woman's lips curled upward, as if she knew the encounter was far from pleasant, yet said nothing on the matter. Instead, her eyes flickered towards the kitchen before she stretched her arms out in front of her.

Instinctively, I leaned back. Then realized she wasn't reaching for me.

She was displaying the silver veins.

"These are a reminder of how far the Crescent Prince is willing to go to secure what he desires."

Cold slithered down my spine, but still, I angled my body forward, observing the branched paths that glimmered as brightly as the moon I had seen lingering in the sky. I settled back in the chair and eyed Telaria warily.

She drew her arms back, tugging on the short sleeves of her dress in a kind of afterthought. The gesture made it seem as though she regretted there wasn't more fabric, more cover to conceal her marks, but I couldn't shake the suspicion this was merely an intended effect on her part. Driving home the awareness of how cruel the Crescent Prince was.

It was simply too meticulous to be anything less.

"Why?" I asked. "Why would he do this?"

Hurt you.

Hurt me, given the chance.

I was growing weary of stumbling in the dark.

A log *cracked* in the fireplace, warmth lapping at me as if I were only gradually thawing.

"How much has my daughter told you?"

"Not nearly enough."

The words were out before I could stop them.

But Telaria only nodded and pursed her mouth into a grave line. Her pine-green eyes turned sharp yet distant at the same time as she looked at the window, as if she were seeing images replay on the canvas of night.

"When I felt your birth eighteen years ago, Ember, right on the Winter Solstice, a blessing from the Stars, I knew I only had a few fragile moments to send forth the spell. Even Ada, the lively child that she was at less than two years of age, had gone perfectly still, as if she understood the rush, the importance of reaching out to you before the veil would thicken. Before we lost you to your world, or to *him*, for good." A fleeting ghost of a smile fell upon her lips, her raspy voice becoming heavier, thicker. "I succeeded. But the Crescent Prince—he learned of the spell."

My spine straightened. "Wait. The Crescent Prince—Mordecai? But he..."

"He's an old soul parading in a young body. I suspect he existed long before my great-great-grandparents had written records of him, his appearance never changing."

I frowned. "He tricked time?"

Between portals folding together different geographical points, blood potent with magic that could deceive all senses, and my own pendant, capable of slowing time, who knew what other powers were out there? His silver shadows certainly looked different from everything I'd encountered so far.

It shouldn't have been so difficult to imagine the concept. And yet my mind rebelled.

"Perhaps he did trick time," Telaria went on. "Or perhaps the Crescent Prince is a creature that was born beyond its grasp."

There were too many voices shouting all at once in my head, colliding with the image of the young man perched atop his stallion. I dug my fingers into the armchair and tuned them out.

Although not without effort.

"So what did he do—when he learned of the spell?" It was

cruel to ask that of her, but I had to know. "And what *was* the spell?"

A memory crept into the forefront of my mind.

"Ada mentioned something about keeping me from coming here. That's the one, isn't it?"

Telaria trailed a finger down one of the veins branching across her left forearm before she turned her attention to me. Her raspy voice held a sharp, fierce edge that mirrored the frigid harshness of her expression. "The spell was to suppress your magic. To keep it locked within your body so that you wouldn't come here until you were no longer a child."

Again, a humorless laugh bubbled inside me.

My magic. In my body. When the only kind in our world derived from precious objects I was forbidden to touch. Seemed to me like there was no need to suppress anything, given our society already did that all on its own. But I refrained from arguing.

With a slight dip of my chin, I acknowledged Telaria's words and asked her to continue.

"My dear, you must understand that it was never my wish to keep you from your birthright. But it was the only way I could protect you. The only thing I could do from here." She spread her arms, encompassing the room. "The spell should have run its course on your twenty-fifth year, when you would be mature enough to take up your destined role—and we would be sufficiently prepared to assist you. But the veil separating our worlds must have weakened the magic, shortening its lifespan."

I opened my mouth, the word *destined* clashing with the echo of how Ada had first introduced me. *Savior.*

Unease slid down my spine. Was I dealing with fanatics?

More than Telaria's perception of me, it was the inconsistencies that set me on edge. I had only seen a slice of this world, but between my own observations and Ada's explanations, nobody seemed to refer to their blood magic as spellcasting. And how was it that Telaria had been able to *send* something to me?

I didn't get the impression the power they wielded was the kind designed to last...

"Should we stop?"

"What?" I snapped my gaze up at Telaria. She was studying my rigid posture, the nails I'd dug so deeply in the armchair's cushion that I was certain a permanent mark would remain.

I unclenched them and shook my head. "No. Please, tell me the rest."

Telaria reached down to stroke Lyra, holding the suspense. Sly woman.

"That night"—she straightened at last—"when the Crescent Prince and his men came to this house and surrounded me, he had known I had influenced you somehow. That this sudden void where your presence had been was my doing. The specifics of the spell, however, eluded him. It was already on the other side of the veil, no traces of it left for him to reconstruct. Only the knowledge I possessed.

"When I refused to break under his guards' torture, the Crescent Prince infused me with his shadowfire, tried to burn the answers from me... But it didn't matter what he did, what horrors he brought upon my flesh. All I could think of was the girl I had saved. Who would save us in turn, when the time came.

"So I gave him nothing. And the Crescent Prince let his

shadowfire burn through my veins, tainting them with his touch and destroying what was mine until nothing remained. I suspect that the only reason he didn't kill me outright is because a life without magic is a far harsher punishment than death. Oh..." She reclined her body on the armrest, half facing the arch. "Tea. Thank you, dear."

I didn't know when Ada had come into the room, but she was staring at her mother, a deep sense of pain lining her lovely features and making the green of her eyes even more prominent. She set down the platter on the low table placed between the two armchairs, took a cup for herself, then sat down cross-legged on the floor.

Closer to me than to her mother, but still far enough away that it seemed she preferred the touch of wild embers licking at the air within the fireplace than our proximity.

Lyra rushed over to her as soon as she settled, sending the cup swaying in her hands. Ada placed it aside, then stroked Lyra's head when the dog leaned her black muzzle against her thigh. Her movements were soft, flowing, yet done with such dedication I couldn't help thinking that she hoped they would take away the hurt still so vivid on her face.

Seeing her like that...

Something within me ignited.

The spell, this world—it all seemed so unimportant compared to the bare sorrow Ada exuded. The haunted cast of her eyes, the way she refused to look at Telaria even when the woman observed her from her perch with an inseparable mix of affection, resignation, and disinterest I would have thought impossible to coexist were I not seeing it with my own eyes.

In the uncomfortable silence, disrupted only as Telaria took her cup from the platter and dumped two spoonfuls of sugar into her tea, my attention slipped back to Ada. Suddenly, I was seeing our initial conversation through a new prism.

I told Mother the spell wouldn't last...

The ecstatic approach that had me running in the other direction wasn't just because she stumbled onto their *savior.* But because she would have proved to Telaria her worth. That she had found me due to listening to her instincts when Telaria believed my arrival was still years away...

A jab of sympathy twisted my insides.

It was painfully obvious Ada loved her mother. Looked up to her with the kind of deeply rooted adoration and loyalty that made a person willing to go to whatever lengths to get the acknowledgment, the praise that would confirm they meant something. That they were noticed. Loved in return.

If Telaria thought she would have been better dead—that it would have been better if she *hadn't* seen her daughter grow, spent these years watching her become her own person, and cultivate this gifted bond... I found that I was harboring a deep resentment for the woman.

I snatched the cup of tea from the table and tightened my fingers around it, hoping to control my rapid breaths. The heat bled into my skin, but I hardly felt it.

I'd always known my parents saw me as nothing more than another prize, a different kind of jewel to bargain with. But that was the way of our world. It had faults, and the Sun knows *they* had faults, a whole lot of them, but in their own twisted, dusty way, my parents loved me.

They wouldn't have chosen a *convenience* over their child.

Had they done so, I would have been locked away somewhere long ago, their reputation spotless.

This—wanting to die rather than being stripped of magic, but able to share your life with your daughter—this wasn't love. The fact that Telaria hadn't actually taken her life didn't erase her wish or had the capacity to redeem her. Not when her desire for death seemed to have spread its poisonous vines, more than likely suffocating every aspect of her life. And Ada's.

No, it wasn't love.

It was selfish. It was cruel.

A part of me wanted to reach out to Ada, but I also suspected she didn't need a stranger's touch. Not now. And certainly not in front of Telaria. So I brought the tea to my lips and took three slow mouthfuls, feeling the rich jasmine flavor slip down my throat.

Wretched woman or not, I still needed my answers.

"Ada mentioned I had magic. Now you say the same." I placed one elbow against the armrest and cradled the cup in both hands. "If my coming here was linked to it, then why don't I feel any different than I did before?"

When Telaria didn't answer, her face a mask of hard edges and harder planes, I ventured on, "You can't tell if it was me, can you? If *I* was the child you spelled?"

There it was. A barely imperceptible flinch. But it held the truth I needed.

Finally, it seemed, I was onto something.

"I'm not the only girl who celebrates her birthday on the Winter Solstice. I'm not even the only one who turned eighteen this year." I placed the cup back on the platter, then crossed my legs, letting my hands fall into my lap as I leaned back. "What if I was just there? When the portal opened? I certainly don't remember anything beyond flirting with Aegan Rosegrave at the party... I could have landed here by mistake."

"No," a voice cut in, and I was surprised to find that the sound came from Ada. Lyra scurried away when she shot to her feet, back held straight, and met Telaria's eyes at last.

"The pendant." She motioned to me. "It has magic. Magic that worked *here*. She wouldn't have been able to use it if she wasn't the One."

By the Sun. The *One*. With a capital O.

I narrowed my eyes at her, then glanced at her mother. It was infuriating, seeing a whole silent conversation pass between them. Especially when it evolved around *me*.

The one person they were excluding.

The leash I'd kept on my temper disintegrated.

"How come you know so much about my world when I've never even heard of yours?" I sneered.

At Ada. At Telaria.

At both of them and their frustrating, secretive ways.

Not a single mention of Somraque in any of the books. Not even the forbidden ones. Yet they knew of us.

Maybe not everything, but more than enough.

"And why shouldn't Soltzen magic work in Somraque?" I plowed on. "It's object-based! A location can't change what they are, or how they operate."

More and more anger seeped into my voice, and for once, I truly didn't care. I gripped the armrests with both hands, balancing myself on the edge of my seat.

"Tell me what's going on, or I'm leaving. Maybe the Crescent Prince will be more forthcoming when I seek him out."

It was an idle threat—I had a sufficient sense of self-preservation to know I needed to stay as far away from him as I could, regardless of the draw—but it worked.

"Don't you *dare*, girl," Telaria snarled. Showing her true

colors at last. "I should have known the Stars would send us our salvation in the form of an ignorant child. You, girl, have the power to grant us freedom, bring the fractured worlds together again. Or, in his hands, become a weapon that will deliver nothing but destruction and pain."

CHAPTER SEVEN

FURIOUS WITH HER TONE, HER INSULTS, AND MORE THAN A little mortified by the grander implications of her words, I shot up from the armchair, nearly upending the table with my knee. My cup tipped over, what was left of the tea spilling across the carpeted floor.

"*What* worlds? For Sun's sake, stop weaving fairy tales when I don't even know *where* I am! And 'Somraque' isn't an adequate answer. I swear to the Stars or whatever it is that you worship that if you don't start explaining *now*, I'm walking out the door."

Not to go to Mordecai, no, but Telaria's eyes flashed nonetheless, creating her own version of all the unspoken currents running beneath my ultimatum.

I was prepared to be patient. But I had my limits.

"Somraque is just one of the three planes," Ada said softly, though not before I caught her sending a stern look her mother's way. "Yours, Soltzen, is another. Ember, please..."

She gestured for me to sit down, a gentle plea in her eyes. After a quick consideration, I obliged.

Whatever Telaria might think, Ada seemed to understand that if she didn't deliver what I sought, our joint path would end here.

As tension continued to coil through the air, though lessening, Lyra padded over to my feet. She rubbed her slender body against me, then bunked down to observe Ada as she shuffled forward and placed her palm flat against the thick medallion rug.

Fire crackled behind her, the embers bringing out the red in her hair, and I couldn't help but think how the fierce image befitted her decision to take the lead—not once looking at Telaria. Although I wanted to remain impassive, satisfaction swelled in my chest.

Ada wasn't meant to live in her mother's shadow.

"Think of the world," she began, "the whole world, not just our respective ones, as the space between two concentric circles."

She traced a finger across the carpet, drawing one rim, then another inside it. As I focused on the invisible annulus, she reached over and snatched my overturned cup to set it in the very center of the design.

"And in here"—she tapped the cup—"is magic. The source responsible not just for mine, or yours, but all three of them."

"What's the third?" I asked, lifting my gaze from the floor to her.

"Words, we think."

"Words?" I cocked my head to the side.

"Something in the voice that gives them power." A pensive expression shuttered her face, then morphed into a look that bordered on irritation. "There are records. About Somraque. Soltzen. Svitanye. They passed down through my family's generations, and we—they"—she glanced at Telaria—"kept them alive. Made sure every descendant learned of the past the majority seemed to have forgotten.

"Unfortunately, some records are more complete than others. The ones about Svitanye are among the latter. What notes hadn't been lost were muddied over the ages before my ancestors managed to gather and protect them. We don't dare assume anything beyond the basics."

Accepting she truly wasn't able to tell me anything more, I nodded. "All right. So we have blood magic, magic objects, and words, all of which originated from the core." I pointed at the cup sitting in the dead center of the imaginary rings.

Lyra bumped her cool nose against my finger. I patted her absentmindedly.

"And you're saying a"—I searched for the word both Ada and Telaria had used—"a *veil* now separates our worlds?"

"If only." Telaria snorted. "The circle isn't a circle any longer. Our worlds are like a shattered vase. Fractured. The fragments scattered, connected by less than a thread. The veil is only another barrier."

It took a moment for the meaning to settle in. The *whole* meaning. Despite the fire burning just as brightly, the temperature in the house seemed to have dropped.

"You're saying my world, this world—they're just *pieces*?"

Telaria dipped her chin, and I was surprised to find there was nothing condescending in the way she looked at me. We were treading on common ground at last.

"Did you ever feel as if there was something...missing from your reality?" The pine hue of her irises darkened. "That the melody of your world was ever so slightly off-kilter? That, perhaps, there should have been something *more*?"

I chewed on my bottom lip as I acknowledged her words. I *had* wondered.

Wondered of the starry sky I'd read about in stories but never saw until now; wondered about the portals, about the edges of the world—and what lay beyond them. But no one else shared my curiosity.

Not that I was even allowed to speak about it openly.

A gentle whoosh of air left my lungs, vines of memories twining around my limbs until I sank into the armchair.

Not no one.

There was Magnus.

While I had been interested in the limitless blue of the sky, he obsessed over another. The ocean. It surrounded our lands, a seemingly perpetual, endless landscape that bled into the day shining from above. No one ever sailed it.

Although people did try.

Every now and then, someone brave enough would venture out onto the languid waves but never returned. And the portals —they didn't even *open* when directed at the ocean. It was a mystery that few wanted to unravel and the majority eagerly glazed over.

"I have," I admitted. "Everything you mentioned, yes, I've thought about it. But only in daydreams and never on such a scale."

It was liberating, to speak of this openly. To not be judged but...encouraged. Telaria seemed content, almost kind, as she waited on the sidelines. As did Ada.

I tucked the loose strands of hair behind my ears and

ventured further. "How can a world just...fall apart? How did we even survive such a thing?"

"We don't know." Telaria sipped her tea. It must have gone cold by now, but if she noticed, or minded, it didn't show. Her attention was directed solely at me. "We assume the individual magics kept the lands from dissolving completely. But the fracture itself... It happened long ago.

"Time has shrouded the true events. If it weren't for my ancestors' chronicles, however incomplete, we would have been unaware that the world existed in another state before this one." She opened her hands, drawing a wide arc in front of her to encompass the current reality.

My gaze caught on the silver.

I still didn't know what Mordecai's part was in this, but I didn't want to break Telaria's cooperative streak by asking. Thankfully, no such pitfalls were related when it came to *my* role.

At least I hoped.

"What makes you think I would be able to return the world to its primary state?" I kept my voice devoid of doubt, of the incredulity that swirled within me and would surely give the wrong impression should Telaria pick up on it. "*How* would I even do that when the only power I possess is this?" I tapped the pendant. Ada had already mentioned it, so there was no point in keeping it out of the conversation.

Telaria looked from the necklace to me, the answer visibly lingering on the tip of her tongue when a rolling vibration swept through the room.

She sprang to her feet, not the brittle old woman any longer, but a warrior. I was so caught up in the sudden change I didn't see Ada move until she was by my side. She pulled me up from the armchair while Lyra growled furiously, yet low, baring canines sharp enough to rend flesh.

"Take her downstairs," Telaria ordered. "Stay there."

"No. They'll wonder why I'm not here," Ada shot back in a whisper-shout, but her mother was already clearing away the tea, leaving only her cup on the table.

Telaria was halfway out of the room when she barked, "What did you do?"

"They saw us. I—I had to magic them, Mother."

"Foolish girl," came the reply from the kitchen, though the harshness didn't seem to be directed at Ada, but the situation at large that I was slowly piecing together. Telaria emerged not a second later, then quickly retook her position in the chair. "If you're lucky, they'll think you drank too much sowhl and got out of control. It wouldn't be the first time now, would it?"

Ada flinched, but her grip tightened on my hand, and the very next moment she was ushering me through a door, Lyra fast on our heels. A stairwell rested at the far end, only Ada turned me right just as I was about to ascend. She pivoted me away from the first steps—

And shoved me into a wall.

No, actually, she shoved me *through* a wall.

An illusion I'd missed, thanks to its nearly imperceptible thrumming and my own heartbeat thumping away in my ears. I hadn't as much as noticed her brandish her dagger.

When I moved my gaze from the translucent sheen of magic we were ensconced behind, Ada was crouching on the floor. She fumbled with the edge of the wine-red carpet, Lyra pressed closely to my side and staying out of the way. We both were.

A soft *snick* cut through the air. The carpet folded over, revealing a trapdoor and narrow stairs leading into utter darkness. I hesitated, eyeing the hole in the ground with no small amount of skepticism.

Enclosed, windowless spaces were *not* among my favorites.

I glanced back at the wall, at the unnamed danger beyond it, then at Ada.

"Go on," she urged, motioning to the hole.

When it became clear I had no intentions of going down there first, she let out a streak of low curses and climbed into the dark. Lyra bumped my legs several times, but it wasn't until the *thud* of Ada's feet stopped somewhere below that I followed. It was a challenge to keep myself from tangling with Lyra. She seemed adamant to take the narrow stairs at the exact same time, although focusing on my balance did make me forget where, exactly, I was headed.

Miraculously unscathed, we came to a stop right at the edge of the soft triangle of light that spilled across the cracked, massive stones that made up the floor. Ada was nothing but a shadowed silhouette, then even less than that when she tapped her hand against the wall and submerged us in total darkness.

Suffocating talons wrapped around my throat. I swallowed to liberate the muscles, but even before I started going through my breathing exercises, the dark lifted.

Small lights flickered to life all around the room. They reminded me of the fireflies I'd read about in one of the books I'd stowed away, only larger. I focused on the smallest one just as it manifested in the darkest corner—a speck of warm, golden yellow that gradually gained volume, like a portal coming into existence in those fragile moments before it snapped into place.

With an amused laugh, I turned to Ada—and noticed her bleeding hand.

All of this—it was her.

My mind struggled to wrap around the idea that someone could conjure false light like this.

Then I remembered that fountain in the center of Nysa. Remembered how the whole town glowed blue in an imitation of what I saw day after day back in Soltzen.

Really, I shouldn't have been surprised. But those illusions had already been formed. Here, I was privy to its inception.

Ada lowered herself onto the blanket spread across the stone floor and braced her back against the far wall. After a while, once I could tear myself away from the breathtaking glow, I sat by her side.

Lyra came last.

She wiggled her hairless body between us, placing her butt in Ada's lap and her head in mine. I chuckled softly. Oddball.

The dog *harrumphed* as if she could sense my thoughts, and I was grateful for it. Because it meant the situation wasn't all that bad. Her warmth bled through my clothes, the gentle weight of her a grounding presence.

After a fashion, I asked, "I take it it's Mordecai's men that are coming to the house?"

"They always do during the celebrations. But especially on the night of the Solstice." She let out a bitter laugh, then coughed. "Lyra!"

The smell hit me just as I wanted to ask what was wrong.

Lyra made herself even more comfortable, stretched out over our laps, while we nearly choked on the vile stench of rotten eggs. Our teary eyes met, and we broke into a laugh, Ada swinging her arm to scatter the gas.

"At least she's comfy," I pointed out.

"Yeah..." Though Ada's laughter died down, echoes of it lingered in the corners of her lips. "The guards—they always seem intent on following me around. Even when I do nothing, they keep monitoring me, waiting for the moment I will. I'm never out of their minds for long."

She sighed, then sought out my gaze.

"Stars, I know this is a lot to take in, a lot from me to ask of you, but Ember... You have to help us. You have to help put the worlds back together. I don't know what Soltzen and Svitanye are like, but we—we've lived under the Crescent Prince's rule for long enough."

"Why did you only ever say his name—his real name—once?" I asked softly.

Ada looked at me, the hurt, the anger naked in the green of her eyes. But her voice—it was nothing but the coolest of steel. "A monster does not deserve the intimacy of a name."

Faint sounds drifted over to us from the rest of the house, but Ada didn't seem to care about the guards' proximity. More than likely, they couldn't even hear us thanks to the magic we were encased behind.

And, despite the awareness of danger walking on pinpricks down my neck, I realized I couldn't be bothered, either. Not when invisible strands of a haunting weight bound Ada and me together.

For the first time, she allowed me a glimpse behind the Mage.

I didn't want to lose the connection just yet.

Keeping my voice barely over a whisper, I asked, "What did he do?"

Ada shook her head, her fingers running through the elegant hairs of Lyra's tail again and again. "Too much. He did too much. And he'll never stop. He—he isn't human, Ember. No one that cruel could be."

She stifled a sob, and I couldn't help the silent admiration rising within me as I watched her piece herself together. Shard after shard.

"The Crescent Prince oppresses our powers like they're something that can be measured and limited. Something we indulge in, instead of a part of us that can *never* be turned off. He doesn't even hide that he murders those who dare break his rules. And if a thousand people rose against him, he *would* bury them all.

"The festivities surrounding the Solstice are just another means of keeping people in line. Not violent, like the rest, but just as vile. He gives them eight days to bask in the magic that could—*should*—have surrounded them every day if it weren't for his edicts. The people are too afraid to say anything, so they take what he offers, pretend it's a gift.

"We're all caged, and we can't... We can't go on like this. But you can change it. The old texts speak of a child born of three worlds. A person who won't be hindered by the tears in reality—whose magic will reach across the planes and bring them balance." Her gaze dipped down to the pendant resting around my neck. "You're that person, Ember. And we're all at your mercy."

CHAPTER EIGHT

THE MEN RETURNED ONCE MORE THAT NIGHT, SEARCHING THE house from top to bottom. Or at least that's what they believed.

I lingered in the hidden chamber, alone, munching on strawberry-flavored biscuits Ada had produced from her pocket right before she went to make an appearance upstairs.

Raised voices overpowered the sounds of their rummaging, but didn't escalate beyond the point of what must have been moderate threats. Presumably, something Ada had already grown accustomed to since the only thing she did when she came to fetch me from the basement was mutter, "Pricks."

I swallowed the last biscuit. "They're gone?"

"Yeah, they're gone." She ran a hand through her hair, tugging on a strand. "We have until tomorrow at least."

Telaria was nowhere in sight when we reemerged into the sitting room, and Lyra was fast asleep atop the armchair I had previously occupied, appearing just as worn-out as the rest of us.

A glance at the grandfather clock positioned by the wall adjacent to the fireplace told me why.

It was late. *Really* late.

I must have lost track of time because it didn't feel as if my sudden emergence in this world had been all that long ago, but with the illusions, the running, the hiding, not to mention the weight of a prophecy that was supposedly about *me*, I knew I wasn't exactly the most reliable person. Even now, my mind continued to work in overdrive, examining the pieces of information and beliefs until they blurred into one large mess I had no hope to untangle.

Ada led me upstairs to a small bedroom with the promise that we would talk more tomorrow. Silence enveloped me as she closed the door, not even the shuffle of her feet audible, although I did sense she'd walked away.

Without the imminent threat of discovery, there was a different quality to the solitude—a pleasant calm that paved the way for the exhaustion to catch up with me in earnest.

Faintly, I wondered whether the guards had searched the chest of drawers, ran their hands across the duvet—as if Ada and Telaria's privacy was something to be taken and given at will. But the thought died before it could grow roots.

I crawled onto the bed, not even bothering to change into the bundle of clothes Ada had set up on the dresser. The single thing I did was liberate my hair from the unruly braid before I fell into a deep, dreamless sleep, not caring that the pillow beneath my cheek was not mine.

A WHISPER CALLING out my name curled around me. It lifted me from the silver-lined depths and into…

Darkness.

I rubbed the sleep from my eyes and looked again.

A starlit sky stretched beyond the window, the shadows leeching into the room kept at bay only by faint orbs of light floating through the space.

Right.

Somraque. Illusions. Endless night.

And Ada.

She was looking at me from where she stood in front of the closed door, her face guarded and posture cautious. One of her arms was twisted behind her back, out of my sight.

"You don't have to hide," I croaked, then cleared my throat. "The magic."

Ada glanced at the orbs, but when I looked rather pointedly at her hand, she let it fall by her side to reveal a thin, already healing slice.

"Didn't want to startle you," she said far more quietly than I expected.

I perched myself on my elbows, and whether it was the sleep still blanketing the edges of my mind or some temporary acceptance of my predicament, I smiled.

"If you'd burst in here brandishing that damned knife,"—I chuckled—"now *that* would have been different."

Ada's green eyes widened, then crinkled, her own mouth curling up. "I've learned my lesson."

She crossed the room in two elegant strides to sit on the edge of the bed. Her hair was pulled in a loose braid that tumbled over her shoulder, her profile softened by the glow of her orbs—or perhaps my own moment of humor—

although a touch of distant pensiveness lingered in her gaze.

I turned my attention to the window just to the right at the foot of the bed and observed the...constellations. Yes, that was what the clusters of stars were called.

"Is it morning?"

"Late morning," Ada replied almost instantly, then added when she saw my gaze drift between her and the night sky, "It must be...odd, for you."

A low, husky laugh left my lips. I threw my head back onto the pillow.

I recalled the blazing light of the sun as it fell upon my skin whenever I drew back the heavy curtains in my bedchamber and left my dreams behind. Remembered the vibrant spill of colors that made my world what it was, a fundamental piece of its ever illuminated beauty. But also one that masked the rigid rules of our society with its effervescent nature.

"Actually, it's kind of comforting," I confessed. "The night."

Ada cocked her head to the side but didn't comment.

I lifted myself back up. "How long did I sleep?"

"A little over six hours. I made breakfast for you downstairs. If—if you want to come."

The slight growl in my stomach was a nice touch, though I didn't really need a reminder to know that I was starving. "Just let me get dressed and take care of...*things*...and I'll join you."

Ada scooted off the bed, the glowing orbs fluttering around like butterflies. "Oh, of course. Stars, I'm sorry. Like my mother said, I forget my manners."

"I'm not that big on manners." I flashed her a smile and swung my feet off the mattress. "But I do need to use the privy. Wouldn't want to get blood everywhere in case my monthlies decided to linger another day and only tricked me with yesterday's lull."

Something eased in the room, as if my words had managed to knit together a bridge across the ravine that, while slowly narrowing, continued to stretch between us. Ada and I might have come from two different worlds, but there were things we both understood.

"At least you don't have to worry about accidentally magicking something," she mumbled, a laugh touching her voice. "My thirteenth year was...unexpected, to say the least."

RELIEVED THAT MY MONTHLIES HAD, indeed, passed, I shrugged off my ruined gown and looked through the garments Ada had prepared for me. Not the nightclothes that still waited on the chest of drawers, but thin hose that fitted me like second skin and a dress in pristine condition.

I turned it around in my hands, then quickly pulled it on. While sconces with flickering embers of *actual* fire illuminated the bathing chamber, goosebumps had nonetheless started to spread down my exposed skin. The exhaustion still etched in my bones must have made me a touch more sensitive to the temperature. I was glad slipping into the dress was an easy affair. No straps or corsets to fasten.

Once the warm, smooth fabric slid over my hips, I glanced at my reflection in the full-length mirror taking up a third of the wall.

The dress was tame, much less flamboyant than the one I arrived in, the color a blue dark enough to pass for black, and the cut a simple A-line without any crinolines or additional skirts to hinder my movement. And yet for its demure, almost simple nature, there was something utterly lovely about it.

It wasn't merely skill that had created this garment, but a keen eye and passion that imbued the fabric, the cut, with elegance and life.

A smile curved on my lips as I ran my hands down the front. But when my gaze skimmed the scoop neckline then caught on the sleeves, reaching just past my elbows, I halted.

While it wasn't exactly frosty outside, if what I'd experienced yesterday was Somraque's actual climate, I still wondered why Ada decided on something that left my forearms exposed. Even if I threw a coat over—

Realization slammed into me.

I let out a surprised laugh.

Magic.

Of course. It was their magic...

I had been too caught up in everything to pay attention to detail—or attempt to explain those I'd absorbed. But now that I thought about it, the seemingly unconnected pieces started to make sense.

My outfit, much like the ones I'd seen in Nysa, wasn't just following some quirky fashion. The design derived from practicality. A way for the people to have access to their skin at all times.

While slashing a blade across the palm—or even a mere pinprick, as Ada had mentioned—seemed to be enough for the majority, it hadn't escaped me that the sleeves of every dress, jacket, coat, or tunic had been wider, making it possible to pull the fabric up at a moment's notice. My mouth curled up at the peculiarity of this world—and at the fact that I was learning.

Good to know that landing somewhere unfamiliar didn't strip me of my observational skills entirely.

I finger-combed my silver hair and left it hanging down since I didn't think anyone in *this* world would mind such a casual style, then ventured out in the hallway and made my way downstairs. Ada was waiting for me in the kitchen—but so was Telaria.

Not a sight I had wished to see so soon after last night, given her chiding tone still crashed through my mind, but one I expected nonetheless. I offered her one of my carefully constructed smiles and took the chair Ada had motioned to before she mouthed "Sorry" behind her mother's back.

Telaria must have given her a false impression that we'd be alone.

I had to stifle a snort. The woman was cunning. I had to give her that.

Ada squeezed a small plate with hard-boiled eggs among the many already laid out on the square-shaped walnut table. Contrary to what I was accustomed to from home, the setting was intimate. Not for lack of space since their house was fairly large, but because the merged kitchen and dining room were arranged with family, instead of appearances, in mind. I bit my tongue before I could ask how long it had been just the two of them here, and guided my finger along the worn, age-soft wood instead.

Bread rolls were stacked on a plate at the very center of the table, a serving of butter and marmalade set beside them. Eagerly, I snatched one of the still-warm rolls from the top and practically devoured it in what my parents would undoubtedly mark as an *unladylike* manner. I took my time with the second, however, slicing it apart with the silver knife and spreading a thin layer of butter with a whole lot of strawberry jam on top.

Ada chuckled silently as I tried my best to eat slowly, but the hunger won.

Much to my surprise, even Telaria waited until I finished the fourth roll and reached for my cup of green tea before she resumed with her agenda of not giving me adequate answers. Once more, she spoke about the prophecy—in even fewer words than Ada had yesterday—but it seemed she was adamant to refrain from calling me the *One*. Which, I had to admit, was perfectly fine with me.

I had always been different. I knew that much. But in Soltzen, *special* was considered as a shortcoming, not something to be celebrated. Besides, I had a hard time coming to terms with just what Ada and Telaria's version of special encompassed.

Savior. In possession of extraordinary power.

It was the one front on which the two women stood united.

But believing in something didn't make it true. Even if I'd had more than my fair share of experiences lately that proved otherwise.

I leaned over to refill my tea when Telaria fell silent at last. The pause was thick with expectancy. My turn to say something. Or at the very least react.

As I set the kettle down, I caught Ada's attention, her fingers tensing around her cup.

"You mentioned a child born of three worlds," I started, forcefully stifling a laugh that wanted to claw its way to the surface at the absurdity of it all. "You mean to say that their ancestors come from Soltzen, Somraque, and..." I searched for the name, but it eluded me.

"Svitanye," Ada offered.

I gave her a grateful smile. "And Svitanye."

"Like yours do." She shifted forward in her seat just when I opened my mouth to argue that she couldn't possibly know that unless her Mage abilities extended to reading a person's origin. "After the world fractured, our magic became bound to our respective lands."

I frowned. "Were the lands separated even before? Had only High Masters lived in Soltzen, Mages, Magicians, and Illusionists in Somraque—"

"No." Telaria's voice was oddly soft, yet lined with unmistakable bitterness. "The magics were native to their respective lands, which is why most people chose to make their homes where they were the strongest. Somraque was—is—the domain of our powers. While a Mage could exist in Soltzen, even possess the full scope of their magic, they would nonetheless feel out of place."

"Wait... But if the different magics work in all lands"—I lifted the chain around my neck, the pendant swaying—"then why was this so important?"

I let it drop back down as Ada stood to clear away the plates, offering her mother the stage.

Telaria handed her cup to Ada, then faced me once more. "Ever since the break, save for the savior, only those native to the land are able to wield magic."

The silence that stretched between us was inky, almost tangible. Even Ada paused by the counter, a plate clutched in her motionless hands.

The truth coalesced into a harsh, solid weight in the pit of my stomach. It didn't need any explanation, but still, I ventured, "So if someone native to Soltzen was in Somraque when the fracture happened..."

"They would have been like me." Telaria rubbed a finger across one of the more prominent silver veins on the inside of her arm. "Powerless."

My chest seemed too tight, too constraining to accept the air my body craved. "What happened to them?"

Telaria didn't flinch as she said, "They chose not to live a half-life."

CHAPTER NINE

THE MOON BATHED ME IN ITS SILVER LIGHT AS I STOLE A VERY much needed moment for myself away from the confines of the house.

I lingered by the wall facing away from Nysa so that all I saw was the endless expanse of rock and the starlit sky. Telaria hadn't tried to stop me when I'd marched outside, and I heard no traces of Ada's approach. I leaned against the cool stones, the touch of winter caressing my exposed forearms.

With every second that passed, the turmoil inside me calmed. There was nothing I could do for those people who had chosen death over a powerless existence, but...

I wrapped my fingers around the pendant, feeling the magic in its core like a heartbeat.

I *was* different.

With one last glance at the moon, its observant face that seemed to watch me with interest, I strode back inside.

Ada and Telaria were both seated, their conversation dying

down before I could make out a single word. I didn't take my place at the table—instead, I remained standing, shifting my attention from one to the other.

"So I have magic that isn't bound to the borders of my land. But surely I can't be the only one? If all three..." *Races* didn't seem right since aside from the power, I really didn't feel as if we were that different from one another. "If all three *people* mixed, there must have been other children, other descendants with a lineage similar to mine."

"There have." Telaria sighed and folded her napkin. "At least my ancestors had sensed them. But none had ever been born in Somraque, or on a Solstice when the veil is thinner. And that flicker of power that came into existence at their births—it never lasted beyond that first flare, rendering them untraceable. So when I felt yours... Preventing you from entering our world had only been part of the importance of the spell. I feared that if I didn't shield your power, if I didn't preserve it in your core, your world would have snuffed it out before it could assert itself, as it did the others."

I pursed my lips and leaned against the windowsill. As hard as I tried, I couldn't recall anyone ever mentioning people in possession of power that varied from what we were accustomed to in Soltzen. Surely one of them would have risen as a High Master if that were the case.

So maybe there *was* merit in her words. Maybe if she hadn't shielded me, I would have been just like the rest.

Not that I had any indication of my supposed powers yet, beyond the use of the pendant in Somraque.

"Let's pretend for a moment"—I blew out a breath—"that I believe I'm the person you have been waiting for. How am I supposed to unite all three worlds?"

Telaria's gaze flickered to Ada. Her eyes widened in realization that her mother was returning her previous courtesy, giving her the opportunity to explain.

Needless to say, I was relieved.

While Telaria had been uncharacteristically straightforward when speaking of the past, I wasn't willing to bet she could keep herself from wrapping the facts in shrouds of mystery. Ada, on the other hand, preferred a blunt approach. And so did I.

Even if it still was, at times, confusing.

"Well," she began, tossing her braid over her shoulder, "there is a story of creation that exists among our people. It has more variants than there are pints of sowhl at the celebration, but our ancestors dug up its core." She glanced at her mother, then sat up straighter, a low-burning passion creeping into her voice. "And we believe it to be the truth. The story, legend—whatever you wish to call it—doesn't say *why* the world broke apart. Not to any satisfying degree, at least. But it *does* mention what held it together. A relic."

A faint pain niggled at the back of my mind, and I realized I'd been digging my nails in my arms, just above the elbows. I forced myself to loosen the grip but didn't interrupt Ada's flow.

"Accounts vary on its appearance. However, all agree that it was some sort of flat, circular disk that carried in its structure the three powers. Its metal held the magic in possession of your people, the particles were bound together by blood, and on its surface were inscriptions. A single item, connecting all three powers into a whole. But *something* happened to make it break.

"As it fragmented into three pieces, so did the world, right along the borders of its native magics. A shard of the relic stayed with each land as they drifted apart. Some of the stories say the new worlds absorbed the fractured disk, and in turn, the pieces kept them alive. Others say the rulers stored them in vaults, guarding them like their most prized possessions. I'm inclined to believe it's the latter."

My hands flattened against the stone ledge. "You think Mordecai"—the name slipped out before I could correct myself —"has a part of the relic?"

"I do." Ada smiled, for once not bothered by the use of his name. "And I plan to steal it from him."

LYRA WAS RESTING in my lap as I watched Ada slide a few more daggers down her clothes—once again a combination of pants and a tunic—all within easy reach. Torchlight illuminated her room, the distinct absence of thrumming only further indicating Ada was saving up her magic. In truth, I hadn't seen her use it at all since she came to wake me up, which made me suspect she had been planning this venture all along.

Though even if she somehow retrieved the relic, I had no idea how she planned to proceed to Svitanye or Soltzen to get the others when my arrival here continued to be an enigma.

I stroked Lyra behind her ears, seeking comfort in her presence while Ada moved from her dresser to the elegant vanity occupying the strip of wall by the window. She twisted up her locks, revealing a scar that ran from beneath the dress and up her neck in a diagonal line, the end lost beneath the hairline.

If her self-inflicted wounds healed so fast, erasing any marks that ever existed, then why did this one stay? Was it possible that their healing worked only when wielding magic?

I shivered.

Just how physical had her former run-ins with the guards truly been?

I'd assumed the conflicts were rooted in illusions, in tricks of body and mind. But the blades the guards wielded were more than just a means to access their powers. And I'd seen enough faded remnants of scars on Masters who'd taken a too-deep look into their glasses of wine before showing off their precious swords and daggers to know the kind of mark Ada had had been put there by nothing less than a blade.

Oblivious to the dark path my thoughts had taken, Ada continued to work in the silent confidence of someone who linked elbows with danger.

She pinned her hair in place with sticks I was fairly certain were sharp enough to draw blood if needed, then secured a few shorter ones beneath the strands. I glanced down at the knives—some visible beneath her clothes, the others hidden from sight. Clever.

If someone tried to strip her of her weapons, they wouldn't think to suspect the "pins." Not when they believed they were cunning enough to locate on her person even those blades she'd gone through a lot of trouble concealing.

A decoy.

I nodded in silent admiration, filing the approach away for later use.

Just as Lyra nudged my hand with her muzzle to alert me I'd neglected her, Ada moved from the vanity to the double-winged armoire. The wood had a touch of honeyed red to it that reminded me of walnut, much like the kitchen table, but its presence boggled my mind since I hadn't seen any trees aside from the peculiar desaturated ones. Then again, I hadn't seen any fields or gardens, either, yet the food I ate—definitely *not* an illusion—had to have come from somewhere.

Ada swiped a black, tailored coat with sleeves that widened at the end off the rack and held it out to me.

Still half submerged in my musings, I blinked. "What?"

"It's yours."

I stared at her, refusing to jump to conclusions to avoid disappointment.

Lyra gave out a grunt as Ada dropped the coat in my lap and the fabric slid across her ears and muzzle. Quickly, I set the coat aside.

"I can't keep up an elaborate illusion from such a distance, and my mother can't protect you by herself in case the brutes return. So *you*"—she gave me a pointed look—"are coming with me."

While it sounded a lot like she wanted to keep an eye on me, I focused on the other blatant issue the decision brought up.

"Won't I attract too much attention? You know, being the *One*"—I created quote marks with my fingers around the moniker—"and all? Wasn't that why you were in such a rush to get me away the previous night?"

Away from the townspeople. Nysa. Mordecai.

And now she wanted me to trail after her in public as she went to build her crew for the heist?

The glaring inconsistency wasn't one I could just dismiss, regardless of how much I hated myself for it. Even if it turned out that there was no hidden agenda in her sudden change of heart— even when I *craved* to get out of the house—I wasn't too keen on sloppy plans. Not when, apparently, there was a whole lot at stake.

Me included.

Ada rubbed the bridge of her nose and threw herself on the bed, groaning. "Trust me, if there was any other way, we wouldn't be doing this. After the mess I made yesterday..."

"If he found the imprint, the Crescent Prince believes you're up to something," I offered, while silently adding *And he's right.*

After all, not only was she hiding me, Ada wanted to break into what was probably the most secure building in Somraque. She claimed that with the Crescent Prince focused on the celebrations, even visiting them, slipping into his castle would only be a question of a few well-placed illusions. Her logic was sound on paper, but it was the *celebrations* part that worried me in this new turn of events.

"I understand this wasn't what you initially planned." Lyra *harrumphed* in my lap. "But if he suspects, won't there be more guards? More surveillance? I get that you're worried they might make a repeat appearance here, catch you at a disadvantage, but while we might blend with the crowd once there, won't they think something's off if they see you walking into Nysa with an unfamiliar girl in tow?"

"Ah." She smiled, and the expression scattered the shadows weighing on her face. "But that's the catch. They won't *see* us coming."

I WAS...ROCKS and a smudge of night sky. Changing, at that.

Slowing down time or weaving a nonexistent, yet opaque wall to hide behind seemed so trivial compared to what Ada had created. And it gave the term "hiding in plain sight" a meaning I hadn't considered until now.

I raised my hand, observing the light blue glow of Nysa where my fingers should have been.

Astonishing.

Ada was a softly thrumming presence by my side—the sound of her magic hushed, but powerful. Even if I hadn't seen how much blood she had sacrificed for the illusion, that alone would have convinced me of its strength. And while I was fairly certain she, as the weaver, could make out me for, well, me, all *I* saw was what any prying eyes turned in our direction would notice.

Nothing but a barren, rocky landscape, and the star-speckled sky stretched above.

In all honesty, it was a bit disconcerting to glance down and not see the swell of my breasts or the tips of my feet, even if I could still feel my body beneath the all-encompassing illusion.

A faint sense of nausea started to burn up my neck, so I trained my gaze on the town, watching it grow larger once more.

Instead of a direct path, we'd taken the long way around, vying for the entry point Ada believed would be the least guarded. We only needed to make it through the outer ring, past one of the arches where the sheer number of people would not only hide our faces but Ada's magic, too—in case she had to use it again.

Since I'd experienced firsthand how subtle the touch of her power could be, I didn't doubt her ability to mask it as part of the ordained illusions.

Her hand, never far, wrapped around mine in a silent command to slow. We were farther east from where I had entered Nysa yesterday, but I would have remembered the patrolling forms creeping alongside the outer rim of the buildings had they been there.

With a gentle tug, Ada adjusted our course to the right. I spotted our way in not a moment later.

The unmonitored stretch of land was by no means large, but with the two wider streets, one on each side, claiming the guards' attention, the shadowed alley wedged between the stone-fronted houses was left unattended.

As we crept across the rock, our shapes taking on the deep sapphire hue that added texture to the darkness, the excitement I had tried to snuff out returned. My first visit in Nysa had been enchanting, if turbulent, and that part of me thirsted for new experiences. Glimpses of all the world—*any* world—had to offer. Right now, that was Somraque.

I longed to see what the second day of the celebrations would bring. Ada had mentioned it was a week-long affair followed by a conclusion on the eighth day, and I had a suspicion the sights changed regularly, building up to the grand finale she'd said was always a party with back-to-back events and performances. Yet underneath it all lay an echo of her bitter words that stripped away the festivities, the glamour, exposing them as a carefully constructed ploy of the very same person who was our reason for coming out here in the first place.

Mordecai.

The name slid like velvet through my mind. Forbidden and dangerous. It wrapped around me in a cocoon of silver light, and for a moment, I couldn't help but wonder how someone so devastatingly handsome could be so cruel. So hated.

I wanted to disabuse myself of the notion.

If my father's parties and lavish dinners had taught me anything, it was that looks were usually deceiving. And yet there was something about the regal prince—something I couldn't explain or place, but made me covet more.

As if there were layers upon layers of brushstrokes, each a painting of its own, if you dared to sacrifice the one above for the other, all the while knowing the image you stripped away would be lost forever.

I still wasn't certain where my path would lead me, whether I would truly try to bring the three worlds together or if, perhaps somewhere down the line, I *would* lose my mind from the peculiarity of my circumstances. But I knew that whatever happened, I wouldn't give Ada more reason to fear the Crescent Prince. I wouldn't hand him myself and destroy the image of the future she was fighting to hold on to, even if I burned to discover what lay beneath the aforementioned layers.

As the narrow two-way alley pressed closer from both sides, my thoughts scattered. Ada's hand tightened around mine. She guided me forward and controlled the rhythm of our steps as we emerged on the other end, weaving an elaborate path along the diagonal streets and the guards' unnerving presence.

We stilled when one looked in our direction just as we wanted to cross the spill of blue light.

We were close. Perhaps close enough for him to sense the magic.

Ada started to retreat, her grip almost bruising as she clenched her fingers. But then the guard looked away, scanning three young women who exited a building, their voices hushed yet saturated with excitement.

We didn't waste the opportunity.

Ada's power silenced our feet as we made a mad dash across the street, detoured through two alleys, and, at last, ran beneath the arch the uniformed guard had been monitoring.

As if passing an invisible line, voices exploded to life around us, the light brighter and the thrumming magic embossed in the air. Ada yanked us in an empty doorway and let go of the illusion, her hand pressed against the stones as she fought for balance. I wrapped an arm around her.

Gratitude flashed across her face, then bloomed into an outright grin when I procured a small, trampled bread roll from the pocket of my borrowed coat.

"Thought you might need it." I smiled and handed her the food. "I'm always ravished after using objects of power for lengthy periods of time."

Namely the pendant. And mostly when I had to sneak not just through the manor, but across the premises, too, to meet up with Magnus. Though the reward had always been worth the exertion.

"You know, I came close to fainting once when I stole a sword from my father's study and tried opening a portal." I bit my cheeks to hold back a laugh. "I barely managed to put the damn thing back in place and get out of there before the servants found me spread-eagle on the floor, clutching a blade more than half my size to my chest. I swore to myself, then and there, to always be prepared for whatever fun life threw my way."

"No wonder you seemed so...accepting when I found you." Ada swallowed one last mouthful and brushed her hands down the sides of her coat. "I would have probably tried to fry your mind, had our roles been reversed."

I chuckled, then ran the tips of my fingers across the silver pendant. "I *did* use magic to give you the slip."

"Yeah, you did. But you're not running now, are you?" she whispered and squeezed my hand quickly before letting go. I looked after her as she strode out onto the street, her coat billowing behind her and an edge of purposefulness to her stride.

When I followed, I felt it, too.

A sense of doing something that mattered. Something that could change lives, make them better.

I'd never been anything more than an ornament in Soltzen. A name and a pretty face, but nothing more.

I caught up with Ada and met her gaze.

No, I wasn't running. Not any longer.

CHAPTER TEN

DAINTY, CRYSTALLINE SNOWFLAKES DESCENDED FROM ABOVE the high table Ada and I had claimed for our own, two small pitchers of what she called *sowhl* keeping us company.

To blend in better, she'd said. But I could see the way she eyed the drink, her fingers dancing around the rim as if she couldn't wait to wrap them around the glass and take a sip.

There was no true need to *blend in* since we were crammed right in the middle of twenty or so tables, every one of them surrounded by people who chatted away while enjoying their chosen beverages, not paying us even the slightest attention.

But I was fairly certain Ada needed that sowhl.

Her excitement was almost tangible, a mix of nerves and eager anticipation I had to actively block to prevent it from becoming mine, too.

With the volatile, although not entirely unpleasant buzzing of the surrounding crowds, it would have been all too easy to get swept away. A part of me wanted to experience the celebrations in full again, but I supposed it was a good thing that I couldn't shake off Ada's words that had exposed the festivities for the breadcrumbs they were, an illusion that went beyond magic.

Nor could I forget why we were here.

A curious observer was the only role, the only liberty I could allow myself.

I dropped my gaze to the honey-colored liquid in my pitcher, inhaling the rich scent. Not sweet, exactly, but more of a sharp blend that seemed to cut through the false day, yet alluring nonetheless.

"So... What exactly is sowhl?"

"A drink," Ada said coyly, seeming to drop her constant, though discreet, monitoring of our surroundings for a moment. "Especially welcomed when you need to warm up your body a bit."

At least that explained why everyone clustered around tables here seemed to be underdressed for the light chill of the afternoon, their jackets and coats draped over whatever convenient free space they could find. I suspected we would need to follow their example soon if we wanted to continue fitting in.

I looked down at my sowhl, then Ada.

Back home, I'd snuck tastes of all the beverages my parents would have been mortified to find me drinking before I came to the conclusion that I favored red wine above all else. For the most part, the bottles in my father's personal cabinet had been positively vile. Especially those he kept on hand for his *esteemed* guests.

I *really* hoped sowhl's alluring fragrance wasn't misleading.

Lifting my pitcher, I lowered my voice and asked, "Is it any good?"

Ada chuckled, but the sound was almost...timid.

"Let's just say I got so carried away when I first tried it that I accidentally brought up an illusion of the whole square burning." She sucked in a breath, then muttered, "While wrapping the people's bodies in heat at the same time."

I stared at her, wide-eyed, my lips pressed closely together to hold back the roaring laughter rising in my chest. "How many did you have?"

Ada dropped her gaze to her pitcher, the corner of her mouth quirking up as if caught between amusement and penance.

"Well?" I nudged.

She glanced at the crowd, then up, towards the blue-veiled stars before training her green eyes on me. "Eleven."

I raised an eyebrow. Whatever sowhl was, I was pretty certain I would have been passed out by that time.

Magnus had called me a lightweight, and unfortunately, he was right. Three glasses of wine were as far as I could go to still be able to form coherent sentences—or not doze off whether I wanted to or not. And wine... It was the least heady drink of them all.

I bit my lip and spied the drink out of the corner of my eye. *Eleven...*

"Our bodies... I *think* they work differently from yours. Or—or not. Maybe it's just the type of power that's different and the effect..." She exhaled and squared her shoulders while I did my best to hold back the amusement. Ada was babbling. And despite all the trouble her faster-than-brain mouth had caused us in the past, it was nice to see her like this.

"One of my ancestors was a healer," she tried again, her words slower this time. "She wrote of how the magic in our veins

affects our system. How it makes us burn through food faster...
and, mercifully, the same goes for our drinks."

"You're telling me that you lit up an entire square to
get *sober?*"

"Not *intentionally*! It was supposed to be just a simple trick...
You know, something to keep my mother from finding out. *Not*
an escort from the Prince's guard back to my house and a fine for
scaring dozens of citizens."

I couldn't help it. I broke out in roaring, choking laughter.
And Ada joined in.

Our outburst gained us a few glances, but the people casting
them appeared to be thrilled that someone was having a bloody
good time, nothing more. They weren't wrong. Tears wetted the
corners of my eyes once I was finally able to stuff some air into
my lungs, although my shoulders kept shaking.

One look at Ada told me she wasn't any better off herself.

Our gazes locked, and another round of laughter erupted. My
fingers tightened around the pitcher of sowhl.

Sun claim me, but the need to try was suddenly far louder in
my ears than the warning that I didn't have any means of erasing
the alcohol from my blood. But given where we were, I was fairly
certain Ada wouldn't succumb to the temptation of another
round, and *I* certainly had no desire to lose even a second in this
world to the haze too many drinks liked to place upon my mind.
Useful at parties, dreadful on days when you didn't want to miss
a thing.

I lifted the pitcher in salute. "Here goes nothing."

Ada watched me with an odd combination of feline curiosity
and innocent intrigue as I brought the glass to my lips, tipped
it, and...

I swallowed down a cough. "*Sun*, that's strong!"

Yet even as I struggled, I couldn't deny this alcoholic thunderstorm had a nice taste to it. *After* one regained the wits the drink had tried to burn down to ashes.

Carefully, I took another sip, this time letting the taste swirl through my mouth before the sowhl slid down my throat, scorching, but bearable. Mischief gleamed brightly in Ada's green eyes.

"Better?"

"Much," I admitted, then bravely ventured to tip the pitcher a third time.

It wasn't all that bad, but I knew one of these was enough for one day. Or a week.

Still, I was grateful Ada had brought me here, even if it was just part of her plan. Somehow, the chatter of people all around me, the laughter, the illusions dancing across the painted-over night sky, and the company of a peer who *wasn't* bullied by her parents until she became their painful model of virtue and grace... It felt good. It felt—it felt like I belonged.

"So this Eriyan we're meeting..." I started, quiet enough to not be overheard. "Who is he? Friend? Lover?"

Ada nearly choked on her sowhl.

"Lover..." She snorted and shook her head. "Definitely no lover. He's an Illusionist. One of the best in Somraque, though don't tell *him* that. Unless you want your ears to fall off from listening to his self-praise. Eriyan can be as full of himself as he's powerful."

"Wait... But you're a Mage. Doesn't that make you, you know, stronger?"

"It does," she agreed, then drank another mouthful. "More versatile, too. But a good Illusionist has the ability to specialize, really hone their skill. And Eriyan—there's no one quite like him when it comes to making people invisible."

"Right you are," a cheerful voice bellowed out of thin air on my right.

I jumped away out of instinct and almost upended the entire damn table as I slammed into it with my side, ribs screaming from the hit.

Ada swore, then scrambled to catch her pitcher, but mine...

It careened over the edge—and hovered in midair.

I FELT MORE than saw Ada shooting daggers at the invisible man who, apparently, decided to down a third of my sowhl before placing it back on the table. With my heart still hammering in my chest, I wasn't sure whether to mirror Ada's expression or laugh.

Either way, I'd recognized the antics for the grand entrance that they were.

Ada clearly hadn't been exaggerating.

Once he dissipated the illusion, I could see Eriyan was thin as a wisp, with messy blond hair and eyes that appeared unable to decide whether they were green or blue. His cheeks had a nice splash of color to them, and his skin, unlike mine, held a warm hue. But it was his wide, blinding smile that truly lit up his face.

And revealed he was more than a little tipsy.

"It's not even evening yet," Ada hissed, likely coming to the exact same conclusion.

"Ada, my love," he drawled and propped one elbow on the high table, "you wouldn't have come looking for me here, at the very best sowhl stand our lovely Nysa can offer, if it were otherwise, now would you?"

Ada scowled at him, but Eriyan's attention was already elsewhere, his eyes turning a shade warmer as he took me in.

"Though if I'd known you were bringing company, I would have at least bothered to brush my hair." He held out his hand. "Eriyan. The bane of Ada's existence."

"Ember." I clasped his hand. "Possible contender for your title."

The sound that left Ada's lips was somewhere between a laugh and a snort. Eriyan seemed thrilled.

"A challenger." He sized me up. "May the largest thorn in Ada's side win."

Somberly, we both dipped our chins, then grinned. I snatched my pitcher, drank a little, then passed it over to him before realizing I was adding fuel to the fire.

Maybe our little contest would be decided faster than I thought.

I mouthed "sorry" to Ada as Eriyan gulped down the rest of the sowhl, but she merely rolled her eyes and shook her head, as if my actions didn't make much of a difference. If Eriyan wanted his drink, he'd get it.

"Are you done?" she asked when he slammed the thick glass down on the iron tabletop.

"I received your flame," he said, gaze flickering my way briefly before he turned around, though I caught the glee resting on his features morph into something a touch more serious. "I suppose it has to do with your friend..."

"I need that fragment, Eri," she whispered. Eriyan's body went perfectly still.

The easiness, the humor... It was gone, erased as if it had never been there at all.

He bowed his head, just the barest of movement, but I could see his concession clearly enough. The hint of disbelief as well.

"You're serious, aren't you?" His composure came together piece by piece, wrapping his carefree demeanor around him like armor. "At least now I know why you were scowling instead of bringing us another round of drinks."

"Go to the Whispers, Eriyan, and burn the sowhl from your blood. We'll meet you there." Ada's gaze settled on me. "We just have one more stop to make."

ALTHOUGH I HAD BRACED myself for it, curbed some of my hunger on the way from the sowhl stand, it was impossible not to stare at all the illusions. To enjoy their thrumming, as diverse as voices, reverberate through my skin.

Some, I recognized from yesterday, but there were more, so many more to behold.

Dresses of crushed ice, lightning that did not harm, but undulated like ribbons in the wind around the bearer...

I felt as if I lost a part of me every time the connection broke off when Ada had to drag me forward as my steps faltered. And whenever we veered away from the stalls, my gaze drifted relentlessly towards those night-tinted tents at the far end of the city with their white peaks drawing me in like beacons.

"What's in them?" I asked once we entered an alley fairly devoid of people, but with the view cutting off just at the right angle to capture those illustrious capped tips.

When she shot me a questioning look, I nudged my chin towards the tents. Her gaze followed.

"Those are the Magicians' domain," she said, then scanned the street to our left before strolling down its cobblestones with a purpose that didn't make her look like the thief she had been yesterday. "A few of them keep to the stalls, tricking your body into believing it's colder than it truly is so that you would consume more sowhl or buy a nice coat, maybe even a shawl. But in the tents...

"You can experience the sun—or at least how we think it feels." She glanced at me, a half-smile resting on her lips. "Probably not all that tempting for someone who'd lived under it her whole life."

"How—how do they make you feel that?"

Ada stopped beneath an archway connecting the two streets, the darkest place there was under the blue light that still shone above, and quickly scanned our surroundings. I did the same, then turned my attention to her when I couldn't spot any visible threat.

A trickle of blood was flowing down her index fingers and I—

I felt *hot*.

My skin seemed to come alive under an invisible force, my whole body warming, growing full with that pleasant laziness that set itself deep in my limbs whenever I lingered out on the grounds, lying with my back on the grass and a book in my hands. And yet I sensed there was something different.

The brush of heat didn't filter through my pores from the outside.

It came from *within*.

I looked at Ada, understanding dawning in my mind. "The

Magicians don't merely create illusions. They actually influence the body, don't they?"

The essence of the sun died down as quickly as it surfaced, and Ada wiped that last drop of blood against her black clothes. She nodded, then motioned me to follow her farther down the road.

"The principle is the same," she explained. "Much like the eyes believe what they're seeing, the body believes the sensations. And reacts accordingly."

Brilliant. Their power was positively brilliant. My admiration must have shown on my face because a smile broke across Ada's lips. She chuckled lightly.

I thought of the sensation that had filled me only moments earlier, then glanced up at the azure dome.

"What?" Ada inquired softly.

Brow furrowed, I nibbled on my lower lip, but didn't respond until the threads and possible explanations rushing through my mind gained form. "Magic is how you grow your food, isn't it?"

For a moment, she looked at me as if I'd said something absurd. But when she nodded, I realized I'd only surprised her.

"The tents are a Winter Solstice exception. The rest of the time"—her voice gained a darker undertone—"the magic they display in there is reserved for crops and greenhouses."

I recognized the silent warning that this was a sensitive subject for her. Only I couldn't just let it go, not with so many pieces that didn't fit—though I sensed why that might be... We walked past more stone buildings, the windowsills devoid of flowers just as Somraque's landscape was devoid of life.

"There aren't any gardens..."

"No." Ada's jaw clenched. "There aren't."

Even if they couldn't maintain a field of magic indefinitely, a few hours of simulated sunlight should be more than enough to sustain the sturdier plants.

I waited until the group of men lingering before a small tavern was out of earshot, then asked, "Is it because of him?"

Ada's entire frame went tense. "Yes."

We carried on in silence, but as we slipped through another alley, more residential than the others, Ada surprised me by saying, "We could do so much if we were free."

The longing in her voice stirred a hollow ache somewhere deep in my chest.

"The greater the magic, the less we're allowed to use it," she went on. "And *always* only under his control."

She trained her gaze on the tents that were once again visible in the distance. But when I studied her face, the hard edges I'd thought I'd find there were softer.

"I envy them sometimes, you know," she whispered before she turned another corner. The bustle from the avenue grew louder to our left. "The Mages, we think ourselves as superior. At least we're raised with that belief. We have both powers at our disposal, and yes, it's an advantage, but... We could never create something as perfect as the Illusionists and Magicians do. Their magic is pure, a single blade that can shape reality into the exact vision or sensation they hold in their minds."

"But I saw you make us invisible, Ada, control those guards..."

If anyone's magic was to be considered as lesser, it was *my* people's.

Affecting time and space sounded intriguing—and before I came here, it was also something I craved to possess. Yet in light of the abilities the Somraquians had, touching objects of power and willing them to perform their little stints seemed... Well, it seemed trivial. Laughable, even.

There was no finesse to it, no imagination. One simply had to slice a sword through the air, think of the location they wanted a shortcut to and, if they were lucky, there it was. A rip in reality, sometimes fit to accommodate a person, at others a crack barely large enough to push a letter through.

Even the rarer objects pertaining to time, like my pendant, or the cufflinks I saw High Master Elaris wear that enabled him to replay an echo of an earlier conversation in case he missed anything, were utterly straightforward.

I scrunched up my nose. No, there was no need to think about my world right now. I would see it soon enough if Ada's preposterous plan actually worked. If I indeed was the savior *and* her theory that touching the fragment would spark up these hidden powers proved to be true.

When I realized Ada had said all she would on the subject of their magic, I asked, "Who's the girl we're meeting? Zaphine?"

"She...ah... We were together," Ada rumbled. I was fairly certain the tightness in her lips had little to do with the current cluster of people at the mouth of the alley we were trying to skirt around.

"Didn't end all that well?"

For a few long seconds, I thought she wouldn't answer. Then her voice reached me past the music and laughter, nothing more than a quiet, "No."

"At least your parents didn't run her out of town," I said matter-of-factly.

Ada turned to me, mortified. She opened her mouth, then closed it again. Finally, she shook her head and groaned. "No, I did all the pushing away myself. No help needed."

I wasn't above prying for more information, but Ada's attention drifted towards a lovely boutique, its windows filled with gorgeous, intricate gowns. Zaphine's shop.

There was nothing that could make this any easier, so I simply squeezed her hand, then followed her across the street for a face-to-face with her own demons.

CHAPTER ELEVEN

"Well, well, well," a stunning girl with rich black hair and eyes as green as Ada's, if a touch brighter, purred once the bell chimed, announcing our arrival. She leaned her elbows on the elegant glass-and-marble counter, the frilly champagne-colored lace of her sleeves spilling down halfway across her fingers. "We don't deal in hearts here, so if you're looking for another one to break, I'd suggest going to the sowhl tent a little farther down the road."

Every inch of the boutique was pleasant to the eye, but the sharp turn in atmosphere made me wish I were anywhere but here. The displayed gowns seemed to press in on us, the air charged with an ominous presence just waiting to combust.

By my side, Ada stiffened.

It was hard to imagine that this was the same girl who yelled at me for giving her the slip. It wasn't even the girl I'd glimpsed in her mother's sitting room... She just seemed lost. Devastatingly so.

I smoothed down my unbuttoned coat and walked over to the counter. Zaphine eyed me warily, her expression unchanging even when I extended my hand—a gesture that belonged to men only in my world, but not in this one.

"Ember Norcross."

"Zaphine Vendela." Her tone was flat, but she accepted my hand nonetheless, perfectly cordial. Unlike the venom beneath her words. "You don't seem like Ada's type."

Behind me, Ada let out a strangled groan.

"We're not together," I offered, relieved by Zaphine's bluntness. At least we didn't have to skirt around the subject.

I moved to the side, rested my forearm against the counter, and discreetly nudged my chin for Ada to move.

Mercifully, she did.

Her gait, however, remained cautious. "Inny, we need your skills."

Something flickered across Zaphine's face at the moniker, an emotion too quick, too complex for me to catch, but the girl quickly regained her cool demeanor.

"I figured as much. Ada the Mage wouldn't be caught dead making a social call."

Ada flinched. "It's not like that—"

"No?"

With each second the brutal silence dragged on, I felt more and more like a third wheel. The parties back at home had given me a lot of experience when it came to giving bickering couples a wide berth, but in a shop as small as this one, with no corners to melt into, I was out of options. My gaze caught a dainty arch leading into what seemed like a chamber, half concealed by a curtain comprised of glittering beads.

Maybe I wasn't out of *all* options.

"You two look as if you need a moment to yourselves." I tipped my head towards the second room. "Why don't I pop in there, and you can talk in the meantime? If that's all right with you, of course."

Ada glared at me, but Zaphine actually seemed pleased. "If you see anything you like, feel free to try it on," she said, gesturing to the long lines of garments I could spy even from out here. "The prices are all Winter Solstice specials. And Ember... Thank you."

The sincere, subtle gentleness I sensed in her voice disappeared the instant I pushed through the beads.

"I haven't heard from you in a *year*, Ada. A *year*. I hadn't even seen you at any of the old haunts, and then you come in here, bringing a gorgeous girl in a dress that *I* made for *you*. Stars, what were you thinking?"

I ran my fingers along the various fabrics of the garments, trying to block out the sound. Silk. Velvet. Chiffon. Wool. All materials I recognized, yet so different from what I was used to. As if Zaphine, through magic or pure skill, had breathed life into them, transformed them from clothing into individual, wearable works of art.

That part of me that was inexplicably drawn to beauty in whatever form or state it existed marveled at the breathtaking designs. At the carefully matched colors that would have struck me as odd, incompatible, if I were not seeing them come together so seamlessly with my own eyes.

But not even that was enough to cordon me off from hearing Ada and Zaphine argue.

Removing myself from their immediate presence had made no difference. If anything, it seemed as if the walls and otherwise all-encompassing silence of the space had only *amplified* the sound.

A quiet groan rolled off my lips. I walked on, drinking in the garments and failing to block out the noise when my gaze fell on another door.

Thank the Sun.

The handle gave way under my fingers immediately. Just for a moment, I hesitated, looking over my shoulder to the delicate archway with its waterfall of beads separating the two parts of the boutique. The voices were there, but neither girl was in my line of sight.

I'd told Ada I wasn't running any longer, and I meant it. For better or for worse, this was my life now—and she a part of it. So when I stepped past the threshold and into the darkened alley, with nothing but the tune of the revelry coming from the direction of the town, I hoped the fragile trust we'd built would be enough to assure her of my intentions.

All my concerns, however, were whisked away in a breath of relief as the door eased shut, granting me solitude. The spill of blue light fell upon the hem of my dress as I leaned against the wall, then let the night, the distant celebrations, and the faint thrum of magic, flood my senses.

There was a slight chill creeping down the street, cooling my cheeks and slipping beneath my cloak until I was forced to button it up and lift the collar higher. We had seasons in Soltzen, but with the constant presence of the sun, I'd never experienced true cold, regardless of what I might have believed. This—this was different.

There was a scent to it, something so sharp and clear it almost stung, only I couldn't bring myself to call it unpleasant. My mind seemed to grow clearer, too, the hazy echoes of Ada's and Zaphine's bickering receding to give way to my own voice. My own thoughts.

Until now, I hadn't even realized how much I craved to be alone—to have, if nothing more, just a few minutes all to myself.

Letting the sensation nourish me, I closed my eyes and rummaged through everything I'd learned.

I was in a new world—no, a different *fragment* of our world I had no idea existed until I plunged straight into it by means I had yet to figure out.

I was a child from Soltzen, a High Master's daughter. But more than that, I was a living intersection of three distinct magic bloodlines. Someone who belonged to all lands, despite the jarring fact that I couldn't seem to actually *use* my heritage.

And I was the one destined to reunite the broken pieces, make reality whole again. *The One.*

A snorting laugh slipped from my lips.

The first two points I could accept. The third, however, would take a lot more convincing. Not that I had any true desire to become Ada's *savior.* I'd barely slipped one pair of shackles thanks to my sudden departure from my land. I wasn't eager to willingly don another.

But on the off chance that Ada *was* right about everything...

I had to see things through to the end.

A bittersweet stench filled my nostrils, scattering my thoughts. I cracked open an eye, then instinctively flattened my back against the wall when I realized I wasn't alone in the alley any longer.

"Are you well?" the stranger asked.

He was in his late twenties, handsome, his jaw strong and lightly stubbled. But his brown eyes were unfocused.

When his breath coiled through the air, I was assaulted by the distinct smell of sowhl as strongly as if he'd soaked me in it.

"I'm fine," I said dryly, hoping it would be enough to put him off further conversation. "Just thinking."

"And what kind of thoughts run through such a pretty head?"

He was closer now, more than bordering on uncomfortable, the heat of his body brushing against mine. There was no thrum of magic emanating from him, yet the crisp air became heavy. Suffocating.

My gaze flickered to the side, to where the door to Zaphine's shop was slightly ajar as if a gust of wind had moved it while I'd been lost in thought. Discreetly, I angled my body towards it, but the stranger placed his palm against the wall, cutting off my escape.

His breath licked my skin. "Come on. It's the Solstice. A girl shouldn't be alone."

"This girl isn't," I snapped, anger momentarily overpowering my unease. "My friend's just finishing her purchase, and once she's done, we're leaving. Without you."

I could almost see his mind working as his brown eyes shifted from dazed to focused, then back again.

"You're lying," he drawled.

An exasperated sound came from my throat even as the hairs on the back of my neck rose.

"Trust me, I'm not."

Keeping my movements slow, unobtrusive, I lifted my left hand towards the pendant tucked beneath my coat. If I could slow him down just for a moment, it would be enough to slip away.

"Fine, fine, you're not." A wolfish smile. "But she's not here right now... We still have time. You don't want to stop the fun so soon now, do you?"

Stop the fun. The words sounded familiar.

Probably because this was *precisely* the kind of fun I wanted to stop.

And I had to do it *now*.

My heart hammered in my chest, but I rubbed my back against the wall, loosening the damn collar I'd pulled up earlier until the lapels parted haphazardly, exposing the neckline of my dress.

The stranger's gaze dropped down to the swell of my breasts.

I gagged on the inside but was grateful for the distraction. My hand slipped up, inches from the pendant—

His fingers snaked around my wrist.

The stranger pinned my arm against the wall, the edge of the stone biting into my skin, then caught the other. I jerked, but whatever strength was in me fled somewhere beyond my reach.

His grip wouldn't budge.

My mind swam, the thudding of my heart suddenly so loud I could barely hear his voice over the thunder echoing in my ears. His body was close, too close, towering over me until I couldn't breathe, couldn't think—

Something snapped.

Not outside, but *inside* me. The charge spread from my stomach, flooding my veins, my lungs, my mind. A cry rose up my throat but never spilled beyond the confines of my flesh. I felt my whole body hum with a force I couldn't name, a storm that thrashed and rolled within me. Until it broke.

Swirls of obsidian black lashed out from my flesh, the alley fading away as all I saw was the hunger blazing in the man's gaze.

Then the fear.

His nails sank into my wrists, a death grip that might have broken bone had he squeezed just a little tighter. But the terror froze him in place as effectively as my pendant would have.

The darkness crept closer, higher, crawling up his limbs, his torso. It shifted and danced, every vine finding a rhythm of its own, yet never becoming anything less than a harmonious whole.

When it reached his chest, the stranger screamed.

His lips parted, the hoarse beginning of his cry tainting the night—and losing its power within it.

Stunned, I watched the shadows fill his mouth, watched them crawl into his nostrils and disappear into his body as it twitched and spasmed. His grip on me loosened, and he staggered back, clawing at his chest as if he could get the darkness out.

But I saw it.

I saw the hint of black appear in the corners of his eyes, saw it spread like spilled ink upon parchment, covering the white, then the brown, until it swept over the dilated pupils and the struggle stopped.

Until there was nothing but the deepest obsidian staring back at me, the man lying faceup on the ground.

Not moving.

Not breathing.

Paralyzed, I stared at the corpse. The tendrils of darkness crept back towards me, disappearing into *my* skin and leaving the alley untouched, as if they had never existed. But the man's eyes...

They remained that endless pit of black.

I bit back a sob and staggered towards the door when a shadow at the mouth of the alley stole my attention. Bile burned at the back of my throat.

Had someone seen what I'd done? Had they seen me...*kill?*

I forced myself to look before my mind folded in on itself.

I froze.

Sapphire eyes, the silken spill of black hair...

Silver danced around his slender form, slowly, so slowly, cautiously, as if it were tasting the air.

My chest constricted.

Him.

CHAPTER TWELVE

His blue gaze drilled into mine.

Even wrapped in terror, on the verge of shattering from the thought of the lifeless body that lay on the cobblestones and the darkness that filled it, the handsome lines of his face seemed to tether me. Ground me. His presence tightened my throat yet willed air to fill my lungs. It was as if I were falling into a spell—and I didn't want to break from it.

My mind descended into silence, the murmur of the avenue becoming insignificant, as did the world around us. What had happened was a mere whisper on the wind, its weight pulled apart by the currents.

There was only Mordecai.

Only Mordecai and the strong, steady pounding of my heart as he looked at me, gazed at me as if I were the most exquisite, singular thing he had ever seen. The silver shadows lapped around his black clothes, as brilliant and as pure as moonlight, the vines growing, expanding in their languid dance—

A hand wrapped around my forearm and tugged me back from the step I had made in his direction. A wretched, silent roar shook my body when those beacons of sapphire were replaced by a sharp spill of artificial light that assaulted my senses, coupled with Ada's frantic voice telling me to *RUN*.

The cocoon shattered.

Aware of Ada's almost bruising grip moving from my forearm to my hand, I cast one last look towards the alley—now just a sliver of blue-tinted shadow visible through the door before it swung shut.

Gradually, I regained control of my limbs. We ran past the long line of garments, but I still stumbled over the threshold when Ada yanked me full force through the clattering beads into the front of the shop.

Zaphine's eyes were wide, back flattened against the wall and hands hidden—undoubtedly ready to bleed, call up her magic if it hadn't been *us* who'd come through.

It was the final shove I needed to shake off the remnants of the daze.

Ada kept barreling towards the door.

Zaphine hesitated for just a moment before she skirted around the counter, then paused, pivoting. She slid her body across the glass, reaching for something on the side the marble front concealed, then pushed herself away to join us on our mad dash out. My heartbeat was pulsing in my ears, a vicious, heavy rhythm I could not only hear, but felt, and almost drowned out Ada's words.

Almost.

"The Crescent Prince."

A sharp hiss ripped itself from Zaphine's lips at the name.

Between one moment and the next, something changed in the way she carried herself, an urgency. As well as fear.

She cast a look over her shoulder, as if checking if some undetectable protections were in place—or, worse, saying goodbye. It lasted no more than a second, then Zaphine trained her gaze up ahead, fabric rustling as we all made for the front door. The night air grazed my heated skin, its bite sharper than what I had felt in the alley.

A cloud of condensation formed as I exhaled.

The lights and the many illusions still swiveled and danced all around us, breaking up the perpetual darkness. But there was a sense of quiet out here that hadn't been present before. A quiet that took the shape of five black-clad men, running in our direction.

With a snarling war cry, Ada sliced her dagger across her palm.

I leaned into her before she could call forth her magic, grabbing Zaphine with my free hand while already clutching the pendant in the other. Ada's eyes flashed in understanding, and then the men's steps were slowing down, the pulse of the city coming to a gentle, yet definite stop.

"It won't hold long," I urged, sensing how faint the magic was, how it struggled to keep our surroundings suspended.

Like paint, stretched so thin it was almost translucent.

The power was unable to truly permeate the buildings, the people, merely settled atop the surroundings like heavy dust—a temporary hurdle time would eventually overcome.

It felt wrong, the weakness, when I knew of the pendant's true capabilities, but it would provide us the advantage we desperately needed to escape.

While Zaphine seemed momentarily stunned as life lingered

in stasis, Ada didn't miss a beat. Her fingers snaked around my elbow without giving up the contact even once, and I tightened my hold on Zaphine, tugging her along those few steps it took her to shed the stupor.

With an assured stride that bordered on running—the fastest we dared to move and not risk losing the touch that bound us— Ada led the way past the guards, their bodies frozen mid-move and hard-set eyes focused on an image that would not be there when they entered reality once more.

Ada paid them no heed. She kept leading us away.

From the too crowded street.

From the Crescent Prince.

Small tremors spread through my flesh as I held on to the waning magic, willed it to last just a little longer—

The hem of Zaphine's skirt barely disappeared into the narrow path between two buildings Ada had chosen when the world sprang back to life.

Shouts ricocheted off the walls, distorted by the music that couldn't have been louder than before, but struck me as nearly deafening.

I couldn't make out what they were saying, but whatever surprise the guards had felt at our sudden disappearance, it faded faster than I had hoped. A series of whistles cut through the air, muting the festivities. It seemed as if the very ground beneath us vibrated with the heavy fall of boots and hooves.

We ducked backwards into a narrow passage. An inner courtyard opened behind us, the still-empty alley up ahead.

"*Stars,*" Zaphine whispered. "What was that all about?"

I lowered my gaze to the cobblestones as she looked at me, the wonder and intrigue written plainly on her flushed face overpowering the uncertainty lurking beneath.

I knew she was asking about the power more than the guards —or *him*. But...

Obsidian shadows filled my vision, the image of the man's contorted features as the coiling wisps of dark seeped into his body, stealing away his life. No, not stealing.

Burning.

Like Telaria would have if Mordecai hadn't stopped. Hadn't chosen to damn her to a magicless existence.

Mortified, I looked at my coat, my hands, but my body remained the same. No whispers of darkness. Nothing but clothing and skin.

"The Crescent Prince found Ember," Ada rasped when I didn't answer. She squeezed her bloodied hand, the furrow on her brow revealing that somewhere, an illusion was forming. "I think he killed someone."

The sowhl I'd drunk rose up my throat. I swallowed as I pressed my back against the wall, but couldn't stop shaking.

Mordecai hadn't killed anyone.

I did.

CHAPTER THIRTEEN

THE TENSION NEVER LEFT ME.

Even when I silenced that primal voice of instinct within me that spoke with utter certainty that the man had lost his life because of me.

Even when Ada's illusions kept Mordecai's men at bay again and again.

The two threads of fear clashed and entwined until I wasn't certain what terrified me more.

The hunt.

Or the inky layer, obscuring the already nauseating truth of what had transpired in the alley.

I forced myself to focus on the surroundings, on Ada's dexterity as she saved Zaphine and me over a dozen times. No display was the same twice, her imagination limitless.

Unfortunately, her body wasn't.

With every minute, she was growing weaker. Although the

thrumming of her power was hushed, the level of its potency wasn't concealed, but cracked wide open for me to read.

I didn't even have to see the tightness on her face or the way her step sometimes faltered to know that she would collapse if she didn't give herself a chance to recover soon.

Zaphine must have come to the same conclusion because when we cut through the slumbering outskirts of the city and towards the mountains, she took over without leaving room for argument. Her magic flowed over our clothes, our hair, our skin, nothing but varying shades of gray and black to keep us blended with the landscape. Camouflage.

Some part of me recognized the beauty of how she worked, of the attention to detail that made her deception almost as perfect as the illusion Ada and I had been cloaked in that had rendered us invisible on our way into town. Still, that awareness was only a flicker of land in the turbulent waves my thoughts continued to be, regardless of how hard I tried to contain them.

I kept flashing back to the alley, some buried thread of darkness niggling at the back of my mind as if there was some shard of reason to it all. But if there was, I couldn't reach it.

Sapphire eyes slashed the knot I had tangled myself into, but only to form another.

The Crescent Prince had been there.

As caught up in the inebriated man as I had been when he'd cornered me, I'd failed to see Mordecai lurking at the mouth of the alley. Could he have somehow called the shadows, masked his own in an illusion of darkness and brought down the man? Made it only *seem* as if they had retreated into my body?

Yet even as the words rolled through my mind, I could taste their falseness.

Taste the answer I didn't want to accept, but couldn't ignore either.

Whatever that was, the obsidian wisps had come from *me*.

I swallowed and lowered my head so that the silver strands hid the expression I simply couldn't school into something even moderately neutral. Even uttering a plain "no" would have been too much of an effort if either of the girls asked if something was wrong...

My brows knitted together.

Could *this* be the power Ada and Telaria had spoken of? What made me the *One*?

Somehow, I found it hard to believe that *darkness* was what would reunite the worlds. Destroy them, maybe. But never bring them together.

Breathless and shaking beneath the warm cloak, I trailed a step behind the two girls as they progressed towards the hulking wall of the mountain, then halted when they disappeared straight through the rock.

I let loose a labored breath.

An illusion. Just another illusion.

And still, I remained rooted to the spot, gaze turned on the fake mountain face.

A crevice opened up inside me. An ugly weakness, with slithering tongues of doubt that would surely flay me alive if I let them.

I didn't ask to come here.

I never wanted to be anyone's savior.

I had no desire to be responsible for their lives.

And I certainly did not want to take them.

The cacophony ripped through me, the volume rising to drowning heights.

Would it make a difference if I told them I did it in defense?
Did I believe I did?

I crammed the words back into the chasm, shoving the darkness inside just as those obsidian wisps had seeped under my skin.

This—this weakness... It wasn't me.

Crying over things that had already happened—

Maybe a time for that would come. But it wasn't now. Not when there was still a chance I could learn something that would shed light on *everything*.

I squared my shoulders and moved towards the illusion, narrowly evading a collision with Zaphine as she popped her head through the false rock.

"Are you coming?" Her green eyes narrowed on me. The expression so similar to Ada's I couldn't help but wonder which girl had picked it up from the other. "Are you all right?"

I nodded, not caring that she had probably seen my struggle through the veil of magic. "Just needed a moment to breathe, that's all."

Zaphine didn't seem all that convinced but disappeared back inside just the same. I followed.

A faint tingle of electricity rushed through my flesh as the face of the mountain wavered like the surface of a lake and let me pass. But while the magic sealed behind me, a sensation I felt as clearly as if I were watching paint spill across a marble floor, the sight remained unchanged.

The rocky desert. The stars glimmering above.

There was no translucent mold of the illusion, nothing to impede surveilling the land from inside.

Tension built at my back, a silent storm waiting to break, and

I realized I'd been gawking at the craftsmanship behind the magic for long enough. I spun around.

I was, indeed, in a cavern. Although one that was illuminated —and furnished. Sparsely, true, but there was a cushioned sofa set by the stone-hewn wall, a rug thrown across the rough ground, and a small, makeshift cabinet tucked in the far corner, flanked by an armchair on each side.

Eriyan's silhouette was a rigid presence taking up the deeper end of the space, his face drawn together in worry. His gaze darted between Zaphine and me, but as Ada wavered on her feet a short distance away, he reacted at once. He rushed over and helped her hobble to the sofa before either of us could as much as move. Ada sank onto the pillows, drained.

With a look over her shoulder, Zaphine joined them in a few trudging strides. But while that glance had been an invitation, I just stood by the entrance, watching the three friends huddle close, feeling like a wolf in sheep's clothing.

"What happened?" Eriyan asked, his palm resting on Ada's forehead. From the strain in his voice, I suspected this wasn't the first time he'd posed the question.

She shrugged away from his touch with enough force to send him tipping onto the rolled armrest, and shot up from the sofa. Zaphine lunged after her, reaching out as if to catch her in case she fell, but Ada swatted her hand aside.

Hurt flashed across Zaphine's face, there one moment, gone the next. Even Eriyan seemed affected by the sudden hostility as he stood to lean against the side of the couch, visibly unable to sit still.

The charge that kept building up in the cavern was broken only when a frustrated groan spilled from Ada's lips and swept through the space as she paced the rock floor.

She didn't cease muttering something unintelligible under her breath as she stalked to the cabinet and, with her back to us, retrieved something from a drawer. Food, I realized, when the scent of dried apples and prunes suffused the air.

None of us spoke while she ate, although Eriyan stuffed his hands into his pockets after Zaphine shot him a warning glare. He'd been fraying the hem of his jacket, the slate-colored strands now dangling from the edge of the fabric.

"How?" Ada slammed the drawer shut and braced her hands on the cabinet. She stayed like that for a few moments, then reclaimed the center of the space. "How did he *find* her?" she hissed at no one in particular.

Zaphine winced, and Eriyan sucked in a breath, his hands balling into fists, though he kept them firmly in his pockets.

"How does that bastard always *win*?!" Ada growled and thrust her fingers in her hair until most of the braid came undone. She tilted her head towards the ceiling, swore, then met my gaze.

Instinctively, I opened my mouth to apologize for leaving the shop, but as soon as the thought of that alley crept into my mind again, my voice faltered, and all that came out was a strangled, almost inaudible cry.

"My mother lost her magic to protect you. She sacrificed *everything*, prepared me for what was coming. All I had to do was keep you safe when you arrived, keep you out of sight until we could move forward." She let out a bitter laugh. "And I led you right to him. *Stars*! Can't anything go right?"

"So he knows?" Eriyan seemed pained by the question. "The Crescent Prince knows we'll go after the relic?"

The heartbeat of silence was loaded with something volatile.

Something ready to combust.

I glanced at Zaphine, the stiff set of her shoulders and rigid spine as she stared at Ada. The suppressed fury rolling off her nearly choked the breath out of me.

"*That's* what you wanted me for?" she erupted. "You're *insane*, Ada! You'll die before you breach his palace. What could you possibly hope to achieve by stealing..." She fell quiet, her body perfectly still. "Oh my Stars..." She looked at me, mouth parted. "You're the prophesied child. You're the One. I—I should have known when Ada brought you, when you...froze...the town...that you weren't one of us."

"You *froze* Nysa?" Eriyan cut in, gaining a glare from Zaphine.

He shrugged and eased back onto the sofa, as if the discomfort that had gripped his entire body only moments before had never been there at all. But Zaphine's attention was already on Ada who was still pacing up and down the length of the cavern floor.

"Why did you bring her with you? Wouldn't she have been safer at your house with Telar—" The soft touch of red on her cheeks paled into an icy white. "Stars, Ada..."

Another silence. Lengthier. Chilling.

I held my breath as Ada drew her dagger from beneath her coat.

"I know," she whispered. Her entire chest shuddered as she exhaled, but her green gaze was dark, filled with singular purpose. "When his men can't find us in town, it will be my mother he'll hunt."

CHAPTER FOURTEEN

"Ada, no," Zaphine cried out. "Don't..."

But Ada was already moving past me and towards the exit of the cavern, the illusion flickering in her wake. With a soft thrumming, her legs started to blend with her surroundings, followed by her hips, her waist...

"Whatever happens," she snarled over her shoulder, "keep Ember safe." She focused on Eriyan. "You know what to do."

With that, she was gone. Out of the cavern. Out of sight.

Zaphine prickled her finger and set the illusion back in place, then let out a streak of curses, sounding dangerously close to the verge of tears. I slumped down on the ground.

She had known. Ada had known what would happen after those guards saw us. What would be the cost of leading Zaphine and me here...

"Do you think he'll kill her? Telaria?" Eriyan whispered as if he were following the same line of thought.

"What do you think?" Zaphine snapped, her full lips drawn tight. "He's already let her live once."

I tuned out the rest of their conversation and leaned against the cool wall, pulling my knees to my chest. More curses and snarls fluttered through the air, reaching all the way over to my spot on the ground, but they bounced off my own thoughts almost effortlessly. Every nerve in my body urged to leave the cavern, to run somewhere far under the night sky. If it would have made the situation better, I would have. Without hesitation.

As it was, I felt guilty enough.

If I could turn back time and keep myself from entering that Sun-damned alley, I would have done it in a heartbeat. But even the most respected High Masters didn't have that power.

The most I was able to do was make sure I wasn't discovered again. That none of us were.

A shape slithered past the corner of my vision. I glanced to the right and met Eriyan's gaze as he settled himself against the wall beside me. Silently, he offered me a pint of sowhl.

A bitter laugh rose in my chest, though the sound died before it left my lips. I accepted the dimpled mug, wrapping my fingers around the glass surface, and inhaled deeply.

This was so much worse than any trouble I had gotten myself into back home.

"Freezing Nysa?"

I cast him a sideways look. "*That's* what you want to know?"

He tugged on a strand of his light hair, a boyish smile softening the underlying strain. I shook my head and drank, barely noticing the taste.

"A man has to size up his competition."

This time, the bitter laugh did break past my lips. "I think you've already lost, don't you?"

Eriyan snorted. "Things you aren't directly responsible for don't count."

But I was. Responsible.

"Ada is her mother's daughter," he offered as my expression fell. His gaze darted up to Zaphine who was pacing around the cavern, tracing a similar pattern as Ada had before. "A survivor. The Aldane women are a tenacious lot."

I sighed, though a kernel of warmth sparked inside me. I sat up a little straighter and folded my legs beneath me, the sowhl resting in my lap. "From what I've seen, I think you're right. It's just... It just feels so wrong. I came here, and everything...fell apart."

"Trust me"—he laughed, the sound harsh—"things have been falling apart for a long, long time. You...you simply sped up the inevitable shitstorm that was brewing on the horizon."

"Well, that's reassuring." I rubbed my thumb over a glass dimple.

Eriyan shifted sideways to face me. Gone was the easy demeanor, but with it also the edge of defeat and concern, as if he'd slipped into a new skin.

One that didn't need armor—because it *was* armor.

"Not everybody cares for our world's true history. Actually, the majority seem inclined to leave it in the past where it's powerless to rattle whatever magicless illusions they put up to block the ugly reality. But those of us who do... Those of us who want a future free from the endless night..." He exhaled and flicked a pebble from the ground aside. "We don't call you *savior* or *One* just because it sounds majestic. We believe in it. Believe in you. And if anyone thought the path to rejoin the three worlds would be easy—well, those people wouldn't be scheming how to break into the Crescent Prince's palace, would they?"

Something rattled in the depths of the cavern. We both glanced at Zaphine, the narrow line of her lips and focused gaze, as if she were seeing all the way to Nysa. To the lone building just beyond the town's edge. Her slender fingers were curling relentlessly, but at least her pacing wasn't quite as frantic. Even if she *had* just kicked a small, empty crate across the floor.

I took a sip of sowhl, then tipped my head back against the uneven surface of the wall, Eriyan's attention on me once more. "How are you this calm?"

"Because I didn't burn the sowhl from my blood." He winked, a mischievous grin tugging at his lips. "And because the Crescent Prince doesn't have you. *We* do."

I was getting tired of my disobedient mind, but couldn't prevent my thoughts from skipping back to those sapphire eyes, so vivid in the demure light of the alley. To the hint of wonder, disbelief, and hunger I glimpsed in them that instant before a guarded veil had snapped into place, as cold as the shadows billowing around his form, when Ada pulled me back.

"Mor—The prince's shadows... What are they?" I asked with a tremor in my voice. "I know what they do. I've seen Telaria... But what *are* they?"

Eriyan remained silent for a few moments, contemplating, then snatched away the sowhl and took a long sip before giving it back. "I try to keep my ass as far away from them as possible, but from what I felt and heard over the years, the shadowfire is some form of magic."

"Not blood magic?"

"If it is, it's not like ours." His fingers reached for the frayed hem of his jacket, then curled into a fist. "I don't think it comes from our world."

He—he isn't human, Ember. The memory of Ada's words swam to the surface.

"So you haven't seen anyone else...exhibit...anything like it?"

"No."

My stomach sank.

"I don't know how he got them. Even Ada with all her old books hasn't been able to figure it out. Maybe, like the magic, *he's* something different. Or found some way to change himself."

"You think that's possible? To change?"

It was hard to keep my voice steady when my entire body buzzed with hope. If the Crescent Prince had altered himself, perhaps he was capable of doing it to another person too. Namely me.

Though even if that were the case, there was no telling whether the change was permanent.

Eriyan mulled over my question. I offered him the sowhl, but he declined it with a wan smile and a shake of his head.

"Anything is possible, I suppose." He rubbed his palms across his face, then groaned. "We have our heads above the surface, but we're still wading through shit. Odorless, camouflaged shit, but shit nonetheless." A chuckle. "Sometimes, the only thing that keeps me sane is the beauty of sowhl."

Zaphine's steps filled our silence.

Thud-thud-thud-thud. Pause. *Thud-thud-thud-thud.*

"What about you?"

I whipped my head towards him.

Eriyan waved a hand at the cavern, the night beyond, me. "What keeps *you* sane?"

Nothing lately.

I bit my lip—

"I can't take this." Zaphine's hoarse, yet sharp, voice sliced the air.

We both looked up at her, at the pained expression on her face... The delicate groove between her eyebrows deepened.

"I can't stand here and do nothing." She reached under the lacy sleeve of her champagne-colored dress and revealed a slender silver dagger. It must have been the item she'd taken from the shop just before we'd fled. "I'm going after her."

Eriyan was on his feet with frightening speed, blocking her way. "Ada told us to wait, protect Ember. You really want to piss her off?"

"I want to keep her from ending up *dead,* Eriyan."

They stared at each other for a heartbeat longer, then Zaphine said, "You can protect Ember on your own. You don't need me here. But if something happens to Ada—" She let out a hissing breath, annoyance manifesting briefly in her narrowed eyes. "Even if she named you her second-in-command, asked you to take over... We won't last without her. Don't deny it. I knew I was leaving my life behind the moment I ran out of my shop, but I have no desire to spend whatever's left of it in hiding. So you *will* let me go, Eriyan, or I swear to the stars I'll shred your balls into ribbons."

Slowly, Eriyan inclined his head, then stepped aside. "Just... Take care. We never exactly saw eye to eye, but I'd hate for you to lose that pretty head of yours."

Humor underlined his words, but Zaphine only glared at him and marched out of the cavern, her long black hair billowing behind her. I pulled my cloak tighter as a gust of wind swept through the space, then observed Eriyan as he unsheathed a small knife from his belt.

Still staring at the mouth of the cavern, he jabbed the blade's tip into his finger. A drop of brilliant crimson appeared on his skin, and the illusion snapped back into place, shielding us from sight once more.

"What do you do when none of you are here?" I gestured to the entrance, desperate to think of anything but Mordecai, the eerie sensation that we were more alike than anyone thought, whether born or made.

Just as I didn't want to think about the argument Eriyan and Zaphine had had—that continued to ripple through the air in muted echoes.

"What? Oh, that... No one ever comes this far out of town. They have no reason to." He plopped down next to me, easing into his laid-back demeanor once more before he motioned to the torches illuminating the walls. The bead of crimson on his finger was gone. "We only need to mask the Whispers when we have light. So, what were we saying?"

I opened my mouth to sputter a new theme, anything to steer the conversation in another direction before the interest I had shown in the shadowfire raised suspicion. But Eriyan was faster.

"The shadows, right." He snatched my sowhl again and drank deeply. This time, when he returned it, I followed his example.

Unlike before, when I had been still too numb, the liquid burned down my throat and sent blood coursing faster through my veins. I relished the sensation. How alive it made me feel.

Normal.

"He razed an entire village with shadowfire once."

The heat fled from my body. "What?"

"I was too young to remember or understand what happened, but my parents whispered about it for years

136

afterwards. And once I met Ada, that terrifying mother of hers..." He winced, then went on. "They filled in the blanks others were afraid to even think about.

"There was talk of overturning his reign. A group of Illusionists, Magicians, even a few Mages—they banded together. Then rallied the villagers who were more than sympathetic to their cause since the restrictions on magic forced them to live on the edge of poverty when they could have easily created more. If only they were allowed. People in Nysa—my parents included—like to accept this comfortable life. They don't have everything, but they have enough that they wouldn't dare risk losing it."

I nodded. Ada had said something along those lines, too.

"Maybe if I hadn't been schoolmates with kids from the country, I would've turned out the same way."

A heaviness crept into his tone, but also something fragile. I handed him the sowhl.

I knew how little it could take for things to turn out differently. If I'd never found those books, if my parents had nipped my dreams in the bud from the day they began...

Maybe I would have been nothing but a breeding mare, hanging on the arm of one of the elite High Masters.

Eriyan gave back the drink.

"The founding group and the villagers," he continued, "formed a plan. No one had ever been able to face the Crescent Prince and win. It was—*is*—suicide to go against him alone. But they thought that maybe if they joined their magic, if they mixed their blood and worked together..." He sighed, the lines around his eyes deepening. "*Nothing* can best such evil, Ember. Forty-three bodies, forty-three minds working as one, and the shadows took them all. That silver of his"—he turned to me, jaw tight—"is nothing but death and torture. You'd do well to stay away from it."

I glanced down, a hollow ache growing in my chest. What if it was already too late?

BETWEEN US, we polished off the sowhl and started to make a dent in the next pitcher Eriyan brought our way. We didn't move from our perch by the wall despite the increasing chill. We hardly even spoke.

He was worried. I could tell, even if he seemed adamant to keep it all concealed under a carefree, if pensive, facade.

Just once he slipped, muttering how everything started with blood and ended with it. I didn't ask what he meant. There was too much on my mind already.

The silence, while not uncomfortable, presented a sounding board for my thoughts. Although I was more than aware there was a good chance I would run myself ragged going in circles, I also suspected the instant Ada and Zaphine returned, any opportunity I had to put the impressions, the outtakes of what I had gleaned into something that at least resembled a coherent whole would evaporate.

So I set down the darkened path and braced myself for the impact.

Mordecai, the power he wielded—it all crashed through me, a pounding more wild and vile than even the sharp taste of sowhl could hope to overcome. But that wasn't even the worst of it.

Oh, I knew that the drunk in the alley had harbored no honorable intentions. Just as I was certain he would have forced me right up against that cold stone facade if I hadn't fought back. Perhaps even killed me, once he was done. But still, I couldn't help feeling as if I had attacked someone who was defenseless, weaker in light of the terror wrought of obsidian mist.

That I—I *murdered* him without a second thought.

I couldn't have predicted what was going to happen, but... Could I have stopped the shadows? Controlled them somehow?

Whether they were mine or merely tied to me through something Mordecai had done, as a part of myself, I should have been able to...wield them.

Swallowing another mouthful of sowhl to camouflage the bitter taste that rose at the back of my throat, I delved into that ugly memory. I blocked the image of the man, focusing only on myself. On that *crack* as something inside me snapped—no, as a wall broke down, releasing the flood of darkness. I had been terrified, yes, but something else had triggered the destruction. Three simple words.

Stop the fun.

Words I couldn't place but sounded all too familiar. A scrape of claws belonging to something I suspected I should know yet remained obscured.

What I did recognize now, was the low-burning rage that swept through me just as the dam ruptured and power flooded my flesh and skin. Different from what I felt whenever I used the pendant, different from the thrumming the illusions produced. Where the magic of the worlds seemed kinder, like sunlight piercing through a thick layer of clouds and illuminating the land, what lived within me, what was *mine,* was sharp like a gust of winter air.

Perhaps I truly couldn't have prevented the darkness from

rupturing the barrier of my skin. But there was no mistaking it for what it was.

Shadowfire.

And it made me feel...complete.

I traced my fingers along the pendant, the three stones set into its silver form, all the same elegant obsidian as the coiling wisps. They had always been a comfort, a shield, and the shadowfire—it had provided it, too.

I bit back a sob and looked down at my body, at what rested inside, fulfilling me beyond anything I'd ever experienced.

The mark of a murderous tyrant.

Was this truly their savior? Someone who unleashes herself on a man with a power he could never hope to survive? Someone who shares the traits of a *monster*? Who *is* a monster in her own right?

Maybe that's why Mordecai wanted me.

To join the worlds. Then burn them.

Between us, no rebellion could hope to survive.

Digging my fingernails into my palms, I opened my mouth, nauseated and ready to tell Eriyan everything when two pairs of footsteps ricocheted off the cavern walls. We both glanced at the entrance, Eriyan's body appearing just as tightly wound as mine felt. He shot up to his feet.

Zaphine ran inside first, her dark hair swept in all directions and dress flapping around her legs. Then Ada. But my gaze only skimmed the furious expression twisting her face before it fell on a single piece of parchment she held in her hands. She marched over, dangling the paper in front of us.

Eriyan swore.

And as I pushed myself off the ground, I knew why.

The note—it was written in blood.

CHAPTER FIFTEEN

Unlike what I had experienced before when Ada had altered my dress, the touch of Zaphine's magic was gentler, more melodic. I would have called it sophisticated, even, if that wouldn't cast every other power I'd seen in a lesser light.

But the undeniable fact remained that Zaphine was an artist, choosing when her brushstrokes were visible or near undetectable.

Her slender dagger with an emerald adorning its argent hilt was in her hand, but she barely used it as a few drops of blood was all it took to shape the magic into whatever she envisioned.

It swept over my face, my body, covering me in thin layers of illusions until the silver of my hair turned a deep brown and my hands weren't mine any longer. The skin now carried echoes of age at least a decade beyond mine, my almond-shaped nails turning rounder to fit better with the somewhat wider fingers, three of them boasting simple, yet elegant rings. My body she strategically filled out in certain parts, while taking away some of my curves in others.

Watching her work, observing the results... It was no wonder that Zaphine was in such high demand for ordained event preparations—a license, as she explained while finalizing her touches, the Crescent Prince himself had given, as he did for every other legitimate business tied to magic. Even so, there was a limit to how many jobs she could take on in a certain timeframe.

It was that restriction, combined with the necessity to use the life rushing through her blood, that had led her to teach herself how to perform without falling on Mordecai's radar.

Beside me, Eriyan was unrecognizable, older, with harsher, although appealing, features and a hint of a belly showing beneath his clothes, while Ada resembled a dark-haired woman in her early thirties. One that oozed quiet confidence, dressed in a simple, form-hugging dress in hues of spring leaves.

The magic thrummed around us, lively and potent, if still nearly imperceptible, its song rising one last time as Zaphine gradually changed herself into another person. Bland, with lackluster blonde hair—the kind of person you wouldn't notice in a crowd.

Another measure, I suspected, to divert attention from her power despite how toned down it already was, now that it settled.

Zaphine checked us over again, and I did the same.

The illusions were unnervingly convincing, the differences staggering. It was more than just our appearances that had changed, but our very presence. Yet despite it all, certain aspects of our true selves shone through—if you looked long enough.

And knew what to search for.

"Changing our voices would demand too much," Zaphine said, the words directed more to Ada than anyone else. She concealed the dagger beneath her now nonexistent lace sleeve. "I should be able to hold our state for an hour. Two at the most, *if* there's no trouble."

"It'll do," Ada cut in, her body already angled towards the exit. But Zaphine wasn't done.

She eyed Ada warily, then addressed Eriyan. "Remember, you're *older*. I'm not sure you're capable of acting mature if your life depended on it, but I'll buy you a pint of sowhl if you at least try."

Eriyan's mouth quirked up. "With an offer like that—"

The *thud* of Ada's footsteps overpowered his words.

My attention slid to her—to the way she held herself; the straight line of her spine, chin up, and a determination to her steps that I couldn't help but admire. No illusion could mask that aspect of her.

Whatever fear or anger that had still marked her posture only moments earlier was gone.

Zaphine approached me and whispered, "You'll be fine, Ember. No one knows you."

I nodded, but my focus was on Ada as she braced one slender hand against the jagged rock at the mouth of the cavern. "The sooner we leave Nysa and form a plan, the faster I can get to my mother."

Mordecai's blood-message flashed before my eyes. He hadn't killed her. He had taken Ada's mother captive—and offered a bargain.

Telaria's freedom in exchange for mine.

A proposition Ada not only *wouldn't*, but *couldn't* accept. We all felt the strain it put her under.

"Now," Ada drawled, shedding the austerity and slipping into her new skin in full, "are we going to waste Zaphine's illusions, or do you chatterboxes intend to move?"

The transformation shuffled us forward. We spilled out of the cavern, Lyra coming to rush up to our side from wherever she had been waiting under the night sky. She ran up to each one of us, seemingly unaffected by the magic we wore, then darted back into the darkness. Keeping her distance, I imagined.

If anybody saw us with her, our disguises would mean little.

Clever dog.

I fell in step with Eriyan while Ada and Zaphine led up front. "So where, exactly, are we going?"

They *had* mapped out a crude course of action before we began with our makeovers, but I had simply been too torn between the leaden sense of responsibility and the dread of that rotten, silent promise the blood-written note carried to catch everything. To catch *anything*, actually, aside from our goal to leave Nysa so we could get our bearings together. Whether Ada had been too caught up in her own thoughts or spotted that I needed a little time to recover, she had left me out of it. After all, it wasn't as if I could contribute much, little as I knew of their world. Though blatantly missing out like that *did* grate on my nerves.

Eriyan glanced back towards the Whispers, the cavern now uncoated as he dropped the illusion, but utterly dark. Just another piece of land.

He was the first to break the silence. "Sorry, what did you say?"

"The plan," I explained, then hastened my step when I saw Ada and Zaphine were quite a stretch away. "I just wanted to know where we're going. I heard you mention a town..."

"Saros. It's just around the mountain." A wistful expression crossed his face. "I'll climb it one day, you know, that dashing beast."

I arched an eyebrow, more than a little surprised by his admission. There was something innocent, intimate in the way he looked at the hulking rock face, the true Eriyan shining through the illusion.

A part of me hated that I had to prompt him for more.

"And Saros?"

"Yes, right, of course." He scanned the moonlit landscape, the blue glow of the celebrations. "Carriages connect it to Nysa. And vice versa. Usually, they come and go as they please, but during the celebrations, they are on a strict schedule to accommodate the people visiting the festivities who don't plan to or can't afford to stay for more than a day. The carriages arrive before noon, leave at half past midnight." A smile touched his face. "Which means they'll be waiting."

We edged across the wasteland, keeping close to the mountain where the shade was deepest. I glanced at the sapphire-tinted town rising in the distance. An icy jewel laid upon a black velvet cushion. Beautiful. And yet the thought of returning to it chilled me to my bones.

"Do we have to cross?" I jerked my chin in its direction.

The thin line Eriyan's lips pulled into was answer enough, but I was grateful when he went on. "There's a square just inside the perimeter on the eastern edge of Nysa. If all goes well, we'll be able to take one of the...ah...less uptight routes that will lead us straight to it."

I raised an eyebrow, noting the slight blush that crept past the illusion. "Less uptight?"

For a moment, I thought he wouldn't answer, but then a wide grin broke across his rugged face. "Brothels."

ERIYAN HADN'T BEEN KIDDING. A little less than half an hour later, we were surrounded by pleasure houses. Unlike the discreet establishments harboring quiet girls with downcast eyes I'd stumbled upon in Soltzen once when I had slipped away during a rare family outing, the women and men here lingered out in the streets, wrapped in coats and wearing little underneath. But what struck me the most wasn't the skin they showed. Or their numbers. It was the ease with which they carried themselves, the laughter that echoed through the darkness, devoid of fear.

They chose this, I realized. They had chosen this way of life of their own free will, and they loved it.

Even the glances they received from the passersby, from people I suspected were their clientele... What I saw was respect, an open appreciation for the work they did.

The light atmosphere of the district was contagious, and I found that I was breathing easier, the tension in my spine present, but much less arduous. It was as if the celebrations in Nysa's center had a twin here in this surprisingly lively pocket of the otherwise somber outskirts, the townsfolk eager for an evening of entertainment that had nothing to do with illusions or tricking the senses. Everything here was real, and the thrumming weaving through the air seemed to come from the people, their laughs and pleasure, not the power coursing through their veins.

For a moment, I regretted our changed appearances, the

impostors they made us into, even if they were not only next to undetectable, but necessary.

Or maybe it was precisely because of that.

But as I drank it all in while we walked down the softly illuminated streets, at least I knew why Zaphine had chosen to age us. With a mature edge to our appearance, we fitted in far better than a group in their late teens and very early twenties ever could. Though by the way Eriyan *almost* greeted a few of the individuals conversing on the cobblestones, I was fairly certain that *his* youth wouldn't have been a problem.

Unfortunately, the recognition would.

"I can't believe he didn't stay!" A female voice came from a small iron table set out in front of a cozy tavern.

I peered towards the two women, both stunning, each in her unique way. One was plump, with dimples and dazzling blue eyes that seemed to shine as bright as the stars above, the other thin as a wraith, with sharp cheekbones and sculpted eyebrows, now slightly raised.

"They're hunting someone, it seems," the voluptuous woman said, coiling a strand of mahogany hair around her finger. "He only stopped for long enough to ask me if I'd seen anything."

"The bastard!" While the exclamation was harsh, her tone was lined with silent humor.

Her friend shrugged. "He paid my wage even when I protested. It's not his fault he got called away..."

"This round is on you, then," the blonde drawled and raised her wineglass by its delicate stem. "You know that, right?"

As their laughter rode the air, my fingers found Ada's hand. I gave her a light squeeze. She nodded, just a gentle dip of her chin, but it was enough to let me know that she'd heard them, too.

We needed to get to those carriages sooner rather than later.

I drifted away from Ada once more when a group of women spilled out of a side alley, casting each other glances filled with pure desire. Eriyan gazed after them a little longingly, then quickly schooled his features when he noticed my attention.

"What? They look good..."

I almost rolled my eyes, then remembered I wouldn't have been any better than him if I did.

"They do," I said instead. "But your youth is showing."

Seeing Eriyan's exasperated expression on a face that wasn't his was as disturbing as it was hilarious.

"But I *am* y—"

I placed a hand on his shoulder. "Forty."

He shrugged, but the easy smile that was starting to shape on his lips died down as he spotted something in the distance.

Not something. Some*one*.

Without flinching, without betraying anything, Ada spun around and threw her arms around Eriyan while Zaphine locked elbows with me. We leaned into each other, doing our best to mimic the free-flowing pleasure and hunger of the people around us, but my face felt tight with fear.

As was Zaphine's.

Our inability to cover up the anxious trepidation brought us closer together—so close that our ragged breaths mixed, just shy of a kiss.

Up ahead, the guards in their black-and-silver attire were blocking off the intersection, stopping the people who wished to pass and scanning them with a critical eye. My stomach churned, and the hard look Ada shot us over Eriyan's shoulder told me my body wasn't overreacting.

Up close, our illusions wouldn't pass their scrutiny. And drawing on the pendant...

Until we were sure the magic left no imprint, we'd agreed I would only use it as a last resort.

In a flash, the grim expression was gone. Ada drew Eriyan to her and slanted her mouth over his, the force of the embrace bringing them over to where Zaphine and I cuddled near the wall. We became a tightly knit group of lovers.

"We'll go through the brothel on the right, take the back door out," Ada whispered just loud enough for us to hear. Then to Zaphine, "Lead Ember through the tavern. We'll meet back up at the square."

Zaphine brushed her lips against my cheek, her voice soft as she said, "I won't be able to hold the spell on you if we part."

But Ada was already moving, Eriyan's rough hands roaming her body as if he couldn't wait to take her behind the velvet curtain cordoning off the brothel interior.

"We'll manage," was all she said before they slithered through the crowd, then disappeared through the spill of crimson.

Zaphine tugged me gently to the left, a smile still plastered to her triangular face. "They won't be surveilling the alleys."

I nodded, pretending I didn't hear the doubt weighing on her voice, then beamed up at her. "So a pint of sowhl before you take me to bed?"

A nervous laugh fluttered from her lips and wove into the atmosphere. "Sounds lovely, honey."

The tavern was submerged in gentle shadows and far more peaceful than I had expected. People, some in pairs, others in threes or fours, were chatting, huddled closely together around the cherry wood tables, as well as the long counter with black and red accents that dominated one of the walls. Decorative beams crossed the ceiling, adding warmth to the otherwise predominant stone. Zaphine and I meandered through the space, aiming for the nondescript back door tucked at the far corner, right next to the clearly marked privy.

Nobody paid us any attention.

This was a place of intimacy, and the patrons, men and women alike, seemed to respect that. Still, I kept my mind focused on keeping up the charade, blocking out any thoughts of those guards, of Ada and Eriyan who were braving the streets without the cover of Zaphine's illusions.

With the silent, yet unmistakable consent weaving between us, I trailed my hand down the curved line of Zaphine's back, and she, in turn, tucked a strand of mahogany brown hair behind my ear, her fingers skimming down the side of my face with gentle affection. But as immersed as she looked from the outside, I could feel the tremors rippling through her body, could read the echoes of fear in every caress she meted out, like an undercurrent no amount of will could overpower. The sensation was familiar.

A sigh left her lips when we reached the door at last. I echoed it.

I spun so that my back was to the wood and let Zaphine embrace me. As I lay my chin in the nook between her neck and shoulder, as if inhaling the sweet, floral scent of her hair, I scanned the tavern.

"We're good to go," I whispered.

The patrons were otherwise occupied—or deliberately

refusing to impose on our moment. Either way, we were in the clear.

Once I disentangled myself from her arms, but remained dotingly close nonetheless, Zaphine pushed down on the handle. She ushered us over the threshold—

Straight into the back of an old woman.

Zaphine and I staggered back, the door ramming into my shoulder as it slammed shut—the *exact* same shoulder that was already sporting a generous bruise from my close encounter with the building the previous day. Without meeting the woman's eyes, we muttered a quick apology, then careened to the side to pass around her.

Our hands entwined, Zaphine pushed forward and deeper into the shadows of the alley. But just as I was about to glide by, the woman's fingers snaked around my wrist, yanking hard.

"It's not hurt that weakens," she said, tugging on my arm and staring at me with imploring, wide eyes. "It is never hurt. Through blood and darkness, we are reborn."

Another tug, only this time, it came from Zaphine.

The woman, however, didn't seem inclined to let me go. Apparently, my body shared the sentiment.

Rooted to the cobblestones, I was perfectly immobile—not just on the outside, but *inside*, too. Only a whisper of something had stirred when the woman first touched me, but faded well before I could pinpoint what it was.

The stranger's features softened, the glint in the intense blue of her eyes muting down—but only for a moment.

"Blood and darkness. Salvation not hurt." She snapped her hand away from me as if suddenly stung by the touch. "No weakness."

She shuffled backwards, then abruptly turned in the other direction, throwing her spindly arms up in the air.

With measured, heavy breaths, I stared after her until the sapphire-stained shadows swallowed her gray-clad form, the alley devoid of life, save for the two of us.

I shuddered, grateful for the heat of Zaphine's fingers still interlaced with mine. But when I looked at her, it wasn't fear that shone through the overlaid features. It was pity.

"It's our magic," Zaphine whispered. "Linked to our blood, it's a part of who we are. If we don't use it enough, it can..." She sucked in a breath, her gaze turned on the depths of the alley as if she could still see the woman there. "If we don't use it, it can mess up our minds."

I followed Zaphine's gaze to the darkness. Only it wasn't the spindly woman I saw, her contorted face and pleading blue eyes. It was the coiling tongues of obsidian black, the cool touch of their fire beneath my skin...

And I couldn't help thinking that, perhaps, my curse was the exact opposite of what had befallen the woman.

IT WAS HARDER to maintain our amorous display after the encounter. Zaphine seemed pensive, and I—I was brooding over *everything*. It wasn't until a lively *thud* of paws reached us from behind, bringing Lyra's gleaming eyes and her puffy ears held high into sight, that my spirits lifted.

Tail wagging, she led us into a dingy street with missing cobblestones creating an almost checkered pattern across the ground. I watched my step, though my gaze kept drifting to the small square that opened up beyond the final two buildings. Zaphine let loose a breath of relief.

Carriages.

We'd made it.

Two shapes lingered in an alcove a little farther ahead, Lyra already trotting in their direction.

Zaphine and I cleared the cracked cobblestones, then joined Ada and Eriyan in their shadowed nook. But when neither of them spared us more than a brief glance as we squeezed up against their backs, a foreboding tingle crept up my neck.

I peered out towards the carriages again, taking my time to note the coachmen's disgruntled faces as they milled around the horses, some feeding the animals, the others leading them by the reins...

Away from the square.

"What's going on?" Zaphine hissed, the earlier pensiveness replaced by sharp urgency.

"We won't be going anywhere tonight," Ada squeezed out. She tipped her head towards the sky and inhaled deeply before looking at us once more. "The Crescent bastard grounded the carriages."

CHAPTER SIXTEEN

SOMETHING KNOTTED INSIDE ME THE INSTANT BEFORE I HEARD it. Before all of us did.

Hooves.

Boots.

The coachmen scurried aside, guards pouring out between the carriages from the streets beyond and upsetting the horses. Riders blocked off the square from the road, fanning out along the width of it.

I pressed my back against the cold stones of the alcove, Zaphine muttering a curse under her breath. But Eriyan and Ada remained still, as did Lyra by her feet, watching as the uniformed men proceeded to open every carriage, every crate stacked neatly nearby that I assumed had served as storage for water and food the coachmen forced to wait here shared.

I had no idea what they suspected to find in such small places, but the guards were definitely thorough.

"Damn it," Ada hissed. The words hung suspended in the air between us.

Horses neighed as wood slammed. Another door. Another carriage.

So lucky.

We were so damn lucky we hadn't already stowed ourselves away in one of the coaches. I wasn't entirely convinced even my pendant would have gotten us out in time.

"We could try leaving on foot," Zaphine offered. Her gaze darted to the night blanketing the land beyond the square. "If we can clear the waste to the river, we could use the forest for cover and make our way through there."

Ada sighed, her frustration almost tangible. "It's too far off course. We'd have to backtrack, *and* it would take us over half an hour at a sprint just to get there." She shook her head. "If the Crescent Prince put all his men to work, it won't take them long to comb through every inch of Nysa. And once they do..."

Zaphine pinched her lips. "They'll expand the search to Saros."

"Precisely." She grunted, jaw clenched. "We have to get there before they do. If they block off all points of entry, we're screwed, but if we beat them to it... They know the town, but not *that* well. We'll be able to hide, or move on to the next one to give them the slip before doubling back."

Her words became more and more clipped the longer she spoke, agitation seeping into her voice and mirroring on her face. As if we were forcing her to explain things to us, not trying to find a way out of here together.

"Why are you so intent on going to Saros, anyway?" Zaphine asked just as I had to hold up a hand lest Eriyan squished me against the wall.

A pool of light spilled from the square and illuminated the chipped cobblestones. I couldn't see what was going on thanks to the wall of bodies but trusted the resolute immobility Eriyan and Ada had settled into.

A quick exchange between two men in the distance, then the light died.

"I have my reasons," Ada said after several seconds had passed, then put a little distance between us. She glanced at Zaphine, then Eriyan, before she returned her focus to the square, making it all too clear this conversation was over.

Zaphine snorted, muttering something about always keeping secrets, but Ada was intent on studying the sight.

I leaned into Eriyan and peered over his shoulder when it hit me. "The mountains."

His temple narrowly missed colliding with mine as he whipped his head around.

"Saros is just around it, yes?" I drew back a little, giving us both some space. "Are there any paths traversing it along the foot of the hill? Shortcuts connecting the two towns?"

A glimmer of recognition sparked in his eyes, but it was Ada who looked ready to answer, lips parted and gaze hard. Probably would have, if Zaphine's gasp hadn't cut through the air.

I felt the gentle thrumming subside before the illusions still placed upon the two of us flickered—then disappeared.

"Shit," she said softly. She extended her slender, once again real, hand. "I don't believe I'll be able to mask us again. Not to the same extent, at least."

Ada's expression grew even tenser. "We need—"

"Sowhl."

"You've *got* to be kidding me." Ada glared at Eriyan, the

distaste so clear on her face momentarily overpowering the outburst I'd sensed building under her skin.

"I don't mean the drink. Well, I *do* mean the drink, but not for consumption. Though I wouldn't mind one right now. You look like you could use it, too," he said to Ada, then licked his lips. "What I'm trying to say is the brewery. The wagons. You know, full barrels arrive, leave empty to be refilled again."

Ada's drawn eyebrows rose up. "You're right. The Crescent Prince wouldn't dare leave his people thirsty."

"There's a large brewery of sowhl in Saros," Zaphine explained when she saw my confusion. "Nysa makes its own drink, but not nearly enough to satisfy the Winter Solstice crowd. There's a standing agreement between the two towns. Nightly deliveries."

"But surely Mordecai"—a heartbeat of tense stillness when the name slipped out—"wouldn't leave the wagons unmonitored." I nudged my chin towards the square, grateful the moment had passed. "He seems like the kind of person to cover all his bases."

Ada's eyes gleamed. "Oh, I'm sure his men will patrol the perimeter. But we have our way in." She looked at the pendant resting around my neck. "Because once we're gone, the power won't matter."

Our "TREK" across Nysa was painfully slow, although we must have been making good time since Ada's mood wasn't quite so salty any longer. Though still a far cry from the spirited nature I'd come to associate her with before our predicament had taken a turn for the worse.

Often, we had to stop and wait for the guards to clear a section, squeezing ourselves into tight slivers of space between buildings or dunking into taverns and shops since using any other magic than Zaphine's was a chance no one wanted to take. Not yet. She was still recovering, but camouflaged us when the sapphire dark wasn't enough to conceal our forms.

We steered clear of the center since Ada believed *that* was where Mordecai would be stationed, muting the pulse of the town into whispers and reminding the people of the power that watched their every move.

I didn't share her confidence. With every new street that opened up before us, I expected to see that flicker of silver, a glint of blue looking our way.

I was glad to be proven wrong. But that, sadly, was the *only* good thing I could name.

My arms and legs ached from frequent, short sprints, from crouching for long, long moments behind whatever offered sufficient cover—even climbing, once or twice, when it became clear that the only way we could go past the guards was over rooftops. An experience I could have done without.

Heights, I liked, but being half pulled, half hoisted up with nothing but stones for purchase and a dress that tangled around my legs was terrifying.

There was no one to catch us if we fell. Just the merciless cobblestones.

Zaphine and Eriyan seemed to share my struggles—him mostly because he, as the tallest of us all, was charged with getting the three of us up first before making the ascent himself, all the while cursing how heavy we were. But Ada kept us moving forward like a seasoned general. She never wavered, never doubted the routes she took, placing faith in us that we would somehow manage.

And after what must have been at least an hour, we did.

Unlike the square with the carriages that opened up onto the vast expanse of the rocky desert while the city hugged it from behind, the wagons were clustered on a flat stretch of land, packed between unadorned buildings and the steep mountain wall. Only two lone torches illuminated the station in a dance of warmth and shadow, the path beyond—if it even existed— drowned beneath the weight of the night.

A few figures conversed softly, their backs to the mountain while another carried water from the well over to his horse. No sight of Mordecai's guards.

Eriyan moved to the front, then stopped when we reached the final line of the buildings. With the torches separating us from the men, we didn't need magic to remain invisible as long as we stayed out of light's reach.

The soft *thud* of paws emerged from behind us, and I was relieved to see that Lyra had somehow managed to follow us all across town. I'd lost sight of her when we moved out of that rundown street, and despite all the problems we were facing, a part of me hadn't been able to stop worrying about the dog. But here she was, safe and sound.

Now, all we needed to do was stay the same.

Lyra brushed up against Ada's legs just as she asked, "What do you think?"

"That one," Eriyan pointed to a covered wagon set on the southern side. It sagged slightly to the left, the dark wood dull from years of use. "The barrels are already loaded, and the horse seems ready to go."

Ada scooped up Lyra and tucked her under one arm.

Zaphine whispered, "Wait."

Ada's gaze cut to her, the frustration returning and darkening the jade of her eyes. Zaphine, however, was unfazed, preoccupied with something in the distance. I had to lean my body to the side to see what had caught her attention.

"The wagon by the well," she clarified. "Two horses, lesser load. It'll be faster on the road."

Eriyan's eyebrows knitted together. He studied the sight before us, then addressed Ada. "She's right. The driver's already inside, too." He grinned. "Looks like we have our ride."

Zaphine mirrored his smile, but Ada's single-minded focus didn't falter as she faced me. "Do you think you can make the magic last long enough for us to slip inside?"

I glanced down at the pendant, feeling its cool surface against my skin.

"If we're fast enough, yes."

"We'll have to be." She glanced at Eriyan. "Grab onto Ember."

When he shot Ada a slightly confused look, I added, "You'll be left behind if you aren't touching me when I freeze time."

For a moment, he only stared at me like he'd been given the most precious gift possible, then shrugged, his mouth quirking up. "All right. How do you want us?"

WE LOOKED RIDICULOUS. It had taken us a couple of minutes to finally find a formation that wouldn't break up the instant we started to run.

Which turned out to be Ada holding on to my free hand, Zaphine looping her arm through the bend at my elbow, and

Eriyan clutching me from behind. Lyra, unfortunately, would have to lose a little time. I hoped she wouldn't be too confused when she came to in a different place, but there was no way to ensure contact with her, as well. This felt fragile enough.

What made matters even worse were the seconds slipping by as we double-checked our positions. I kept casting glances at the wagon, begging it not to move before we closed the gap.

Ada and Eriyan delved into a hasty discussion about what we would do if the magic dropped before we reached our destination, how we would handle it if any of them lost their grip and succumbed to stasis.

I knew I should have participated, but my mind seemed to let go of everything but the sensation of the pendant resting in between my fingers, the will I always poured into it to activate its magic. There was something about this world that hindered its abilities, but maybe if I forced enough of myself into the metal, if my desire to freeze the flow of time was stronger...

"Ready?" I asked, clutching the silver tighter.

Silence. Then three mumbles of agreement.

I blew out a breath and—

We moved.

We moved like one across the dirt and rocks, sprinting beneath the starlit sky, through the ocean of utter tranquility. Absolute quiet.

I felt a presence inside me coming to life, connecting me with the pendant and feeding its magic so seamlessly I nearly stopped just to take in the effect. But my gaze caught on the sleek wagon Zaphine had pointed out, on the empty sowhl barrels that would be our way out of imminent danger.

So I didn't stop. My steps didn't falter.

Ripples of excitement that spread through the others echoed in my heart.

We rushed past the men and women tending to their own stock, past the horses with their still eyes and stiller manes, not slowing down until the white flap of fabric pulled halfway aside loomed just before us.

Careful not to break contact, Eriyan's palms braced me from behind as Zaphine, Ada, and I leaped onto the wood, far enough to make room for Eriyan but not so far as to tear away from his grip. Still, his weight rammed into my back when he followed suit and sent me careening forward. I caught my footing a hair's width from the nearest barrel, then paused so that all of us could catch our breath.

The instant I was certain we wouldn't tip anything over when we moved, I dipped my chin. I forced us all to take a step back and put some more space between us and the merchandise to discern the safest path.

Magic flowed through my consciousness as my presence did through the pendant. I entwined the threads to make it last longer, then focused on my surroundings once more as we shimmied between the barrels as deep into the darkness as we could.

Only then did I let go, the world taking a collective inhale as it burst to life.

Soft voices rose, the neighing of a horse joining in. The sounds covered our quick climb into the empty, although still moist and *definitely* sowhl-smelling barrels. Eriyan took the one behind me, Zaphine the one to my left, and Ada was just about to tuck herself into the one positioned on my right.

Or she would have if someone hadn't cleared their throat rather pointedly.

My body went taut, Lyra releasing a low growl. I looked away from Ada as she half dangled atop the barrel to the figure now blocking the square space of the flap. A man.

Lit from behind, I could only make out the most basic traits, but there was no doubt about it—he was looking straight at us.

Instinctively, I reached for the pendant, but the voice that filled the somber space cut me off.

Because it wasn't coming from the newcomer.

It was coming from Eriyan.

And he was *laughing*.

CHAPTER SEVENTEEN

THE MANIFESTATION OF WHAT WE FEARED THE MOST draped us all in heavy chains of dread. Only the sound of Eriyan's laughter still cascaded through the twilight. It morphed into a snort, then a muffled yelp when Zaphine reached over and slapped her hand across his mouth.

Between one moment and the next, the fury etched into the lines of her face turned into a cringe. Her gaze darted back to the man blocking the wagon, and she let her hand fall away.

Eriyan could laugh all he wanted. Bellow even.

We were caught either way.

My fingers sought out the pendant, but still I hesitated, Ada's rule to avoid turning to magic hammering inside my skull, a twin beat to the pulse thrashing in my ears. We'd already used it once. And only because we believed we would be well on our way out of here by now.

I released the necklace.

One man. He was just one man against four.

And with every second he stood there, one hand braced against the wooden beam, he was giving us a chance to attack.

So why did no one move?

Muscles tensing, I readied myself to—

I didn't know what, exactly, I would do, but *anything* was better than letting fate take its course.

"*Stars,*" the stranger said. He ducked his head deeper into the wagon, revealing a mass of tousled, dusty blond hair. "Eri, is that you? Why the fuck are you soaking your ass in my stinking barrel?"

I glanced over at Ada who was watching everything with a stern face. She wasn't pulling out her dagger, which was a good sign, but the sharp cut of her jaw and fingers clenched on the rim of the barrel she'd scurried in sometime over the past seconds revealed she wasn't at ease yet.

"Dantos, you son of a bitch." There was a series of creaks, then Eriyan was shoving through the barrels, his lean form twisting lest he topple something over.

For a moment, I entertained the notion that he was going to tackle the stranger, but instead, Eriyan stilled right at the demarcation line between shadow and light.

"I'd hug you, you bastard," he drawled, voice low, "but we're kind of on the run here."

Zaphine snorted. "Sure, why don't you spill *more* of our plans..."

"Spill our plans?" Eriyan turned around, then motioned the coachman to crawl up into the already too crammed space. "I found us the perfect ride out. Or, well,"—he waggled his eyebrows—"the ride found us."

Head bent at a slight angle, the man slapped Eriyan on the

back—and kept his hand there. "Not a single letter all this time and you expect me to hand out favors?"

"As if *you're* any better." Eriyan scoffed, mirroring the stance. "Everyone knows I'm not to be trusted, but you, lovable oaf, were supposed to make up for my shortcomings."

A thread of bitterness seeped into his otherwise light tone, and as if sensing the slip-up, Eriyan plastered a grin to his face, then spread his arms wide. "I'm more than willing to let you make it up to me now..."

"I swear to the Stars, Eriyan, if you don't start making sense, I'll twist your rutting insides," Ada snapped.

Both men whirled on her, twin expressions of false innocence entwined with mock annoyance adorning their features.

A small laugh escaped my lips. "Now you know how *I've* felt this entire time."

Ada glared at me. Then glared at Eriyan. But I heard Zaphine chuckle in the darkness by my side.

Good to know that we *all* appeared to be losing our minds.

But Eriyan—he definitely took the cake. He wrapped one arm around the man's neck—the man who, I noticed, was about his age, but powerfully built, with corded muscles testifying he was no stranger to physical labor—and grinned at us all.

"Ladies, let me introduce you to Dantos. My cousin."

AFTER WE EXCHANGED a few less than coherent greetings, Dantos said to Eriyan, "I should have known the barricades had something to do with you."

Eriyan clicked his tongue. "Such low opinion of me, cousin. I'm wounded."

Dantos only stared at him.

Long enough that Eriyan threw his hands up. He winced as he skimmed the knuckles of one hand across the taut fabric stretched over the wagon, but quickly caught himself.

"Fine, yes. But not *directly.* I'm just helping this time. And now"—he gave him a pointed look—"so are you."

Although Dantos shook his head, his shoulders moved with silent laughter. Like Eriyan, he was handsome, with the same eyes that seemed to shift between blue and green. But where his cousin appeared a little disgruntled, like a scholar who, well, drank a little too much sowhl after a long night of sticking his nose in the pages of a book, Dantos was a peculiar combination of rugged and polished. It suited him.

"Right." He exhaled. "So I suppose you need a ride out of town without the Crescent Prince or his flunkies noticing?"

"If it wouldn't be too much bother," Eriyan chipped in with a sheepish smile.

"You were *always* a bother, Eri. That's why our parents kept us apart, remember? But"—he raised a calloused hand—"I always liked you just as you are."

Eriyan leaned against a support beam. "Is that why—"

"We really need to get going," Ada snapped. Which earned her a scowl from Eriyan in return. "You can chat all you want once we reach Saros."

Tension surged through the wagon. Dantos swept his gaze from Ada, to Zaphine, then finally settled on me. Could he sense I lay at the heart of it all?

I fought the impulse to cringe and shy away, deciding on something else entirely.

"Please," I said. "The guards *can't* find us."

Out of the corner of my eye, I noticed Ada roll her eyes. She was hiding her pain well, but the effort seemed to have worn her patience thin. Luckily, she didn't sneer at anyone, simply settled back down in her barrel with Lyra, her brows drawn.

"Saros, eh?" Dantos asked, then nodded, more to himself than us. "All right. I'll take you."

"Thank you," I whispered.

Eriyan hugged his cousin in earnest and started to make his way back to his barrel, but Dantos—he didn't leave us just yet.

Expression thoughtful, he cast a look over his shoulder to the torchlit darkness beyond, then back at us. "There's a guardhouse set a little farther down the road, so make sure you stay in the barrels, though I doubt there'll be any real trouble, just regular patrol." An echo of a smile flirted with his lips. Like he knew something we didn't. Oddly, my instincts didn't act up.

Whatever it was, it wouldn't harm us. Right now, that sufficed.

He scratched his forehead, that ghost of a smile turning into a rakish grin. "We've already had a visit from the guards, threatening us with the usual excruciating death should we take anything beyond the town line but our stock. Good thing you're my stock now."

WHEN DANTOS'S command to the horses rose beyond the sturdy white fabric, and the wagon started to rock gently on its way towards the outpost, I found it a little easier to breathe. Metaphorically speaking, at least.

I sat at the bottom of the barrel, my knees tucked close to my body and arms wrapped around them, my nose buried in the fabric of my coat to stave off the invasive, sour stench.

Briefly, I fought off a hysterical laugh at how absurd all of this was, but when my memory jumped back to the voiceless scream, the obsidian-filled eyes, and the coiling wisps of night retreating into my body...

I stopped the images before they could reach the regal features of the Crescent Prince. The immaculate, entrancing casing that concealed a monster.

Too similar to how my appearance, the ideal of who I was supposed to be, concealed *me*.

I hugged my legs tighter, wishing Lyra was with me in the barrel. Animals were supposed to sense evil, weren't they? So perhaps, since she always looked at me with nothing but pure affection in her eyes... Perhaps there was some other explanation for the swirls of obsidian that had unspooled from my skin.

Another explanation—but the outcome would remain the same.

A man, lying on the ground, his lifeblood replaced by endless black.

I shuddered, almost relieved to hear Dantos tap on the fabric —our agreed-upon signal for the outpost. My mind snapped to attention, calming my breaths until they were inaudible whispers in the dark, muffled further by the thick coat. I couldn't hear the others, nothing but the low rattling of the barrels stirring the calm. Normal.

The wagon slowed, then stopped—just a solitary tap of the hoof from a restless horse up front.

A second went by.

Another.

"Dantos Ellerian." Papers rustled. "Brewery of Saros."

Whatever answer the man gave sifted through to my ears as nothing more than a grunt. Footsteps retreated, but when another voice curled through the night, I realized there wasn't just one guard.

There were two.

"Headed back already?"

"Wanted to avoid the rush," Dantos replied, no note of panic or traces of tremors in his voice. He lowered it a notch. "Besides, I figured I would catch you before the end of your shift."

The stench, the cramps that had taken up residence in my legs—it all faded as Dantos's words registered.

He *knew* the guard.

"Got anything for me?" The man's hushed tone carried over.

I wondered if Ada heard. What she would do if she did...

But Dantos simply said, "Tomorrow. If you can send in your brother while I'm unloading, I'll set a barrel aside."

"What time?"

The tension in my spine loosened. Grew into gratitude when Dantos drawled on, annoyance plain in his voice, "If your *comrade* doesn't take forever to verify my papers, I'm hoping to fill these beauties up tonight. I could come half an hour before the others, make sure we aren't interrupted."

The man barely sounded his agreement when footfalls marked the second guard's return.

"You check out." Papers rustled again. "Your license expires next month. Make sure you renew it if you want access."

"Of course." Dantos.

I heard him settle into his seat up front, a whisper of reins—

Then footsteps.

"Oy," Dantos shouted, a tightness seeping into his tone before he replaced it with a trained demand. "What do you think you're doing?"

But those footsteps—they kept marching towards *us*.

CHAPTER EIGHTEEN

"I NEED TO TAKE A LOOK AT YOUR LOAD. THE PRINCE'S orders."

"Now you listen to me," Dantos shot back as the *thud* of boots grew closer. "Your men already rummaged through my wagon. Twice. You'd think they were scraping sowhl off the wood the way they were going about it." He huffed. "Now enough of this nonsense. I still have to clean them out and fill them up, not to mention take care of my lady, if you know what I mean. The night isn't young any longer."

"You dare defy the Crescent Prince." A threat. Not a question.

"Who said anything about defying? I'm just trying not to get my ass whipped when I stumble home in the wee hours of morning. I'd like to keep my head as it is. Attached to my shoulders."

Silence.

"Let him go, Kalian," the other guard drawled, sounding fed

up and bored at the same time. "Make a fuss now and you'll lengthen *our* shift, too. I stared long enough at your rutting face for one night, man..."

"Prick," the guard spat, but the sound was fainter—farther away.

"Your finest," the other whisper-crooned to Dantos, who snorted in return.

It seemed impossible, but the wheels squeaked beneath us and the wagon swayed, taking us deeper into the desert.

As I slumped against the damp wood, Dantos muttered, "As if I ever bring anything but the fucking best."

FOR A LONG WHILE, nobody spoke. We didn't even crawl out of our barrels, as if we were still slowly coming out from the daze, fighting off the nightmare.

Dantos hadn't said anything, either, perhaps slightly rattled by the close call. If that guard hadn't intervened...

I didn't allow myself to think about it. We were on the road, past the patrol, and all I felt was a deep gratitude for whatever side dealings Dantos had going on that had eased our passage.

I half expected Eriyan to call him out on it, though given how low the voices had been, I wasn't certain how much of the conversation had translated. Or if Dantos had even wanted us to know.

I certainly wouldn't point it out. After all, I was the last person to flash around other people's secrets...

So I remained crouched, trying to push the ache building up in my legs and my back from my mind, and submerged myself in the calming rattle of wheels once more as I imagined Nysa fading in the distance.

"*Stars*, this stinks," were the words to finally bring us all to the surface.

I untangled myself with a groan and peeked over the rim. My lungs greedily sucked in the somewhat clearer air, my vision spinning for a moment.

"No better than you, Eri," Ada fired back at a grimacing Eriyan. The look she gave him was laced with disgust, but the corners of her lips were turned up, and blunt relief made her eyes flicker brilliantly in the somber light that filtered from Dantos's lantern through the protective fabric.

"I must say I agree," Zaphine grumbled. "On both accounts."

She hoisted herself up on the edge of the barrel, scowling down at her crumpled dress. A frustrated breath later, her mouth twitched. She cast a sideways glance at Eriyan.

"Makes you see your beloved sowhl in another light, huh?"

Eriyan's jaw dropped. "What? That would be like judging food based on what you leave in the toilet."

Zaphine graced his response with a flat stare. I struggled to hold back a chuckle. "Are you even aware of the shit coming out of your mouth?"

"I was talking about the one coming out of your—"

Lyra spared us all as she let out a little yelp, squirming in Ada's hands. I smiled at her, then at Ada. She'd been observing me for a while, but I pretended not to notice. I was just happy to see her faring a little better.

"How are you holding up?" she asked.

"I think *I* should be the one asking *you* that..."

She cradled Lyra tighter, then pressed a kiss between her ears. "I'm doing what my mother would want me to."

A non-answer if there was any.

Still, I nodded, encouraging her to go on.

"She was aware of the danger she would face when she cast that spell eighteen years ago. Just as she knew that was only the prelude to the battle that would follow. And so do I. There were always going to be sacrifices. Shielding you. Getting that fragment..." Her spine straightened. "But it will be worth it, in the end."

"I—" The words died on my lips. All three of them were looking at me—no, four, if I counted Lyra—their faces expectant, relieved, even after the disaster we'd barely pushed through.

If I said I was a murderer, that I was more like Mordecai than they could ever imagine, that light would wink out. Ada would deny it, try to convince me otherwise even if a part of her knew I was right. Because if she didn't believe...

Then all of this, including her mother's sacrifice, would have been in vain.

Eriyan would probably understand, but hide it beneath a thick layer of humor. And Zaphine—we had already plucked her out of her life. She'd stand by Ada regardless of how much she hated it.

They would all stick with me.

Until the illusion—the one not their magic, but their *minds* spun—would crumble. Until the truth would burn down their hope to obsidian ashes.

This would accomplish nothing. *I* would accomplish nothing.

And yet, shrouded perhaps to allow individual interpretation, I voiced the one question they had to hear.

"What if I'm not who you think I am?"

Ada opened her mouth right before a vicious *rip* cut through the air.

A dagger sliced through the fabric stretched over the wagon, its sharp tip sinister in the somber light.

Zaphine let out a startled cry, nearly falling off her perch atop the barrel. I leaned over and steadied her with one hand, but didn't take my gaze off the blade that continued to hack at the material, slicing and gnawing at it until a wide rectangle of it flapped down. Dantos's face peered through, along with a gust of chilled wind.

I stifled a laugh as Zaphine unleashed a long, filthy string of curses.

Dantos wasn't affected in the least.

"I got bored," he said matter-of-factly, his gaze skimming over our group. "Besides, I never meet anyone new up in Saros."

"New? What about old?" Eriyan pressed a hand to his supposedly wounded heart. "Don't I matter?"

"You matter by default." Dantos's attention flickered over to Zaphine. "But you sure don't look as good as her. Or spew such colorful profanities."

SINCE WE DIDN'T dare risk leaving the barrels entirely, not even when it seemed the trip would be blissfully uneventful, my legs were stiff when we arrived in Saros. I jumped off the wagon and landed on unsteady feet, then slowly worked the kinks from my body. The others followed my example.

Once I had faith a cramp wouldn't attack me out of nowhere, I diverted my attention to what lay beyond the brewery's courtyard.

Saros.

The town seemed eerily quiet, as if there were barely any souls left wandering the streets. With the moon above us shining as brightly as it had from the moment I came to my senses, lying in an undignified heap out there in the waste, I had no idea whether it was still night or early morning. No telltale heavy blinds on windows like in Soltzen to mark the time. Just sporadic lights, burning here and there, that could mean anything.

"The prince will have a *lot* of unhappy people on his hands," Dantos said.

I arched an eyebrow when I realized he was speaking to me.

"The town," he continued. "You were watching it like you expected something different. I don't blame you."

My mind sifted through the odd bits I'd gathered over the past two days, but either I was too tired, or I was simply missing a link.

I frowned. "What do you mean?"

"Saros isn't usually this quiet. Stars, it's positively unnerving most of the time with everybody loitering around as if they got nothing better to do. And some truly don't," he added, softer. "But they *all* flock to Nysa during the Winter Solstice. Most can't afford to stay there, but that won't stop them from doing everything they can just for a taste of the celebrations. The oblivion."

Right.

"And now they're all trapped there," I finished for him.

Dantos inclined his head, then walked over to the wagon.

I glanced at Ada, wondering if this came as a surprise to her or if she'd known we would be among the few living souls in the entire town. Hiding when you had nothing to hide behind wasn't a comforting thought, but Ada simply shrugged.

Whatever she had planned, she clearly wasn't worried.

A loud *thud* spun me around. Eriyan was standing halfway inside the wagon, helping his cousin get the barrels down. He passed a smaller one to Zaphine, then dragged the next to the ledge.

I joined them just as Dantos heaved it up and set it by the low wall cordoning off the brewery. "Need an extra pair of hands?"

"Wouldn't want to keep you from your business," he said softly. Behind him, Ada looked ready to agree.

But while I knew she wanted to get whatever it was we came here for over with fast, Dantos had saved our skins. It felt wrong not to pay him back in any way we could. Getting the barrels ready for cleaning was a good start.

Zaphine, Eriyan, and I were apparently of the same mind.

When Dantos accepted that nothing could shake our resolution, he cracked a smile and teamed me up with Zaphine, while Ada—of her own volition—went up to join Eriyan. Between the five of us, we were done in no time at all, though Dantos caught me flexing my aching fingers.

"Hazard of the job," he commented, flashing his own worn skin.

I smiled at him but clamped down on my response. Truth was, I would welcome calluses and chipped nails over being a High Master's decoration any day. Something I'd confided in Magnus once when his rough hands had roamed my body.

The memory warmed my chest.

He'd understood. Understood that wealth meant little when it was fashioned into shackles.

"If you need a place to stay, you can always come with me." Dantos's voice pulled me from the molasses of a different life.

Zaphine shoved away the hair that had fallen in her face and peered at him through narrowed eyes. "Won't your *lady* mind?"

He motioned to the darkened building of the brewery looming behind us, a proud smile blooming on his face. "*This* is my lady. The only thing she'll mind is you refusing a drink."

A corner of Zaphine's lips curled up, and Eriyan let out a snort.

"Still can't believe it." He squeezed past us and leaned against a barrel, his arms crossed. "All this time, our parents claimed *I'd* be a bad influence on *you*. And then you go and become the champion of the brew." He laughed. "Stars, how many times did I drink your lovely poison and didn't even know it?!"

Dantos flashed him a blinding grin, but his gaze quickly flickered to Zaphine before it came to rest on his cousin once more. "Find me when whatever it is you're up to blows over. All of you. I'll bring the sowhl."

BEFORE WE PARTED, Dantos gave us directions to a tavern that would still have its doors open in the slumbering hours between late night and early morning. He'd even hinted we wouldn't be too conspicuous since the place was one those who weren't keen on the revelry in Nysa liked to frequent. I was still a bit skeptical but trusted Ada's lead.

She was oddly complacent, didn't try to rush us or steer us anywhere else as we walked through the silent town to the tavern hidden in a street just off the main road.

At first, I couldn't figure out her sudden change of heart, but the reason presented itself soon enough.

I was *famished.*

We *all* were.

The adrenaline must have masked it before, but the instant the four of us huddled around a corner table, my stomach growled viciously, the sound accompanied by pangs of hollow pain. It was a wonder I'd managed to get this far without collapsing, especially after using the pendant—and pushing it to its limits.

So much for my *always prepared* outlook.

At least I wasn't the only one who'd messed up, setting out of the Whispers without pocketing any food at all.

To think that *we* were supposed to get into Mordecai's palace when we obviously failed to take care of ourselves was hilarious. In a disquieting, and more than a little discouraging, way.

We threw ourselves on the broth like vultures as soon as the barkeep set it in front of us. Hunched over our bowls, we ate in utter silence until the last of the bread was gone and the dishes wiped clean. Even Lyra was preoccupied down below the wooden bench, unleashing herself on the scraps of meat the cook had more than happily sent out from the kitchen once he learned who they were for.

It wasn't until a young serving girl cleared the dishes away and brought us four small pints of sowhl that Ada leaned forward, the look on her face hinting at what could only be a speech.

I wasn't wrong.

"You all know getting out of Nysa wasn't the only reason I wanted to come here," she started, voice low enough for the other late-night patrons to not overhear.

"Finally, she spills the beans." Zaphine turned her gaze

towards the beamed ceiling as if thanking the Stars before she leveled it on Ada. "So why *did* you drag us out here, love?"

"I couldn't tell you before—"

"Nothing new there," Zaphine remarked under her breath, and despite her quiet manner, the bite in her tone was clear. "Still afraid to let people in lest they rattle your single-handedly made decisions?"

The atmosphere took an uncomfortable dive.

I made room for Lyra on the bench next to me, focusing on the warmth of her muzzle as she laid her head in my lap. I ran my fingers down her spine, but not even that was a sufficient balm to keep me from feeling like a wretched third wheel.

"Well?" Zaphine pressed.

I laid my free hand on top of hers before she could escalate. "Please, just let her speak. We're all tired and on edge." An understatement. "The sooner we get this over with..."

Her mouth tightened, but she inclined her head, dark hair spilling over one shoulder.

A temporary truce.

Ada took a sip of her sowhl, paused, then downed what had to have been at least half. Her voice, when she spoke, was nothing more than a compilation of hushed tones I suspected had little to do with the public setting.

"Don't panic, but... I want to recruit Ivarr."

Both Eriyan and Zaphine went perfectly still, a different quality to their reactions, yet nonetheless, one that infused me with a distinct feeling that I was once again missing some vital information.

Contrary to past experience, the gap didn't take long to fill this time around.

"You want to recruit the most notorious Magician to our

cause?" Zaphine exploded in a furious whisper. "Have you lost your mind? You honestly want to tell the man who's one drop of blood away from kicking the Crescent Prince off his evil throne about the *One?*"

I flinched at the moniker, even more so at the way it was thrown out as if I weren't sitting right here. Yet the old wound that started to weep thanks to being treated like I didn't have a voice of my own faded into the background in light of the steel determination Ada was projecting.

She'd slipped into the role of the leader, and unlike the numerous instances before, the transformation was complete.

"I do," she said simply, as if Zaphine weren't shooting daggers her way. "If we want to get the relic *and* rescue my mother, we need him."

Zaphine's manicured nails dug into the table. "What was it that you said to Ember? That Telaria knew the dangers? That *you* knew this mission would demand sacrifices?" she hissed. "We were supposed to slip inside the palace unnoticed, try to get your mother out, but *only* if it wouldn't put us in more danger that we're already wading through. And now you're adding a killer to the team? Putting us *all* at risk for...Telaria?"

Not a hint of emotion reflected on Ada's face. "The Crescent Prince made sure we have to up our game if we want to succeed. Or haven't you noticed Nysa has turned into nothing but grounds for a hunt to the death?" She leaned back and crossed her arms. "Ivarr can incapacitate impressive numbers of men at a single time."

"And is just as likely to do the same to us and snatch Ember for himself," Zaphine parried. "He's an assassin, Ada. He'll promise us one thing, then stab us in the back—"

"He won't. There is nothing and no one he hates more than

the Crescent Prince and the limitations he placed on his magic. He'll work with us to steal the relic."

Zaphine let out a frustrated breath. She looked at me, a flood of conflicting reactions rushing across her face, then turned to Eriyan. "Of all the times to run your Stars-damned mouth, now would be it."

His blond brows lifted.

They stared at each other until a laugh escaped his lips, so at odds with Zaphine's sharp edges.

"Well, I for one think it's a brilliant plan." He raked his fingers through his hair, another laugh rippling through the air. "No, actually, it keeps getting better and better."

"Better?" Zaphine stiffened. "You knew, didn't you? Why we were going to Saros?"

My fingers stilled on Lyra's spine. I half expected, or maybe hoped, he would deny it. But all Eriyan did was offer a casual shrug.

"Our darling leader might have mentioned it while she was dragging me away from the lovely people at the brothel."

"And you didn't think to talk her out of it?" Zaphine snapped, her voice pinched.

Eriyan's gaze slid to Ada. Then back. "She's worse than Lyra with a bone. You should know that, since you dated her." A bland smile. "I'm rather fond of keeping all of my fingers, thank you very much. Besides"—he lifted his hand and called for another pitcher of sowhl—"isn't this wonderful?

"Refuse lodging in favor of finding a place to stay in a foreign town all on our own. Convince a notorious Magician assassin to join our cause. Then storm the most guarded palace and steal from the cruelest, bloodthirstiest prince in existence. What could possibly go wrong?"

CHAPTER NINETEEN

ZAPHINE'S SMILE BRIGHTENED ON HER FACE, THICK EYELASHES batting as she chatted up a middle-aged man who looked at her with heated interest. While not an imaginative tactic by any means, one that was working nonetheless.

The man tried to act casual, but the attempt was pitiful and only made it that much more obvious just how the beautiful Illusionist affected him.

Despite everything we'd been through, Zaphine was radiant. Her black hair cascaded down the lace-filled back of her dress, a silken strand draped over her shoulder and bringing out the flawless porcelain skin, the soft pink of her lips. But most of all, the allure rested in the way she carried herself, so at ease with her femininity.

It didn't surprise me Ada had fallen for her.

Or that the Mage was currently busy looking anywhere but at her former lover.

I glanced to my right where she stood beside Eriyan, Lyra

sitting at her feet and—probably to Ada's relief—demanding affection whenever the atmosphere in our little shadowed corner turned from laid-back to something a bit more on edge.

We'd chosen this spot, close to the tavern we had emerged from some manner of minutes ago with the Saros native in tow, to let Zaphine work in peace. To be honest, it was more as if we'd settled for it, given how Zaphine had taken initiative. She'd left us little choice but to play along unless we wanted to plunge headfirst into yet another argument.

After the truce we'd come to, no one did.

Thankfully.

I drew my coat tighter around me as wind howled through the empty town. It distorted whatever Eriyan and Ada had begun to mutter among themselves—more secrets, if I were to venture a guess. I couldn't bring myself to care. Not when up ahead, a touch of hesitation swept across the man's lean face.

Zaphine, however, didn't flinch. If anything, her demeanor became even more gracious, the charm that came to her naturally now pronounced, changing her into someone different.

Not an illusion, no. What Zaphine did was a simple act of masking your true self until not a breath of it escaped, all the while building the lie on a solid foundation of reality. Something I'd had eighteen years to master back at the Norcross estate.

At last, the man nodded. He handed Zaphine an ancient-looking key, then, with a lingering smile sent her way, tucked his hands in his pockets and marched past us into the alley that would take him back into the tavern's cozy atmosphere. The moment he was out of sight, Eriyan, Ada, and I surged forward as one, Lyra trotting a few steps behind.

"Well?" Ada asked. "Do we have it?"

I peered towards the weathered, two-story building perched

on the rocky terrain, the last bastion before the wasteland took over.

"We do," Zaphine said flatly. But the simmering fire in her eyes revealed she wasn't done just yet. "Once I agreed to help him add a few *lady* touches to the damn thing after he finishes remodeling, he waived the fee entirely." Her face scrunched up into a grimace, nose wrinkling. "Men. So gullible, it's repulsive."

Eriyan let out a choked groan, backpedaling into the shadow and away from Zaphine, but she went on as if he didn't exist at all. Her gaze narrowed on Ada. "I don't know *how* you stand them."

Ada's eyebrows went up, her lips struggling not to form a smile. "You seemed pretty chummy with Dantos back in the wagon..."

This time, the sound that burst from Eriyan's mouth was a clear gasp of wounded disgust. "Oh, Stars..."

"He's a...a finer specimen than most," Zaphine squeezed out, then lifted her chin higher. "Not that I care."

I swallowed down a chuckle. Ada just plain laughed.

"Sure you don't." She leaned against the wall, one ankle crossed over the other. "And I'm certain you won't be bothering Eri about getting you a second face-to-face with his dazzling, sowhl-brewing cousin."

"Hush." Zaphine tossed the keys to Ada. "Come on. I'd much rather go see the nice little rundown crap of a house I've just acquired for the next couple of days, don't you?"

IT WAS... Well, it was standing, at least. The building had more holes than it had walls, and the windows were boarded shut, though not all of them. Some still had chipped glass dangling from the frame, letting in the cold air through the jagged cracks. The two Illusionists, however, were confident they could mask our presence here by cloaking the building in a veil of darkness, and Ada agreed to expand a little of her magic to heat up our bodies if the press of winter became too much to bear.

Out here, with the distance separating us from Nysa, the chances of Mordecai actually picking up on their power were playing in our favor. And if he did, as Ada assured us in the next breath, we would be long gone by the time the cavalry arrived.

Of course, all that would have to be *after* she returned from convincing Ivarr to join our cause.

The next point in her itinerary.

I braced myself against a chipped, white-painted vanity, the scent of damp wood invading my nostrils, and gladly waited on the sidelines for the argument to unfold.

"You know I won't let you go alone." Zaphine skirted around a pile of rubble dumped on the rug that had seen better days. She didn't stop until she was bare inches from Ada's face. "At least between the two of us, we stand a chance of stopping Ivarr's murderous ways for long enough to get away if he decides to try something."

"He won't get paid for our deaths," Ada countered, voice calm, though her arms remained crossed. "Ivarr isn't the type to whip out blood for nothing."

Eriyan snorted. "Now if *that* isn't the worst reassurance I've ever heard..."

"How?" Zaphine touched a hand to Ada's shoulder. "How can you be so sure he won't lash out? How can you say with certainty that there *isn't* a price on our heads?"

"You think the Crescent Prince would go through...unofficial channels?" I asked.

She drew her lips in a tense line. "He could have ordered one of his men to do it..."

Ada shrugged off Zaphine's touch and sighed. "Look, you can come with me, but only if Eri feels comfortable staying with Ember alone."

"As long as *I* don't have to go, I'm fine," he grumbled but flashed me a come-hither grin. "Besides, I like someone who can handle her sowhl."

I chuckled as Ada barreled straight through the rubble and buried her finger in his chest. "I swear to the Stars if you so much as *think* about getting another pint—"

"Fine, fine." He threw his hands up in the air. "No drinking on the job. But what if *Ember*—"

"No," Zaphine and Ada snapped at the same time. Then, in a tone that left no room for arguing, Ada added, "Now that that's settled, shut up before I decide to trade your life for Ivarr's services."

Eriyan plopped down into a frayed dark blue armchair, his fingers creating a legato of *taps* against the rolled armrest. Ada walked over to me and took my hand in hers.

"Eriyan likes to babble far too much, but in case anything does happen... Stick with him. He knows what to do. There's a reason why I told him about Ivarr before I shared the plan with you and Zaphine." The corners of her eyes softened. "He's been in on this whole save-the-world mission from the start."

I swallowed past the unexpected tightness in my throat and dipped my chin. "Are you sure you need to do this?"

The smile she gave me was close-lipped, but the resolve in her gaze was unyielding. "I do."

She let the echo of her words linger between us a little longer, then nodded to Zaphine before marching out one of the larger holes in the walls. I watched them go, noting that despite Ada's command to stay, Lyra was already on the move, her lithe body stalking through the darkness.

With nothing else to do but wait, I curled up in the armchair beside Eriyan's, pulled my coat tightly around myself, and tried to get some sleep.

A STIRRING in my chest ripped me from a spill of dreams I couldn't recall. I gasped, blinking at the utter darkness we were tucked in. No flickering lights hovering beneath the ceiling like the stars high above. Nothing but shadows and a cool draft, winding through the cracks.

Eriyan, too, must have dozed off.

His steady, low breaths twined with the chilly currents. Definitely asleep.

Slowly, I reached out to him, fumbling with the worn, sturdy fabric of the armchair until I found the warmth of his skin. I squeezed his hand.

"Eriyan."

"Mmm-hm?"

"Eriyan," I whispered a little louder, "wake up."

"Oh, Stars," came his mumbled response. "Did I fall asleep? Ada is going to *skin* me..."

I clutched his fingers tighter, the cool, slithering sensation growing in my chest, as if it wanted to reach out. To find something. Or someone.

"Ember?" His thumb slid across my skin.

"Would you—would you mind checking if everything is all right? I would go, but..."

"No blood magic," he offered, then covered our entwined hands with his free one. "Sure. I'll go take a look."

When he started to draw away, I stopped him—just for long enough to whisper, "Be careful."

Eriyan climbed out of the armchair, his silhouette nearly indistinguishable from the backdrop of the night. I stayed curled in my seat, listening to his footsteps echo across the floor, then fade when he stepped through one of the many cracks and into the wind beyond.

With every second he was gone, I held my breath, certain I would hear him cry out.

A thousand curses drifted through my mind as the horrid anticipation kicked my mind back into a fully functional state.

Why did I send him out there alone?

We should have hid, stayed together. I didn't have blood magic to conceal me, but I wasn't helpless.

Splitting up suddenly felt like the worst possible mistake.

But Eriyan—he returned mere moments later, whole and, apparently, untroubled. He lit one of the torches that had somehow survived the passing of the very same years, possibly decades, that had gnawed on the building, and bathed the battered surroundings in gentle light.

"Anything?" I asked, though if he was risking the warm glow of the fire without a barrier of illusions shielding it from sight, we had to have been in the clear.

Still, that slithering weight in my chest remained. Eriyan glanced down to where my fingers had curled into the cushion.

"No trouble," he said softly, meeting my gaze. "Just the night.

But I must admit, you are quite a sight in the torchlight, Ember."

It sounded like he was tasting my name, rolling it across his tongue as if this were the first time he'd said it. The sensation in my chest bloomed, a brush of cool wind sliding over my insides with a kind of hidden affection.

I looked up at Eriyan, and somehow... I *knew*.

Between one heartbeat and the next, I was running, cutting across the room and aiming for the night stretching beyond. I exploded through the crack, my fingers still fumbling with the buttons on my coat to get to the pendant, cursing myself for not preparing sooner—

A wall of muscle sent me staggering back. Two pairs of hands captured my arms, pinning me in place while Eriyan—the *illusion* of Eriyan—walked up to me. With grace that was too pure, too beautiful for what it revealed, the blond hair and blue-green eyes faded away, Eriyan's simple clothes turning into an immaculate black coat with silver embroidery and a stiff, high collar that brushed against a chiseled jaw.

"You're a hard person to find," Mordecai said, gazing at me with those piercing sapphire eyes.

Recognition flared within them.

A monster.

A monster who had found his kin.

CHAPTER TWENTY

I DIDN'T HEAR ANYTHING BUT THE THUMPING OF MY HEART. Not from within, but from somewhere beyond me.

As if I'd been thrust deep into my body where reality, the convoluted, threatening mess it had become, held no sway.

A twin pulsing then—this distant awareness beating in tune with the organ concealed beneath my ribs.

The roar of blood was a thousand waterfalls ensconcing me, urging me to break free and act. Only my limbs, the contours of my skeleton... They remained motionless. As if my bones, my flesh, my skin belonged to a corpse—so at odds with the raging disembodied presence I had become.

One that felt everything.

But could do nothing.

Or, perhaps, feared the extent of the destruction I could unleash if I were willing to ruin myself in the process.

The guards' hands that prevented me from running or reaching for the pendant were light. A grim decoration.

They didn't have to physically restrain me, not as Mordecai stood so close, his power suffusing the air like an opulent perfume. There were no silver shadows undulating from beneath his immaculate clothing.

Only him.

Stoic. Calm.

A hauntingly beautiful picture, wrought of nightmares and dreams alike.

His cool gaze slithered across my face, down to my body— only faintly touching the chain and the tip of the pendant that had slipped free from my coat—then back again. Revealing nothing. A marble wall without cracks, too flawless to be natural.

I was shivering under the weight of that dark sapphire, goose bumps spreading across my skin even as heat invaded my cheeks and built up an uncomfortable knot deep in my stomach. It was the latter that drew me back from the depths until I was once more present in every inch of my useless limbs.

But something—that presence, the pooling frost of shadowed wings across an icy lake I felt when sleep had faded away... It stilled.

Worse.

It beckoned me to close the distance still lying between the Crescent Prince and me.

A sliver of darkness that did not belong to the unyielding marble passed across his face, as if he'd felt it too. Felt it, but did not want it. A mere moment later, it was gone, leaving me alone in the thrall of magnetism I couldn't explain.

I closed my eyes and ground my teeth as I fought to shake off the spell.

Then I remembered.

Eriyan.

Frantic, I scanned the darkness for any sign of him, dreading what I would find yet needing to know at the same time. But we were on the wrong side of the building. Whatever Mordecai had done to him...

"Escort her to the carriage." His velvet voice sailed through the night, smooth and demanding.

What will I had left reared inside me, gathering force.

When the guards' fingers tightened on my arm, I pulled back, then threw myself forward. The grip loosened, losing purchase, the guards now a step behind. Two...

My strength fled from my flesh.

All of it.

Panic surged in my chest, choking off my breath as I tried to fight the guards from entrapping me again, only to find myself being dragged to the side like a limp doll. What—

There. One of the uniformed men waiting in the distance sheathed his dagger. A Magician.

I looked down at my treacherous body in horror. I couldn't will it back to power. I could hardly do anything more beyond keep myself upright. It was the only thing I had left—to not collapse before them. The one satisfaction, one victory I refused to hand over to them on a platter.

They guided me around the corner of the building, past the single wall where there hadn't been windows or gaps for us to spot their approach.

Had the proprietor betrayed us after he'd given away the keys? Or had it been the magic that was supposedly safe to use, taking on the role of a far more powerful beacon than Ada had anticipated?

Ada.

I hoped she and Zaphine were still with the assassin. That they would run instead of fall into whatever trap I was certain would wait for them upon their return. And Eriyan—I didn't allow myself to think about that easy smile, the blue-green eyes that saw far more than he ever let on.

I only nurtured the anger, cradling it inside me until its time came.

An elegant black-and-silver carriage waited just a short stretch from the building, the phases of the moon—much like the ones I had seen crawling up Mordecai's neck that first evening in Nysa—etched onto the door. With frustrating ease, the guards lifted me up and placed me on the lacquered leather bench. I jerked when they began to climb up behind me, tears of fury scalding my cheeks as my attempts to lash out with a foot and send them sprawling backwards failed. There was no use fighting the Magician's hold. And my entourage didn't exude any particular caution as they ascended.

I wasn't a threat.

Breath after breath, I forced myself to calm down and assess the situation with a clear head. It took more effort than ever before to shape my thoughts into something that resembled reason. Cold sweat was prickling at my brow by the time the chaos raging in my mind faded into something I could sift through—but it did.

When the last guard piled into the carriage and perched himself on the bench opposite mine with the other two enclosing me one on each side, I was done struggling. Done yielding to that primal instinct raking its claws down my insides. With the magic weakening my muscles and overpowering my will, I needed to accept that *this* wasn't my moment of plight. The Magician wasn't in the carriage with me, so even if I managed to somehow slip past the three somber-faced men, I had no delusions he would fortify his hold on me long before I cleared the rocky land.

No, I had to conserve my strength. Had to keep my wits about me.

Mordecai might have planned my capture well, but people always made mistakes. Even monsters.

To my surprise, the carriage started moving before I caught a single glimpse of him. I peered through the single square window to see where the Crescent Prince had gone.

Only it wasn't him I saw.

Two figures were running across the tenebrous landscape, faint echoes of their shouts reaching all the way to my ears.

Ice coated my lungs.

I wanted to scream at them that Mordecai was still out there. Roar at them to turn around while they still could.

With me in his grasp, he didn't need Ada any longer to see if —*when*—she would find me just so he could snatch me from her. And Zaphine...

The glacial darkness within answered, rolling and grazing my insides, offering me to take what I wanted. To obliterate this threat. All I had to do was say yes.

And yet whenever my thoughts touched the Crescent Prince, bringing his regal features to mind, the obsidian battle cry turned into a velvet murmur.

I gasped, torn between the two forces, my eyes tearing up as I saw Ada pull a dagger—

The carriage rocked on the uneven terrain, and my vision blurred. The horses hurtled forward, Ada's and Zaphine's forms fading in the distance, then disappearing out of sight, only the stars witness to their fate.

DESPITE MY RESOLVE TO keep my wits about me, I barely remembered the ride to Nysa. That last glimpse of Ada burned too vivid, too potent within me, the uncertainty and fear of the worst a barrier between my mind and soul no thought or sound whispering from the outside could survive. I had to let the numbness fade on its own lest it would claim me completely.

Once the guards eased me out of the carriage in the enclosed courtyard trapped between the looming mountain rock and what could only be Mordecai's palace, I forced myself to take note of my surroundings. Still, my attention drifted, blown from my grasp far too often by the icy gusts of dread.

Behind us, a solemn figure atop a stallion, his diamond-blond hair illuminated by the pale moonlight and the echoes of blue streaming from the heart of town. The Magician.

But no Mordecai.

The thought remained a heavy weight in my mind as the guards took me through a looming gate, my body still not my own.

The Magician followed, though the echo of his boots on the stone floor was unhurried, as if he had no fear the distance would extract me from his clutches.

Sporadic torchlight lifted most of the shadows, and contrary to what I had expected, the corridor, while used, was well-kept. Presentable. A part of the palace rather than a path to whatever horrors would shape my captivity.

Then again, the Crescent Prince himself was ruination

encased in silver and onyx. Enthralling to the eye, pestilent to the touch.

A wide stairwell with an iron-and-silver railing curved to the levels above when we emerged into a grand hall, the worn stones gaining elegance. Light fended off the press of night, yet failed to infuse the refined space with warmth.

My entourage herded me up, deeper into the palace and down a corridor that was somehow lavish and modest at the same time. I was still no more than a toy, pliant to the Magician's will. Door after door whisked by. All closed. Lifeless.

It was only after they locked me in a spacious chamber, scented lightly of jasmine and neroli, that I felt my strength return.

A second—that was all the time I took to suck in a breath and shake the remnants of weakness from my flesh. Then I was running across the carpeted floor, right to the arched, double-hung windows overlooking Nysa in its blue glow. My fingers fumbled with the latch on the centermost one, the tremors I was unable to control hindering my movements.

Eventually, I eased open the glass.

The clear night air rolled over my skin. I braced my palms against the ledge and leaned over to see if there was a way down, my nose leveled with the wall—

No.

No.

The line of stone was as far out as I could reach.

I ran my trembling fingers over the unnervingly solid air, then brought up my other hand. Tracing and patting, I explored every inch within my reach. Nothing.

The invisible barrier stretched up from the outer edge of the window, spanning across its width.

Once there was no more space for me to cover, I dragged over the chair set beside a simple desk and climbed on top of it. Balancing on my toes, I stretched until my fingers brushed the curved arch. Only to drive the point home.

The translucent wall spanned across the entire opening, not a single crack marring its unyielding, ethereal structure.

I climbed off the chair, and although I had no true hope, repeated the process on the left window. Then the right.

The result was the same.

A weak cry wrung itself from my lips. I shoved aside the chair and pressed my forehead against the barrier, breathing deeply as tears started to fall. I didn't know how long I stayed like that, helpless, defeated. Sick with myself for even thinking my escape would come in the form of an unprotected window, if a fair distance from the ground.

With each new tear, hate stirred in the pit of my stomach.

Hate. And something colder.

I bunched my fingers into fists.

Being a crying, weak mess would get me nowhere. I had to get back to what I knew. *Think* my way out of the situation.

Drawing away from the wretched barrier, I closed the window and traced my hands along the sill. Magnus had once said that people are always alone. That while he was glad he'd found me, shared a part of his life with me as I had with him, we shouldn't be afraid when all else fades and the only thing that remains is *you*. Granted, he had been referring to being at ease with oneself instead of using the company of others as a shield to hide behind, but his words—they rang through my mind for a reason.

I had never been scared of being alone.

But ever since my arrival in Somraque, the others *had* been crutches. Veils and dimmed lights I could hide behind. I had contributed, yes, but at the same time, I had retreated into the background to let them take charge. Understandable. Yet not entirely excusable.

I was alone now. Just as I had been for the better part of my life.

There was comfort in that.

As was strength.

Every exhale rebuilt the adamant foundation I had allowed to crumble. As its familiar presence ensconced me, muting the useless emotions and creating an environment in which I could hear myself think, I stepped away from the window, then turned to peer at it from afar.

The most visible way out. That's what it was.

But it certainly wasn't the *only* one.

Palaces were built like mazes, designed to protect those who rested within. In part achieved through numerous passages, including those hidden that, more often than not, branched off from every single chamber on the premises. Long before I had taken to using them to my own advantage, I had studied books our library harbored—in one of those sections I wasn't supposed to access—that covered the topic of underground tunnels and stairwells encased within walls. I was more than a little fascinated by the intricately constructed labyrinths that were the cornerstone of every larger residence.

Even in a world where powerful men wielded portals, the need for a purely physical means of escape remained.

So why should this world, this palace, be any different?

A fresh burst of confidence filling my veins, I turned from the window and, for the first time, truly took in the room. A large bed rested against the wall on my left, a vanity cabinet taking up one side of the opposite corner in close proximity of the crackling fireplace. Behind me, occupying the space beneath the window closest to the bed, the utilitarian desk and chair I had already acquainted myself with, the latter still haphazardly tilting against the wall where I'd shoved it earlier.

Sparsely furnished and with no tapestries or peculiarities in the walls, there was little chance of a hidden door.

My gaze flickered over to the arched, short hallway on the right of the fireplace. Flames cast flickering shafts of light and darkness dancing across its stones, obscuring most of what lay beyond, although I could see the lip of a bathtub in the distance.

Maybe the bathing chamber would yield better results. Sometimes, the least expected route was the right one.

I stalked across the soft carpet towards the archway and barely set a foot between its narrow walls when the door behind me unlocked.

Retreating into the chamber, as if merely standing in the passage could give my intentions away, I pressed my back against the stones. The fire blazed before me, and the touch of winter licked at my spine where the night slid past glass. I ignored the way my heart seemed to thrash in my chest as the lean figure manifested on the threshold.

A pause, then Mordecai strode into the chamber.

His coat was gone, replaced by a black shirt, its top buttons undone and revealing the stark moon tattoos contrasting with the paleness of his skin. His spill of black hair was wild, as if ruffled from the wind after a long ride—which it most likely was. My throat constricted as a crack snaked along my intricately constructed wall.

A thought slipped through.

Of that building in Saros.

Then another, of Eriyan, never returning, Ada and Zaphine lost to the night...

Instead of letting the images weaken me, I fed on them.

I lifted my chin to meet Mordecai's gaze.

And held it.

CHAPTER TWENTY-ONE

NEITHER OF US BREACHED THE FIELD OF QUIET.

Demanding news of my friends, demanding my release—it would have been useless. A waste of breath that would only weaken my position and solidify his.

As for Mordecai...

I suspected whatever silver lines of thought he followed were his and his alone.

We were as far from standing on equal ground as two individuals could possibly be, but the resolute silence gave the impression of a standstill in this fleeting battle of wills.

I had already given too much in Saros.

As I hid behind an armor of dark scales that encompassed not only my body, but my mind, too, I studied the Crescent Prince. The warm light of the fire cast shadows across his unreadable face. I wondered how someone so young could have lived through the ages. How he could remain untouched by the crawl of time that etched deep grooves into the earth. How he evaded the death that claimed generation after generation...

A singularity.

Like the moon, I thought, my gaze flickering to the stark tattoos adorning the column of his neck. *Eternal.*

And yet there was something utterly human resting on his features. Traces of exhaustion that spoke of a man who had survived a long journey, yet knew this wasn't its end.

I didn't know what to make of his willingness to show vulnerability, as small as it was.

"The wing is yours." His voice rang through the chamber, though his body remained locked in its regal stance.

It was only those sensual lips that stirred, drawing my gaze, and holding it there. Mesmerized.

I forced myself to look up and ignore this irrational reaction —refuse to let it anchor. But as his velvet voice resonated through the air once more, I knew that had been only a minor victory in the long line of battles his presence would thrust my way.

"You may move around the wing freely, but should you try to escape..." A hint of a smile as that unnerving sapphire cut from me to the window, to the draft seeping through which could only mean I hadn't closed the latch all the way. "You already know well how futile it would be."

He sounded almost playful. Cruel but not... Not entirely.

I sucked in a breath—a chink in my armor—deep enough that my chest strained against the dark blue fabric of the gown, mercifully obscured by my coat. Our standstill was tipping in his favor, but not by means I had thought he would use. Even when it became clear the dungeons weren't my final destination, I had still expected something befitting the image of the Crescent Prince Ada, Telaria, and Eriyan had drawn.

Intimidation. Torture.

Doing whatever it took to call up from the depths these powers I had yet to meet, so that he could harness them for the still unclear purpose that had made him hunt me in the first place.

But for the myriad of outcomes my mind had supplied, none involved this...tranquility and etiquette.

These silences that pulsed between us as we stood apart, with our gazes locked onto one another, as if uncertain.

Fearful of what our proximity would bring.

While I refused to believe it, a voice inside me crooned that Mordecai knew about my darkness. My *shadowfire*.

Perhaps like did call to like, but it also made it weary.

Made *him* weary.

Yet the coldness inside me, that darkness I couldn't deny, seemed to purr. A predator, soothed by the presence of another. I didn't want to think about it.

Not with him still looking at me, as stark and vast as the night itself.

Exploring what rested within me now wouldn't give me direction. The only thing it would achieve would be to strip me of my already weakened shields and leave me at the mercy of the alluring dark.

But for all the roaring conviction to level the scales he had tipped, I couldn't bring myself to utter a single word.

"I presume you are tired from your travels," he said, his tone the same velvet, if a little stiffer than before. "I shall leave you to rest, Ember, in the hope that you will join me tomorrow for a late breakfast, your strength replenished."

I ignored the jab, the memory of the humiliation at being handled as if I were nothing more than a hurt, helpless dove with the Magician's power infesting my flesh.

"Don't patronize me," I said coolly. "Or are such low attempts at establishing dominance part of the Crescent Prince's grand arsenal?"

I could have sworn that was amusement, brightening the sapphire that now roamed down my cloaked body before coming to rest on my face again.

Appearing a lot more stoic than I felt, I waited for retribution that never came. Mordecai simply turned around, his hand on the doorknob.

As his fingers closed around the ornate crescent moon, I released the question poised at the tip of my tongue. "Why? Why all this?"

Not a plea for answers, but a command.

Mordecai turned, looking at me over his shoulder. "It's fitting, the name." A ghost of a smirk on his lips I had no doubt the flash of unguarded confusion that had swept through me fueled. "Ember," he said with sinful intimacy. "Fire. Like you."

He was out the chamber faster than I could recover, nothing but the sharp line of his back filling my vision before the door closed, submerging me in silence.

Somehow, the weight of the lifeless room and the heady scent of jasmine seemed far more oppressive than it had been before.

"My lady," a gentle, lilting voice called out.

I opened my eyes with a start—and instantly regretted my

decision. They ached as if I had rubbed them with sand, the echoes of last night's tears I had refused to, but had shed nonetheless as I crawled into the queen-sized bed, still blurring my vision.

The memory came to me in a burst of images and sensations.

How I had been unable to stand even a second more awake in this too comfortable chamber, drowning in the crush of thoughts and plans and ideas that cornered me yet drew me in too many directions. A captive guest of an undetermined future.

Even when the hushed currents of winter that drifted through the slightly open window had dispersed the jasmine and neroli—a mocking echo of the garden that had been my refuge in the life I had left behind just to stumble into a convoluted variant of it—the walls had continued to close in on me.

I blinked past the burning ache, slowly bringing the figure lighting the sconce by the door into focus.

A girl.

She wore a simple, three-quarter-sleeved black dress, her auburn hair swept back in a bun to reveal a youthful face. She couldn't have been older than sixteen. Gingerly, I pushed myself up, then tossed the unruly silver strands over my shoulders and dipped my chin in consent for her to approach.

On silent feet, the girl walked over to the bed, but kept a respectful distance. "My lady—"

"Ember," I corrected. Titles and displays of servitude, being treated as if I were something more just because I had been born into privilege, had always chafed me. "Please, call me Ember."

The slight widening of her hazel eyes revealed that was unlikely to happen, but she nodded regardless. "My name is Merayin. I will be tending to you during your stay in the palace."

Her words were most likely no more than a formality, and yet they gave me hope that this *stay,* as the word suggested, wouldn't be indefinite. Although it pained me to even consider just *what* the Crescent Prince had in mind, if it were to lead me beyond these walls. My head felt groggy enough without the added strain.

Merayin lit another one of the sconces that had dimmed while I slept, then faced me once more. "Breakfast will be served in half an hour, my lady. Should you need my assistance to bathe, I am at your disposal."

I shook my head. I preferred not to be tended to, save for when my hands alone weren't sufficient to squeeze my body into some of the more ornate, celebratory dresses the Norcross gatherings and parties demanded. I wasn't about to change my stance now.

Besides, half an hour was hardly a generous amount of time. I would need every minute of it to rebuild my armor and think through what pitiful options I had.

Mordecai had found cracks in my composure far too easily yesterday. Maybe it would have been wiser to decline, ask for my breakfast to be delivered to my chambers—but that would be more than just admitting defeat.

It would mean depriving myself of answers.

"Thank you, Merayin. But I'll manage on my own." I mustered a smile.

Although the girl seemed a little taken aback, she schooled her face with impressive speed and gave a curt nod. "Then I will wait for you in the hallway. The dressing room is connected to the bath." She gestured towards the archway. "If you find nothing to your liking, please let me know, and I will arrange something else."

It was my turn to stare at her blankly. Only for a moment—if a longer one than it had taken her. "I will ring you for aid if I require it, Merayin."

She seemed pleased by my answer and hurried out the door, though not before dropping into a swift, elegant curtsy. The instant I was once again alone, I sank back down onto the pillow.

As I drank in the simple, yet elegant beauty of the vaulted stone ceiling stretching above, I shuffled through my thoughts, discarding threads until only one remained.

No different.

This was no different than the numerous occasions I had been forced to take meals with *reputable guests* my father had invited to the Norcross estate. No different from all the times I had dined with my parents alone, using silken words to slip through the cages they had thought to trap me in.

I flashed back to the previous night, the guards' hands resting on my arms, the unbreakable shackles of magic—

I had never been a fighter. But brute strength wasn't the only way to win a war.

Although my stomach recoiled at the idea, I pushed off the bed and wandered into the adjacent bathing chamber.

Half an hour, Merayin had said.

Not much, but it would do.

WHEN I STRODE out into the hallway with comfortable minutes to spare, Merayin couldn't mask her surprise. Forgetting about propriety, she took in the gown, my proud, straight-backed stance, her eyes flashing softly as they absorbed the image I chose to project, clearly struggling to accept the transformation.

I had to admit, even *I* had been taken aback when I had glimpsed myself in the floor-length mirror. But unlike me, Merayin had only ever seen my ragged, worn state. I definitely had the advantage of knowing just how far I could go.

And, in a way, managed to surpass it.

As she had promised, the dressing chamber had offered plenty—and then some. All the same size, as if Mordecai had taken my measure in that alley and had a seamstress create an entire wardrobe tailored to me in expectation of my arrival.

The thought was slightly unsettling, but it belonged to one of those mental threads I had roped together and set aside for a later time.

Thankfully, sifting through garments was such a familiar task that it wasn't *too* hard to silence the unwanted voices.

The dress I had picked out was a lovely burgundy velvet creation that narrowed at the waist and fanned around my legs. Its neckline was simple, a sweetheart cut that cupped my breasts, the pendant just brushing over the edge of the fabric. With the warmth coming from the fireplaces, the three-quarter sleeves weren't a nuisance, so I had forgone putting any kind of cardigan over the gown, not wanting to hide even an inch of its striking beauty.

Unfortunately, as much as I reveled in the feel of hot water erasing the grime and sweat from my skin, I hadn't had the time to wash my hair. But I *had* found another solution.

Much like the wardrobe, the vanity was well stocked, an array of cosmetics laid out for me to use. Including plain powder. I'd applied it to my hair to soak in the remnants of sweat weighing down the strands, then brushed them out, but not before I used just a touch of the same product on my forehead and chin. There was nothing worse than an unwanted shine to undermine the composed, regal yet alluring, image I was going for.

Somehow, I suspected I would need all the help I could get to last through the meal.

With that done, I pinned the strands of hair in the front away from my face, but kept the rest undone, the wave of silver now cascading down my back like an ocean of frost. I had even gone as far as to faintly line my upper lash line with kohl and added a touch of rouge to my lips. My cheeks, however, I left pale, the freckles scattered there remaining visible.

"You look lovely, my lady," Merayin whispered.

I didn't bother to correct her. Or think too much about *who* I had gotten dressed for.

Just another social appearance, I quickly reminded myself.

The fluttering tightness in my stomach, however, wasn't convinced.

Still, I inclined my head and offered the girl a smile. "Thank you, Merayin. Please, lead the way. I wouldn't want to be late."

The guards joined in the instant we left the wing. They trailed behind us up the elegant stairwell of carved, polished stone, their gazes, although discreet, burning into my back.

Not appreciating my form, but assessing the threat.

If they were waiting for me to lash out, attempt an escape, they would be sorely disappointed.

I was the epitome of politeness and grace, holding up the hem of my skirt with a trained hand while keeping the other on the curved railing as I climbed higher and higher up the winding stairwell, all the way to the uppermost level of the palace.

When we reached a double-winged door, Merayin dropped into a curtsy, then stepped aside. This was as far as she went, apparently, though her position didn't remain vacant for long. The older of the two guards, a stout man with salt-and-pepper hair, moved past me to open the doors before he fell back in line with the other.

Not looking ahead but down, lest I lose my nerve, I strode past the threshold. I'd half expected my armed entourage to follow, but it was only my steps that sounded, the heels clicking against the black-veined white marble floor.

I lifted my gaze at last—

And barely stifled my surprise.

The chamber—it was made of transparent glass.

It stretched between powerful stone columns and dominated the ceiling amidst slender lines of iron, leaving nothing but the clear night sky above me, the thousands of stars scattered across the dark canvas. Brilliant, but not as bright as the moon, a pure, undiluted silver that drew the eye.

Yet was not without competition.

Mordecai was a vision of alabaster and obsidian, sitting behind a round table. Not grandstanding like the ones I was used to from home, but intimate, designed to seat no more than two. His posture was straight, screaming of cool, calculated control, his attention—not on the food before him, but *me*— revealing turbulent, stormy depths that infused the regal appearance with a hint of something that could not be tamed.

His gaze swept across my dress. My hair. My lips.

And, finally, locked on mine.

As I experienced the full force of that sapphire, I forgot about my plan, forgot about the part I was supposed to play.

It was as if the Crescent Prince possessed the gravity of a portal, drawing me in until my reality was gone, replaced by another. It would have been so easy, too easy, to give in to the spell. To let that treacherous tugging within my chest claim what it wished. Grant it its freedom.

The *click* of the doors shutting saved me from succumbing to the impulse.

Whatever game he was playing, I had no doubt inviting me here, to this chamber where the allure of the night could sidetrack me, had been a deliberate move on his part. His unnerving insight into me was irrelevant. Even if I *hadn't* spent my entire life dreaming of its existence, the vastness of the star-speckled canvas would have taken the breath out of anyone who had only ever known the punishing brightness of the sun.

While I hadn't feared it even before, as I suspected someone from my world might, observing the night from the warmth and the safety of the chamber somehow turned it into living art.

Or a frame to offset the true masterpiece.

Him.

It was that, more than anything, that kept me rooted to the spot. But thankfully, having concealed the onslaught of sensations that raged inside me, the situation worked in my favor. Just a small whisper of authority, to stand while he remained seated—not a prince, commanding his subjects, but the observer I had allowed him to be.

In light of that, willing a smile to soften my lips was second nature.

And yet my voice came out hoarser than I had expected as I said, "Good morning."

I hid away my wince and strode forward without waiting for an invitation, the dress rippling around my form like liquid wind.

Mordecai's gaze burned into mine. "Please, sit down."

A light twitch grasped his body when I claimed the seat opposite him—as if he remembered the gallant thing to do would have been to hold the chair out for me. If he were anyone else, it would have been endearing.

The Crescent Prince played off the involuntary jerk as if it were nothing, flicking an invisible lint off the sleeve of his jacket with those elegant fingers instead. He peered at me, his profile stark in the cool light of the white-flamed lanterns.

"Did you sleep well?"

More politeness. More tactics I had grown up with, designed to conceal the festering reality beneath.

I swept my gaze around the space, taking in the pillars supporting the glass, the land beyond...

No, I hadn't slept well.

But my pain was my own.

"I have," I replied, returning my attention to him at last. "Although I must admit I am a little...confused, as to the terms of my presence here."

The words seemed heavier than I had wanted them to be, strained, as if the lie within them refused to lay low.

The One. That irritating voice grew. *He wants you because your power is unparalleled.*

I sighed. Inwardly to silence the voice. Outwardly to pave the way for my apparent confusion.

At least *that* wasn't entirely a lie.

"When I fled," I started and angled my head gently to the side, "I believed your guards were hunting me for the...man"—I couldn't bring myself to say *corpse*, even if my ploy depended on admitting murder—"in the alley. But I must admit, I had expected a dungeon for my crime, not this."

I waved my hand towards the table, then myself, bringing Mordecai's gaze once more to the fine cut of the burgundy gown, the single strand of shimmering argent hair that coiled down the side of my chest. Only instead of the usual response the display would have evoked, an elegant cruelness touched the strong line of Mordecai's jaw, his expression almost bordering on amused.

A tyrant, maybe. But not so drunk on power as to underestimate an opponent.

Perhaps the first I'd ever met.

"The dungeon would have been a far better fit for him than you," he said smoothly, though I sensed the sharp edges shaping the very foundation of his words. "His death was well deserved."

Was it?

An imperceptible flutter of tightness across his mouth. "I saw your fear..."

The hands holding me against the wall. The sickly reek of his breath, too close. Violating.

As he would—

Death over a dungeon.

I refused to admit it, refused to accept that I thought...

I thought Mordecai was right.

A tremor spread from my core as my stomach revolted. I needed to occupy myself with something, anything but the insight I had gained.

I *agreed* with him.

Of its own volition, my hand reached for one of the peculiar, violet-hued strawberries nestled in a silver bowl. I turned it over between my fingers, then tasted the fruit. I didn't have the strength yet to resume the conversation.

Once again, the Crescent Prince was winning.

And maybe... Maybe I should let him.

As soon as the thought crossed my mind—and on its wings, violent refusal—his sonorous voice dominated the air.

"He would have paid for his actions either way. But you do not need the rulings of the law to protect you, do you, Ember?"

It was an effort not to choke on the succulent fruit. I felt my mask slipping and quickly patched up the cracks. He was baiting me. But he hadn't revealed the full extent of his knowledge yet.

Even when my instincts were screeching to just admit to myself that I harbored no secrets before him, I had to hear it from his lips.

"As I said"—I reached for another strawberry, ignoring his question—"I would like to know the purpose behind my stay here. Unless all you desired was a breakfast companion, which I find hard to believe given your efforts to secure me."

Mordecai cast me a look that shattered my pathetic charade for good.

Silken words and manners cut as sharply as diamonds were of no use in his presence. Perhaps he would have let me play this game until he grew bored, until my tongue was twisted into a knot from all the honeyed half-truths I would have spun. But that look—that cool glint in the blue of his eyes. He was giving me a choice.

Honesty. Or deceit.

I crossed my arms. "I *would* like to know why you brought me here. Why take me from Saros only to grant me *this*?"

This time, when I motioned to my appearance, there was no seductive elegance to it. Just the rawness of being unable to find a kernel of sense.

Mordecai leaned back in his chair, his head cocked sideways as if my surrender had loosened some of his rigidness, too. "You know why I want you."

My throat bobbed, thoughts catching on the word *want*, the

way it coiled through the air, brushing against my skin and seeping beneath my clothes.

"No, I don't," I forced myself to say. "I don't know why *any* of you are crowding me. I'm a High Master's daughter." A bitter laugh bubbled from my lips, and I didn't bother to mask the distaste as I spat, "My only value is in *breeding* to continue the prestigious Norcross line."

A shadow passed across Mordecai's face, but it was gone before I truly caught it. He laughed darkly, the sound rich and silken, yet thunderous all at once. His gaze leveled on mine, leaving me breathless in that split second when everything seemed to still—

The air around us was awash with silver.

The shadowfire came at me in a crushing wave. It pressed from all sides until the world was nothing but the blinding argent, every inch of my skin covered in its touch. I tried to scramble away, tried to push myself from the chair, from the table—the need to flee clamping up my throat. But I couldn't.

I couldn't move.

I couldn't even scream.

Only the darkness within me responded.

The shadows radiated through my flesh, coiling through the endless silver and parting it like a veil until the outlines of the chamber became visible once more. I was still surrounded by those dancing tendrils—argent and obsidian alike—but what rendered me immobile now was the realization that the shadowfire, Mordecai's shadowfire, wasn't trying to hurt me.

Mortified, I looked at the wisps of unnatural flame, light and darkness twirling around one another and inching ever closer, like two dancers, drawn by the music and the heat of their flesh.

Life. Not death.

Mordecai hadn't attacked me. He had simply forced an invitation my icy obsidian was unable to refuse.

The answer I had been searching for.

The end of my secrets.

And the beginning of a path only he could unveil.

My gaze found his among the flickering, billowing embers, our bodies bathed in their respective flame. Silver on black. And black on silver. Mirror images, with the blue of our eyes the focal point of this peculiar universe we had created.

His face remained guarded, but a corner of his lips turned upward, followed by a slight lift of his brow.

Almost lazily, he twined a single elegant tendril around mine, promising to close that final sliver of distance and grant our powers their wish.

"Do you still believe you are only a High Master's daughter, Ember?"

CHAPTER TWENTY-TWO

THE OBSIDIAN AND SILVER COLLIDED.

I wasn't even aware I had gasped, but I *heard* myself do so from somewhere deep within. Like in Saros, my conscience seemed to come from a different place.

Only now, my body wasn't numb.

The strange, double awareness only became *more* prominent as the icy sensation transformed into tight, pulsing heat that spread through my body, suffused my cheeks, and left my mouth dry.

It was...overpowering.

With a deep inhale, I crawled back into my flesh, choosing *this* awareness over the other. But while muted, it remained, feeding me impulses I didn't want to acknowledge as mine.

How *good* the touch felt.

How my every nerve came alive, burning with the need for more—

A loud *crack* snapped through the room.

Wide-eyed, I looked across the table, only to realize it was farther away than I had thought. I was standing, my hands balled into fists and my shadowfire pulling away from the brilliant silver until not a trace of it remained. Contained beneath my skin once more.

Color bloomed high on Mordecai's sculpted cheekbones as his own shadows retreated, his unguarded bewilderment vivid in his gaze as we stared at one another, the overturned chair the single visible testimony of what had come to pass. I swallowed, still feeling the remnants of that searing heat in my core.

My mind was nothing more than a jumbled mess of contradicting thoughts, and the more I tried to make sense of everything, the more I was lost. All I knew was that in all my life, I had never experienced something quite like this.

Being powerful, yet laid bare at the same time.

Raw.

Equal.

What I could never become in Soltzen, I was granted here.

A lure. It had to have been some sort of lure.

But why, then, did it feel so right?

Not trusting my voice, I shook my head and marched towards the door.

I couldn't stay with him. Not in this room. Not when his very presence beckoned me to unleash the shadowfire and drown myself in whatever *that* had been.

It would...consume me.

My fingers were already poised on the ornate gibbous moon handle when Mordecai's voice slithered up from behind. "Your charming friends... They do not know of your gift, do they?"

I ground my teeth, my hold on the iron tightening.

"No, I suppose they wouldn't have tried so hard to save you if they were aware of the darkness residing within. Their precious savior. The manifestation of their prayers, their dreams. But those who follow beliefs are often blind to the truth."

Wasn't that precisely what I thought? What I feared?

A dangerous chuckle. "No, your friends do not know who their savior is at all."

I whipped around, still clutching the handle.

Gone was that flicker of bewilderment, the hint of a blush that had adorned his features. He was the Crescent Prince once more. Cool. Collected.

Lethal.

And yet I recognized the offer in his tone—the willingness to give me answers no one else was able to provide.

The sole thing that remained undetermined was the payment I would have to provide.

It went against everything Ada and her mother had tried to drill into me in the short time we'd had together. But as the memory of the man lying dead in the alley surged to the front of my mind, there was no room for doubt left.

I *had* to know how—why—I had this darkness. What it might mean.

Perhaps the price for the knowledge would be the knowledge itself, ruining me. But it was still a kinder fate than living in shambles, never knowing when the next piece would collapse.

I exhaled, then walked back to the table and picked up my chair. I set it down with such force it skidded across the marble, tipping over—

My hand lashed out. The impact reverberated up my arm,

but I refused to let my expression waver as I righted the chair, then sat down.

Mordecai's attention never left me, just as mine didn't veer from him, even as I snatched the porcelain cup and its saucer then poured the still hot tea from the delicate teapot set within easy reach. The amusement teasing the corners of Mordecai's eyes, while lasting no more than a heartbeat, made me itch to throw the cup straight at him. Though with the way tremors continued to zing through my hands, I wouldn't be at all surprised if my tantrum backfired.

Whether he sensed how close to the edge I was or not, Mordecai waited patiently as I composed myself, as if he had all the time in the world. Well, I supposed he truly *did*...

I turned my attention to the tea, sucking in the sharp aroma of ginger and watching the orange-tinted surface slosh as I brought the cup to my lips. I forced myself to drink slowly, to flush away the wayward, unpredictable impulses with every sip until I felt more like myself again.

Only then did I set the cup aside.

"Whatever it is that makes them believe I'm this...this *savior*..." I lifted my gaze to his, gauging his reaction—or rather the lack of it. "The shadows aren't part of that power, are they?"

Mordecai didn't answer. Instead, he waved an elegant hand at the food spread between us. "Eat something."

"I'm not hungry."

"Then you will not get the answers you seek."

I opened my mouth. Closed it again. He was being serious.

A flutter of amusement that struck me as just a touch hysterical flowed through my mental tones. Sun damn me, but I'd much rather have him as my jailor than an overbearing caretaker.

My thoughts hurtled back to the Norcross residence. I snorted inwardly.

The two could definitely be one and the same sometimes.

Relenting, I took one of the smaller pastries off the silver plate. My stomach was tight with an inseparable blend of unease and misplaced excitement, but I pushed myself to eat bite after bite, the chocolate filling melting on my tongue and lessening the tremors. I snatched another between my fingers. The nausea that rose at the mere thought of more food made me wince, yet I ate it whole, down to the last crumb.

Throughout my struggles, Mordecai gazed at the outlines of Nysa visible beyond the glass. He was turned partially away from me with one arm braced on the backrest, the other resting casually on the table.

A vision of pensiveness, distant and unreachable.

I couldn't help but wonder how much of it was a front. And how much his own way of accepting that what he had hunted for centuries, if Telaria was to be believed, was now in his grasp.

He would receive no sympathy from me, yet as I ate the third—and last—pastry, observing him from beneath my lashes, it took a lot of effort to stifle the whispers of kinship that rose.

In our own way, we had both found ourselves in a new reality.

When I poured more tea, I made just enough noise to lure him from his thoughts.

"What have you learned of me so far?" he asked, his tone without inflection.

I peered over the silver-lined rim, debating whether to lie or tell the blunt truth. My previous attempts at sweetening our circumstances had crashed and burned miserably, and although I was still tempted to take the tried path that had always eased my life back at home, I accepted that Mordecai was beyond that.

I placed the cup back on the saucer but kept my fingers curled around its warmth.

"Surprisingly, not that much," I said. "But not one ounce of it was good."

The almost imperceptible twitch of his lips convinced me that if he hadn't stopped the expression from forming, I would have glimpsed a bitter, resigned smile on his face. Or maybe it was just my imagination, seeing things and hidden depths where none were to be found. It didn't matter.

"I do know," I continued, steering the conversation back where I wanted it, "that you're the Crescent Prince. The oppressor ruling Somraque. And—*supposedly*—the only one in possession of the shadowfire."

This time, a tentative smile did touch the corners of his lips. But his eyes—they burned like molten sapphires. I sucked in a breath, entranced by the kaleidoscope of thunderous emotions his body betrayed nothing of.

"Not anymore," he said softly.

His words were enough to rip me from my daze.

I blinked, unsure what stunned me more. The way he looked at me, his expression caught somewhere between shielded admiration and respect. Or the light pleasure in his tone, entwined with gentle surprise that revealed he, too, hadn't known. Not before that alley.

Which meant that the shadowfire was mine, and mine alone.

The thought of a monster finding his kin hadn't been unfounded. But why, then, did I feel anything *but* one in this fragile atmosphere that had woven between us?

And neither... Neither did he.

As small cramps started to tug at my fingers, I let go of the tea and laid my hands on my lap. "Where does it come from? What *are* the shadows?"

Nothing but death and torture, echoed Eriyan's voice.

"I trust your boisterous company has spun many tales about me, but while some perhaps came close, I presume none were the truth. Not when it comes to my—*our*—power." Mordecai leaned back in his chair, my eyes following the graceful movement before I managed to stop myself.

It was only then that I realized—

"*Our* power. But you—you aren't like me." When he cocked his head to the side, I went on. "Maybe my bloodline is what Ada made it out to be. But I'm still native to Soltzen. I don't..."

Think you belong there, I finished silently, unable to mute the thought that followed on its tail. *And neither do I.*

Mordecai saved me from wading farther down a path I wasn't entirely sure I was ready to take on.

"I come from an ancient people, Ember. Immortal people."

He waited for the words to sink in.

Not a spell, or a trick.

No, Mordecai wielded something far greater than that.

Eternal life.

"The three faces of magic," he continued once I gave him a weak nod, "birthed three children. Three races, if you prefer the term, each with their own powers, but meant to live as one. Some who command blood, some who command words, and some, who have no magic in their bodies, but can control objects in which it resides."

I bit my lip. The three worlds. I hadn't doubted what Ada had told me, yet hearing it confirmed a second time... It brought reality closer, made accepting it more manageable, somehow.

Especially as the message remained unchanged despite coming from two opposing sides.

"Somraque, Soltzen, and Svitanye," I said quietly.

"So you know." Mordecai inclined his head, a brushstroke of respect softening his features.

Something I had no doubt my words would erase. "I didn't until Ada explained."

I waited for whatever backlash would come for my brazen, liberal mention of her name. But all he did was incline his head again before he sat up straighter.

"The Aldane family has knowledge, but not as complete as they would like to believe." He eased himself back and ran his thumb across his lips, his gaze drifting to the moonlit night blooming beyond the palace, then seeking out mine again. "What you learned of the worlds and its people is true. But magic—it created a fourth race. One, unlike any before, existing solely with the purpose to rule. To keep the volatile faces of magic in balance, and punish those who would abuse the power for their own gain.

"The Ancients, as they used to call us, were never a large people. But with our strength and with immortality saving us from the ailments that plagued others, we saw no need to inflate our numbers. Not at first. Magic, in its nature, strives for balance. It is pure, whole, and created the world in its liking. But as it manifested physically, it also grew wild. The ethereal heart did not predict that men, with their mortality and fragile bodies, would not only show incredible resilience to the passing of time, live longer with almost every generation, but spread.

"The population grew, and we didn't. The Ancients bore only a few children—no more than one a century if fate was kind. So as those very centuries passed, our numbers became small in comparison to the three people of magic. But worst of all, we learned that not even immortality could save us from a violent death."

Caught in the magnetic sound of his voice, in the story I had never heard, never read, yet somehow felt to be true, I had gone utterly still. I took a hushed, shuddering inhale when silence swept between us, but the coldness in my chest persisted as those last two words lingered, imprinting on my very heart.

Mordecai's features were drawn, an impenetrable wall, yet I sensed the phantom weight he carried with striking clarity—as if I, too, was placed at its mercy.

As if that haunting ache flowed in my blood just as vividly as it did in his.

My throat was raw as I asked, "What happened?"

Mordecai ran a hand through his dark strands and sighed. "The Ancients feared the loss of control. What it might mean for the world if it were to wrench itself from their grasp. But they alone couldn't hope to uphold their roles as protectors for long. Desperate, they sought other consorts. Individuals who did not only possess the capability to fall in love with an immortal but whose magic was strong enough, so that they would, perhaps, be able to bear a child of mixed heritage, in which our power could live on.

"My parents were already bonded, as were many others. They couldn't bring themselves to part, or accept someone else into their union, though some tried. But they all aided their friends, watched that belief in a bright outcome flourish—then wither.

"Very few succeeded in having children who embodied our traits, and with each new generation, the magic—the *true* magic belonging to the three people—grew stronger, weeding out the presence of our power until it became dormant, nothing but a useless sliver of past with no hope of manifesting. The Ancients tried, again and again, but failed to produce more offspring of our nature. It appeared that the magic had adapted, learned how to suppress our traits long before a child was born.

"Those who still carried the essence of my people never revealed it." Brimming sapphire met my gaze. "Until you."

CHAPTER TWENTY-THREE

IT WAS A GOOD THING I WAS SITTING DOWN WITH THE WAY my knees went weak, my mind spinning in circles far more sinister than if I had drunk an entire barrel of wine. Or sowhl— something I actually wouldn't mind having a pint of right about now.

But when I thought of the last time I tasted it, clustered around the tavern table with everyone buzzing, if a little tense, about plans that had gone so wrong only hours later...

I locked that thought, that part of me away.

I cared for them, worried for them, but... Was I any better than Ada? Any better than the rest if I allowed myself to believe that had been friendship kindling among us?

Exhaling, I lowered my gaze to my lap, to my hands entwined there, white-knuckled and shaking, all the while acutely aware of Mordecai's focus on me. Or rather the way he was pretending he *wasn't* studying every fine tremor that rippled through my flesh.

The descendant not just of all three people, but of Ancients, too. Of his own race.

On some intuitive level that refused to be ignored, I knew he hadn't lied. Not about my heritage. Nor about the world as it had once been.

Regardless of what the others had said, regardless of who he might have become, Mordecai didn't wrap his history in tailored veils of distortion.

Or mine, as it turned out.

But that didn't mean I trusted him. Couldn't...

I reached for the now lukewarm tea, hoping it would calm my unsettled stomach. Mordecai continued to give me space, going as far as exchanging his seat at the table for a spot in front of the glass, his silhouette nearly blending with the night, yet standing apart. Solitary.

Not any longer, I thought, but the humorless laugh that fluttered through my mind choked.

I sipped the tea, struggling to keep it down.

When Mordecai had still been speaking, I had been ensnared by the oddly familiar unknown. Now, I fell prey to it. The obsidian inside me stirred as if to comfort me.

I wanted to scream.

Shadowfire. The mark of Ancients. The mark of a man who had gained the hatred of an entire land. I buried my head in my hands, for the first time wishing with all my heart that all of this was only a dream—that I would wake up in my own chamber, my own bed, with no regrets save for the abundance of wine I had consumed that had cast me into such horrid depths of dark-hewn sleep.

But there would be no such mercy.

And, as I met Mordecai's gaze as he turned halfway

towards me—as I *truly* looked into those ancient, sapphire eyes and saw my own form reflected within them, I knew I wouldn't have accepted the fabrication over the truth, however tempting.

Gingerly, I rose from my chair and waited for the spell of dizziness to pass. Once I had faith my body wouldn't betray me, I strode over to the glass. To him.

With each step, the tension locking my spine lessened, and by the time I reached the edge of the marble floor, coming to stand as close to Mordecai as I dared, I could almost appreciate the view. I traced one finger along the glass, following the contours of the lively town pulsing beneath us. I couldn't help noting how that simple, unhurried move made something in *him* loosen, too.

"What you speak of," I said, dropping my hand to my side. "It must have happened ages ago. My people, they have no stories of your existence." Nor were there any of the three worlds, aside from those children's books I had guarded like treasure.

But they had mentioned no lands. Merely drawn images of a reality different than the one I had been born into.

Something dark crept across Mordecai's face, but his voice was still the same velvet spill as he said, "I was only a child when the world fractured. It's surprising any stories of that time remain at all, let alone ones of a race that had all but gone extinct."

Only a child.

His words roused something inside me. Urged me to look past the youth, past the vision of the dark prince that he was...

Beneath those carefully laid layers, I saw, at last, the marks I had been blind to before.

Whispers of the centuries, perhaps millennia, he had lived. Not in solitude, but isolation.

The cold shadow where a heart should have been—*had* once been—transformed by the ungrateful privilege of having to witness it all.

The kindness burned away by the passing of time that deepened the gashes of loss instead of sealing them.

The image I uncovered layer after layer didn't make him into more of a monster. It didn't make me shy away.

If anything, I caught myself leaning closer, eroding the distance between us.

I locked away the impulse before it could thrive.

Whatever it was that I felt for him, this—this draw... I couldn't let it win. We might share the shadowfire, but it didn't have to mean I was *like* him. I was still Ember. High Master Norcross's daughter and *possible* savior. Between those two things, I had enough titles to my name. *Ancient* was one I didn't dare take. Not even as my very soul seemed to ache for it.

For him.

Bracing my fingers against the cool, clear glass, I shook myself mentally and threw enough insults around in my head to sober me up. Mordecai was a poison. A slow, clever poison that crept up on you long after you believed you had already walked away unscathed. I'd seen enough people succumb to their desires only to have them burst into flames right before their eyes.

I snorted and let out a bitter laugh. By the Sun, I needed to choose my words better. I didn't think the particular flames in my possession would burn away what that inexplicable part of me yearned for.

Though I had a suspicion *I* would be left in ashes if I were to give in.

With one last breath that sounded unnervingly like a dying echo of my laugh, I released the glass and moved to lean against the nearest pillar. Mordecai remained where he was.

"I understand that my mother's bloodline had to mix with my father's to produce a child born of all three worlds," I said carefully, keeping my voice perfectly leveled. "That their union was the key for these powers everyone keeps speaking of, but I have yet to see manifest that which will...ah...make it possible to reunite the lands." I shifted against the pillar, but couldn't find a comfortable position. Though I imagined I was at fault for that, not the smooth, chiseled stone. "Alone, one bloodline or the other wouldn't have been enough."

A curt dip of Mordecai's chin.

I tilted my head towards the starry ceiling, thinking through my words before deciding against softening the edges.

"Telaria bound my magic." I didn't look at him when I said her name, ridden with guilt that, until now, I hadn't even considered Ada's mother was locked somewhere in this palace. But even more so, guilt that I couldn't inquire about her just yet.

"Whatever she did," I went on, seeking constellations I had no names for, "prevented me from exhibiting any traits of my heritage. Based on what Ada said, my parents wouldn't either—just as anybody else who is not born of all three branches of magic is incapable of tapping into power beyond that of its native land. But..." I chewed on my lip and lowered my gaze to the dark veins spreading across the marble. "But for me to be one of the Ancients' offspring—why? Why would the power show in me when my family is so utterly normal?"

Mordecai was perfectly still when I looked up. No, not only still, but *stiff*. Whatever flicker of warmth I had seen in his eyes had fled, leaving nothing behind but an icy landscape where no life could hope to prosper. Posture regal, he stalked towards me, his honed body towering over mine as he barely left any space separating us.

He pinned me with an unrelenting stare. "You would do well to stay by my side, *savior*."

Despite the calmness, his voice hit me like a blade to the gut.

"*Normal* is a word that can easily be skewed. I would not wish for it to be the last lesson you ever learned."

He strode towards the door, each demanding *tap* of his silver-tipped leather boots against the marble slicing into my skin, making me feel small. Insignificant.

"We commence training tomorrow."

I looked over my shoulder to find him standing by the door, one hand on the handle, the other curved behind his back.

"Your friends have done enough damage as it is. And the world has been paying more than long enough for your people's crimes."

CHAPTER TWENTY-FOUR

For what felt like an eternity, I did nothing but stare at the night sky, hoping I would never learn the meaning behind Mordecai's words and knowing that I would always be incomplete without it.

I probably would have stayed longer if Merayin and the two guards hadn't come to escort me from the chamber.

Accepting that Mordecai would spill his secrets when he chose to and not a moment sooner, I let go of my incessant pondering. Because there was one thing he'd already confirmed —one thing I had to try even if the mere idea of doing it set me on edge.

I waited until Merayin's steps faded, then disappeared in the vastness of the palace beyond my wing.

I planted my feet wider apart, then surveyed the bedchamber. To seek out any hidden magic that might be used to spy on me.

To stall.

With a grunt, I curled and uncurled my fingers, then shook the stiffness from my spine.

The way Mordecai had spoken of Zaphine, Ada, and Eriyan... He made it seem as if they were alive, if not unharmed. I had to trust they were out there somewhere, devising their plan to break into the palace, only now adding another person to their list of what—and who—they needed to liberate from within these walls.

Mordecai had offered me insight. Sincerity. But only to a point. And the way our conversation had ended...

My future, if it remained in Mordecai's hands, was murky. Whereas Ada, with all her scheming and secrets, had had no reservations spelling out what the endgame was.

Just as I had to believe she was alive, I needed to have faith that her determination to reunite the worlds would overpower her shock when she realized I wasn't the savior she expected. When she came—when they all did—I wanted to be ready to aid them. Even if it demanded wielding a weapon to fight our way out of here.

I closed my eyes and centered myself, much as if I were trying to reach for the power of the pendant.

Only my fingers didn't wrap around the silver. It was my *mind* that moved, delving into my core to where that seed of ice rested, once again still now that I was free of Mordecai's presence.

I tried to remember what had happened that day in the alley —not the event, but the emotions, the sensations buried under the avalanche of my discomfort. When that proved fruitless— and my stomach grew increasingly queasy—I tried to recall what had stirred when Mordecai had bathed me in silver, strove to recreate the moment...

But despite my efforts, the darkness within me remained silent. Placid. Nothing but a dormant shade, uninterested in my call to emerge from the depths.

A frustrated groan spilled from my lips. It bounced off the walls and—

Ruffled the air?

I backed up against the bed until my legs hit the frame, my gaze fixed on the point by the fireplace that seemed different. That *thrummed.*

Breathless, I watched the air coalesce and form a shape, the stones behind it now bathed in colors that grew more opaque, yet never solidified. But I recognized the silhouette, then the features, the translucent jade eyes that stared at me, as if surprised this, indeed, was real.

"Ada?" I took a step forward.

No, not her, but an apparition of her. And yet relief washed over me as if she truly were standing before my eyes.

"How?"

"Later," the echo of her said. "The projection won't last long with the prince's defenses eating at my strength. We will get you out, Ember. But before we do"—flicker—"search for the remnant of the hallow. However"—flicker—"and whenever you can, search for it."

"I don't even know what it looks like—"

"You'll know when you'll see it."

She winked out of existence, the air once more undisturbed.

Well, that *was helpful...*

And judging by the way she assumed I had free reign of the palace, she must have...spied on me? Saw, somehow, that I wasn't locked in some cell but had been given rooms of my own?

Or had she known all along how Mordecai would treat me?

I threw myself down on the bed, sinking into the mattress. I buried my face in my hands, then swore when I remembered the cosmetics I must have smeared. *Some days...*

With a grunt, I got up again and moved over to the vanity to repair the damage. After I salvaged what I could, I pulled my hair up into a bun to keep it out of the way and walked out the door.

The wing was mine, Mordecai had said, and while I doubted he would leave something as precious as the relic within easy reach of his captive, I hadn't yet inspected every inch of the chambers I had been assigned for a possible passageway tucked out of sight. I strode down the hallway and pushed through the last door in the line. It was as good a place as any to start.

And it certainly beat moping in bed.

I PAUSED my snooping only when Merayin and another servant brought my meal three hours after midday. I ate it in one of the chambers at the far end of the wing, where the large windows overlooked the endless waste and no lights disturbed the vast night sky. It was odd, how there were no reflections in the glass with the chamber illuminated by numerous fires burning in iron sconces along the walls.

A different make, perhaps, than the one that was always alive with sun-fueled images back at home.

Absentmindedly, I speared another morsel of meat as my eyes narrowed. It made sense.

However it was that Somraque manufactured its glass, the result made sense.

In Soltzen, the reflections were just another wall. Another

means to ensure prying eyes couldn't glimpse what unfolded within the boundaries of the estate.

Sun forbid anyone would catch a High Master unguarded.

I snorted and helped myself to another serving of roasted potatoes.

For all the issues Ada had pointed out, Somraque was, in a way, far freer than Soltzen. I'd seen how people were at the celebrations—perhaps ignorant by choice, but also full of wonder. Open. They wouldn't use offshoot manifestations of nature to hide behind.

I didn't stop looking out the window until I ate my fill, but the second the food was cleared, I resumed my search of the wing.

For long hours I explored, leaving nothing untouched, but all I managed to find were paintings and baubles, expensive rugs, and a few books scattered here and there, as if someone had discarded them, too immersed in the story they had finished to return the tomes to their respective shelves.

I couldn't imagine Mordecai acting so...casual and uncontrolled. It must have been one of the servants, using this wing as a private refuge before my involuntary stay here had driven them out.

By the time the grandfather clock in one of the two sitting rooms at my disposal alerted me the day was crawling to an end, I returned to my bedroom and took the leisurely, thorough bath I had been putting off for long enough.

Mercifully, Ada didn't appear while I was soaking in the grand claw-foot tub. I gave myself over to the warmth, the caresses of the gently sloshing water as the slight annoyance of not finding anything of importance gradually fled from my skin. Wrapped in a white silken nightgown, I dried my hair by the fire, then slipped into another dress—a flowing gown of cool-toned lavender velour, with form-fitting lace sleeves that, unlike the fashion prevalent in Somraque, reached just beyond my wrists. I debated leaving my silver strands down, but the dress was too striking, too sharp to allow such informality. So I fastened them up with a series of jeweled pins, then reapplied the cosmetics to my face to bring out my light blue irises.

I smiled at my reflection, but the expression was grim.

Whatever irrational impulse had guided me over the past hour, it appeared to have made me into a female variant of the Crescent Prince. Where he was nothing but stark contrasts, with no color in sight save for his eyes, I embodied the pale hues of winter, as lovely as they were harsh.

I let that glacial smile stay on my face as I rang for Merayin.

THE CHAMBER beneath the stars was doused in candlelight. Everything inside me quieted at the sight, at the warmth and the gentle darkness that embraced me like an old lover, the smoky scent carrying undertones reminiscent of oakmoss.

I half expected Mordecai to peel from the shadows gathering by the pillars, yet I remained alone, with nothing but the whispers of fire dancing with my breaths.

Every click of my heels ricocheted through the emptiness as I approached the table, and my disappointment transformed into intrigue.

The porcelain-and-crystal setting was laid out for one, but where Mordecai's plate had been in the morning, a dark bundle waited, a note perched on the very top.

Tomorrow.

That was all it said. A single word, written in immaculate cursive on a cream-colored card.

I placed the note aside, then carefully took the bundle in my hands and let it unfold. My lips parted.

Garments.

Similar to the guards' uniform, only finer, more refined—and tailored to a woman's physique. *My* physique.

I knew what they meant, the hint they revealed of the nature of the *training* that waited for me tomorrow, and yet I couldn't bring myself to hate them for their taunt. Perhaps because I wasn't entirely certain they were meant as one.

My fingers trailed the supple, yet strong material of the tunic, skimming over the silver embroidery running down the side, from the top of the breast to the very hem. Moon phases. Each made out in stunning detail.

Still clutching the tunic, the black, skintight trousers that went along with it, I lowered to pick up the thigh-high leather boots stored beside the table. I sank down into Mordecai's chair.

I cherished the fine make of gowns, enjoyed wearing them, the way they felt like armor in disguise. But all that was my own twist in attitude, turning the gilded shackles into strength.

But these... These were clothes designed with an intent beyond flaunting my body to gain attention of highborn men.

Designed for someone who was not a mere passive observer.

I didn't return to my chambers until late that night, pondering over the slice of clarity that had cut through my thoughts until I realized what this peculiar sensation was.

One I had felt whispers of, then lost—but now bloomed.

Purpose.

CHAPTER TWENTY-FIVE

THE HALL WAS WIDE, WITH A TALL TRAY CEILING A SHADE lighter than the slate-gray walls, and what little furniture there was was pressed against the walls to produce additional space. I was dressed in the uniform Mordecai had given me, my hair braided back, and feeling more than a little out of place.

I wasn't a fighter. My body merely stored the one thing I had always considered as the closest approximation to a weapon I could have—my mind.

Unfortunately, even *that* had lost some of its edge lately, riddled with betrayal whenever I thought I had regained the reins once and for all.

As useless as it was useful.

My eyebrows knitting together, I looked up at Mordecai who was staring at me with those intense sapphire eyes, his face perfectly devoid of emotion. Stoic.

He wore a tailored jacket that showed off his broad shoulders and honed torso, and for the first few moments when he had strode into the room, it had been an effort not to gawk at how good he looked. The latest of the aforementioned betrayals. He, on the other hand, had spared me only the barest of glances, though I could have sworn there was a tightness in the way he marched over to a low, locked chest of drawers to procure the bone handle dagger I now had in my hands.

My gaze dipped down.

Familiar. Its presence was familiar even if the blade itself was not.

"I sincerely hope you're not so foolish as to think of using it on me." His voice brushed against my ears.

I blinked, more than anything surprised that the thought hadn't even occurred to me. The lack of skill shouldn't have been an obstacle for intent, at least.

Although his remark did confirm my suspicions that this would *not* be the kind of training I had envisioned on my way down here.

"The blade is from my world, isn't it?" I asked as I rotated the dagger, its unmarred surface catching the light. "How did you get it?"

Mordecai raised an eyebrow. "I have some relics of other lands in my possession."

I didn't as much as twitch at his words, despite the pointed way he'd said *relic*. As if he knew of my supposedly covert explorations.

Maybe. But it didn't matter.

I was confined to my airtight prison of a wing anyway, and if he'd ever let me out... Well, then that would prove he wasn't aware of my side mission after all.

I slid a finger down the blade. "Right, I forget you're old."

Mordecai barked out a laugh. The lightness of it caught me

unprepared, but just as I managed to shoot him a questioning look, he was already pulling the walls back up, slipping behind the impervious facade once more. Although, I was glad to notice, not *entirely*.

A hint of his amusement remained, lurking in the gleam of his eyes and the slightly upturned corner of his lips, as if he couldn't control the disobedient muscles.

"I suppose I am," he said smoothly. "And so is the dagger. You should have no difficulties opening a portal with it."

"I—"

"A small one," Mordecai continued nonchalantly, like he wasn't just giving me the power I'd been denied my entire life. He clasped his hands behind his back. "Just to another room within the palace."

As if the translucent barrier would let me get farther.

A gleam passed across his eyes. "Try my bedroom, if that will give you additional motivation."

I snapped my gaping mouth shut. Bastard. The Crescent Prince was a bastard, and yet the slight twitch of his lips sent me into a spill of laughter.

When I finally recollected myself, I adjusted my grip on the bone handle, marveling how it felt; how the magic embedded inside it, the steel it extended into, seemed to call out to me. *Me.* It didn't care about my gender or where I stood in the social hierarchy. It was simply a well of pure, undiluted power, wishing to be used.

And Mordecai had given it to me.

I peered up at him. The smattering of satisfaction made his flawless features more sensual, and in that moment, I couldn't bring myself to care for his agenda—that he had more likely than not only extended this courtesy to reach the fragments

Soltzen and Svitanye harbored. The time for that would come. I knew as much in the marrow of my bones. But this—this slice of power he'd granted, it was *mine*.

An uncut jewel perhaps, but one I would quietly cherish.

A breath whizzed from my lips as I grounded myself and focused on the magic, pulling to the forefront everything I had gleaned about portals, the theories and practices I'd read about but could never properly test. The time my father's prized sword had knocked me on my ass hardly counted.

I centered myself, letting nothing but the thought of his bed—

The bastard.

I glared at him for planting the damn image in my mind, but Mordecai feigned innocence. As if there was even a sliver of that about him. I shook my head and tried again.

No bedroom this time. The chamber under the night sky anchored in my thoughts, the visual reinforcing my will. Magic stirred, reverberating from the dagger into my arm while a current of it traveled the other way. I sliced the dagger through the air before me, a shimmering slash taking form—

And fading.

"What the—"

The portal collapsed before it even truly opened.

"Are you having performance issues, Ember?" The velvet voice rubbed against me from the side.

I cut Mordecai a look dripping with disdain and shoved the dagger in his hands. "Then you try."

His fingers brushed against mine as he wrapped them around the hilt, the touch faint, yet heady. I pulled my hand away and brushed it discreetly against the hem of my tunic, as if that could scatter the heat still lingering there.

In the end, it didn't take much to forget about the effect the feel of his skin had on me. Just a slice of the blade through the air and—

A portal.

Mordecai had opened a portal in a matter of *seconds*.

It was small, just a gaping wound in the fabric of reality, but through it, I had no difficulties seeing the silken black sheets glistening in opulent candlelight.

"Bastard," I whispered.

A chuckle greeted my word before the portal folded in on itself. I turned to him, my gaze drifting between the ages-old object of power and the *smirk* resting on Mordecai's lips.

I stuffed the kindling admiration as deep down as I could, and said, "I don't see why you need me when you can do perfectly well by yourself."

He twirled the dagger between his fingers, lazily and with the confidence of someone who'd had centuries to perfect the movement. He opened his mouth, then hesitated, as if whatever reply he had waiting to chuck my way was too impulsive. I crossed my arms and gave him a pointed look when he fell into the cool, slightly disinterested act once more, erasing any traces of the prince who had presented me with a glimpse into his bedroom.

I couldn't tell whether I should be relieved or frustrated.

"Try." He held out the dagger to me, hilt first, but I kept my arms just as they were. Crossed.

"Not before you explain why it has to be me to get you onto the next plane." A roll of surprise brightened the sapphire, then vanished. "You owe me that much."

It had to have been madness that allowed those final words

to curl into the air between us because Mordecai's gaze turned murderous.

He advanced on me. "Don't think your pretty shadowfire will be sufficient protection should you push me to my limits."

"I have no intention of pushing you anywhere," I countered, just as coldly as he. "But if you want my cooperation, I want answers in return."

"*Sunshine*, you are in *no* position to make demands."

Bare inches separated us, icy anger pulsing off his body and bathing mine. The dagger lay idly in his hand, a silent threat, should I push further.

I did.

"You're not going to kill me. Whatever your endgame is, you need me alive to work the fragments. And possibly willing."

My throat bobbed as I said it, but my words rang hard and true through the empty space.

Mordecai lifted his hand, his thumb fleetingly brushing against the corner of my lips. "Oh, you will be willing. When I dangle your friends' lives in front of you. When I burn them until their eyes turn silver. Do not tempt me, Ember. Do not think the liberties I give you make me less of a nightmare than they undoubtedly whispered of."

I swallowed but didn't dare back away. Even when his breath grazed my lips—when he leaned down, his head cocked to the side and nothing, absolutely nothing human was left in his gaze.

He shoved the hilt into my hand. "Now open a portal."

I TRIED. And I failed.

Mordecai pushed me, again and again, standing to the side

like a commander overlooking his troops. But this world, or maybe the unwillingness within me, kept that rip from opening. I felt the magic with unchallenged clarity, had no difficulties tapping into that brilliant well...

But it didn't change the fact that I was simply unable to do what Mordecai demanded.

I'd heard that not all men were able to wield both powers. That some had an affinity purely for space manipulations, while others were attuned solely to those of the temporal variety— though the objects pertaining to the latter were incredibly rare.

Someone with a single affinity would be unable to make anything but the smallest of manipulations outside their element, if at all. The potency of the object they were wielding would be irrelevant. If the connection wasn't there to begin with, nothing could will it to life.

Maybe my specialty was time, and time alone. The pendant —I *had* used it in Somraque, as faint as the magic might have been. But this... The dagger just didn't cut it.

A bitter laugh danced through my mental tones at the choice of words. I sank down onto the hardwood floor, lay my back against it, and stared at the recessed ceiling. I heard Mordecai move, but didn't avert my gaze from the two-toned stones that comprised the perimeter—darker—and the central rectangle— lighter—situated several inches higher. It was a thing of beauty, but I could hardly spare a thought on the elaborate design.

I closed my eyes.

My failure should have, by all means, been a good thing in the current situation. If I couldn't rip apart a segment of reality, a prerequisite to bridging the lands, Mordecai wouldn't get what he sought. Not through me.

And yet at the same time, I felt so frustratingly inadequate.

I *had* to learn how to do this.

Otherwise, I would end up stuck in this world, Ada's mission to retrieve and reunite the pieces burned down to ashes, and Somraque permanently under Mordecai's reign. Not that I expected I would see much of the future if I outlived my usefulness.

Some situations were simply bad whichever way you turned them.

"Ember."

I peered to the side. Mordecai was sitting next to me on the floor, his long legs crossed and back slightly hunched. Not the demanding prince any longer, it seemed.

"You opened a portal once. Not just a minor one, as mine are, but a gateway between *worlds*." He fixed me with his sapphire stare. "You'll succeed again."

I lifted myself into a sitting position and tucked my legs beneath me. My fingertips danced along the gleaming leather of my boots, but I looked up at him as I confessed, "I can't remember. I can't remember *anything* about that night, Mordecai."

He stiffened, a vulnerability creeping into his gaze. Several seconds passed before he said, softer than should have been possible given our earlier fallout, "We'll find a way."

"And then what?"

Mordecai didn't answer. He simply stood up and offered me his hand. After a heartbeat of hesitation, I took it, warmth erupting where skin met skin. He pulled me up to my feet. His fingers lingered on mine for a second longer before faint, gentle tendrils of silver started to lap from the back of his hand.

Instinctively, I flinched and backed away, but Mordecai

steadied me. His grip tightened, not enough to hurt, just to keep me from bolting, while his free hand came to rest on my hip.

I sucked in a breath, unable to do anything but hold his gaze as my mind fractured under the tenderness of his touch, the surety it infused me with.

"Don't fear it."

I glanced at the wisps of silver and shuddered. It wasn't *them* I feared.

Mordecai's breath danced across my lips. "The shadowfire is more than a weapon. It's a shield."

The silver washed over our entwined hands—a kiss of winter, a breeze of northern air. Serene.

"The choice of how you wield it is yours."

My gaze dipped down to his mouth, to the way his lips moved so softly, harmoniously as he formed each word, as if he were crafting it anew.

"But it will always be a part of you. A companion. A protector."

My own darkness rose. Tendrils of obsidian uncoiled from my waist and snaked up Mordecai's arm. He shivered, the tremors traveling through his exhales, each vibration crashing into my skin like the waves of the ocean.

"Let them run free," he whispered.

The warmth of his hand on my hip faded, and he was pushing away, the silver following until there was only me, surrounded by undulating embers of the darkest black.

A ghost of a smile haunted Mordecai's lips, one my own mirrored. He stood perfectly immobile, only his shadowfire dancing in tune with mine, coiling to the rhythm of our hearts. Our souls.

I remembered then.

The alley.

The reek of alcohol.

Recoiling.

A tightening in my chest.

Darkness.

The man's mouth contorted into a scream, a gateway for the shadows to steal the flicker of life.

My smile died on my lips, the shadowfire dispelling into nothing.

Mordecai was by my side as I staggered, whatever stability I'd felt now breaking down to brittle rubble. I buried my head in his shoulder and bunched my fingers in the crisp fabric of his jacket. I couldn't hold back the pain any longer. His arms encircled my back, his chin coming to rest on the top of my head while I trembled and wept, letting out the turmoil I'd tried so hard to keep at bay.

Everything, *everything* poured out of me.

The nightmares, the fears. The shame.

And Mordecai embraced it all.

He trailed a hand up my back, all the way to my neck, then traced his fingers along my quickened pulse, again and again, the caresses building up a melody that called me up from the jagged depths and cradled me until my lungs functioned again.

Safe.

Even if the world was not, with Mordecai, *I* was.

He placed a finger beneath my chin, gently lifting it up, but didn't speak. He'd said enough.

"If—if it's my choice... Then why did that man..." I closed my eyes, another tear laying a scalding path down my cheek. "If *I* wield the shadowfire, then I *wanted* his death."

"Perhaps," Mordecai whispered, releasing my chin to brush a

loose strand of hair behind my ear. His fingers lingered. "But not all deaths are equal. Not all make you evil."

I lifted my gaze and sought out the intensity of his. My fingers dug into his jacket as, instead of away, I leaned *in*.

A breath.

That was all that separated his lips from mine.

"My lord..."

Silver exploded from Mordecai as he tore away from me. He snarled at the newcomer neither of us had heard approach. "*What?*"

The guard backed against the wall. His terror was palpable, even when I struggled to adjust to the sudden, harsh absence of Mordecai's warmth.

"There—there's a disturbance at the celebration."

CHAPTER TWENTY-SIX

A DIFFERENT GUARD ESCORTED ME BACK TO MY WING AFTER Mordecai stormed out of the training chamber, his shadowfire whipping behind him in angry tongues that cast the hallway beyond the threshold in pale, cold light. I had the distinct impression the sudden drop in temperature had little to do with the issue he had been called to straighten out. But what said issue had prevented.

He hadn't looked at me as he left, though the stiffness of his spine, the slight angle of his body—they gave the impression that it had taken a lot to contain that glance.

And I...

I wasn't entirely sure how I felt. About any of it, actually.

Once inside my wing, I sat down on the edge of my bed, half expecting Ada to show up and announce the disturbance was their way of getting Mordecai to leave the palace. I presumed he had no particular interest in the festivities now that he already had me trapped between his walls. His absence must have been noted, but even more so, had complicated infiltrating his stronghold.

After all, Ada's plan relied heavily on Mordecai's attention turned elsewhere and his forces spread out. That part hadn't changed even *after* we'd lost the element of surprise—thanks to me.

I shifted on the bed, gazing absentmindedly at the fire as I waited.

No apparition came.

In fact, *nobody* came until Merayin and an older servant with a kind, grandmotherly face brought my meal on the first chime after noon. I cast one last look at the room, then walked outside before I could ponder on whether that was relief I'd felt when it became clear Ada wasn't coming for me just yet.

I ate in my usual spot, with one of the books I had found the previous day keeping me company. To my surprise, it wasn't poetry or tales spun as if plucked from dreams adorning its pages, but *theory*.

On magic.

The leather-bound tome was old, its paper thin and ink slightly faded. The language was archaic, too, but after a few minutes of reading out loud and immersing myself in its sound, I found a way to decrypt the words I hadn't understood initially.

After I finished my meal and notified Merayin I was done, I took the book, along with a cup of tea, to the larger of the two sitting rooms. Bedecked in blue and silver accents, with upholstered, comfortable armchairs, and a view of Nysa just slightly less impressive than the one in the chamber of glass, it had quickly become my second favorite spot in the wing.

Ensconced in silence, I continued my studies.

The book carried no mention of a child born of all three

faces of magic, but there were some intriguing details about the specific manifestations of power. Not entirely unexpected, most pertained to blood magic—on how Illusionists were able to breathe life into their imagination, how Magicians were attuned to the ways of the flesh, able to reach deep inside and artificially stir reactions. It was fascinating, but it wasn't what truly held my intrigue.

My fingers traced down the page depicting a sword, lines of text spreading on each side of the illustrated weapon.

Portals.

All Mordecai had told me, all I had pieced together on my own back at home, was true. The knowledge should have been sufficient to slice open a rip right in the interwoven threads of reality. So why was I failing?

What was I missing?

If I *had* an affinity for both geo and temporal alterations, then, by all means, I should have excelled under Mordecai's guidance.

Musing, I set my finger as a bookmark between the pages.

I'd overheard two heirs at a party once, saying that the High Masters were full of shit—that power wasn't given, but a muscle that had to be flexed, again and again, to develop the needed strength. Dangerous talk... And something that most likely would never have happened if they weren't thoroughly drunk. But maybe their words had merit.

Unfortunately, nothing in the book backed their theory, let alone provided hints as to how one should train said metaphorical muscle.

I closed the book with a gentle *thud*, then carefully rubbed my aching eyes to avoid smearing the faint line of kohl accentuating the corners.

Fine. Maybe I wasn't able to wield portals—not *yet*, if I allowed myself some hope—but there *was* something I could do right now.

The remnants of my tea had gone cold during the time I'd spent with my nose stuck between the pages of the tome, but I drank every last drop of the delicious ginger flavor as I gathered the courage to stand up. I moved farther away from the armchair and table, finding a position on the thick rug that offered the most space.

One exhale.

Another.

I closed my eyes and reached for that icy lake inside me.

Now that I had a better grasp on how it felt, *where* those stirrings had always come from, finding it was easy. I ran my ethereal hands across its placid surface in light, loving caresses.

A companion. A protector.

Mordecai's words slithered through my mind, his smooth voice grounding me and washing away the fear that was still keeping me contained. The moment those barriers fell, the moment I accepted the shadowfire as a part of me, it answered.

Like an animal, reassured that I had no intentions of fleeing should it reveal itself, the darkness came to meet me.

My eyes flew open, a soft gasp fluttering from my lips as small, playful tendrils of lustrous dark rose from my hand. I lifted it closer to my face, the movement careful—not because I feared the power, but because I was afraid of doing anything that might disrupt this kindling bond.

The obsidian tongues coiling through the air grew bolder, wilder as I smiled. My skin was cold where they unspooled from it, yet the sensation wasn't unpleasant.

If anything, it felt right.

Fulfilling.

As if a part of me that had been missing for too long had returned at last.

The obsidian spread up my arm, the tips of the highest embers reaching just above my elbow—like a lively, resplendent glove. I savored its touch of ice, savored the way its tongues seemed to react to my every thought. Calming as I contemplated them. Then becoming vigorous once more as I let a kernel of joy weave its way from the depths of my heart.

Mine.

The shadowfire was mine.

I didn't snuff it out when I went to stand by the window and gazed at Nysa's blue-tinted rooftops spread out below.

Whatever the disturbance Mordecai had gone to deal with was, it didn't seem to impact the pulsing core of the celebrations. The vibrant heart of the town.

Nysa was stunning. From above, the illusion of the blue sky was far more translucent, letting the life that teemed under its dome seep through.

I couldn't see the people milling in the streets, but I could *feel* them.

The thrumming of their magic and lives alike, carried on the air and sifting through the slightly open window as clearly as if I were standing among them. I leaned into its caress, wishing— wishing I could share their joy. The normalcy of a pint of sowhl, with laughter bubbling from the clustered tables. The easiness of knowing there was no greater plan lurking in the depths, only the carefree enjoyment of the evening.

"Would you like to go?"

I whirled around at the voice, my back colliding with the edge of the wall where the stones dipped to nestle the window.

Mordecai was leaning against the doorframe, his sapphire eyes turned on me, and hands resting in his pockets. His black hair was tousled as if the wind outside, caught in the throes of passion, had dragged its fingers through it, and painted a stark contrast to the immaculate way his clothes molded to his body.

The quickening *thump* of my heart pressed against my ears, the memory of how he'd held me in the hall as I broke down, then pieced myself back together, washing over my mind. The memory of what I had almost done, too, that desire to obliterate the last of the distance...

"I didn't mean to startle you," he said, still not moving from his perch.

"You didn't," I admitted, wondering *why* that was. Why I didn't lie to provide grounds for the spell of silence I'd fallen into when I'd seen him. "I was just...thinking."

"So?" His gaze drifted past me to the window, then slowly settled on mine again. "Do you wish to go? Partake in the festivities?"

The shadowfire died down with nothing but a few embers still flickering at the tips of my fingers.

"It's not like you would let me," I said, quieter than I intended.

Mordecai shrugged and peeled away from the doorframe in a ripple of grace.

"Perhaps"—he crossed the room in four elegant strides, stopping just beyond my reach—"there is another way."

CHAPTER TWENTY-SEVEN

THE GUARDS STANDING WATCH AT THE EXIT OF MY WING hesitated only briefly when Mordecai dismissed them before he took me up the winding stairwell. Wordless, I trailed behind him, my gaze resting on his back as he climbed stair after stair, then turned right on the landing. The opposite direction of the chamber under the sky.

I didn't know what he was planning, but something about the way his demeanor had changed when I agreed to his offer kept me from asking. He was as impenetrable as ever, only now, it wasn't the stance of a merciless ruler that crafted his armor, but a resolve to retain my interest—as if he feared I would change my mind along the way.

He needn't have bothered.

Still, Mordecai didn't look back at me, not once, as he strode down a short hallway, then curved his fingers around an ornate handle—this one a full moon rather than the crescent ones dominating the entirety of my chambers—and opened one side of the double-winged doors. Only then, once he stepped to the side to let me pass, did his gaze slide over me. Over the pendant resting atop my chest.

But I was too stunned to pay him attention.

Driven forward by what spread before me, I stepped into the most exquisite ballroom I had ever seen. Ornate pillars rose from the polished floor, each of them crafted to appear as if spirals of clustered stars were reaching for the sky. And between them—nothing but glass and the infinite night. As with the chamber where we had taken our meals, the ceiling here, too, was clear. Only there were no slender iron beams supporting the glass. Nothing. As if the ceiling weren't there at all.

I felt, more than saw, Mordecai walk up to me. His presence was a brush of heat against my back, and involuntarily, I closed my eyes, savoring this stolen touch. It—it didn't feel like betrayal any longer.

I shivered as his fingers undid the band securing my braid then slowly, tenderly, tangled with the strands to let them fall free across my shoulders. Fleeting, faint caresses traveled down my arms before Mordecai spun me around so that I was facing him, his touch lost, but only for a moment.

His hands were tender on mine as he placed a small, silver dagger in my palm, then closed my fingers around the hilt.

My gaze flickered up to his.

The intensity of the sapphire was startling in the demure light of the room. With an expression too complex to read, Mordecai brushed his thumb against my skin, then guided my hand, and the dagger in it, to the palm he held upturned in the nearly nonexistent sliver of space separating our bodies.

He pressed the blade into the pale, unmarred skin.

When he felt my attempt to move away, his grip on my hand

tightened. Not hurting. Not forcing. But steadying me, steadying the dagger as he drew a sharp line of crimson, the thrum of his blood saturating the air and reverberating through my very core.

I didn't dare move as it spread, ensconcing the ballroom, *transforming* it. The magic's caresses swept over my skin, the uniform I hadn't bothered changing from morphing into a flowing gown of midnight blue, with only the glint of gold breaking up the rich color. The aureate details branched down from the bodice all the way to the hem, as if the stars themselves had found a new home there.

Mordecai's blood-kissed hand slipped from mine, his other liberating the dagger from my grip and casting it aside. But as I followed its trajectory, as I expected to find it clatter onto the black marble floor, I saw—

Nysa.

The town's square with its fountain of starlight rose around us, the sounds of revelry, the smell of sowhl and night filling my senses. I drank it in. The people lingering by the tables, chatting, laughing; the sweep of wind bringing a touch of cinnamon and apples as those who danced to the gentle, magnetic music whirled around.

And when I looked at Mordecai, I realized he, too, had changed.

His regal clothes were gone, replaced by an elegant, utterly black tailcoat that emphasized his shoulders and honed waist, the collar of the stark shirt beneath low enough to reveal the black moon tattoos trailing up the side of his neck.

Not the Crescent Prince. But a King of Darkness.

My breath faltered, and heat crept into my cheeks as his gaze swept down my body, then came to rest on my face. His expression never wavered from the chiseled, stoic display, but his eyes...

There was life in them. Wonder.

He offered me his hand, now no longer bleeding. "Care to dance?"

I wasn't entirely certain if I could move, and yet my fingers found his. Mordecai led me through the crowd as if we were truly among them. He sidestepped couples already in the music's thrall, but while he *was* observing them, it was me who had his attention. Not only to measure my reaction, but... But perhaps to replace the death-touched memory of when we had first met with one that could have been ours, had the circumstances been different.

The sentiment was one I shared—and let anchor inside me.

When we arrived at the square of space in the very center of this dreamscape, the obsidian within me shifted.

Ripples of longing. Anticipation.

Only the sensations didn't originate from the shadowfire.

It was *me,* sending the lapping waves along the lake.

The heat of Mordecai's palm was searing where he positioned it on the curve of my waist. He drew me to him, then eased me into the flow of the hauntingly beautiful melody until my body found its own way.

Even then, he didn't let go.

And neither did I.

The illusion—the *world*—around us blurred, my thoughts, my senses belonging to Mordecai and Mordecai alone. I was ensnared, captured in the embrace of his magnetic presence.

I didn't want to break for the surface.

With every turn, we came closer, his gaze never leaving mine, as if he, too, had succumbed to the opulent infection of the spell.

I slipped my hand from his grasp to trail my fingers up his arm, his shoulder, then higher, shifting with each new gliding step until both my hands rested around his neck. Until his found their place at the small of my back, the heat of them drawing me in.

Silver shadows unfurled from Mordecai's back like the most exquisite wings, and my own answered in turn.

Softly craning my neck, I gazed up at him from beneath the fall of my lashes. Those half-parted lips beckoned me. An invitation I yearned to accept.

Behind me, around me, shadowfire fanned. We were a dance of argent and obsidian, dark and light, wishing to become one.

I belonged to the night.

And this time, nothing would stand in the way of its claim.

CHAPTER TWENTY-EIGHT

It was my lips that found his.

A touch so gentle it barely existed, yet it enveloped every inch of me, radiating through my veins and crackling through the very shadows that reached towards the starlit sky beyond the illusion. Mordecai's fingers tightened on the small of my back. I leaned into him and took his lower lip between mine, tasting the night.

"Ember..." he whispered as I let go, just enough to look up into his softly dazed eyes.

Beautiful. He was beautiful. Carved marble crowned with ink.

Mordecai brought one hand up to my face. He brushed away a strand our dance had tossed carelessly over my shoulder, then drew a gentle, curving path down my cheek, my jaw, before sweeping up to my mouth. His thumb lingered in the corner, my smile growing as I entwined a single vine of obsidian shadowfire around the silver of his.

My darkness and his moonlight met.

Mordecai shuddered, then leaned down, close enough for me to feel his breath play across my lips, to sense his heartbeat pulsate through the fragrant air between us. His gaze dipped down to my mouth, catching on the corners still turned up in the ghost of a smile lingering there, gradually receding as it gave way to something else.

A raw, yet fragile hunger his own expression mirrored.

Around us, beyond the veil of shadowfire, the illusion of Nysa flickered, the starlit night seeping through. A discrepancy. A fluke. But one that produced a result far more stunning than the flawlessly crafted sister-realities alone could.

Low, husky laughter escaped me. *Fitting.*

The man before me, my own response to his touch, and the undeniable, unbreakable desire he stirred within me... The sum of what we created was a discrepancy, too.

Yet for all the layers that did not match, I couldn't help but think of it as anything but perfect.

Mordecai raised a brow in silent question. But I couldn't—I couldn't put the swell of everything rushing through me in coherent sentences. So I simply twined one hand in his dark strands, letting the other explore the breadth of his chest. When I felt his pulse beneath my palm, I didn't go farther.

I gazed at him, *feeling* him—

Between one heartbeat and the next, Mordecai slanted his mouth over mine. He pushed my lips apart until I was drowning in the taste of him, ripples of pleasure enflaming my core as his tongue stroked mine. My clothes reverted to the black uniform when one of his hands snaked up my back, but I didn't care.

Not as he guided the other lower, fingers digging into my flesh.

A tremor rushed through his frame as I moved into him.

We stood with nothing but our clothes separating us, and I opened up for his kiss, giving as much as I received. More and more embers of our shadowfire curled around one another, thunder echoing off the glass walls.

His fingers found their way to the nape of my neck, across the silver chain, tensing, then—

Gone.

Mordecai staggered back, his sapphire eyes wild and breathing frantic. As was mine. The silver tongues lashed out around him, untamed, uncontrolled. Frenzied.

As he reeled them in, as my own calmed, my lips still burning from his hunger, reality slammed back into my mind in a tidal wave that obliterated the haze. I watched my own reemergence through the pain clouding Mordecai's gaze, but it did not stop me from mourning the loss of tenderness as his features became an immaculate, harsh landscape again.

Mourning it more than I feared the threat of doubt—the hurt I wanted to deny, but couldn't—whispering my ruination.

"We try the portals again tomorrow afternoon," he said with cold indifference, though the velvet of his voice was hoarse.

A nod. That was all I could give him as he strode out of the ballroom, the shadowfire no longer following in his wake.

MORDECAI WAS absent from breakfast the next morning. But so were the guards.

While I couldn't leave the palace—even if it weren't for the sentries on the perimeter or the solid wall of air still blocking off the windows, I wasn't as naive as to believe he would drop *all* precautions—it seemed Mordecai had nonetheless decided to lift some of the restrictions.

After his abrupt exit the previous night, I had to admit the absence of my watchers had taken me by surprise. Merayin, however, didn't as much as bat an eyelash when she escorted me upstairs. To the grating silence.

I didn't have the nerve to think about the ballroom on the opposite end, so I dug into the food, decidedly steering my mind in another direction.

This new lack of confinement would greatly aid my cause of finding the damned relic. I had to fulfill my end, but even more so, I desperately needed to distract myself. To *leave* this place before whatever madness had driven me to kiss Mordecai yesterday—to take things further, had he not retreated—sank its talons deeper and erased what little sanity I was holding on to.

Not madness, a voice whispered.

I frowned at it and stuffed it down into the deepest, darkest pocket of my mind.

Darkest, it crooned in echo.

I crooned, I realized with horror.

Darkness.

Where I belong.

By the Sun... I fled from the chamber and down the stairs, the guards on the landing—not standing sentry, but conversing —barely glancing my way as I pushed into a wing. I didn't know where I was going, only that I wanted to get away from that wretched voice. Escape its merciless clawing before it took down every reinforced wall I had built during my sleepless night.

It was easy to lose sight of things, isolated as I was with no counterweight to balance the scales. Easy to convince myself

Mordecai was the only person I could show my true face to—who wouldn't see me as a monster because he, too, was one.

I pressed my back into a shadowed alcove and closed my eyes, breathing deeply.

No, I was being unfair.

I had long ago ceased to think of him as such. I wouldn't revert to prejudices and blind conviction just because I was panicking. Because I was *hurt*.

My fingers outlined the contours etched in the stone encompassing me from three sides.

The truth always had many faces. I had never accepted only one and discarded the rest simply because they didn't fit into the way I viewed the world. What if—what if what I felt was just as true, just as right as what Ada saw? That our juxtaposed experiences were all valid?

The image of our joined shadowfire danced at the back of my eyelids. Darkness and light. United opposition.

Perhaps Mordecai was capable of kindness. Perhaps he even...*felt* something for me.

But none of that changed what he was to the rest of Somraque.

And what Somraque saw in their ruler didn't change how *I* felt when I was with him.

A mess. It was all one great mess, but in this chaos, I found my way. My plan hadn't changed. I only needed to be careful not to give in to this incessant tugging that craved the Crescent Prince's company. *More* than just his company.

Yes, Mordecai and I were alike. But only to a certain point.

I was still tucked in the alcove when two maids exited one of the chambers down the hall, their voices carrying to me as they moved towards the next set of doors. Keeping myself as immobile as I could, I kept out of sight and listened to their lightly accented speech.

"Yours will be northern wings on this, and the next floor up. We take shifts every fortnight. During your next rotation, you will aid Vanaan in the kitchens, as well as make sure the stableboys have everything they need. If not, you make a note of it and report to me, understood?"

"Yes." Footsteps, then— "You—will you not clean here?"

"The prince's private study?" The first voice huffed, though there was a stiff undercurrent to the amusement. "My dear, you will want for nothing in the palace. But if you want to keep those golden curls on your shoulders, I suggest you *never* attempt to enter that chamber."

I pressed myself deeper into the alcove, angling my head so that not a strand of silver would show.

"He—he cleans it himself?"

Another huff. This one devoid of emotion. "I don't care what he does, and neither should you. Understand?"

"Yes, Viensa."

"Now," the first voice—Viensa—continued as they walked on —right towards where I was secreted away in the shadows. "Have you spoken to Merayin yet? You are to lodge with her and Salla. Those girls are loud, but don't let them bother you..."

A gleam of golden hair.

A second figure. Smaller. But with a demanding quality etched in the straight line of her back, the profile marked with age but no less sharper for it.

Words resonated through the air, but none registered as I stood there, plastered against the stones until they warmed under my skin.

The breath that whizzed from my lungs when they cleared

the hallway at last was long—too long. My head was a little dizzy from the lack of oxygen, so I had no choice but to rest against the wall for a few moments longer despite the impatience ratcheting up inside. The instant I felt like myself again, I peeled from the shadows. I spared nothing but the barest of glances at the several doors pressed into the corridor before I hurried in the other direction.

Seven.

Seven doors.

It was a start.

MERAYIN BROUGHT me lunch with the notice that my training session with Mordecai was postponed until the next day. I wondered whether he had been called off to deal with another disturbance, or if the sudden lack of pushing me to open portals had something to do with the previous night.

I didn't linger on that slippery slope of thoughts for too long.

I finished my meal, rereading certain passages from the book on the theory and application of magic, then, when Merayin returned to clear away the dishes, asked her where I could find more. She directed me to a chamber in the wing opposite mine. I thanked her for the information but didn't go looking straight away. Instead, I retreated to my bedroom and locked the door behind me.

After a few seconds of waiting for the slight tremors that still plagued me to pass, I called to the shadowfire.

Mordecai might not have felt like training me, but I certainly had no desire to wait around. I had never been good at that sort of thing.

The obsidian answered almost instantly, the tongues flowing from my skin and up towards the ceiling. I studied them, the way they moved...

I willed the icy lake to rise. Then calm. And rise again.

There was no double awareness now, nothing to startle me or break my concentration. Nothing to stand in the way of my wishes.

Gingerly at first, I infused the cool depths with my desires.

A single vine, extending farther than others.

Wings of obsidian flexing at my back.

The shadowfire fanned as I laughed—the burst of disbelieving joy translating as smoothly as any command I had given.

We were one. And as I let that fact settle in my core, I ventured further.

Even the weakest of thoughts manifested itself in the way the shadowfire coiled through the air. Attuned to my instincts, my reactions, as well as strands of rational commands, it was seamless. Faultless.

Protection, Mordecai had said.

And I believed him.

Inch by inch, I willed the obsidian to spread, to ensconce me in its darkness until I couldn't see the walls of the chamber any longer. Only a glimpse of the ceiling remained high above me, surrounded by a flaming circle of the deepest black where the embers reached towards one another but failed to touch.

With an exhale, I released my hold and folded the power back inside my body. Good.

When the time came, I wouldn't be defenseless.

CHAPTER TWENTY-NINE

SOMETHING SLITHERED OVER THE EDGES OF MY AWARENESS. Any traces of sleep I had been cocooned in for the past hours evaporated immediately, my body prone under the covers.

But the shadowfire—it waited.

Kept my fear at bay.

The chamber was dark with only a single fire burning beyond the archway, quiet, the night—the time of it, not just the endless star-sprinkled sky—still in full bloom, though crawling towards morning. While I trusted the shadowfire to shield me, I still didn't move beyond tilting my head to survey the room. Nothing was out of place, and yet—

The peculiar sensation intensified.

If it weren't for the utter lack of sound, I would have missed the muffled thrumming, the mark of magic that coalesced. I latched onto it with every scrape of my awareness—and found its heart.

Right at the foot of my bed.

"Ember..." A weak voice.

I pushed myself up into a sitting position, the duvet pooling around my waist. "Ada?"

The illusion of her formed before my eyes, fainter than the last time I saw her. *She* looked thinner, too, with bags under her eyes and deep-set grooves encasing her mouth. Even her fiery hair was lackluster, curls sagging across her shoulders and down the simple, slightly ragged tunic.

Worn from the use of magic, I realized. *From being on the run.*

"You sure know how to choose your timing," I said dryly, just to get *some* emotion from her.

The jade in her irises warmed. Good enough.

"It's easier at night. Less interference."

But also more chances of discovery the longer she kept it up, I suspected. Still, I couldn't help asking, "Are you all right?"

Ada didn't deign to answer. Her gaze was drinking in my image, undoubtedly noting the stark opposite my well-kept state was to hers. It was an effort not to fidget, draw the covers higher and hide the pristine nightclothes hugging my skin.

"Did you find the relic?" Her voice cut through my guilt.

I shook my head. "But I think I know where it could be. I intend to investigate as soon as Mordecai leaves the palace."

The illusion flickered. "Do you need a diversion?"

"If you can manage... But if it's more trouble than it's worth, I'll find another way. Swear to me you won't take any unnecessary risks, Ada."

I still had no idea whether they had lured Mordecai away the last time—if it had been on purpose, had they stood behind the disturbance, or rather an unexpected, obstructive turn of events. The thought didn't sit well with me, and I hated the idea of them sticking their necks out—again, or for the first time in this capacity. Unless... Unless they were *absolutely* certain they would be in the clear long before Mordecai's wrath descended upon the town.

Ada glanced around, though I got a distinct feeling it wasn't my chamber she was seeing, but the reality in which her true form existed. "We'll get it done. This afternoon."

"This afternoon?"

Soon. So soon it bordered on impulsive.

The leaden weight in my stomach grew heavier. I reminded myself that Ada was skilled. That she wouldn't get caught—or let anyone else fall.

But the fact that this was the *second* question she chose not to answer concerned me.

What was it that Eriyan had said? *Worse than Lyra with a bone.*

Ada was an immovable force. I just hoped her nature didn't blindside her. A single chink in her armor was all it would take...

Pushing aside the grim thought, I studied her, confirming she *was* interacting with her own surroundings. It was almost staggering, the difference, when her attention homed in on me once more.

"I can't linger." A flicker, as if to back up the statement. But when her backlit form solidified again, her gaze was far clearer than before. "We plan to breach the palace on the last night of the celebrations, when the festivities reach their peak," she said, then added, softer, "We're getting you out, Ember. Can you hold on until then?"

The phantom heat of Mordecai's lips on mine scorched my memory. I let loose a breath and nodded. "I can."

Ada cocked her head to the side. For a moment, I thought she was going to comment on my hesitation, however brief it might have been.

Because there could be no mistaking my reluctance, even if I tried to mask it into fear, then conviction, as I said more soundly, "I can hold on for three more days."

Mercifully, she only dipped her chin after a few torturous seconds, the illusion of her turning more and more translucent.

"I'll try to contact you when we have the details."

"Be careful," was all I said as the colors faded, leaving me alone in my bedroom once more.

I slumped back down on the bed, then burrowed my head in the pillow. But as hard as I tried, the incessant roll of my thoughts refused to give way to sleep.

For all my supposed affinity for time, I sure was running short on it.

⠀

"AGAIN, EMBER. TRY AGAIN."

I cut a sharp look at Mordecai where he was standing by the wall, the gleam from the sconces reflecting off his hair. With his arms crossed and cool disinterest shaping his features, I could almost believe his lingering on the sidelines had nothing to do with maintaining his distance from me.

Almost.

While *that* was a relief, my continued, constant failure to open a damn portal certainly wasn't.

Even after I'd scoured the small, but well-stocked library yesterday for any books I could find on magic—not as many as I'd hoped—and read even the most marginal of mentions on how to command space, I still couldn't push that damned gap open.

Mordecai's instructions bore no fruit, either.

It was becoming frustrating, to say the least.

In order to reunite the fragments, I would have to actually get my hands on them. Svitanye. Soltzen. If each land harbored a piece of the relic, the first step to locating them was to *be* on the same plane.

Doing Mordecai's bidding or working with Ada—it made little difference if I couldn't progress from phase one.

But most of all, it was the deadline breathing down my neck that set me on edge.

There wasn't that much point in escaping if Ada broke me out of the palace *before* I mastered this ability. With Mordecai overseeing my training, there was at least a chance we'd work out my *performance issues* eventually. Alone, that hope dwindled.

I chanced a look at him—at that flawless mask—and suppressed a groan.

I *couldn't* leave before I succeeded...

Mordecai would hunt us—of that I was certain—and we would be stuck in Somraque, the *savior* completely useless. More than useless, actually. A dead weight.

Without being able to wield blood magic, I could hardly hold my own if it came to us being on the run. I thought of the pendant, tucked beneath the black uniform, its surface warm against my skin.

Sun damn me, even if I had to shred myself to pieces, I *would* do this.

The innate vibrations of magic spread through my exhausted body, linking me with the blade I held in my hand as seamlessly as if it had been the pendant. But this part had always been easy.

Gritting my teeth, I channeled every thought, every ounce of power into the dagger as I sliced it through the air and broke up the threads that held reality together to fuse new connections.

Darkness gaped, thin and sharp, but even as the air shimmered, even as I willed it to grow, to open up until I could glimpse my own bedchamber lying on the other side—the cursed thing collapsed.

Sun...

"One would think that for all your people had done, this majestic bloodline of yours would not be so damn pitiful," Mordecai sneered.

The iciness in his tone whirled me around. I clutched the bone handle tighter. "*What?*"

"You Soltzeniens think you're so grand"—he pushed off the wall, each stride slow, demanding—"that your magic is above what comes from the body, *cleaner.*"

I inched back, suddenly *very* aware this anger encompassed more than just my current inability.

I forced myself to stop moving lest it fueled that predatory wrath.

"And yet"—his eyes flashed—"you fail to complete even the simplest of tasks. Is there *nothing* you can do right?"

Thunder boomed in my ears, my breaths deepening in tune with the fire igniting in my veins. I should have asked what he'd meant, why this hatred for my people, for Soltzen, the buried echoes of some sort of history that hadn't released him from its clutches—or one he had chosen to shackle himself to. Yet all I heard was the poison dripping from his words—the viciousness now directed at *me.*

I exhaled, only it wasn't serenity that filled the vacancy.

"You know what? Screw you, Mordecai. I haven't been here a *week*, and you expect me to do something I have not only never been trained for, but haven't been allowed to even *think* of for eighteen years? I don't know if your knowledge of the other worlds is that rusty—although I doubt it, given how you like to insult us every chance you get—or if you're just that self-absorbed. But I'm a High Master's daughter, Mordecai. *Daughter.* Sun, how many times do I have to repeat it to you people!

"All my life, I was nothing but a tool to my father. Trust me, if you think I'm pitiful now, then you can't even imagine what I would have been like if I hadn't fought him every damn step of the way." I threw the dagger at one of the armoires lining the wall, and the tip embedded itself deep in the wood. I didn't even have it in me to be surprised. "My father had his purposes, as I'm sure you have nefarious ones of your own. But I am *not* an object to be wielded and taken advantage of at your convenience. I'm done. I'm done being everyone's pawn."

CHAPTER THIRTY

Mᴀ ᴍᴏᴏᴅ ᴡᴀs ᴘᴏsɪᴛɪᴠᴇʟʏ ꜰᴏᴜʟ ᴀꜰᴛᴇʀ I ʟᴇꜰᴛ Mᴏʀᴅᴇᴄᴀɪ ᴀɴᴅ marched up to my chambers. Not even his stunned, if tested, silence could curb the storm raging within me.

Merayin made her presence scarce, staying for no longer than what was necessary for her to bring me lunch—then clear away the plates. It was unfair to her, I knew, but that part of me that would have cared... It was locked under impervious layers.

I didn't regret anything I'd said down in the training hall. Perhaps only wished I'd uttered those words sooner.

Some *savior* indeed.

Tendrils of obsidian shot from my flesh, lashing out at the air and twisting in tune with my anger—but also honing it.

Instead of succumbing to the impulse to lay waste to this wing, this palace, the chaotic drive narrowed, coating my thoughts in merciless ice.

Maybe the three worlds deserved to rot. Maybe the reason they had broken apart in the first place was because this supposed harmony and balance magic sought was too deeply corrupted by the people to ever liberate itself from the twisted, festering depths of our reality.

The price for greed. For the inadvertent death of the Ancients our forefathers had caused—an immortal people they had attempted to eradicate, yet lingered on by a thread, just as tainted as the rest of it.

I was more than inclined to let them all pay.

Why should I give everything, anything, when the world had not extended the same courtesy?

A knock sounded at the door.

I glared at it, contemplating blocking the entrance with shadowfire and be done with it.

In the end, I hissed, "Yes?"

The door swung aside, revealing Mordecai's form, but the Crescent Prince didn't enter. His gaze skimmed the darkness swirling around me, the fury I could feel resting on my face.

"I came to apologize." He hesitated. "May I come in?"

I snorted and fixed him with a hard stare. "It's your palace."

Mordecai remained on the other side of the threshold. He raked a hand through his hair, looking...lost.

I hated it—I hated *him*—but I gave him the consent he wanted in the form of a curt nod. The shadowfire, however, I left on display.

With evident caution that, on some disturbing level, pleased me, he walked over to the book-strewn table, as close as he could without coming within reaching distance of my obsidian flame.

"It was...uncalled for. What I said earlier." He met my gaze. "I was too hard on you, and for that I am truly sorry."

My shadowfire calmed as the sincerity of his tone struck me deep in my chest. "Then why were you?"

He strode past me to the window, his hands tucked behind his back, fingers clenched. "I've waited for millennia for someone who possesses the power to open gates between realms. Ages of monitoring every atom of air for that trace of magic... I have grown impatient." He turned around, the sapphire falling on my face, darkening. "All that time, I have spent in solitude. I—I am not used to being around other people."

The truth. But not the entirety of it.

"And I suppose that doesn't have anything to do with you *terrorizing* your own people?"

A shadow flickered across his eyes, his body stiffening. "I have some business to attend to this evening, but I would very much like to have lunch with you tomorrow, Ember. I might not be able to give you all the answers, but those I can... They are yours, if you want them."

My eyebrows rose, a refusal dancing on the tip of my tongue.

I angled my head. "Fine."

I SPENT the hours after midday in a small chamber overlooking the inner courtyard, the pile of books I'd hauled along with me stacked on the table by my side. One of the tomes lay open in my lap, but I was hardly paying attention to the words as I kept glancing at the window, waiting to catch that glimpse of lean darkness cut through the somber light.

Between Ada's distraction and Mordecai's own business, whatever it was, I was eager to start exploring. And if I indeed found the relic, well, it would be *my* choice what to do with it the instant I was liberated from the castle walls. Portal or not.

The soft clicking of hooves snagged me from my thoughts. I peered over the windowsill, watching the rider atop the black stallion speed across the courtyard, his guards in tow. Despite everything, I found myself holding my breath at the sight, my gaze fixed on the straight line of Mordecai's back, the dark hair that undulated in tune with the smooth, liquid motion of his mount.

Devastation personified.

The moniker seemed fitting. So fitting, in fact, that the thought extracted me from whatever thrall I'd once again succumbed to even before he cleared the gateway.

Casting the book onto the armchair I vacated, I rushed out into the hallway, then down its length, grateful for the uniform I was still wearing as I hurtled myself in the proper chamber and sprinted across to the window with a clear view of the path leading to Nysa. I spotted Mordecai instantly, his stallion aiming for the town as the guards rode in a spacious, yet firm formation around him.

I exhaled. This was it.

Quickly, although seemingly without haste, I made my way towards the wing harboring Mordecai's private study. As I passed a few servants and guards, I kept my chin high and my steps filled with intent, as if I had every right to walk the palace grounds. Mercifully, I truly did.

All the time I hadn't spent brooding, I had made sure to explore the palace, letting the people here grow accustomed to my presence. And now, even as I took a turn into the wretched wing—the single place I *hadn't* entered since that day—they paid me no more attention beyond a perfectly normal acknowledging look. After all, no one had explicitly prohibited *me* from entering this section. Or its rooms.

I tried three of the doors, but even before I peered inside, I knew they weren't the answer. The maids had their orders, but I didn't for one moment believe Mordecai would leave his study unlocked.

Nevertheless, I checked each and every one on the off chance my hunch was misleading.

I spared the contents—a sitting room, a smaller version of the training hall, a workspace, though one that didn't seem as if it were in use—only a brief glance. The fourth, however, I slipped inside, driven by the cascade of light footfalls.

A servant... A maid, by the sound of it.

The moment I was inside the room, I cursed myself for the impulsive reaction.

Even if she had run into me in the hallway, I could have feinted going somewhere and that would have been it. If I'd had enough time to enter the chamber and shut the door behind me, then I could have easily moved *away* from it, too.

I smothered a groan.

When the footsteps neared, I pushed deeper into the room, though I didn't take my eyes off the door just yet. No, this was still salvageable. As long as I kept the panic—and with it more ill-conceived decisions—at bay. If, by chance, she walked in and saw me pressed up against the wall like a thief or standing pinned in one place, *waiting* for discovery, it would raise far more suspicions than appearing busy in—

The bedroom.

I swore under my breath.

What were the chances that from all the Sun-damned chambers, the one I stumbled into just had to be a seductive spill of velvet and silk?

My gaze flashed to the large four-poster bed dominating the

middle, an empty wineglass perched on the carved nightstand, a book, its pages worn as if Mordecai had read it countless times, beside it. Between it and the first of the windows, an archway similar to the one in my own bedchamber veered out of sight.

I looked away before visions of his body, bedecked in traveling droplets of water overtook my mind—

Only to find I had done myself no favors.

With no other furnishings, nothing save for the chiseled phases of the moon cresting along the midnight walls, my treacherous attention returned to the bed. My cheeks heated viciously as I couldn't stop drinking in the black lining, the mound of pillows scattered about all too invitingly. It was easy to imagine Mordecai sprawled across them, his hair blending with the silk and his skin bringing forth a stark contrast from where it peeked from beneath the sheets.

I shook myself mentally, then dug my fingernails into the palms of my hands before I could do something foolish. Like run my fingers over the alluring black expanse.

The *click-click-click* of the maid's low heels produced that final jolt that saved me.

I had forgotten about her.

Forgotten that I was supposed to have come up with a believable excuse to be in this chamber. But I didn't dare crawl onto that bed, pretend I was here...for him.

My inner battle stretched on for so long, I would have been discovered in my worthless, unprepared state a dozen times over had I not been granted a reprieve.

Those steps, while still loud, still close, were growing fainter.

On silent feet, I stalked back to the door and listened. Followed the maid's path to the landing.

A greeting.

A second set of footsteps.

Then...

Gone.

Counting the seconds to make sure no surprises lurked on the other side was a test of my nerves.

My hand trembled when I reached for the handle at last, but the wait had been worth it. There was no one left in the corridor but me. In fact, the entire wing was doused in silence.

I didn't waste another moment.

After trying two more doors, I found one that wouldn't give way under my touch. Out of instinct, I glanced around to make sure that I was, indeed, alone, then produced two slender pins, the silver strands I had swept away from my face now tumbling down the side of my neck.

Ada wasn't the only one with weapons in her hair, even if mine were designed for frowned-upon deeds of a different kind.

It was second nature to straighten the pins—and have my way with the lock.

My father had quickly taken to sealing his doors in hopes of keeping me out, so I had been forced to uncover early on how proper leverage and just the right touch could help me to overcome those obstacles. Thankfully, Mordecai wasn't using the same magic that barricaded the windows in conjunction with the lock. Otherwise, no amount of skill would have made a difference.

The distinct *snick* was like music to my ears. I carefully pushed open the door, slipped inside, then shut it firmly behind me.

Again, the discrepancy between my expectations and reality stunned the breath out of me.

I pressed my back against the wood, my chest swelling as I beheld the grandeur.

A library. Mordecai's study was a *library*.

Not the kind of bare-boned collection we had at the Norcross estate, or the cobweb- and dust-covered trunks from which I'd pilfered those tales of night. It wasn't even the display of carefully organized tomes Merayin had shown me to—

But an actual temple of books.

My lips parted as I swept my gaze across the two levels of the chamber, all of them filled with looming bookcases where not a single inch of space remained between the beautiful cloth- and leather-bound volumes. The space was illuminated by lanterns, every single one of them crafted with an artist's devotion to detail.

It was... It was as if I had stepped into another world.

A silent, husky laugh bubbled from my lips.

Another world within another world.

A massive, dark-wood desk dominated the middle of the space, one brocade armchair resting on each of the longer sides. The smooth surface, as well as the chairs, were littered with discarded books, much like the ones I had found up in my wing. Sun...

It hadn't been servants after all. But Mordecai.

Spending hours in the chambers I now occupied, perhaps gazing down at Nysa while resting his eyes between paragraphs —much like I did—was not an image he projected. Even in those moments when he was not the Crescent Prince, only Mordecai, there was still...something about him. Something that, perhaps, showed promise of an entirely different side, but not to the extent this revelation had taken it.

And yet for all the peculiarity, the vision also rang true.

I bit my lip. No, now wasn't the time for any of this.

I forced my booted feet to move, coming closer to the desk when something caught my eye on the upper level. It peeked from above the long line of bookcases pressed against the banister, just a wash of color and thread that did not belong to the marvelous tomes. I climbed the stairs to the next floor, realizing it was far larger than I had first imagined.

Mordecai must have modified this part of the palace—or my own perception of the layout was skewed—because what had at first appeared only as a small semi-circular landing actually curved to the left and opened up into another chamber. As much as I itched to explore it, it wasn't there that my steps took me, but straight ahead to the tapestry on the wall I had spied from below. It was enormous, as tall as the bookshelves and as wide as three of them pressed together.

A map.

A map of the world.

Not Somraque or one of the other fractured lands. But the world as it had once been.

The two concentric circles Ada had drawn that day with her finger were now in front of me, yet where hers had been a simple illustration to help me grasp the mechanics, this was crafted with beautiful detail and enriched with colors time had touched, but failed to fade.

I traced my fingers across the left-side curve, Somraque, then followed the line as it spilled into Svitanye before finally reaching Soltzen. Three individual lands, the only separator between them a thin line the artist had drawn. And in the heart of it all, an ornate orb. Magic.

I didn't know how long I stared at the map, how long I let it break apart everything I knew and etch this depiction of the past—of the future we could have, if I succeeded, into my very heart. I traced the circular outline of the world once more, then pressed my fingertips to the elaborate orb, my nail catching on a groove that lurked beyond the thick layer of interwoven threads.

I sucked in a breath.

Too easy. This was too easy. And yet when I lifted the tapestry, rolled it onto the narrow ledge running alongside its top, I saw the small latch in the stone.

By the Sun...

I hooked my fingers into it and pulled. The stone moved away from the wall, taking several others right along with it. They surged towards me, then slid to the side until what lay before me wasn't a wall any longer, but a room.

Modest in size and cast in darkness, it harbored numerous artifacts on the narrow shelves stacked from the floor to the flat ceiling. I stepped aside, letting the light from the library pool into the chamber, then ran my gaze across these treasures, all with the air of ages past to them, regardless of how pristine they looked.

All from the time the world had still been whole, it dawned on me.

Jewelry, weapons, sculptures—

A familiar crest.

I stepped inside without thinking about repercussions. The stale air drew around me like heavy curtains, but thankfully no malevolent magic lay in wait.

Still, my lungs felt tight with the lack of oxygen as I stared at the sword, at the image etched into the pommel I would recognize anywhere. The burning sun, a blade running down its center.

My family's sigil.

Pushing past the deafening pounding in my ears, I reached

for the weapon, almost a twin to my father's, wondering what kind of power it possessed when something tugged at my core. A silent, yet unmistakable call, beckoning me to answer.

I spun on my heel and nearly rammed into the shelf as I searched for the source. Nothing stood out, but I walked across the shaft of light spilling down the length of the floor, following the general direction of the sensation.

More echoes of a past time, more objects brushed clean of dust, but for all their history, none struck me as important. Not in the way the tug was suggesting.

And yet...it intensified when I came to stand in front of the shelves.

As if something—

As if something were blocking the signal.

I shifted aside a small, peculiar-looking statue. Nausea churned in my stomach as everything inside me muted for a horrible second while my skin touched the stone. Grimacing, I set it aside, then teetered backwards as my senses returned to me and that bond, that pull of guidance, slammed into me with unbarred strength.

I steadied myself with a hand against the wooden ledge, but looked, far too fast, at the space I'd cleared. My knees went weak. My mind swam with the sudden rush of blood and lack of oxygen at the same time. Barely holding it together, I lifted my trembling fingers—almost not daring to touch the broken fragment, a third of what had once been a disk.

The relic.

I swallowed deeply and did my best to ignore the lethal blend of trepidation, relief, and...power. Dormant power, but one that set my insides alight.

A sob wrenched itself free from my throat, and I reached forward, obliterated that sliver of distance—

Only to find my hand snatched back with such force my already precarious balance shattered.

I staggered, catching myself on one of the shelves with my elbow, but the other arm remained immobile, pinned by a coiling strand of silver, wrapped tightly around my wrist and whispering of death.

CHAPTER THIRTY-ONE

"You can thank your friends for this." Mordecai's sharp, icy voice coiled around me, just as tightly and unyieldingly as did his shadowfire.

My gut, my lungs—everything inside me froze over. Even the shadowfire went numb under this oppressive, glacial wrath that pulsed from Mordecai.

I'd met the Crescent Prince at last.

And I wasn't sure I would survive the encounter.

That *anything* could.

The cold radiating from him was leagues beyond even the worst outburst I'd seen, my skin burning beneath the shackle of silver.

"I suppose *I* should be the one thanking them," he continued in his cool whisper. "If they hadn't acted out, I would have never raced back here to see if *you*, darling Ember, were all right. Safe."

He spat that last word, fury catching on its edges.

I opened my mouth, but no words came. My body was locked up so soundly, I couldn't even shiver.

His backlit form stalked closer, blocking the exit. Not that I was capable of running. Not that he would let me cross that threshold alive.

The near-black sapphire of his eyes scrutinized the terror that must have been etched in my face, but there was no response—no flicker of emotion, as if he were beyond such a mortal thing.

Faintly, I sensed the hard edges of the shelves digging into my back. I hadn't even realized I'd inched back, ensnared in the dispassionate brutality of his gaze.

"Tell me, what did you intend to do?" He prowled across the stones, another vine of shadowfire snaking around my waist, preventing me from moving away as he crushed the distance between us, one harsh step at time. "Steal the relic and take it to your band of misfits? Or perhaps destroy it, to keep me from unleashing your powers upon the world? From *exploiting* your potential?"

The way he said it—it was as if he were recounting someone else's words.

Ada...

What had he done? What had we *all* done?

A glint of steel caught my eye, but the scream died in my parched throat as Mordecai unsheathed the bone handle dagger, the lethal bite of its blade hovering mere inches from my body.

One thrust and it would be over. The blood he had searched for so long spilling across the smooth stones...

Tears burned at the back of my eyes—dread and frustration at this utter helplessness alike—but didn't fall.

Mordecai's free hand replaced the shadowfire digging into

my waist and crushed me against his rock-hard body the instant he shifted away the blade. With unbarred strength, he spun me around, then pinned my back to his torso, the dagger now in line with my throat.

But not on it.

I swallowed.

"You think this is some game?" he whispered into my ear. "You believe you and your friends are so noble, fighting for a just cause, keeping the darkness at bay..." I trembled as his lips brushed against my skin. "As if you could ever hope to comprehend what true darkness means."

With that, the dagger cut through the air, and I was plummeting, losing the reality around me as Mordecai shoved us both through the thin wisps of a portal.

BARREN LAND MATERIALIZED beneath my feet. Mordecai's steel grip held me upright as I struggled for balance, but there was nothing comforting in his touch. A prison ensconcing its captive.

My jaw clenched, I braced myself against the whipping wind that had begun to ratchet and lifted my gaze from the desolated rock to—

Nothing.

I flattened myself against Mordecai's chest.

It was not the dark of the night that rose before me, but a canvas so black it was colorless. Endless.

Alive somehow.

And lethal.

The shadowfire that had been paralyzed before now

retreated, folding itself in a tight mass of obsidian that urged me to do the same. To flee. To take us away from here—

"The Void." Mordecai's voice slithered past my ear as he motioned to the terrifying darkness with the tip of the dagger. "The barrier lining the edges of Somraque."

His heartbeat reverberated into my back, but I was too busy controlling my own to think of how at odds the heavy pulsing was with his icy words. With every ounce of strength I still possessed, I hung on to the eroding threads that were keeping me from yielding ground to the animalistic, primal response the unnaturalness of the Void that extended bare inches from my toes was bringing to the surface.

I didn't think I could reclaim my humanity if that fear consumed me whole.

Sweat coated my forehead in spite of the chilly wind, bile rising at the back of my throat. I wanted to plead. Beg Mordecai to take me away—

His fingers tightened where they dug into the side of my waist, just below the ribs. He pressed me tighter against him— comforting or securing his grip, it made no difference. It was a kernel of strength I latched onto with all I had.

If he murdered me now, it would be a mercy.

"The people here accept the Void as if this were how the world was always meant to be. They fear it, but they also look the other way. A terror they don't understand, but believe is powerless to touch them as long as they don't acknowledge it." The cool touch of the dagger lay against my thigh, almost imperceptibly traveling higher. "They are too absorbed in their short, fleeting lives to look beyond the realm of comfort and their own pleasures. Even the old Mage bloodlines, with their fucking high opinions of themselves, seek the truth without wanting to accept what lies within their grasp.

"The Void, *savior*, is growing. Like a river eroding the earth, it spreads inward, feeding on our reality. In a few centuries, perhaps millennia—if we are lucky—it *will* consume us all."

I braced myself against the rage pouring off his body as he shoved us closer, so close that there was nothing but that pit of black filling my vision.

"*This* is the nightmare, Ember, that none of us will wake from," he whispered.

Then I was sucked back, a scream wrenching itself from my lips and dying in the distance as the sound remained trapped on the other side of the portal while we were once again in the library, standing just outside the vault.

I barely forced my mind to stop spinning when Mordecai turned me around and backed me up against the wall. Shadowfire fanned in a wide, glorious arc behind him.

He trapped me between the cold stones and the fever of his body, those sapphire eyes burning as they locked on mine.

"Did you truly believe"—his words grazed my lips—"that *children* could hope to reunite the realms before the Void finishes its hungry crawl? Children who are no more than yet another facet of this ignorant population, feeding the darkness precisely what it needs to spread?"

CHAPTER THIRTY-TWO

"W-WHAT?" I STAMMERED, BUT THE SOUND WAS WEAK. FEEBLE.

Too many forces ripped at my mind, my heart cleaving—two pieces, a million, I could hardly tell. I was bleeding from the cut of Mordecai's words, drowning in terror of the gaping hole in the fabric of reality that was the Void—from the image of that darkness spreading, devouring this world until no trace of it existed, as if it had never even been.

No more illusions. No starlit sky. No jesting over rounds of sowhl.

Nothing.

It wasn't the obsidian of shadowfire that blackened my vision. With a silent scream, I closed my eyes and sought that lake within me—the ally who shared my fears. And would walk alongside me.

When I, at last, wrenched myself free from the pit, Mordecai's turbulent gaze greeted me.

"What do you mean, feed it?" I asked again, then dared to touch my fingers to his elbow. "Mordecai, I don't understand..."

The sapphire storm continued to blaze, yet something... thawed. Far from a reconciliation, but I—I wanted more than answers.

I wanted him back.

A tick worked in his jaw. He leaned back, his body still keeping me pinned to the wall, but allowing a sliver of space to slip between us.

"Every time magic falls out of balance, the Void grows—and the beast will continue to expand, devouring everything unless the worlds come together. The three branches of power even each other out. A great accumulation of magic, a concentration of power beyond what suffices for a normal life could still tip the scales, but the margin is wider. And the consequences not as grave. Here, now, every ripple out of line carries to the Void— and, in turn, brings it closer. The world truly *is* broken, Ember. It's broken, and it's dying from its own jagged ends." His gaze dipped down, then slowly crawled back up to my face. "I had wanted to tell you this. I *would* have told you this over our meal. But you had no intention of listening to me, did you?"

My fingers fell from his elbow.

"No intention of accepting *why* I needed to use you, because all you heard was that single word. *Use.*"

Deep-set anguish flashed in Mordecai's eyes, and he tore away, encircling the landing before returning to stand before me.

No restraints this time. Just the weight of his once again glacial anger as the chiseled mask fell back in place, keeping me there, immobile and shaking.

Only now, it wasn't *him* that coated my veins in ice.

"Who we are does not matter, Ember. The Void does not

care for the person. Only for their power. Power that can either feed it. Or destroy it. And you, my dear, are the only hope we have."

I flinched at his bitter, scathing tone.

It was torture, but I stepped away from the wall, my shadowfire eerily still within me.

Waiting to see what I would do.

I lifted my gaze to his to let him know that he couldn't insult or threaten me into backing down. I wasn't one of his subjects. And if we were all fighting for the same goal...

"Why should I side with you, Mordecai?" I demanded. "You want to stop the Void, claim you have a better chance of maneuvering me in a position to merge the fragments than Ada, and, fine, maybe with your resources and experiences, you truly do. But what would happen after?

"What would happen if I *did* reunite the worlds—would you rule them as you do Somraque? Will you have not only your people living in fear, but *all* of them?" I didn't know when my voice had risen into a shout. My words crashed and rolled between us, ricocheting off the too quiet library walls. "Your people might have been the keepers of balance once, but you... How could I give you the key to controlling all three worlds, deliver them to you after the atrocities you have committed—"

"Atrocities?" He barked a dry laugh, the coiling silver flaring behind him. There was danger in the curl of his lips. "*You* want to speak of atrocities? The daughter of the people, the men with no magic in their bodies or minds, who had not only rebelled against the Ancients and slaughtered them in cold blood, but who in their incessant greed *broke* the world? Condemned it to this pitiful existence we're now forced to live in? You don't know the first thing about atrocities."

CHAPTER THIRTY-THREE

I FLINCHED AWAY, MY THROAT CLOSING UP. BUT MORDECAI wasn't finished. He prowled over to me until I was pressed against the wall again, his shadowfire concealing the library behind him.

In the gleam of silver, his words cut harder.

"Oh, it was the men of Soltzen, the people of your beloved sun who envied those with magic so alive in their flesh, who had plotted and schemed. Spread poisonous whispers of the dangerous superiority the others possessed until their kinsmen saw nothing but a threat in those they had once deemed friends. Family even." He seethed. "They smeared their true standing among the races with well-crafted lies of oppression to band their kinsmen together. Ripped open festering wounds they had inflicted *themselves*, then bandaged them so that no one on the outside suspected the dark path they had taken. Bidding their time to strike.

"But not even their precious objects of power could eradicate the masses, no matter how much they wished it were otherwise. So when they accepted that they couldn't raze the Somraquians and Svitanyians, they turned on someone else instead. An *easier* prey, but one they knew would lead them to their ultimate goal nonetheless.

"At that time, the Ancients were so few in number they were scattered across the world to fulfill their sacred duty of maintaining the balance. The Soltzeniens sought out those who were the most remote first, then gradually tightened the noose. They spread out the killings so they would not raise any alarms, covered their tracks by utilizing tactics that evaded discovery. What was a death here and there among a people whose numbers were already dying? Who had already been shunned for their differences, for the role they played within the world? But most of all, what did heaps of lifeless corpses matter when there was no one to find them until it was too late?

"One after the other, they picked them off without mercy until only two families remained. Two bloodlines who did not tend to the lands, but the temple safeguarding the hallow—the embodiment of the heart from which all life, all power originates."

I braced myself against what I knew was coming, braced against the cold wrath burning in Mordecai's voice...

Only a child.

Only a child who had slipped through the massacre, but not unscathed.

Whatever defenses I had cultivated the rawness that now gaped from beneath Mordecai's mask stripped away, obliterated. Leaving me bare before him.

"Your people slaughtered them all. Even the infant and two children the Ancients were keeping safe within the temple walls to, above all else, protect them until they were strong enough to face the world and its wild manifestations on their own. And as their bodies bled out on the ground, as their shadowfire ceased to flow, the murderers—the *conquerors*—stole the relic.

"They joined their power to open a portal with a single entry point, but three different paths leading from its core. One to Somraque. One to Svitanye. One to Soltzen—where part of the temple had stood. They cast the hallow into its gaping mouth, let the magic rip it apart—and with it, the world. Like the doors of the portal, meant to succumb to the deliberate fault in the design, like the relic, unable to withstand the opposing forces that carried nothing but destruction, reality, too, had fragmented, entrapping its people. And its magic." The storm-wrought sapphire took me in. "So do *not* speak to me of atrocities, Ember Norcross of Soltzen. Not when your land is built on the blood of innocent lives."

I closed my eyes, battling for breath as my chest wanted to cave in. But as Mordecai's voice resonated in my mind, as those final two words echoed, again and again, the cold inside me stirred.

The wisps of shadowfire shot from me and shoved Mordecai away, back to the center of the landing.

"Innocent lives?" I cried. "What about those *you* took, Mordecai? You speak of crimes, of genocide, and a death sentence of the world, but do you truly believe that just because someone has done something that much worse, it gives you the right to murder people? To intimidate and torture them at your will?"

Hurt flashed across his eyes, a flicker of a ravine wrought of endless, haunted depths, but was quickly buried under a cascade of turbulent fury.

"I *made* myself into a monster because of them. *For* them," he roared. "Every death, every wound I inflicted was to keep them from bringing the Void upon themselves." He raked a hand through his hair, clawing at the strands as a brutal hardness overtook his features. "I tried to plead reason when I uncovered the border of our lands was not only death, but a parasite. The Mages wouldn't listen. They believed it was a lie —a means to secure my rule over them, to keep them obedient. So I did. They had revealed their fears. I played upon them."

"You razed an entire village!" I countered even as my legs felt weak beneath me. The truth of his words sank deep into my gut, cleaving me in two. But I couldn't just let it go. "If *mass murder* is one of your means to instill fear, then you're no better than my kinsmen!"

His shadowfire blazed, the bookcases disappearing behind the argent.

"They bound their magic together, believing it would be enough to overthrow me." His fingers twitched by his sides. "Illusionists, Magicians, Mages—their power is linked to their blood. Their *lives*. The disturbance—I felt it too late. Their web of illusions kept me from sensing the festering rot lurking behind the heavy veils." He strode up to me, sapphire eyes burrowing into mine. "Do you think I enjoyed purging the magic from them? Enjoyed purging the land onto which it leaked? I burned them *alive,* Ember. Every single one of them I burned alive, then forced my shadowfire to follow the taint of magic, obliterating *everything* it touched.

"Yes, I became a nightmare for the people of Somraque. And their deaths, their screams—they became mine."

The words died in my throat as his eyes simmered with the

centuries of hatred. For who he had become, for those who had spilled first blood—I couldn't tell.

Mordecai's head dropped, a defeated, painful laugh rolling from his chest. "Do you know what stings the most?"

I stood my ground as he finished his prowl towards me, his lean, powerful frame filling my vision.

"I accepted the past, the future—the enmity that leeches the air beyond the palace as wildly as the desire for my death I see in their eyes. If I had a choice, I would do it again. All of it. I would be the monster that haunts their dreams just so they can wake into another day.

"But what I can't accept, Ember"—his fingers fell upon my face, cupping it gently—"is that after all I have done, after the ages I have waited, I can't take the solution lying within my grasp. Even for them, I can't force you against your will more than I already have. And that"—his lips brushed against mine —"is the one thing I cannot live with."

He pulled away, as quickly and as quietly as the heated imprint of his kiss, the shadowfire trailing down the steps behind him like the maritime flag of a ship sacrificed to the horizon.

CHAPTER THIRTY-FOUR

For once, the quiet failed to soothe me. I lay tucked beneath the covers, staring at the vaulted ceiling and going over every word that had left Mordecai's lips.

A nightmare.

A monster.

Built from the selfless desire to keep this world from falling into the kind of darkness it could never emerge from again.

Telaria's silver veins flooded my mind, as if birthed from the haunting image of the Void. Then the sharp anger lining Ada's words whenever she spoke of the Crescent Prince. The contempt, not only hers, but Eriyan's, Zaphine's, for the seemingly unwarranted restrictions on their magic.

But underneath it all, fear.

Fear of the repercussions for breaking Mordecai's laws—something the majority might not speak of overtly but carried in their hearts nonetheless.

Mordecai had played his part well. Too well. The stance of a merciless ruler had leeched into reality, tainting him with the blood of his victims.

The sacrifice of a few to save many.

I didn't think he'd meant for the unrest to come so far. But I suspected that, aside from the tragedy at the village, whatever rebellious notions arose were still a lesser threat to Somraque's precarious health than having the entire population doing as it pleased.

I groaned and rubbed my hands across my face. Regardless of Mordecai's crimes and choices, he was unequivocally right in one regard. *Children.* We had tackled the matter like children, plunging headfirst into this mess without considering what lay beneath the surface.

By focusing solely on the dangers surrounding Ada's plan in *this* world, on keeping me safe, infiltrating the palace, and retrieving the fragment, we had been blind to the fundamental flaw gaping in the depths.

How were we supposed to find the piece of the hallow kept in Svitanye when no one has ever stepped foot on that land? When we didn't even know what waited for us there beyond *some kind of voice magic*? And that's *without* taking into account the fact that Ada hadn't even considered my inability to open a portal without an object of power in my hands. She hadn't mentioned the dagger in Mordecai's possession or gave any indication she had an alternative stowed away somewhere.

It wasn't enough.

I hated to admit it, but our knowledge was disgustingly inadequate. *We* were disgustingly inadequate for such a task.

Even if we somehow traveled to Svitanye, succeeded in finding the broken relic, and jumped worlds again—I had no idea where in

Soltzen the fragment could be. There were several High Masters, not merely my father, all holding their own estates and people, all fiercely protective of their treasures. And with me being the only one with active powers the instant we left Somraque behind... We would probably end up executed for attempted larceny long before we found whoever was even in possession of it.

In Soltzen, I would sooner be a liability than an asset, even if I tried to charm my way up their ranks. Sooner or later, the only solution left would be to kill everyone who stood in our way, and that—

That wasn't something I could live with.

I didn't have Mordecai's steel, the experiences that had made lethal force a necessity. One life claimed by my obsidian was one too many already.

I flinched at the memory, even when its weight seemed so... inconsequential, compared to everything. In light of knowing that if the Void spread, another darkness would have claimed the man had he survived mine. And so many others who, unlike him, in no way deserved death.

A frustrated grunt rippled from my lips.

Mordecai was right. There was a far greater chance for the worlds to unite once more with him by my side.

He, at least, had power that would endure crossing through the portal, had insight into history because he had *lived* it. And yet...

I'd felt it. The rage.

Mordecai might want to keep Somraque safe, but I had no doubts he would pay my people back for what they had done. The worst part was that, in a way, I understood. I despised myself for it, but I understood.

I rolled over onto my stomach and buried my head in the pillows.

I wished I were able to say that I couldn't possibly imagine my kinsmen walking down such a dark path, but with the rigid rules of our society, with the High Masters accumulating power while the common people were forced to live without it...

It wasn't such a stretch, truly.

For all I knew, they just might start another war, threatened by what a world reunited would bring.

Sun, I didn't know what I was to do.

I needed more time—needed Ada to flicker into existence at the foot of my bed so I could tell her to abort their rescue attempt until I sorted all of this out. Balanced the scales *I* was tasked with protecting.

But my wish went unanswered. Only the pounding of my heart and the thunder of my thoughts kept echoing through the chamber. I tossed around, then threw the covers off with a snarl, and stalked into the bathing chamber. I wrapped the flowing black nightgown I'd kept there over the ivory camisole I had on, and tucked my feet in a pair of low-heeled slippers.

Ever since I landed in Somraque, I was a game piece set between two opposing forces who failed to see that they were fighting for a common goal.

I wasn't merely caught in the eye of the storm. I *was* the storm.

I fastened the belt and slipped from my chamber.

Nobody could make this choice for me. Nobody could take it away, either.

My footsteps echoed softly as I descended the wide stairwell, the palace and its stillness an embodiment of the dead of night. Not daring to let my musings seep through the painstakingly constructed confines I had stuffed them in, I let my body take me where I needed to go.

But once I reached the proper corridor, once I was standing just outside the door I had to enter, I hesitated. The stirring of the icy lake inside me was telling me Mordecai was inside.

Like a coward, a small part of me had clung to the hope that I would find the chamber empty, even when I had known that would not be the case the very second I had donned the robe, my decision made. A shuddering exhale left my lips.

I knocked, just a single rap of my knuckles against the wood, then pushed down the half-moon handle and stepped inside.

Torchlight illuminated the demure chamber, a dance of light and shadow that fell across the silken black sheets and the contrasting white of Mordecai's torso as he lifted himself from the bed. The covers pooled around his waist, revealing more of his honed body. The rise and fall of his chest.

"Ember?"

The surprise in his voice was a deep, dark melody that played across my senses. I shivered, my fingers digging into the doorframe I'd gripped for support, but I didn't move a single inch farther into the room.

Nor did I retreat.

"I want to save Somraque. The world. I will work harder on the portals, and I won't stop until I succeed, but"—I sucked in a breath, grateful the darkness by the entrance masked the way my gaze kept drifting along the tattoos, the breadth of his shoulders, the taut abdomen my lips yearned to explore—"as a token of good faith, I ask you to release Telaria. I expect an answer by tomorrow."

I turned around, one foot already out in the corridor when Mordecai's velvet tone slithered against my ears.

"Ember..."

But I didn't stop. I couldn't. Not when the pull of the shadowfire was so strong. I ran down the hallway, then up to my wing, not slowing until I hurtled myself in my bedroom and locked the door behind me.

Not to shield myself from the threat beyond.

But to contain it within.

WHEN MERAYIN CAME to wake me the following day, she didn't arrive empty-handed. She rolled a cart stacked with breakfast food and a steaming kettle of tea up to my bed, but that wasn't all this unexpected meal contained.

I snatched the folded note off the plate the moment the girl left me to eat in peace and traced the immaculate cursive with the tip of my finger.

Mordecai would be waiting for me in the training chamber in two hours' time.

Enough to eat. To prepare myself.

Propping myself against the pillows, I went through my meal slowly. The novelty of eating in bed was not lost on me, but it didn't interfere with my devotion to clear my head of any and all thoughts save for the portals.

If anything, it helped.

The process was far from simple, yet as I lounged ensconced in the warmth of the duvet—in a way almost isolated from the rest of reality—the newly found resolution shone that much brighter. It helped me hone my mind, secret away the many jumbled threads and trails until all that remained was the knowledge of inanimate magic and my own affinity for it, rising above.

When I left my wing, this time wearing a violet gown instead of the uniform, I allowed the shadowfire to lap down my skin. With the tendrils released, my chest felt lighter, the strain I had often sensed grazing my insides becoming nothing more than an echo that held no sway over me. Precisely as I wanted.

There was a passage I had read—and reread—in one of the books, a footnote made by the author, indicating that she believed magic was at its most potent when its bearer accepted not only it but themselves, too. While I was still far from confident in my skin, I also knew that all the previous times I had held that bone handle dagger with Mordecai's eye trained on me, I had been hiding.

As stunning as the uniform was, it was meant for someone who needed the freedom of movement—someone I *would* become if we made it onto the next plane. But between these castle walls, I truly did not require the garment's almost authoritative air just to perform magic.

I had successfully—and foolishly—convinced myself the change in attire would give me strength when all it did was sap it away.

So when I walked down the stairs, accompanied by a myriad of discreet gazes on me, then took the corridor that would bring me to the hall, I held my chin high, the dress billowing around my form as elegantly as did the shadowfire.

This was who I was.

Not a doll forged after another's ideals, but a lover of the endless shades of beauty, the girl of moonlight—and now the darkest night—who had never thrived under the sun. Because she couldn't.

There had been no place for me—not there, not in Somraque either. Until now.

Until I *claimed* it.

Mordecai stilled when I pushed through the doors, his gaze catching on the flaming obsidian. He drank it in, then the exquisite garment. Blunt adoration deepened the sapphire when he met my eyes. His lips parted, gently, but no sound came as I strode over until we were face-to-face—he a wisp of darkness, and I a storm.

"I have released Telaria this morning," he said at last, then produced the ancient dagger from behind his back.

"Good." I kept the surprise from seeping into my features and motioned to the blade. "Then we can begin."

THE SLASHES GREW LARGER, if no more than two fingers' width. At first, they were simply rips in space, leading nowhere. But after the eighth attempt, I could make out the outlines of various chambers in the castle.

If I was fast enough.

What irked me the most, however, was that none of them held long enough to push even a trinket through to the other side.

Mordecai didn't lose his temper as I tried and failed, and regardless of the undercurrent of frustration, neither did I. Instead, we fell into a steady, comforting rhythm, with him creating a portal after several of my attempts so that I could feel the magic in the air before resuming with my task. All the while, I kept the shadowfire coiling around my body, its soft curving a reassuring reminder that I wasn't powerless. That all of this—it wasn't a mistake.

After what must have been my fiftieth time connecting with the dagger, Mordecai reached out. His hand covered mine, the warmth of his skin seeping into my fingers that continued to clutch the smooth bone.

"Enough, Ember. You have done enough for now."

I hesitated for a moment, then allowed him to take the object of power away. He placed it atop the low armoire by the wall and angled his head towards the large double doors set a short distance away from it.

"Come."

I fell in step with him. Neither of us spoke as he pushed down on the handle and led me—

Outside.

I was *outside*.

A soft smile touched the corner of Mordecai's lips as I let the open air of the courtyard fill my lungs, marveling at how good it felt to stand under the dark sky without the glass barrier dulling the impact of the night. He motioned to a bench nestled between two dark, oddly twisted trees, but as I moved to go there, Mordecai didn't follow.

I looked at him over my shoulder.

"Wait for me," was all he said before he strode back inside the palace, the *thud* of his boots the only sound breaking up the peaceful silence.

If there were any guards monitoring the perimeter, no trace of them disturbed the air.

For long moments, I simply stood there, halfway between the doors and the bench, tasting this small freedom with gratitude while tongues of obsidian coiled around me. Then, languidly, I called them back, willed them to return to the icy lake resting inside my core. They did. And they remained silent. Satisfied.

I hid away a smile and went to sit on the bench. The stone was cold against my back as I leaned into it, the dress not entirely sufficient for the brisk weather that appeared to have set upon Nysa, but I didn't care. I was too caught up in how wonderful it felt to be out here, to see the architectural jewel with its many windows and carved stones from the outside instead of stealing glimpses of the courtyard while locked within the palace's walls.

The slow, confident footfalls alerted me of Mordecai's return. My eyebrows rose at the sight.

The Crescent Prince was carrying a pint of sowhl in each hand, and draped over the bend of his right elbow— Was that a coat?

I stood to take the drinks from him and set them on the bench, then relieved him of what indeed *was* a coat. For me.

"Thank you," I said as I wrapped myself in the warm black wool. "For this and the sowhl."

A ghost of a smile flirted with his lips. "Well earned, I must say."

"Earned through failing?" I swooped down on the bench and laughed, but the sound came out just slightly bitter. My fingers closed around the pitcher.

Mordecai eased himself beside me. He cradled his own glass in his hands, the proud lines of his face softening. "Failure is inevitable. In everything we do. It's what you make of it that matters."

"But what if it doesn't go away?" I met his sapphire gaze. "What happens if I'm unable to open a portal into Svitanye?"

I'd finally learned, after outright asking somewhere between my thirtieth and fortieth attempt, why it had to be that particular land when I had an already established connection with Soltzen. Not only was it my home, but if I had crossed through that part of the veil once, then maybe I could do so again far easier than taking an entirely new route.

My theory, Mordecai had admitted, was not wrong, but it didn't take every crucial aspect into consideration. He suspected we would not be able to retrieve the fragments and make them work, lest we did so in their natural order—to which I had already established a starting point, thanks to my fleeting contact with the relic.

Night gives way to the break of dawn, dawn spills into day, then the light falls into the embrace of darkness once more.

It was hard to imagine this fluid transformation of the sky, even when I *had* read about it. Far harder, in fact, than it was to accept Mordecai's reasoning for the sequence of the retrieval.

I presumed that was in part because echoes of that former life were still sprinkled throughout our existence, but had taken on an entirely different meaning. I struggled to reconcile the old with the new. Like the Solstices that, as Mordecai had explained, had once marked the longest night or the longest day, yet now only announced the arrival of a new year or the cusp of summer.

Odd, how a person's mind could be wired to not reject improbabilities that had proven themselves all too real, yet when it came to semantics concerning terms that were rooted in everyday life...

Something glitched.

But it wasn't the only reason why Mordecai's logic was easier to accept over the thought of a constantly changing sky.

The truth was that I trusted him in this. Implicitly.

And, perhaps, when I had touched the fragment, however briefly, some ancient kernel within me had *sensed* we could only move forward from our current standing point.

Which meant we would have to greet the dawn.

Mordecai brushed his fingers across my temple, then, when I didn't protest but welcomed the affection, trailed a path down to my neck and cupped it gently. "If you're unable to open a portal, then we keep trying. Until the end, Ember. We'll both be here to see it, after all."

I frowned, caught between his words and the oblivion his touch offered. It took more willpower than I wanted to admit to not let the latter prevail.

"What do you mean? I thought you said Somraque still had centuries—"

"It does. But so do we."

"Wait." I jerked back. Mordecai's hand slipped from my neck and fell into his lap. "I don't have centuries..."

The pureness of his sapphire eyes spoke otherwise. I tipped the pint of sowhl, drinking deeply before I looked at him again. "I *age*, Mordecai. And if this Ancient blood had been passed down for generations, surely one of my ancestors would have shown signs before—"

He shook his head, then lifted his fingers to my lips. He traced the edge of my mouth, planted a trail of fleeting caresses all the way to my throat, to the pendant resting just below, and tapped it lightly.

"When Telaria felt your birth," he whispered, my pulse quickening beneath his touch, "she sent an ages-old curse—irregular, singular magic her family had managed to preserve despite the odds—to suppress your powers through the thin veil separating our worlds. To keep you from me, to protect you from exhibiting your magic and revealing just how unique you are to your people. But she wasn't the only one who reached out.

"I knew which Soltzen bloodline you belonged to—could sense the three powers of the lands coursing through your veins, but I didn't know *where* they were keeping you. Telaria made certain of that. All that I had felt—it winked out of existence, as if someone had doused the stars from the sky.

"I couldn't reach you if I couldn't find you." His voice dropped, a knot of anger and remorse, twined with bone-deep defeat. "Before I fell prey to my wrath, my instincts seized control. This"—he trailed his finger along the edge of the pendant—"is a family heirloom. Crafted by the Ancients and *for* the Ancients alone. When I cast it through the veil, with nothing but the impulse to find its rightful owner roaring in my mind...

"It wouldn't have come to you, Ember, if you weren't a true member of my race. Not merely in possession of shadowfire, but immortality alike."

CHAPTER THIRTY-FIVE

IMMORTAL.

I reached for Mordecai's fingers, closing my own around them—and the pendant beneath. Too many impossibilities.

I tightened my hold.

Too many impossibilities cracked open to reveal their cores of truth. Sun, I almost didn't know what was more absurd.

That I had never questioned why no one had noticed I had an object of power dangling around my neck. An object that had been with me for as long as I could remember, no clear origin to its presence, only a deep sense that it was *mine.*

That I had not once thought about its crescent-moon shape, even after I had found myself surrounded by Mordecai's symbol —by the Crescent Prince himself.

Or the unimaginable depths of what it meant, that the heirloom had chosen me, had stayed with me—and, as it appeared, would remain for a long time to come.

A weary, disbelieving laugh clawed up my throat but didn't break the surface.

Mordecai's breaths painted the silence between us, so quiet I knew he was controlling every single exhale, as if a stronger force could blow away the thin strands I was holding on to.

Maybe he was right. Only I didn't fear the reality he'd uncovered as he peeled away the gilded layers of falsehood. I wanted to *understand* it. Yet for whatever reason, my mind continued to fall short as it tried to bridge the gaps.

So maybe it *was* too much—but between the familiarity of his skin beneath my fingers, the presence of the pendant and the shadowfire alike, both now a part of me I couldn't imagine living without, I was determined to try.

"You said that it was instinct, but did you suspect?" I whispered, then louder, "Did you suspect I was more than just the savior when you sent it to me?"

Mordecai shook his head. Just a faint move from one side to the other, but the look in his eyes, the slight sheen of silver that offset the sapphire spoke that while the surface seemed calm, he was anything but.

"Some primal part of me hoped," he confessed, the velvet of his voice vulnerable. "With someone of your power, someone with mixed bloodlines, there was always a chance... But it wasn't until I saw you, until I saw the shadowfire, and then it..." His gaze dipped down to our entwined hands pressed against my chest, the pendant resting between them. "Once we came face-to-face, I knew who you truly were. I knew that I... That I have found another."

"Why didn't you tell me I was..."

Immortal.

An irregularity.

A bitter half-smile sculpted his lips. "As if that would have gone over so well."

"Well, not straight away." I frowned and dropped my hand from his, but didn't retreat. "I meant after..."

"When, Ember?" he asked quietly. "When you were struggling with your own self, facing not only the burden of being a savior, but one who possessed the shadowfire I had to force from your core that first morning? When you already had your mind full, thinking through the implications of having power like mine—power you had believed to be evil?

"I saw the turmoil in you, Ember, when I told you of your heritage. Even after you learned that there was more to the shadowfire than destruction. But then, your obsidian was merely *one* trait in which we aligned. How could I have told you that for all the other magics alive within you, you are, at your very core, a full member of my race? That you're even *more* like me when you were fighting to decide whether I truly was the monster everybody warned you about?" A laugh no louder than a whisper. "No. You needed to decide for yourself how you saw me first. Not shape your perception based on how you wanted to see *yourself*."

I bit my lip. "And if I had chosen to fear you? What would you have done then?"

"I do not believe you are the fearful type."

While his tone was playful, the censure beneath...

He leaned closer, his black hair falling across the sharp edge of his cheekbones. I brushed it aside, wishing it would be as easy to sweep away those echoes of doubts built on longing —and pain.

He would have let me go. Not from the mission. But his heart.

"Perhaps," he went on, "it would have been better if you *had* feared me."

My fingers stilled, lingering just above his ear. "Why?"

Mordecai pulled back and closed his eyes, a long shudder rippling through his body as he exhaled. "Any savior who came into existence, including you, was supposed to be a means to an end. A tool, Ember, nothing more. When I found out that I couldn't use you, regardless of what you believe—regardless of what *I* had *wanted* to believe..."

He lifted his gaze to mine. The kaleidoscope of contrasting forces silenced my remark.

"I meant what I said. Even thinking about how easily I would sacrifice everything I had fought for for *you*..." The sapphire darkened. "Ember, I made my peace with the blood on my hands a long time ago. But I would not wish to see it become a stain on my soul."

Because of me.

Because I wasn't a prisoner he could exploit, but someone who could not only condemn his sacrifices to a status of meaningless slaughter but condemn the world, too, while he stood by, reluctant to bend me to his will.

My chest constricted. I wanted to comfort him, promise him that I was here, that I would open that damned portal to Svitanye.

As for the rest, for those words building up inside me...

I was afraid of what such an admission might mean. What if merely acknowledging out loud that I was an Ancient in every way that mattered would unleash into the air something that had already started slipping through the cracks, changing reality, changing *me*, forever.

It was a path I wasn't able to take.

Not until I knew the difference it would make would be for the better.

"You mentioned that Ancients were created as a fourth race," I ventured. "As a means to uphold balance."

"We were." His voice was careful, guarded. And it only encouraged me to follow the unspooling ribbon of thought.

"What you did for me in that ballroom, bringing the celebrations to life... You possess the same capabilities as Mages. *And* you can open portals."

"Only ones confined to Somraque," he added. "And only for a limited time."

"But you *can*, so it's safe to assume all the faces of magic belong to you. Perhaps not as wholly as within others"—my memory drifted back to Ada, to her wistfulness when she talked of the purity of Illusionists and Magicians, how they were, in their own way, stronger than her—"but they are there."

My fingers touched the pendant. "If this is your heirloom, Mordecai, not just a Soltzenien object of power, then maybe it's as free of restrictions as you are."

His brows knitted together. "It has only ever manipulated time."

"Just as I have never used anything beyond inanimate magic," I countered. "But if I'm an Ancient"—at last, the word rang through the night—"and all magic is mine, too..."

My thoughts stumbled over one another, the avalanche they created too violent to separate them into neat threads. I sucked in a breath, then exhaled, aware of Mordecai going stiff beside me. As if he, too, struggled with the onslaught of connections kicking into place.

I lifted my gaze to the stars. "What I'm trying to say is that... I've only ever used inanimate magic, but the well reaches much farther than that. The Ancients as a *whole* possess capabilities beyond the initial natural laws."

I looked at Mordecai—the burning sapphire, the coiling tightness of him as he came to the same unbelievable conclusion.

"You mean—"

"That maybe, like me, the pendant just might do more than we both believe."

CHAPTER THIRTY-SIX

MORDECAI'S GAZE DROPPED TO THE SILVER PENDANT WITH ITS three black stones, observing it as if he were seeing the necklace for the first time. A gentle frown appeared down the center of his forehead, but he held his silence.

Waiting for me.

I took a sip of my now-cold sowhl just to chase away the excitement that had dried my throat. I brushed my thumb along the rim of the pint, a stray droplet wetting my skin.

"Your gift," I said, because that's precisely what the pendant was, "was the only object of power I had on me when I woke up in Somraque. If no one else is capable of opening portals between worlds—just me—then it had to have been this"—I lifted the necklace, the crescent-moon shape of it swinging before I let it drop back down—"that brought me here." I shrugged. "I still can't recall the events of that evening, but I do want to try, see if I can somehow replicate what happened."

Mordecai rose and offered me his hand, eyes bright. "Then let us try."

As he led me back inside, I couldn't ignore how different it felt. I wasn't returning as a captive, but entering the palace of my own free will. Still, I wished I hadn't left the sowhl behind, cold as it was. Because on the heels of the nearly overwhelming sense of freedom—not merely physical, but that of my actions—came a far more bitter thought.

All this time, I had the answer right in front of me—*on* me, actually... Maybe the time hadn't been right before. Maybe I had had to shed the cloak concealing who I truly was in earnest for everything to align, give me the grounds needed for making the right decision...

But it was a hard truth to swallow nonetheless.

"Ready?" Mordecai's voice wrapped around me, embracing me for an exquisite moment before it dispelled in the vastness of the hall.

I nodded.

He let go of my arm and took two long strides away from me, offering space. I wanted to tell him to stay, to keep his fingers entwined with mine, but I also knew that I had to do this on my own. It was my power. My object.

Perhaps even my fate.

I grabbed hold of the pendant. The broad strokes of torchlight against the walls, the solid floor beneath my feet, even Mordecai—everything faded as I focused on the lively core pulsing beneath the silver. Only this time, I didn't reach for it blindly.

I didn't seek out the ethereal touch that had answered the first time the necklace had revealed its power to me when I had been in need of running away.

Instead, I pushed my awareness deeper, past those willing currents, all the way to the pendant's heart. As the strength of it infused me, I nurtured the bond, *became* that sensation, then channeled everything into a single point in the air up ahead.

Slowly, my surroundings returned, though I didn't avert my gaze from the ripple—the shimmering, irregular circle, no larger than a marble.

At first.

As I poured more and more of myself into it, it expanded, revealing a glimpse of the ballroom with the smooth elegance of an artistic unveiling.

My breath hitched somewhere in my throat as details sharpened, turned vibrant, *real*, as if I could truly reach out and trail my fingers across the ornate columns framing the night beyond.

I was so focused on the stars carved in those impressive pillars, feeding on the memory of how Mordecai and I had danced—how the heat of his body had played against mine, then the brush of his lips—that it wasn't until his soft gasp ruffled through the air that I realized what had happened.

The portal.

It stood.

***

I TRIED AGAIN and again and again, and every time the portal not only persisted but grew larger. Eventually, the cut in the fabric of reality was tall and wide enough for a man to slip through.

I glanced sideways at Mordecai and extended my hand in silent invitation.

His skin joined with mine. Gently, I led him forward, my breaths quickened from knowing what I was about to do, as well as having him stand so close, his grip filled with quiet support.

I had stepped through portals in my past life. At first whenever my father wanted to make a grand appearance at some party or another, then on the arms of my suitors, eager to impress. Of course, that was *before* I had tarnished my reputation —my worth, as they deemed it—by having an affair with Magnus.

Yet for all those past experiences, I had never gone through a portal of my own making.

Magic lapped at my face, my body, the pendant warm around my neck, vibrating in an enchanting tune that seemed to spread through my very veins. I clutched Mordecai's hand tighter and took the step.

Only for a fraction of a moment, I felt it when reality was ripped away from me, but as the ballroom materialized beneath my feet, the night sky filling my vision, there was no sense of disorientation. No lightheadedness or palpitations. Just a strong sense of rightness.

I let out a little laugh and turned to Mordecai when he emerged through the portal behind me.

His sapphire eyes shone, the corners of his mouth lifted in a surprised smile and lined with tender innocence I had never seen on him before. He cupped my cheek with his free hand.

For what seemed like an eternity, all he did was stare at me.

And then I was wrapped in his arms, breathing in his scent as he held me close.

"You are brilliant, Ember," he whispered into my hair and kissed me gently. "Brilliant."

Darkness shot from my back as I blushed. A low, rumbling

laughter rose in Mordecai's chest as he drew me into another embrace. My own lips twitched in response.

Once the resonance of his laughter faded, I pulled away just enough to meet his eyes and reeled the obsidian shadowfire back under my skin.

"It's still far from a gate to another world," I pointed out, but Mordecai simply traced his fingers down my jaw, then followed the contour of my neck until they skimmed the pendant.

"Try opening one into Nysa."

My eyebrows knitted. "But the barrier around the palace—"

"Won't stop your power."

The impact of what his words revealed rendered me speechless. But before I could put my thoughts in order, Mordecai's lips brushed against my cheek.

"Perhaps I'm a fool. But I want the choice to be yours."

CHAPTER THIRTY-SEVEN

MY FINGERS WERE TREMBLING AS I FOUGHT TO SUBDUE THE wild silver strands into something that at least resembled an elegant hairstyle. Freshly washed and recently dried, they were a pain to work with, though my own skittishness more than likely made matters a lot worse than they would have been otherwise.

Tinkering my appearance had always been a soothing task, not one that only unraveled me further.

Then again, I supposed I had never been quite as invested in the outcome of whatever event I was readying myself for as much as I was now.

On *so* many levels.

I pinned two slender braids together at the nape of my neck, adding volume to the top, while letting the rest of my hair flow freely down my back. The cascade of argent matched the details on my dress—stars scattered across a rich blue-black velvet, with embroidered lunar phases decorating the plunging neckline. Unlike the rest, the full moon at the very center was merely a rounded border of silver thread surrounding the circle of pale skin, my pendant resting atop it.

I blinked and stared at my reflection in the mirror. I had known the outfit was daring, a statement in itself. But I hadn't been quite prepared for how striking the end result was. I looked...

I looked as if I had stepped from the night itself.

Not merely that, but as if I were *made* from it.

Or *for* it.

The fluttering tightness in my stomach intensified.

No, I wouldn't back out now. A part of me might be intimidated by what the dinner meant, what it could—or would—lead to, but it had been my lips that had uttered the invitation.

Because I *wanted* this. All of it.

And sometimes, standing on the brink of your deepest desires was terrifying.

With one last exhale, I curled my fingers around the pendant and cut open a portal to the airy chamber under the sky. Focusing on the feel of the magic calmed my nerves, yet when I stepped through, when I saw Mordecai standing beside the table, dressed in a silver-and-black tailcoat, his dark hair swept back, and sapphire eyes blazing, my chest constricted.

I let the portal collapse behind me and exchanged one magic for another. Both helpful, not harmful to this land.

With each step I took towards him, I unfurled the shadowfire, shedding any and all pretense until I stood before him as I truly was. The obsidian flames danced around my frame, some even coiling around my arms and down the atypical fitted point sleeves like the most peculiar, but sumptuous jewelry.

In silence, Mordecai took it all in—my kohl-lined eyes, the midnight gown, the elegant wisps of darkness.

Yet for all the details his gaze lingered on, not once did he hide that beneath them—or with them—he saw *me*.

Ancient. Savior. Oddity.

A girl who had always been in love with the night, then became it.

A smile touched his lips, and then *I* was the one left staring as the brilliant silver of his shadowfire engulfed him. Though I didn't know how it was possible, he was even more devastatingly handsome, the sharp angles of his face making me clench my fingers as I fought the urge to trace those chiseled lines.

It would be my undoing to give in.

The time for that would come.

I was grateful for the table that created a barrier between us —even more grateful when Mordecai waved his hand and offered me a seat. He claimed his own on the other side, but his attention never wavered from me, as if he couldn't stand to look away even for the smallest fraction of the moments passing silently between us.

"I wanted to thank you," I said before the sapphire weight would scatter my thoughts. "For giving me a choice."

Mordecai's body stiffened, the heat in his gaze becoming a guarded landscape crafted of ice. I fixed my stare on him, willing him to step beyond those walls regardless of what he believed my decision was. But Mordecai remained immobile, only the slight rise and fall of his chest letting me know he was still alive.

I sighed, drumming up the courage to utter the words that raked their talons within me as only the truth ever could— hating myself that with every second I hesitated, I was fueling Mordecai's discomfort.

But I needed him to not only hear this, but *listen.*

"I want to do what's best for the world. Best for all of them. I will fight to keep the Void from spreading, join the fragments as I was meant to," I began, the ominous words eddying the air. "But I wanted to speak with you first. Before I can move forward."

A gentle, yet curt incline of his head was all the answer I received. I swallowed and smothered the impulse to hurry.

No missteps allowed on the precarious path I was treading.

"My friends, as you like to call them, weren't idle after you took me from Saros and brought me here." I didn't want to tell him *how* I knew, and, mercifully, Mordecai didn't ask. Explaining Ada's apparition or deceiving him—neither option would aid my cause. "They intend to rescue me tomorrow, when the finale of the celebrations is at its peak. *And,*" I added hastily when I saw the shadows descend on his face, "I want to stop them."

The stillness that washed over him now was different than before. Not the shielded caution I had seen him turn to time and time again, but rather the relief-lined surprise that made his features softer. More open than perhaps he had ever allowed himself to be.

"You have my trust, Mordecai." I entwined my fingers in my lap, looking down as I fixed the cracks in my composure as the force of his disbelief, the raw emotion and affection running beneath it, crashed into me.

"Even I can't tell for certain when you stopped being my enemy and became an ally instead. More than that." Color flooded my cheeks, my own hunger for him reflected in his gaze. "All I know is that somewhere along the line, it hadn't been merely my feelings for you that have changed, but our entire relationship. If it hadn't—I don't think I would have found my way. And I dare to say that neither would you.

"Our beginning was not inspirational, but it *is* inspiring. The agenda we'd kept hidden, the misunderstandings that we could have so easily avoided... I don't want to be caught up in that any longer. Not with you. Not with anybody else." I squared my shoulders. "That's why I want to open a portal to Nysa, locate Ada, and reason with her. We are *all* working towards a common goal.

"She might not know of the threat the Void poses and is focused on liberating magic instead, but whatever her motivation is"—I didn't have to speak it for both of us to know it was *him*—"she wants the same thing. Find the three fragments of the hallow. Then restore the world.

"No one knows what we will have to face in Svitanye. Or Soltzen, for that matter. Ada, the rest of them... They're resourceful. Yes, we will have power on our side even beyond Somraque that they won't, but magic isn't the only strength that exists. They *would* go to the ends of the world to set things right. As would we.

"If I could speak with her, explain... I think we could form a truce. Temporary, if nothing more. I don't expect you to trust one another—I could *never* ask that of any of you—but I still believe we have a greater chance of succeeding together than apart."

Mordecai cocked his head to the side, an emotion I had no key to decipher falling upon his features. "Your faith in us is beautiful, Ember. But I do not believe they will be able to put our differences aside. Even for something as important as this."

Not an outright declination.

But a denial of hope—the very same one that kept churning in my stomach.

I could present my case. But I couldn't force the outcome.

I stared at him for a long moment, then slid my hand across the table, palm up. Mordecai's gaze flickered from my silent offering to my face before he leaned forward, the warmth of our skin meeting under the starlit sky.

"No matter what happens, no matter what Ada's answer might be, I *will* come back, Mordecai." I tightened my grip on his hand. "I'll come to you. I promise."

His thumb caressed the side of my palm. Gently, he lifted up our entwined hands and leaned forward to place a lingering kiss on my knuckles.

I couldn't help thinking that, regardless of my reassurance, he was saying goodbye.

CHAPTER THIRTY-EIGHT

DESPITE THE HOLLOW ACHE IN MY STOMACH, DESPITE IT BEING part of my initial plan, I couldn't bring myself to stay for dinner.

Shaken by how final that kiss had felt and driven to prove him wrong, I strode out the moment his lips had left my skin—and opened a portal just beyond the doors.

The shadows were no longer billowing behind me as I emerged in the familiar sitting room.

No stirrings marred the stagnant air, no voices, though the dying embers in the hearth showed that someone had been here recently.

But what convinced me more than anything that Ada's house was truly vacant instead of simply appearing empty was the utter lack of thrumming—seconded by the fact that Lyra hadn't come running. I was certain she, at least, would have picked up on my presence in a heartbeat and guided Ada over, just like she had that very first time.

I turned around in a semicircle, looking at the house without truly seeing it as my instincts offered up another location.

As far as I knew, Ada could be *anywhere*. But—as impossible as it was to even consider it—I thought I *felt* her magic. The unique thread that was hers in an entire tapestry of power.

Before I could doubt myself, I drew on the magic within the silver and opened a portal to the Whispers.

I saw them in the birth of the looking glass—those few precious moments before the portal became a doorway, visible from the other side.

Ada's fiery hair was unmistakable in the torchlight, her back turned partially to me as she helped fasten an already sheathed knife around Eriyan's hips.

Battle gear, I realized when the image widened, encompassing Zaphine who was handling some mean-looking pins that would undoubtedly serve not only as a means to draw her own blood but anyone else's, too, should they come too close with ill intent in their hearts.

At a distance behind her, a man I didn't recognize was examining his own assortment of blades. Was that the assassin —Ivarr?

I didn't know why, but an attractive, dark-haired man in his mid-twenties was *not* how I had pictured the Magician.

As intrigued as I was, dwelling would have to wait for another time. The passage before me opened.

I stepped into the in-between, then emerged on the other side, finding myself not in the atmosphere built of sharp concentration and precise, if hurried, movements, but the unnatural calm before the storm.

Muscles tense and spines stiff, they sensed my presence among them before they saw me.

The man I suspected to be Ivarr seemed ready to launch an attack. Ada stayed him with a hand as she whirled around, then all but broke into a sprint towards me.

The man's figure relaxed. As did Eriyan's and Zaphine's.

"Ember!" Ada's smaller form crushed me in an embrace. "By the Stars, you're here. How? How did you escape?"

She leaned back and scanned me with a critical eye. But if she saw anything peculiar in the way I was dressed, it was buried under the staggering weight of her relief.

"We were just coming for you." She laughed, an edge of hysteria I wasn't used to hearing from her permeating the sound. "But you—you opened a portal, didn't you?"

I skimmed over the rest of them briefly before meeting Ada's gaze again. "I didn't think you would come until tomorrow."

"That was the plan until—" Guilt lined the tight press of her mouth. "My mother. After the Crescent Prince released her, she..."

"She blabbed about you to every soul the damn woman could find," Zaphine hissed, her tone vicious. "You can imagine how the people reacted. Even Ivarr"—she waved a hand at the Magician—"was too late to control the damage in an acceptable way."

"What do they intend to do?" I demanded, though my heart already laid out the most likely scenario.

Zaphine shot Ada a pointed look, Eriyan looked positively torn, and Ivarr just stood there. Impassive, if perhaps a little amused.

But Ada... She could barely meet my eyes.

"They're going to storm the castle. Tonight." She exhaled, a tremor running down her limbs. "They—they would rather see you die than become a weapon in the prince's hands."

CHAPTER THIRTY-NINE

THE ICY LAKE WITHIN ME FROZE, AS DID MY ENTIRE BODY. Only my mind worked in overdrive, struggling to swallow her words.

"What?" I whispered, though I wasn't entirely certain my voice even broke beyond the whirlwind of a cage that had no clear key for unlocking its doors and escaping.

It wasn't so much the masses' desire for my death that tumbled through my thoughts. Or Telaria's betrayal—even if both did chill me down to my very bones. But the fact that Mordecai hadn't even mentioned something sinister was unfolding in Nysa.

Then again—how could he have known?

He had spent the entire day with me, helping me master the portals. The progress I—*we*—had made was monumental, a step closer to salvation that had, until earlier, felt more like a far-fetched dream than a possibility. Mordecai had devoted himself to the cause. And in the brief repose between our session and the dinner, after my invitation to join me for a meal we had both known would be a pivotal point, I doubted he had troubled himself with the town caught in the middle of the celebrations.

His guards were out there, monitoring the illusions. It should have been enough. So why didn't they—

My throat dried up, a low pounding building in my temples.

I looked at Ada—those jade eyes transforming a shade darker in my mind.

Telaria hadn't only spread tales about me to the people. She was *leading* them.

I jerked away from Ada as that final piece fell into place.

The old hag might not have magic of her own, but she had knowledge. Plenty of it. If she had instructed the mob to lay off their powers until the last moment, if she had made sure that whatever magic they did use was well within the restrictions Mordecai had set, then the guards wouldn't have taken notice. And Mordecai—there was no reason for him to suspect anything was amiss.

My gaze swept across all four faces staring at me. The dark-haired man assessing, while the others...

They thought it was fear for my life that had locked up my muscles. But all I could see was the vision of a hate- and fear-fueled group, advancing towards the palace under the banner of Telaria's vengeance. And within those walls...

I wasn't their sole target.

I had to go back. Had to warn him.

Ada's fingers snapped around my wrist as I reached for the pendant. "It doesn't matter what they think, Ember. You're here. We can hide, go to another town when Dantos returns."

"Hide? You want to *hide*?"

"Just until this blows over."

I tore myself away and seethed. "The Void is *growing*, Ada. It feeds on your magic and is swallowing your world inch by inch. What if the attack goes out of hand? What if there isn't a place *left* to hide in on the fringes once their destruction takes a different turn?"

Ada stilled, and Eriyan swore softly behind her. The dagger he had been fumbling with clattered onto the ground. He picked it up, resolutely looking at everything but me.

My jaw went slack, though the anger prowling through my veins burned brighter.

They had known. Known about the threat and dismissed it, just as Mordecai had said. Just as he was right about—

I reined in that part of me that broke, along with the hope now scattered around my feet in useless shards.

Mordecai had always been their enemy. The only threat that mattered.

Coming here was a mistake.

But maybe I could still turn it to our advantage.

If I was fast enough.

Zaphine shifted behind Ada so that she was in my direct line of sight and pinned me with a hard gaze. "What do you mean it's *growing?*"

"We don't have time for this. I swear I'll explain everything later unless Ada"—my gaze flickered to her, then back to Zaphine—"wants to fill you in on what she's been ignoring. But we have to *stop* those people before they disrupt the balance further."

"None of it will matter if we reunite the worlds," Ada countered.

I had to hold back with everything I had to not claw at her face. "You're right. *NONE* of this will matter if your mother and

339

her mindless followers destroy the relic during their attack! Did you even consider that?"

Ada lunged for me as I stepped back, her hands shackling my wrists. But the voice that caught my attention was not hers.

"That's why he wanted you?" Ivarr.

Remaining calm seemed impossible, but I managed to nod. "To save Somraque."

"Then claim all three worlds for himself," Ada snapped. Her nails dug into my skin. "We'll find a way—"

"Are you even listening to yourself?" I sneered.

"Are *you*?"

I looked at Eriyan, the hard set of his face. And Zaphine's beside him.

"You're siding with a tyrant," he went on, but the words got buried under the roar of blood in my ears.

"WE DON'T HAVE TIME FOR THIS!"

As my voice swept through the cavern, all it left in its wake was silence. Tense, coiled silence.

"Let me go, Ada," I warned. "I have to tell Mordecai."

"No." Her fingers tightened. "You've just got out. I can't let you leave. Not for...for *him*."

I stared at her, marking the concern, the pain lingering in the rich jade. She thought I was the one betraying her—because she didn't know, *couldn't* know. And would never understand unless she saw it herself.

So I showed her.

As soft as the morning mist, the shadowfire rose from my body. Ada staggered back, the others sucking in a collective breath as the tendrils snaked through the air, enveloping my form in a halo of a starless sky.

"What has he done to you?" she whispered, dread gnawing at the words.

I let out a bitter laugh. "Mordecai hasn't done anything. This is who I am. *This* is your *savior*."

I felt the thrumming magic rise in the back where Ivarr stood at the ready, felt Zaphine and Eriyan's horrified gazes on me...

But worst of all was the fear pulsing from Ada in violent, crushing waves.

Not just fear. Terror.

And disgust.

"If you care for this world at all, stop the attack," I hissed, ignoring the weight in my chest, how broke my heart was. "It's not just for him, Ada. I'm doing this for all of you."

I cut open a portal and stepped through without looking at them a second time, but their silent judgment...

It lingered.

CHAPTER FORTY

I EMERGED IN THE CHAMBER UNDER THE SKY, MY SHADOWFIRE whipping through the air with the maelstrom of emotions I couldn't allow myself to feel. My mind sharpened into a blade, only one task left that had my utmost dedication.

The table was still there, prepared for us to dine, with plates of food and a bottle of wine that belonged to another life set upon its gleaming surface.

But no Mordecai. Not even a note.

I tried to convince myself that he had just stepped out, didn't linger, alone and idle, while I was occupied elsewhere. Only I could taste the putrid undertone of wishful thinking on my tongue.

Just as I could sense the amassing thrumming of magic, reverberating through the very foundation of the palace.

They were here.

My attempt at diplomacy had gained me nothing. I wouldn't let it cost me everything in one sweep, too.

The paramount fear that had paralyzed me at the sight of the Void settled upon me like a murder of crows.

If the promise of annihilation had been a wraith blotting out the stars before, it now glutted on the very air I sucked into my lungs. But it hadn't won yet.

Honing the trepidation until it became a driving force, I bolted out the door, searching the corridor for the first glimpse of a black tunic I could find. There were none on this level, the utter vacancy of life almost palpable, etched within the ethereal tapestry of power I had called to mind again. The threads, an ensnarled mess now, all blurred together, but the pull propelled me downwards, across the steps my feet barely touched—

The thrumming rose just as I saw a russet-haired guard on the landing. The same one Ada and I had run into in Nysa.

Tristan.

Blood glistened on his white skin, his gaze fixed on nothing in particular, yet seeing—*projecting* whatever magic he had brought to the surface towards the knot of threads dominating the lower palace floors.

I all but threw myself at him.

I caught him by the shoulder before his steps could take him farther down and spun him around. "Mordecai—the Crescent Prince, where is he?"

"I don't know."

Lie.

A lie even as his amber eyes skimmed the obsidian. He tried to slip from my grasp, but I looped a thin veil of darkness around his upper arm.

"Where. Is. He."

A tick worked in his jaw. I tightened the shackle—

"Tristan."

"Down. Last I saw him he went down to hold the line with the rest of the guards."

I released him with such force he staggered.

"Keep your magic to a minimum," I ordered over my shoulder as I ran. "And don't waste it."

The voice that had come out of me was foreign, yet mine. I didn't have the luxury to dwell on the change as I took two steps at a time, my senses tuned not on the dark stones of the castle, the distant clash of steel, or the audible thrumming—too loud, too violent—but on the superimposed reality I had no doubts was the Ancients' alone to navigate.

But the threads had only grown helplessly knotted, their edges tattered and bleeding into one another, disfiguring the centermost part of the tapestry. I couldn't see or sense Mordecai's among them, so I listened to the whispers of the ice within me, seeking that draw I felt whenever he was near. Yet even as I searched, the webbing of power became more turbulent, convoluted, and with it, the thrum of blood magic ascended to a deafening buzz that made it hard to think, let alone hold the high level of focus the task required.

With a groan, I threw my consciousness back onto *this* plane and kept running.

I descended stair after stair, ignoring the sprawling wings on either side, the few guards that had remained behind while the others—

I stopped so abruptly I nearly plummeted headfirst down that final flight.

The uniformed men formed an ocean that coalesced on the landing. My eyes watered under the pressure of magic clogging the air.

This wasn't one line of defense. It was the *only* one. And if they failed, if the masses breached the living wall I felt extend throughout the ground floor...

No, Mordecai wouldn't be here among them. Too many blind spots for his control to reign supreme.

If he thought I was still away, safe—if for no other reason than Ada's own need for me—then he would be protecting the one thing that mattered most while his men fought here, still within reach.

Grounding my teeth, I bunched my fingers into the star-sprinkled skirt of my dress and sprinted back up. My steps grew less certain with each passing second, the press of magic eroding my concentration and coordination alike. Nausea rose in my stomach and bile burned at the back of my throat, my vision blurring in the corners as tears that had nothing to do with emotions weighed heavily on my lower lids.

My shadowfire curved around me like armor, but while it helped ease the pain that seemed to burn from within my very cells, the talons of terror refused to cease puncturing my chest. My heart.

Because I knew what this was.

Knew what it meant, this foreboding torment that grazed my insides as the clashing magic of the masses and the guards ratcheted up yet another notch.

Mordecai had said the imbalance fed the Void. But just how much of it did it need? How much sustenance had the wretched thing consumed by now?

Already, I could feel reality fraying at the edges. Curling inward like paper caught in the thrall of fire.

This wasn't merely *seeing* the threads of the tapestry deteriorate, then vanish in earnest. It was as if my entire being was attuned to this world, and each fragment of land the Void devoured stole a piece of me away.

Sun... I had known Mordecai was telling the truth, had felt it in the way his words had coursed through my mind and veins when he had spoken of what it had taken him to hold the Void at bay. But I could have never imagined the horror of watching the world slip through your grasp while you were powerless to prevent it—save for one way.

Through burning the offensive magic from existence, right down to the very last ember. Securing life by invoking death.

Caught up in the full weight of the sacrifice Mordecai had made to keep the world safe, the price he had paid time and time again, I noticed the figures blocking off one side of the landing a fraction too late.

I whirled around, my shadowfire blending with the dress, and hurtled myself in the other direction to lead them *away* from the damned corridor—and Mordecai's study.

Mercifully, they followed.

But they were also gaining ground.

My muscles screamed in protest as I pushed myself to move faster, but the languid life I had led at my father's estate continued to punish me. A layer of darkness clouded my vision, white spots flickering across what little I could still see. I clenched my jaw and kept going. I only needed to slip away from their sight for long enough to open a portal and close it before they could follow through. But the architecture of the castle made it next to impossible to shake them off.

There were none of those hidden passages I had dreamed of, no forks in the long line of hallways to slow them for even the smallest amount of time. And when I turned the next corner—

Magic.

Magic hit me like a wall, obscuring the castle and replacing it with an illusion so thick I had no hopes of seeing through.

But worst of all was the burning in my lungs.

I gasped, sucking in air that simply was not there any longer.

A Magician's power. Pure. Unrivaled.

My knees gave way beneath me. When I crashed onto the hard ground, I understood.

The darkness overtaking me now could end my suffering.

But another would be my salvation.

As a sob wrenched from my dying body, I reached for the icy lake and willed its obsidian to rise in a tidal wave that would incinerate it all.

Burn *them* all.

CHAPTER FORTY-ONE

THE FIRST ROLL OF POWER RETURNED THE AIR.

The second dispelled the illusion.

More figures surrounded me than I had anticipated—so many, that it was clear they hadn't snuck into the palace, but killed their way through the perimeter.

The wrath that twisted their faces didn't falter at the sight of my shadowfire. Didn't change as I sent it barreling towards them.

Only the cadence of their magic shifted, thrumming and bouncing off the hallway walls violently enough to shake the polished stones beneath my feet. Poisoning Somraque.

In that fraction of a second, I found myself in Mordecai's skin—in that village where the braided twine had tugged and pulled at the grander structure, unraveling the design for the Void to consume.

I didn't have Mordecai's finesse. Nor did I possess his experience.

But my shadowfire needed no instructions.

And the people—they were powerless against my will.

The obsidian tendrils crawled up their forms, spilling into their mouths and filling their bodies with icy darkness.

Cascades of screams filled my ears, then the muffled struggle, when the shadowfire blocked off the sounds, swallowing them as it spread down their throats. With every new blackened vein, it charred their magic.

But it was too little, too slow.

Even through the shrieks, the labored, pained groans, they persisted. The Illusionists fought to ensnare my senses, submerge me in nightmares, realities designed to break my mind, while the Magicians assaulted my body, lashing out at my skin, my organs, until I could taste the coppery bite of blood on my tongue.

The shadowfire swayed like willows in the wind as something crawled from the depths of my memory and broke through the thick layers of ice, stone, and iron I had placed upon it. It obliterated the bonds, enveloping me in images, sounds, and scents. I barely had time to sink the obsidian deeper in my attackers, give it free reign over their diminishing lives before—

I WAS STANDING in the hallway leading away from the main hall, just a few steps shy of the passage concealed behind a statue—a shortcut to my father's prized wine cellar. Music crawled through the cracks beneath the heavy double doors, along with select voices of the guests who had taken it upon themselves to dominate the party.

But here, away from the stage, where boasting meant nothing, we were blissfully alone.

A husky, slightly breathless laugh slipped from my lips as Aegan Rosegrave leaned into me. His eyes, a rich blend of greens shot through with strands of amber, flashed when I pressed my back against the wall, then brought my hands to the fine panes of his chest the forest green jacket only pronounced.

I played with the golden embroidery, fingers traveling along the paths it mapped out, never taking my gaze off him. Off the smile that curved up in a single corner of his mouth before he dipped his head, his breath a quiet caress. A promise he fulfilled the instant my hands traveled up and found their position at the back of his neck.

The warmth in my veins spread into my flesh, and then Aegan's lips were teasing mine, the slow exploration becoming a tempest as I responded.

He tasted like wine, like the laughter we had shared during the endless dancing when the blur of movement and the rhythm we had given ourselves over to had offered us the illusion that we weren't scrutinized by an entire hall of busybodies.

Of all the High Masters's sons I had met, not one had come close to the easy, enchanting nature the Rosegrave heir possessed.

Aegan had drawn my eye from the moment he'd stepped into the hall.

There was something different about him, as if while he played the role of heir, he wasn't truly caught in the never-ending game of spotless appearances and power. He walked the edge of what the High Masters tolerated as acceptable—that much had been evident from the way the very texture of the atmosphere surrounding him shifted as he toured the room.

And when my father presented him, with far less enthusiasm than he extended to the two suitors vying for my hand who lingered behind him like vultures, I knew Aegan was the one I wanted to spend the evening with.

With a moan, I opened my mouth, wanting to taste more of him. His kisses had turned lazy, yet thorough, exploring me as if he had all the time in the world. My father would skin us both if he found us like this, but losing myself in Aegan's arms, even if only for a moment—it made everything bearable.

My fingers curled around the nape of his neck, my other hand coming to rest on his shoulder as my back arched, body pliant under his affections.

Divine oblivion.

The usual scrutiny of the guests wasn't the only thing I was eager to forget. They all... They all ogled me as if I were some prize to be won, while at the same time questioning if I was worth it, constantly separating truth from lie, fragments of both carried on the endless winds of gossip.

My father knew how to spin tales to make people desire something or someone they otherwise might not have.

Every word that had filtered through the heady fig- and patchouli-scented air had left me more nauseated by the minute —the various High Master's offers of more riches, even objects of power, to reconsider their low-ranking sons for the match...

And my eighteenth birthday had made it all that much worse.

I had at last reached the wretched age when my father could hand me off to a husband, no questions asked. He was eager to let someone else deal with my *disobedient* nature.

Tonight, I was nothing more than goods to barter.

But Aegan—he saw me. Without a word, he took my hand

and invited me onto the dance floor, the weight of the conversations falling off my shoulders with the very first time he spun me around.

"Aegan," I whispered as we came up for air, my cheeks hot and breathing ragged. "This was... Thank you."

I smiled at his answering grin, though I knew the expression faltered a little around the edges when I thought of what my next words had to be.

"I think we should return to the party before anyone misses us."

The grin adorning his face turned into a roguish smile. "But we're not *nearly* done..."

It was impossible not to react to the sultry drawl of his voice. But stealing off for a few kisses was one thing. What Aegan was suggesting, however...

"We really should get back," I said as steady as I could. "If my father or one of his men come looking—"

"Then I'll claim you as my wife."

There was no hint of amusement in his features, nothing to indicate he was anything but serious.

A laugh bubbled from my chest, and there was nothing I could do to stop it. I leaned back, watching those amber-speckled green eyes with interest.

"You can't possibly believe he would allow that." I squeezed his shoulder. "What you want—what I want, for that matter—carries no weight. He's already narrowed his pick, and he won't take you into the fold."

"He will." Aegan traced his tongue up the side of my neck. He bit my earlobe, gently, then drew back, the amber in his gaze reflecting the sunlight that spilled in a thin shaft down the corridor.

"Your father played off your little affair with the help well, but not quite well enough to fool me. Or a handful of others who, I must say, are intrigued by your *reputation*, if for the most part disapproving. I don't care who you fucked, Ember," he whispered, his hand lifting the hem of my gown until he touched my bare thigh.

My muscles grew stiff.

"Once your father learns that I took you right under his roof, once everyone does... Well, he'll find that his chosen ones don't want you anymore. And that the list of his daughter's precious suitors dwindled down to one." A wolfish smile. "I think it's a fair bargain, don't you?" He traced a finger along my collarbone. "I marry the only child of the great Norcross line without groveling at anyone's feet, and you can do whatever—*whomever* —you want behind closed doors. So take me up to your room, Ember. Unless you're the kind of girl who prefers the rush of lifting her skirts in public?"

It felt like time had slowed as his voice rang out, bearing the offer that would have been the perfect escape if it weren't for this...this crass, demeaning way he'd delivered it.

I wasn't only a means to an end to him, but a tattered doll he could do with as he pleased after he made me into a pariah.

A partnership I would have accepted. But this was a worse cage than even those my father wanted to lock me in.

"No, Aegan. I *don't* want that," I said with what I hoped was steel in my too-thin voice. "I'm going back inside."

"Come on, love." The hand he'd kept on my thigh rose higher, gripping me harder when I tried to move away.

"Aegan, stop," I squeezed out through gritted teeth as nausea rocked my insides. "Just because we kissed doesn't mean I—I want *this*."

353

"No?" Again, that hand moved. Up. Up. "But your body says otherwise. You wanted to fuck me from the moment we came together on the dance floor. So don't stop the fun so soon, darling, and don't pretend you don't like it. You know you'll be thanking me when I'm done."

I shoved against him, my pulse rising in my ears, but Aegan was bigger. Stronger. Slamming his free hand over my mouth, he hooked one finger beneath my undergarments, pulling them away to—

A *snap* cleaved my entire being.

My vision was blurred from the tears I couldn't keep from falling, but even through the shimmering haze, I saw them.

Shadows. Growing between us and crawling up Aegan's muscular form, their curved, coiling tips forcing open his hunger-ridden mouth and spilling inside. He choked, as if the darkness had substance.

A spasm rocked his body. I gasped as Aegan staggered back, but I didn't run, *couldn't*, pinned to the wall by the sight of him clawing at his throat, his chest, until he landed on his knees, his face contorted in primal, raw fear.

But it was his eyes that chilled me the most—only a flicker of the amber-touched green remained, and then it was gone, the obsidian all that was left as he fell on the ground. Unmoving.

"Ember, where have you gone—"

I heard my father's voice, but couldn't see him past the darkness.

Past the darkness surrounding me.

My knees buckled.

Nor past the one that claimed my consciousness and swept away the rest of my father's words.

WHEN I AWOKE in a damp room illuminated by torchlight, my head nestled in stale hay, the only indication of the time that had passed were the dried trails of tears pulling at my skin. My throat was hoarse, muscles aching as if I'd been running—

But *I* hadn't run anywhere.

It came to me then, flashes of images, phantom remembrances of touches that made my body recoil. And the darkness. Aegan's lifeless body on the ground, the mark of his death written in cold obsidian.

I closed my eyes and tried to breathe past the rising panic— only to fall into the talons of a new one.

The stale, somewhat damp air, ridden with the smoky essence of fire...

There was only one place in the manor I could be.

The dungeons.

As I cracked open my lids and twisted my head, the ages-old bars cut across my vision.

Not just the dungeons. But a *cell*.

I thought I saw the edge of my father's coat swish up the stairs on the opposite side of the rank chamber, but even as I blinked to scatter the fog still clouding my sight, he was gone.

Focused on those weathered, time-licked steps straight ahead, I hadn't noticed I wasn't alone until four guards pushed into my prison through the door on the right-hand side. Their heavy boots pounded a merciless rhythm that reverberated through me and worsened the pressure already crushing my temples from within.

A cry that was too weak to surface shook my body.

I twisted my shaking legs beneath me. My hands scraped for purchase.

The stones cut into my skin as I clawed at the wall, a warm trickle of blood snaking its way across my palms.

Just as what little space there had been left between the guards and me dissipated, my fingers found a small ledge. I sobbed and lifted myself onto my feet, making a shuffling retreat into the farthest corner. But it didn't matter.

Half submerged in shadows the torchlight failed to reach, there was nowhere I could run.

I couldn't keep my chin from trembling as I looked up at the faces I recognized, had known all my life, but were staring at me as if I were a stranger—no, worse. A threat.

But I wasn't—

I didn't—

I...I didn't understand any of this.

My mind was a shredded mess, offering no answers. I wanted to scream, would have, if the hostility emanating from the men weren't so thick I choked. The two that were standing the closest moved forward—to *hold* me, I realized as their backlit figures neared—while the third blocked my way, keeping the last guard from my sight.

Only I didn't need to see him to know that it was a blade he drew, its cold *snick* as he unsheathed it slicing through the unraveling knot that was my mind.

"Please, no. No, no, no..." I cried, but the guards kept advancing.

The pendant grew warm against my skin, as if in reminder that I wasn't powerless, that I could still escape as long as none of them touched me. With the last remnant of my strength, I wrapped my hand around the gemstone-adorned silver and called to its magic, wishing it would save me. Pave the way to safety.

I GASPED AS I RESURFACED. The corridor was utterly still, my shadowfire coiling around me in protective wisps that soothed the turmoil and restored clarity.

Bodies were strewn across the ground, but it wasn't them I saw as I raised my hand—as I turned it around, gazing at the now unmarred skin. I clenched my fingers, forming a fist.

I knew.

I knew how to open the portal to Svitanye.

CHAPTER FORTY-TWO

THE THRUMMING CONTINUED TO GROW, ROLLING THROUGH the ground with a destructive viciousness that sent chills sweeping down my spine. I didn't dare open a portal, not when the world was this frail.

It wasn't that I feared a rip in reality would be precisely what unraveled the cords still holding it together, still keeping the Void at bay. What stayed my hand was the uncertainty of whether the threads the portal wove together would hold. If I were to end up trapped in the in-between...

Not a fate I was keen to meet.

So I ran.

I ran through the palace, cursing the beautiful gown that tangled around my feet and forced me to slow as I hurried down the steps of the smaller, secondary stairwell.

And up them once more, when the townsfolk came surging from the level below.

I had hoped to circumvent the mass of attackers making

their way up the main stairs—hoped to buy myself and Mordecai what little time I could instead of leading them straight to him.

Maybe I still could.

Cursing, I gritted my teeth and took the corridor on my left. The layout of the palace locked in place within my mind, the paths I had explored during my stay here filling the dry schematics like liquid gold setting into a mold.

One last avenue to explore. One last route to hold off death.

I just hoped the people hadn't flooded it on their march *to* it.

Voices boomed behind me, rising in tune with the surge of magic. My dress caught on an overturned dresser someone had tossed from the freshly wrecked room I'd spied from the corner of my eye. I yanked the material free, but too late to save my balance. My ankle tipped.

I crashed down, skidding across the floor until I collided with an open door. Frantically, I pulled myself inside the faintly illuminated chamber and crawled behind a massive cream-and-gold sofa, bearing smudges of already dried blood. The prints were small, delicate—and this close to the servants' stairwell I was trying to reach, I couldn't help but think of Merayin. Was she safe? Were the others?

I'd never thought to ask Mordecai if he had prepared for an attack like this.

He cared for the people in his employ. It was evident from the way Merayin harbored no fear, only respect for the Crescent Prince. Surely he had ensured a safe—

The presence of my pursuers slammed into me.

I pressed my back against the silk brocade, keeping one arm plastered to my lips so that the raspy breaths wouldn't give me away. Even with the chaos brimming outside, they seemed too loud—a signal just waiting to be heard, to bring them to me.

As I listened to the *thud* of their feet, almost by the threshold now, I wrapped the shadowfire around me. It burned low across my skin, hidden safely behind the backrest should anybody peer inside, yet as ready to strike as if it were flaring freely around my form. Bile burned at the back of my throat at how easy it was—how easy it *had* been—to lash out with a power designed to burn through theirs.

And how wrong.

My insides twisted into a painful knot that I didn't know how to unravel. My way had always been paved with sly words and a cunning mind, not the ability to wield death.

But here, without it, I was helpless.

I didn't want to be a killer.

Regardless of what I had already done, of the lives I had taken, I was terrified of embracing a role where lethal force became second nature. Murder a solution, instead of that last resort I would use only when I was left with nothing else. And even then, used with regret.

What if taking this leap would not only unleash death upon others but slaughter the person I was now?

I closed my eyes, remembering Mordecai's words. The small laughs he had shared with me, the light in his sapphire eyes. The tenderness I would welcome for an eternity to come if I were granted it.

A monster does not deserve the intimacy of a name. Ada's condemnation slithered through my mind.

Perhaps. But to me, he had a name. He had light, coiling around the darkness. Two entities that could not exist separately, only together.

And so did I.

When the men charged into the chamber, I didn't hesitate.

My only regret was not learning how to control this power sooner, to teach myself to stop right on the cusp of a life forfeited.

But as I remembered Telaria's words, the bitter resentment and cruel wish that had broken Ada's heart even when she struggled not to show it, I also knew that the people of Somraque would welcome death long before they would take on the burden of continuing an existence devoid of magic.

So I accepted the scars unleashing the obsidian would bring, accepted that I would carry their deaths within me for as long as I lived—and broke down their magic until nothing remained.

The front line fell in a blaze of darkness.

The second called for reinforcements.

There was no flavor to their deaths, no reek of blood or approaching decay. But my stomach churned regardless.

Where the Void was a sentient, brimming emptiness, the bodies my shadowfire left behind were eerily hollow.

And still, I pushed, the shadows of the lit sconces flickering in answer to my own as the obsidian consumed everything and anyone, smoothening the ensnarled patch of the tapestry—a flatland now, ensconced among frayed ridges.

My pulse was frantic as I weaved through the labyrinth of corpses, then rushed out into the corridor and aimed for the servants' stairwell. I only encountered three more townsfolk, hands full of loot—loot they dropped to draw blood and wring to life illusions, false realities with their only goal to trap my mind.

They weren't fighters, so I didn't fight them.

I only shoved them aside with a whip of solid darkness, then moved my feet forward, the unadorned railing of the stairwell already coming into view. I lunged for it and clung to the iron to keep my feet from slipping across the polished floor, when the world around me spun, my chest heaving.

Clenching my jaw against the pain, I fought to snap my surroundings back into focus, but the Mage's power held, eroding control of my body and toying with my perception.

But through it all, I heard it.

The press of men, the echoes of their feet squeezing me into a corner. As I drifted in and out of the thralls of the illusion that assaulted me with blinding light, I glimpsed their faces. Hostility carved their expressions, twisted them into perpetual snarls, rivaled only by a hunger that went beyond their fight for freedom.

As a thousand thorns raked my insides, I recognized two of them. The couple from the celebrations. The image of the future I had known I would never have now distorted, stepping forward to aid holding the reins of my destruction.

Whatever kindness, whatever serenity I had seen in them when they had walked with their elbows linked and observed their children, had peeled away to birth the single-minded drive crafting a downfall that would cost more than they knew to pay.

More than they *could* pay.

My skin crawled with the violent thrum of power, the taint of blood suffusing the air until I could taste it on my tongue.

Or perhaps it was mine, the crimson spilling every time I coughed, struggling to lift the damaging weight off my lungs.

I grappled for the wall, but my fingers were unable to find purchase in this world that refused to stop spinning. And when it quickened its pace, when the images of the true surroundings I'd managed to glimpse blurred beyond recognition, followed by the whorl of consecutive illusions, my senses finally failed.

My knees crashed against the stones with a cruel *crack*, but I barely felt the pain.

Within this spiral, my body was hollow. Spent. If the icy lake existed within me, it was beyond my grasp.

My protector. My companion. Gone.

It seemed even the Ancients had limits to their power.

And I had plummeted over the edge of mine.

With trembling hands, I clutched the pendant. Its magic greeted me, trickled into my fingers in a silent offer to draw on it.

Only there was nothing left inside me to answer the call.

Whatever the Soltzeniens believed, whatever all those books I had read taught, they were wrong.

Inanimate magic didn't lie only within the objects.

It wasn't just a passive affinity within us, allowing us their use, but a silent power—a spark that needed to ignite the process.

The magic in our flesh couldn't be wielded on its own. But without it, the objects... They were worthless.

I tried, again and again, to rouse its flare. Softly, forcefully, desperately. Nothing.

The people closed in, something I didn't see, but sensed as their magic lashed out across my skin in a blaze of cold. Of searing heat. And one of silence. Of a power that wrapped around my heart, containing it so tightly it ceased to beat.

I gasped and sprawled onto the ground, my hands trapped beneath me—one on the pendant, the other on my chest. Utterly still.

Darkness crept across my already shot vision. It whisked away the whispers of crimson-tinted stones I glimpsed through my half-closed eyes, then my thoughts, but not the image they conjured. The single impression I would take with me to whatever waited beyond.

I smiled as the ethereal glow of silver broke through the night, spreading across the world I was losing, and filling my unbeating heart with warmth.

With love.

CHAPTER FORTY-THREE

MOONLIGHT. THE WORLD WAS ENGULFED IN BRILLIANT SILVER moonlight.

I couldn't tell if the divine blaze existed behind my closed eyes or in earnest—couldn't feel my body enough to mark the difference.

But that was peace I sensed within me.

Details sharpened, the seemingly endless argent now comprised of an army of embers. Furious. Protective. A force no one could hope to restrain as it spread its majestic wings and swept away the chains weighing my limbs.

The pressure lessened, and my body turned until I lay on my side, though I didn't move beyond that small shift in my position. My bones, my muscles—they were distant. But even more so, I was rendered immobile, mesmerized by the stark silhouette that emerged from the vivid glow of the moon.

The smile on my lips grew as I drank in those chiseled

features, the sapphire eyes that slid into focus, gradually, as if stepping through a thick mist.

The shadowfire flared, and Mordecai knelt before me.

I didn't remember, but I must have shifted again, because those were faint outlines of the ceiling I now saw, creating a dark backdrop for the tongues of silver that coiled like a crown around Mordecai's head.

He leaned forward, then captured my mouth with his.

His fingers dug into my back where he held me, his warmth, his taste spilling onto my tongue and awakening the power within, irradiating my blood with its potent presence. I was aching for breath but only brought him closer, losing myself in his kiss as I wrapped my arms around his neck, unwilling to let go.

Not now. Not ever.

He shuddered and slid one hand to the small of my back, then lifted me off the ground to mold our bodies together. He filled my lungs, my senses, my mind, the crescent moon pendant growing warm against my skin—

"Mordecai." I pulled away from his kiss. "We have to go. Get the fragment—"

His hand cupped my cheek, silencing my words before he trailed his thumb along my lips.

It came away bloody. As was—

As was his mouth.

Each brush of the kisses we'd shared smeared in crimson.

It *had* been my blood that had stained my tongue before. But I didn't...

I didn't *feel* broken.

From the drawn lines of his face, I knew Mordecai was divided—the shadowfire deep in the thralls of battle in the background, while a kernel of it still infused my flesh, coaxing out my own shadows to tend to those wounds Mordecai's fingers were unable to trace.

He didn't let his distress show, but his voice gave away every nuance of torment that slowly seeped into relief as he said, "You need to rest. I'll take you—"

"No." I sucked in a lungful of air and curled my fingers into the lapels of his tailcoat. "Mordecai, you don't understand. I know. I know how to open a portal to Svitanye."

Hope softened his features for a moment before the fragility leeched away, replaced by the sharp lines I had come to love as much as the light. "How?"

"My blood. The pendant needs my blood to create gates between realms."

Without words, Mordecai detangled his body from mine and helped me rise. A shadow cut across his face, but he looked away before those depths yawned open.

And when the curtain of silver retreated, when the familiar desk, the bookcases greeted me—

When did we end up in his study?

Had he drawn me through a portal without my awareness? Or had I found my own way here while trapped in the whirlwind that had wanted to scrape my life away inch after vicious inch?

Behind us, his shadowfire spread in a wide arc. It blocked the door—cordoning off this sanctuary from the thunder beyond. I tightened my grip on his arm. We had to hurry.

But as I made a move for the pendant to freeze at least those threatening to break inside, Mordecai caught my hand.

"Save your strength, Ember." His voice was clipped, leaving no room for arguments.

And neither did his stride as he led me up the stairs.

He was concealing something from me. I could read as much from the somber flavor his presence had taken, but while my body had recovered, it still took nearly all my concentration to guide my weakened muscles up the steps without faltering.

A sheen of perspiration coated my forehead when we reached the tapestry. Mordecai's mouth tightened as he noticed, the shadowfire that rippled behind him and set a burning path all the way down the stairs thrashing in response. But his expression—it shuttered, gaze once more focused on what lay right ahead.

With a swift move, he slid the depiction of what we were fighting for aside, then hooked his fingers in the groove of the concealed door. The slice of wall shifted, but before it opened fully, a quake rattled the ground.

Mordecai's arm snapped around my waist. He pulled me to him as he steadied us both against the frame, then curved the silver in a protective shield over our heads. My stomach rolled uneasily, the bite of bile once again creeping up my throat. But most wretched of all was the tightness of my power, the way it thrashed against my insides like a caged animal, willing to do anything to be released.

"The Void isn't only eroding the edges, is it?" I asked, my voice barely more than a whisper.

Sorrow darkened the sapphire. "No."

The thrashing intensified as a heaviness lay upon my chest. It spread through my veins, as if it were a part of me that was withering, but I knew better. I held Mordecai's gaze as the palace around us trembled, the touch of his hand on my hip the only tether I still had in this world.

The ethereal tapestry's tattered, interwoven threads were now speckled with particles that had broken off from the devouring mass that was the Void, like pollen carried on the wind.

I leaned into Mordecai. "They're breaking Somraque apart."

The people.

The grains of nothingness and its insatiable hunger.

"They are." His voice was quiet, so at odds with the thunder of magic crashing through the air.

A flicker of light pierced the chaos of my mind, and I gripped his arm.

"This is because of us. Because of *me*." I frowned, then lifted my chin to face the full weight of his gaze. "If we go to Svitanye, if we leave this place, they won't have a reason to fight any longer. Somraque will be damaged, but not on the verge of destruction if the magic calms. And if we work fast enough—"

The ghost of warmth that touched the corners of his lips cracked my heart. "It's too late for us, Ember. And too late for nature to take its course."

Instinctively, I backed away, but the arm he kept around my waist held firm. And one look at the shadow I had glimpsed earlier but now reigned upon his features doused my objections.

"Even if I were certain losing Somraque wouldn't destroy its sister lands, I couldn't let it fall. I need to purge the source of magic from existence, give it at least a chance, however small, to endure this final dark age." He traced his knuckles down my cheek. "Or perish trying."

A DEAFENING SILENCE swallowed my mind. All I could see was that profound sadness, cut only by a single ray of light, that filled the sapphire of his eyes. The way he gazed at me, the way he held me, as if it were the last time.

I shook my head, breaking the confines of the spell. "No."

"No," I repeated when he said nothing, the plea sharpening into a command. "I'm not leaving you, Mordecai. Whatever it takes, we'll stand together."

Die together, if we have to.

The world shifted and pulsed beneath us, the quake growing more violent, wrenching the threads of reality and snapping them apart, one by one. Gobs of power drifted as they lost their anchors, the Void ravenously slithering into the gaps and snapping its venomous teeth.

"You don't have a choice, Ember. Not in this."

He tore away from me before I could stop him, casting aside the shelves the quake had brought down. A sob wrenched itself free as I watched him disappear behind a veil of silver. The very same silver that guarded me—but also kept me from moving beyond the circular patch of ground visible underneath my feet.

I couldn't do this. I couldn't do this without him.

Didn't *want* to.

Even now, the moments devoid of his presence seemed to stretch far longer than it should have taken him to retrieve the relic—a cruel glimpse at what it would be like to continue this path without him.

Perhaps even my life.

He'd sacrificed so much already. Why did he have to give *everything*—

There were no tears left to scald my skin when Mordecai manifested, a vision of alabaster and onyx haloed by moonlight.

The barest line of silver brightened his eyes as he forced the fragment into my hand and closed his fingers over mine. "Fulfill your destiny, and I will try to uphold mine."

As soon as I accepted the weight of the wretched piece, Mordecai wrapped me in his arms and crushed his lips over mine. He kissed me deeply, passionately, infusing me with all that was still left unsaid between us. All we could have had. I clutched the fragment in one hand while tangling the fingers of the other in his hair, as if by holding on to him, he would be unable to slip away.

And still, he did.

"Please, Mordecai, don't make me go without you." My words suffocated on the pain that ripped through me as the warmth of his lips faded from mine.

"I love you, Ember." He pressed a chaste kiss to my forehead, and I felt a familiar vibration bloom into existence to my left. "Go now. I do not wish for you to remember me as a nightmare, too."

I looked into his eyes, but he was already pushing me away, his grip unyielding as the presence at my back strengthened.

"I love you, too, Mordecai," I whispered, and then I was falling, sucked through the rip in space, with the Crescent Prince nothing but a fading image, etched into the ruins of my heart.

CHAPTER FORTY-FOUR

THE IN-BETWEEN HELD ME. REFUSED TO LET ME OUT ON THE other side, as if my mute roar—that last hope I carried within me—caused it to pause. Rebel against its order.

But I couldn't go back. That path of argent was sealed.

There was only forward.

As I gave myself over to the fate that had not been of my choosing, the portal cast me out.

Like my beginning, so was my end.

Sharp pieces of rock bit into my palms, the landscape covered in darkness. But whereas that first night I had brimmed with wonder, I now felt as if there were a ravine cutting right through my insides, straining to snap me apart once and for all.

I calmed the vicious tremors.

Cradled the pain, the anger, until it was vanquished beyond that edge where it could consume me no longer.

A cold wind blew against my cheeks, and I looked up, seeing

the barren land, marred but still whole, spread before me. And in the distance—

Nysa.

No longer tinted blue by the illusion of a clear sun-kissed sky, but wrapped in a half orb of silver. The brilliant light pulsed, strongest in its core, then fading into translucence. My fingers dug into the ground, nails scraping against soil and rock.

Mordecai.

The well inside me shattered, and I doubled over, gasping for breath as the silver burned, creeping across the night sky. He was wrong to send me away. Wrong to place this on himself.

Not a monster.

Never a monster.

His actions weren't a reign of terror. They were a sacrifice. Selfless. His role of a protector shrouded in nightmares that would paint over reality, forever writing him as the villain while I held the true pages of this tome.

My shattered cry of fury and anguish was met by a gasp.

I grabbed the fragment from where it lay on the ground beside me and shot up to my feet. My shadowfire threatened to rise to the surface as I whirled around.

And froze.

Ada's wide green eyes were staring at the argent glow engulfing Nysa, her lips parted and body taut. Four more figures stood in the darkness behind her, every one of them just as immobile. Ridden with distraught and fear set over a canvas of disorientation.

But when Ada's gaze wavered, when it fell on me, then took me in, truly saw me, a ray comprised of nothing but relief beamed through. It irradiated the devastated lines of her face, shifting something inside her as if a lifeline had manifested where there had been nothing before. She broke into a run and threw her arms around me, her body shuddering in painful silence.

She had suffered loss, too. But that part of me that responded to the girl who had come so close to being a friend—it couldn't pass through the entangled, thorned weeds that the sight of that silver, the depths behind it, had grown from the barren land.

"Thank the Stars you're all right," Ada whispered, her tears glistening under the moonlight as she stepped back.

My lips parted instinctively, only no sound came. I couldn't bring myself to utter a lie.

I was many things. More than even I could comprehend.

But I was *not* all right.

So instead of replying, I glanced at Zaphine, Eriyan, and Ivarr, now joined by Dantos, all keeping their distance, faces ashen. But there was something else there, too, as they stared at me, not the blaze of silver in the background—something that fed me the necessary strength to walk towards them, Ada falling in step by my side. My fingers tightened around the broken hallow I kept concealed behind my skirt of flowing night.

"How did you get here?" I asked, my gaze passing over the remnants of confusion I recognized—and hoped I wasn't interpreting wrong.

A frown slashed across Ada's forehead. "We were on our way to the palace to"—her voice faltered—"to help when something ripped us from our path."

Not something. Some*one*.

Mordecai.

He did this. For me.

The wall of shadowfire, the time that had threatened to consume me when Mordecai had stepped into the hidden chamber—he hadn't only retrieved the fragment.

He had ensured I would not have to brave this path alone.

I swallowed and steered myself in another direction before I crumbled under the weight of it all. Ada's eyes darted towards Nysa, the jade clouding over as if she were thinking of going back.

To fix or to worsen the situation, I didn't know.

And I didn't give her the chance to tip the scales either way.

"He's buying us time," I said. "To get to Svitanye. I know how to open the portal. And I have the fragment."

The nearly unanimous sharp inhales were the only sound that broke the silence following my words. Following the sight of the relic I revealed.

I met their gazes, each and every one of them, so that there was no mistaking the resolve coursing through me.

I hadn't accepted the role they wanted me to play. I became it.

Breathed life into something that had only been an ideal, and gave it flesh.

As my statement crafted the very structure of the air, I turned to Ada.

"I'm going to Svitanye. With or without you, I'm finishing this. However..." I sucked in a breath, shoving down those final echoes that screamed in protest, that urged me to open a portal, only not one to another world, but to the moonlight-encased keeper of my heart. "I would like you to come."

Ada glanced towards the argent blaze again, and I knew it

was our last encounter in the Whispers that was replaying in her head as her jaw tightened. But when she looked at me, then dipped her chin, her expression was clear.

"Of course."

"Yes," Zaphine said, her answer echoed by Eriyan and Dantos.

Ivarr simply inclined his head, but there was a decisiveness in that single gesture that spoke more than any words could convey.

I turned to Ada. "Give me your blade."

Concealing the tremors in my hands, I stuffed the fragment behind the band of my stocking, the metal cool against my bare skin, then took the dagger from Ada and sliced it across my palm.

Blood welled, dark under the starlight. I focused on its warmth, on the feel of it. And drenched the pendant in crimson.

The need to reach Svitanye formed in my mind; no image, just the sensation that was oddly tangible as I held on to it, allowing it to sweep over every other thought, every desire still alive within me.

A short distance to our right, the air shimmered, folding apart the threads of reality until light brimmed through the endless night—a smattering of purple sky and fire-touched clouds. A doorway through the veil.

I locked it in place and gave them a curt nod. "It's safe to enter."

The Magician strode up to the portal first. He lingered for only the briefest of moments before he squared his shoulders and stepped forward, something akin to respect reflected in his eyes as our gazes met. The portal swallowed his body. Eriyan went next, casting a glance in my direction—seeking reassurance, I realized.

That much, I could give.

A smile touched his lips in response. "I hope they have sowhl," he muttered, then let the cut in reality engulf his form.

Dantos and Zaphine approached the portal with more caution, but as he grabbed her hand and gave it a squeeze, I could see the determination unfolding through her. Spine straight, Zaphine stepped into the next world, taking Dantos with her.

"Your turn," I said to Ada.

My gaze skimmed the land, but no flash of white greeted me. Wherever Lyra was, she had to have been safe, since Ada merely licked her chapped lips and glanced at the portal.

"I really am glad that you're all right, Ember."

My throat closed up at the words she didn't have to utter for me to hear. *I'm sorry.*

But that kernel of myself still trapped beneath the weeds was unable to break free.

I nodded. "Go."

The tails of her coat whipped in her wake as she left this reality, and then I was alone, only Nysa burning quietly in the distance, the silence of Mordecai's shadowfire drowning out the thrum of magic.

"I'll come for you," I whispered into the night. "When the world is right, I'll find you again."

I closed my eyes and allowed the last tears to flow.

As a cool wind whisked them away, the icy lake inside me calming, a faint glint of silver caught the edges of my awareness. But when I opened my eyes, there was no one there.

Only the cruel, beautiful sky, the moon shining down upon me.

Clutching the pendant tighter, I stepped through the portal and left Somraque behind.

But not the memory of its prince, entwined with the very essence of my being.

ACKNOWLEDGMENTS

A massive thank you to the incredible people who helped shape Evenfall into what it ultimately turned out to be.

Lindsey R. Loucks, our copy editor extraordinaire, and Michelle Rascon, the newest addition to the kickass word-wizards team. Thank you both for the saves, the polishes, for being the keen eyes no author could hope to exist without. You rock!

Merwild, we can't even begin to say how grateful we are for your incredible cover art. You brought Ember to life in a way that went beyond our wildest imaginations. Thank you.

And, of course, thank you, dear readers, because all of this is possible only because of your love for the worlds printed out in black and white.

We'll see you all in Svitanye!

ALSO BY GAJA J. KOS

KOLOVRAT UNIVERSE
PRESENT

BLACK WEREWOLVES SERIES

Urban fantasy

Novels:

The Dark Ones

The 24hourlies

The Shift

The Ascension

Novellas:

Never Forgotten

Chased

NIGHTWRAITH SERIES

Paranormal romance

Windstorm

Blackstorm

Nightstorm

FUTURE

LOTTE FREUNDENBERGER SERIES
Urban fantasy

Shadow Moon

Darkening Moon

Transient Moon

SHADE ASSASSIN SERIES
Urban fantasy

Shadow World

PARADISE OF SHADOWS AND DEVOTION
Standalone paranormal romance

DESTINY RECLAIMED
Urban fantasy standalone novella

ROMANCE

SILVER FOX CLUB
Steamy May December standalone novellas

Cotton Candy

9 789619 437452